# LONDON
# AFTER
# MIDNIGHT

*Selected & Edited*

*by*

# Peter Haining

BARNES
&NOBLE
B O O K S
NEW YORK

*FOR*
*JOHN KELLY*

First published in Great Britain in 1996

Copyright © 1996 by Peter Haining

This edition published by Barnes & Noble Inc.,
by arrangement with Peter Haining

1996 Barnes & Noble Books

Printed and bound in the United States of America

ISBN 0-7607-0345-0

96 97 98 99 00 M 9 8 7 6 5 4 3 2 I

QF

# Acknowledgements

The editor and publishers are grateful to the following authors, their agents and publishers for permission to include copyright stories in this collection: Grace Publishing Inc for 'The Knife' by Robert Arthur; A. P. Watt Literary Agency for 'Fu Manchu and the Frightened Redhead' by Sax Rohmer; Associated Newspapers Ltd for 'The Funspot-Street Affair' by Thomas Burke; Greene & Heaton Ltd for 'The Girl Who Loved Graveyards' by P. D. James; Davis Publications Ltd for 'The Most Hated Man in London' by Patricia Moyes, 'Dangerous Game' by Michael Gilbert and 'Karmesin The Murderer' by Gerald Kersh; London Magazine for 'Flight From Fleet Street' by Carter Dickson; Daily Mail for 'The Day Lucky's Luck Ran Out' by Allan Prior; The Bodley Head Ltd for 'A Little Place off the Edgware Road' by Graham Greene; Peters, Fraser & Dunlop for 'People Don't Do Such Things' by Ruth Rendell; The Estate of John Rhode for 'The Elusive Bullet'; Victor Gollancz Ltd for 'The Bottle Party' by H.C. Bailey and 'The Cave of Ali Baba' by Dorothy L. Sayers; HarperCollins for 'Aces High' by Peter Cheyney; Aitken & Stone Ltd for 'Yellow Iris' by Agatha Christie; Random Publishing Group for 'Trent and the Fool-proof Lift' by E. C. Bentley; Chatto & Windus Ltd for 'The Border-line Case' by Margery Allingham; Curtis Brown Ltd for 'The Santa Claus Club' by Julian Symons; Express

# Contents

# LONDON AFTER MIDNIGHT

The Santa Claus Club JULIAN SYMONS 285

The Incautious Burglar JOHN DICKSON CARR 298

The Bones of the Case R. AUSTIN FREEMAN 317

# Introduction

IN LONDON, ON most nights of the week, as darkness falls, the shadows draw in and street lamps begin to come on, groups of walkers can be seen setting out on guided tours of the city. Some are heading for a look at the capital's great buildings of historic interest; others to see its famous statues and monuments. But a few – the braver souls – have chosen to follow much darker routes which explain the terrible deeds and awful villainies that have given London an infamous reputation in the annals of crime.

Some of these men and women, half-expectant, half a little nervous, have chosen tours with titles like 'Ghosts of the Old City', 'Ghosts of the West End' or even 'Ghosts, Ghouls and Graveyards of London'. Then there are others intent on hearing all about the brutality that once went on behind the prison bars at Newgate, or else the unspeakable acts of torture committed in the dungeons of the Tower of London. Perhaps, though, the most stout-hearted of all have chosen to walk the same dimly lit, cobbled alleyways of Whitechapel where, a century ago, Jack the Ripper stalked his prostitute victims before disappearing into legend . . .

It was on one such tour that the idea for this book was born. For in the area of London bound by Limehouse to the east and Bayswater to the west are to be found not only a number of infamous 'black spots' stained with the blood of some terrible and well-recorded crime, but also the familiar apartments and offices of a group of the greatest sleuths in crime fiction. Within these two extremes lie the streets where Jack the Ripper and Sweeney Todd practised their deadly arts and, close by within walking distance, the Baker Street of Sherlock Holmes, Hercule Poirot's Park Lane, fashionable Piccadilly where Lord Peter Wimsey lives, and Dr John Thorndyke's rooms in the heart of the legal district at the Temple.

*London After Midnight* offers a unique fictional tour around this heartland of London: both the places where actual crimes were committed and the imaginary residences of the city's band of crime fighters. It is a journey that has been made all the more fascinating by the fact that most of the authors of the stories lived in London, thus enabling them to bring to their tales a special sense of authenticity and atmosphere based on personal experience. Indeed, so intimate is their knowledge of London's dark secrets that although the journey is one which can be walked as easily in an evening as the stories may be read at a sitting, I would recommend only the stout-hearted to try. At least after midnight, that is!

All of these tales of crime and detection evoke the mood of the city at night when the streets are deserted, the lights are low, and honest men and women are in bed. Each aims to provide the reader with the same kind of *frisson* offered by an actual guided tour – without the need to leave the comfort of your armchair. I hope that they live up to a claim made by one of the capital's late night tour guides who always tells his followers before they set off into the darkness: 'You will laugh, you will scream, you will never forget!'

Peter Haining

# SECTION ONE
# BLACK SPOTS

# The Knife

## ROBERT ARTHUR

*There is surely no more appropriate locality to begin a tour of London's black spots than Spitalfields, adjacent to Whitechapel, which for many years was known as the heart of the city's criminal underworld. It was from here that hordes of villains would strike out to prey on the law-abiding citizens of the metropolis – picking pockets, committing burglaries and carrying out robbery with violence – and then disappearing like wraiths into an almost impenetrable warren of tiny, evil-smelling and hugely congested courts and back streets. Despite the lawless nature of their inhabitants and the insanitary conditions which existed everywhere, the names of the streets were in striking contrast: Dean Street, Flower Street and Dorset Street to name but three. The last of these, on the edge of Spitalfields, was known for years as 'The Do As You Please' and the police were said to avoid it, unless they went there in numbers. Quite simply, throughout the nineteenth and early twentieth century, Dean Street, Spitalfields was reputed to be 'the most evil street in all London'. It is no surprise, either, to find it associated with that most famous of all London's crimes, the reign of terror of Jack the Ripper . . .*

*Dorset Street, then, is the setting for this first story of London after midnight, told by Robert Arthur (1909–1969), an American writer, editor, radio and television figure who was a long-time associate of Alfred Hitchcock. The two men visited*

*London on several occasions, and it was while Hitchcock was in
England filming* Stage Fright *in 1950 that Robert Arthur took
the opportunity to follow up his interest in the legend of Jack the
Ripper and tour his haunts – a walk that subsequently inspired
him to write the story of 'The Knife'. It was first published in
America and adapted for the weekly radio programme* The
Mysterious Traveller *in November 1951. Popular and much-
anthologised as many of Robert Arthur's stories have been, this
marks the first book publication of his ingenious and chilling
variation on London's most infamous series of murders . . .*

EDWARD DAWES STIFLED his curiosity as long as he could,
then he sidled over and lowered his large bulk carefully on to
the chair opposite Herbert Smithers. Leaning on the table, he
watched the other man clean away rusty mud from the object
in his hands. It was a knife, that much was apparent. What
was not apparent was why Smithers was so intent upon it, in
its present condition. Edward Dawes nursed his glass of half-
and-half and waited for Smithers to speak.

When Smithers continued to ignore him, Dawes drained
his glass and banged it down with a gesture.

'Doesn't look like much, that there knife doesn't,' he
remarked disdainfully. ' 'Ardly worth cleanin' it, I say.'

'Ho!' Herbert Smithers retorted, and continued to work
delicately with the point of a fingernail file at the caked dirt
on his find.

'What is it?' Gladys, the Three Oaks' buxom barmaid,
asked with open curiosity as she collected the empty glasses
in front of them.

'It's a knife,' Smithers vouchsafed. 'A rare antique knife
wot belongs to me because I found it.'

It was now Mr Dawes' turn to say, 'Ho!'

'Thinks it's valuable, 'e, does,' he stated to the room at
large, though it was empty save for the three of them.

'It don't look valuable to me,' Gladys said frankly. 'It looks
like a nasty rusty old thing that ought to be put back on the
rubbish heap it came from.'

Smithers' silence was more eloquent than words. Discarding the file, he now moistened the corner of a grimy handkerchief with saliva, and rubbed at a small scarlet spot in the end of the still-obscured hilt. The spot enlarged and emerged from the grime as a faceted stone which glowed redly.

'Why, it's a jool!' Gladys exclaimed with quickened interest. 'Look at it shine. Maybe it's real.'

'Another half-and-half, if you please!' Smithers said pointedly, and Gladys flounced off. The swing of her well-curved hips disclaimed all interest, but her backward glance revealed what the swinging hips tried to deny.

'A jewel!' There was a hollow quality in Dawes' disdain now, and he leaned forward to stare as Smithers rubbed. 'Not likely!'

'And 'ow,' Smithers asked, with composed logic, 'do you know?'

He breathed upon the red stone, polished it with his sleeve, and held it to admire it. Like a red eye it winked and glittered, seeming to gather into itself every crimson gleam from the tiny grate fire in the corner behind their table.

'Prob'ly,' he remarked, with the quiet dignity befitting one who has just come into wealth, 'it's a ruby.'

'A ruby!' The larger Mr Dawes seemed to choke on the word. 'And wot would a knife with a real ruby in its 'ilt be doin' out in plain sight on the street for you to find?'

'Wasn't,' Smithers said succinctly. He picked up the file again and began digging the dirt out of the crevices of the intricately worked handle. 'It was in a pile of muck where they're fixin' th' drains, down Dorset street. Prob'ly been in th' drains no tellin' how many years.'

His small figure straightened inside its shabby covering of clothes; his thin lips tightened.

'Look at th' rust an' muck on it!' he challenged. 'That proves 'ow long it's been lyin' there. Nobody can't claim they lost it in th' blitz.'

Reluctantly Mr Dawes conceded the point.

'It's good steel, though,' he added. 'Still got a point to it, rust or no rust.'

'Only a minute ago,' Smithers pointed out, 'you said as 'ow it wasn't worth while cleanin'.'

Having removed enough of the encrusting dirt to show a slender, ornate hilt and a long tapering blade, he let his finger close about the weapon. The hilt slipped naturally into the curve of his palm. He swung it a little, made a practice thrust-and-cut.

'It 'andles like it was part of me,' he remarked dreamily. 'Sends a kind of warm feelin' all up me arm, just to 'old it. Tingles it does, like electricity.'

'Let me try,' Mr Dawes suggested, all disdain forgotten. Smithers scowled and drew his hand back.

'It's mine!' he said, a new truculent note in his voice. 'Nobody else is touchin' it but me.'

He thrust-and-cut again, and the red stone in the hilt flashed fire.

Smithers' thin, pinched face was flushed, as if reflecting the firelight, and he swayed, as though suddenly a little drunk.

'It's worth a 'eap,' he said huskily. 'This 'ere is a foreign knife, a old one, and it 'as a real ruby in the 'andle. I've made a find, I 'ave.'

Gladys set down two glasses and forgot to complete her mechanical wiping of the table top. Smithers held the knife steady, to find the brightest possible glow of the stone in the hilt, and Gladys stared at it with covetous eyes.

'Maybe it is a real ruby at that,' she said. 'Let me have a look, ducky.'

Her moist, outstretched fingers touched Smithers' hand, and the little man whirled, was on his feet.

'No!' he shouted. 'It's mine, d'you hear?'

'Just a look,' Gladys said eagerly. 'I'll give it right back, promise.'

She followed him a step, coaxingly, and the flush on Smithers' pinched features deepened.

'I tell you it's mine!' he cried shrilly. 'An' no pretty face is gettin' it away from me. D'you hear! D'you hear!'

And then all three of them, even Gladys, were deathly silent, staring transfixed at the winking red eye which now of a sudden stood out some five inches from Gladys' heart, Smithers' fingers still gripped about the hilt. Gladys' eyes grew wide and wider.

'You stabbed me,' she said slowly and distinctly. 'You stabbed me!' And then with no other sound but a queer rattling noise in her throat, she crumpled. Her body struck the floor with a crash that seemed to shake the room, and sprawled there emptily. A little red tongue licked across her breast and spread hungrily.

But even that, for a moment, did not change the position of the two men – Smithers standing, the knife left in his hand by Gladys' fall, and Dawes half risen, his hands on the table, his jaw slack.

The power of speech returned first to the little scavenger.

'I didn't do it!' he cried hoarsely. 'I never did it! The knife stabbed her! 'S truth, it did! And I couldn't stop it.'

Then recovering a semblance of self-possession, he flung the knife down. Turning, he stumbled sobbingly toward the door and was gone.

Edward Dawes moved at last. Breathing hard, as if after a long run, he stood up. The knife lay at his feet. He listened. There was no sound, no outcry. He stopped. When he straightened, he held the knife gingerly in his hand. Mechanically, his gaze darting to the door and back, he wiped the blade on half his evening paper. Then he wrapped it in the other half. A moment later he was moving at a shambling run for the door.

His plan, formulated quite without conscious thought, was simple. The lodging house run by his wife was directly across the street. From there he would phone the police. He was taking the knife to protect it as evidence. When the police arrived, he would turn it over to them minus the stone in the hilt. If Smithers, on being caught, mentioned it, he would swear that it must have been knocked out and lost when the knife was thrown to the floor.

Who was to prove different? . . .

Still breathing hard, Edward Dawes pried at the glittering red stone with the blade of a penknife. He was in the kitchen, just outside which was the phone. He had perhaps three minutes before the police got there in response to his call. He worked with the sweat pouring from his brow and his heart thudding as if he was exerting himself to the utmost.

Two minutes more. The prongs that held the stone were stout. His penknife slipped and cut him. He cursed under his breath, and went on working. The blood from his cut made his fingers slippery, and a moment later the knife shot from between them and clattered to the floor, the steel blade giving out a ringing note.

Dawes stooped, his bulk making the movement difficult, and snatched at the knife. It eluded him and skidded a foot away. A minute left. He followed it, not even taking time to curse now, and had it in his hand when his wife entered and stopped just inside the doorway.

'Edward,' she began shrilly, 'I heard you at the phone just now. What nonsense were you talking about a murder at the Three Oaks?'

Then she took in the whole scene as he straightened up – his flushed and furious face, the knife in his hand, the blood staining his fingers.

'Edward!' she shrieked. 'You've killed somebody! You've killed somebody!'

He took a step toward her. There was a singing in his ears, and a strange warmth shooting up his arm. A reddish mist floated up before his eyes, hiding his wife from him.

'Shut up, you bloody fool!' he shouted.

His stout wife became silent at that, except for a blubbery gasping through which words seemed to be trying to come.

Then the reddish mist cleared, and Edward Dawes saw that she was lying on the floor, the hilt of the knife standing out from her plump white throat just beneath her chin, the red eye in the end of it winking and blinking up at him, holding him transfixed so that he did not hear the pounding on the outer door. Nor, a moment later, the sound of it opening. Nor the tramp of heavy official feet coming down the hallway . . .

'That's it, sir.' Sergeant Tobins' tone was respectful, to a full inspector. 'Killed two women inside ten minutes, it did. Two different men used it. Both of them claim they don't know why they did it.'

He smiled, as if to say that he for one would never be taken in by such a claim.

'Hmm,' The tall, gaunt man turned the knife delicately between his fingers. 'Indian workmanship, I see. Sixteenth or seventeenth century.'

'Get that, Miss Mapes?'

The plain, middle-aged woman standing at the inspector's elbow nodded. 'Yes, sergeant.' She made a few squiggles in her notebook.

'It's been cleaned up some, Inspector Frayne,' Sergeant Tobins ventured. 'No prints on it. Anyway, they both confessed.'

'The stone?' The tall man tapped the hilt. 'Is it real?'

'It's a ruby, right enough,' the thickset sergeant agreed. 'Badly flawed, though. Has an air bubble right in the middle of it, shaped like a drop of blood—' he coughed delicately, 'like a teardrop, I mean.'

Inspector Frayne continued turning the thing. Pencil ready, Miss Mapes waited.

'It's a genuine rarity, all the same,' Frayne said. 'Glad you asked me to look at it. Probably brought to this country by one of our Tommies after the Sepoy rebellion. Bit of looting done after it was put down, you know.'

Miss Mapes' pencil scribbled busily.

'Found in a drain, wasn't it?' the inspector asked. 'Been there a long time, that's plain. Which of them found it – Smithers or Dawes?'

'Smithers, sir. Funny thing, that. He was cleaning it, hadn't 'ad . . . had it more than an hour, when he used it on a barmaid. Then Dawes cops it and ten minutes later sticks it in his wife's throat. And both of them said the same thing, when we questioned them.'

'They did, eh? Just what did they say?'

'Well, sir, they said they got a warm, tingly feeling just from holding the knife. It came on all of a sudden like when they got angry at the women. They didn't know why they got so angry, they just did . . . and just like that the women were dead! They said—' Sergeant Tobins allowed himself to smile— 'that they didn't have anything to do with it. That the knife just sort of moved by itself, with them holding it.'

'They said that, eh? Good Lord!' The tall man stared at the knife with a new interest. 'Sergeant, just where was the drain in which this thing was found?'

'Dorset street, sir,' Sergeant Tobins stated. 'Near the corner of Commercial street.'

'Dorset street, did you say? Inspector Frayne's voice was sharp, his eyes alight. 'By George, I wonder . . ."

Neither Tobins nor Miss Mapes interrupted. After a moment, Frayne put the knife back in its box on Sergeant Tobins' desk.

'I was having a brainstorm,' he said, smiling. 'This knife – well, do you know what happened on Dorset street a good while ago?'

Sergeant Tobins shook his head.

'I seem to remember reading about it,' he said. 'But I can't just put my mind on where.'

'It's mentioned in one of the largest files in our record department. It happens that in November of 1888 a woman was brutally murdered – with a knife – in Millers Court, off Dorset street. Her name was Marie Kelley.'

Sergeant Tobins stared.

'I remember now,' he blurted out. 'Jack the Ripper!'

'Exactly. His last murder, we believe. The last of twelve. All women. He seemed to have a special, venomous hatred for women. And I was toying with the thought of a murderer hurrying from that spot in the dead of night, with a blood-stained knife in his hand. I could see him dropping it into a drain opening as he fled, to lie there until now . . . Well, as we say, a brainstorm.'

Sergeant Tobins watched the door close, then turned.

'The inspector would do great writing thrillers,' he said with ponderous humour. 'A regular imagination for it, he has!'

He picked up the knife, gripped it firmly, and struck a pose, winking broadly.

'Be careful, Miss Mapes!' he said. 'Jack the Ripper!'

Miss Mapes giggled.

'Well now,' she breathed. 'Let me look at it, may I Sergeant Tobins, if you don't mind?'

Her fingers touched his, and Sergeant Tobins drew his hand back abruptly. His face flushed and a fierce anger unaccountably flared up in him at the touch of Miss Mapes' hand. But as he stared into her plain, bewildered face, the anger was soothed by the pleasurable tingling warmth in his right wrist and arm. And as he took a swift step toward her there was a strange, sweet singing in his ears, high and shrill and faraway.

Or was it the sound of a woman screaming? . . .

# Fu Manchu and the
# Frightened Redhead

## SAX ROHMER

*From Spitalfields it is a walk of less than a mile through Stepney
to Limehouse and the base of Fu Manchu, the 'Devil Doctor' of
innumerable books, films and TV series, who is said to be 'the
most sinister villain in history'. This Chinese master-criminal
who operates from the East End of London using his vast wealth,
intelligence and occult powers in an all-consuming quest to rule
the world, also shares with Professor Moriarty an enduring position in London legend despite also being ostensibly a fictional
creation. I say ostensibly, because his creator, Sax Rohmer, main-
tained that he was actually based on a real villain named 'Mr
King' who operated in Limehouse controlling the gambling, drug
smuggling and criminal activities in the Chinese districts of
London. Although this mysterious criminal was never brought to
justice – and Rohmer himself did no more than glimpse him one
foggy night in Limehouse – his organizational skills and use of
the dreaded tongs to terrorize his victims, were immortalized in
the series of Fu Manchu novels and short stories published
between 1913 and 1973. Fu Manchu's great adversary on the
side of the law is Sir Denis Nayland Smith who works in association with Scotland Yard to try and bring him to justice. But
the sinister Oriental in his yellow robe, black cap and moustache, with his mesmeric eyes and mastery of disguise is always
just one step ahead . . .*

*Sax Rohmer (1883–1959) became interested in the mysterious*

*East while he was a young man, but it was bravely accepting a newspaper assignment in 1912 to write about life in the sprawling and dangerous (for Caucasians) Chinese colony of Limehouse which first brought him into contact with the criminal elements who would later inspire much of his fiction. An old Chinese merchant living near the docks with whom he became friendly also told him many stories of life in China which proved invaluable. His inside knowledge of the drug trade which he described in 'The Yellow Claw' (1915) and 'Dope' (1919) proved instrumental in the government taking action on drugs and helped to clean up Limehouse in particular. Despite the enormous popularity of Fu Manchu, the character did not make Rohmer a wealthy man, due mainly to his extravagant lifestyle. Interestingly, the author once claimed that a figure who called himself Fu Manchu materialized in his room one day and denied that it was he who had given him his fame. 'It is your boast that you made me,' Rohmer later claimed the figure had said to him, 'but it is* mine *that I shall live when you are smoke.' The story hereunder is set in the heart of Fu Manchu's Limehouse empire, and was originally written for the American newspaper* This Week *in 1959. Curiously, Rohmer's original title for this account of another of the 'Devil Doctor's' evil schemes was to have been 'Secret of the Flying Saucer'!*

SHE WOKE IN completely incomprehensible surroundings. There was a vague smell of what she thought might be incense, a strange heaviness of all her limbs. 'Where am I?' 'Who am I?' were questions which danced mockingly across her brain. Then came helpless fear, fear of the silence, the void around her. Had she been abducted? An accident? Was she suffering from amnesia? She lost control, wanted to cry out – but couldn't utter a sound.

And then, to crown growing panic, she became conscious of a presence. Softly came a voice, a sibilant, commanding voice: 'You are quite safe, Miss Merton. There is no danger.'

That voice! Its strange tones magically awakened her memory. She knew herself. She was Pat Merton. She knew the voice and where she had heard it before. Clearly, as though a veil had been raised, she remembered the crowded room in the Mayflower Hotel. A reception for Bruce Garfield and some of his colleagues was being held there. But his old friend Nayland Smith was arriving from Hong Kong and had wired him to meet his plane on a matter of vital importance, and so Bruce had phoned, asking her to rush over to the hotel and apologise for his unavoidable delay.

Bruce's colleagues assembled at the reception knew Pat and introduced her to some of the dignitaries in the throng. One of them was a Swiss scientist whose name she now failed to remember. But she recalled that he wore tinted glasses. Feeling rather uncomfortable as his voice droned on she had decided to leave, and then – this memory was crystal clear – the Swiss gentleman had removed his glasses, and a stare of long, narrow emerald-green eyes was fixed upon her. Apart from a hazy impression that he saw her from the hotel to a cab or car, the rest was a blank. But this was his voice. And then almost silently a tall figure appeared beside her.

Pat's inclination, as she looked up, was to scream. But a sense of horror, or, rather, of supernatural dread, reduced her to passive submission. This was the man she had met at the hotel, but he had changed. As the Swiss scientist, he must have worn a wig, for now his massive skull was only sparsely covered by hair. It was a wonderful face, the face of a genius, but of a genius inspired by hell.

He spoke softly, watching her, and his words soothed her terror strangely.

'I regret that you were overcome by the heat of the room at the Mayflower, Miss Merton. I took the liberty of bringing you here and restoring you.' His eyes seemed to grow larger, to absorb her in their green depth; but she recovered in time to hear the words, 'My car is at your service.'

The cool night breeze outside refreshed her as a courteous chauffeur in smart uniform made her comfortable in a limousine.

Numbly, she began to study her surroundings. The chauffeur had navigated several narrow, sordid streets. From one dark alleyway she had seen Chinese faces peering out in the gleam of the headlights. Over the low roofs there was a glow of night labour; she heard the hoarse minor note of a steamer's whistle. This was the East End dock area, of which she knew nothing.

Now they were speeding along a wide, straight thoroughfare, almost deserted, toward a part of the city with which she was acquainted. She had a glimpse of the Mansion House. There was Ludgate Hill . . . They were in the Strand . . . Charing Cross . . . Piccadilly.

The car pulled up. The chauffeur opened the door. Pat stepped out and found herself at the entrance to the Mayflower Hotel.

'Two o'clock!' Pat said in astonishment, when the night doorman told her the time.

'Yes, miss.' He looked at her in an odd way. 'You are staying here?'

'No, I'm not. Will you please call a taxi?' Bruce will be frantic. She must get to him.

Pat opened her handbag, momentarily wondering if her money was still there. Everything was in order. She tipped the doorman and gave the taxi driver the address of Bruce's flat in Knightsbridge. As there were frequent occasions when she had to go there while Bruce was working, she had a key.

Bruce occupied a mews flat which Pat had helped to furnish and decorate. When the taxi pulled up, she saw that the windows were lighted; there were sounds of excited conversation coming through an open window. She hesitated for a moment, rang the bell.

The voices ceased. Then came footsteps on the short stair. The door opened.

'Pat! Pat, darling! Thank God you're safe.' Pat went into Bruce's arms.

She was so emotionally exhausted that he had almost to carry her up to the living room. The first person she saw, a tall lean man with sunburned skin, white streaks on dark hair above his temples, and grey eyes, she knew and welcomed: Sir Denis Nayland Smith, former Scotland Yard Commissioner and one of Bruce's oldest friends. The very man she had hoped would be there.

'A nice fright you have given us, young lady,' he rapped in his crisp fashion. 'Four divisions of the Metropolitan Police are combing London for you. This is Inspector Haredale of Scotland Yard' – indicating the third man – 'who has been directing the search.'

The inspector was so typical a police officer – fresh-coloured, frank blue eyes and a grey toothbrush moustache – that Pat could have guessed his profession. When the excitement of her unheralded, dramatic appearance had calmed down, Nayland Smith spoke.

'Before you attempt to explain your disappearance, let me bring you up to date about what has happened since you vanished from the Mayflower Hotel. Garfield found nothing remarkable in your leaving after giving his message of apology. After the reception, I went to my flat in Whitehall Court and Garfield came here. He made an unpleasant discovery.'

He paused to relight his pipe which had gone out. Bruce crossed to Pat's chair and sat on the arm, his hand resting on her shoulder. 'Don't let what has happened bother you, Pat. You're in no way responsible.'

But Pat, looking from face to face, sensed that whatever had happened during those lost hours was intimately tied in with Bruce's flat.

'A report of a paper read by Garfield before a group of scientists a week ago,' Nayland Smith went on, 'had reached me in Hong Kong. It outlined his revolutionary theory of travel in outer space without rocket propulsion. He spoke of a scale model on which he was still working – and I knew he was in deadly danger.'

'Why?' Pat whispered.

'Because I knew that Dr Fu Manchu was in London. Scientists all over the world have been disappearing. What they had in common was that each one was working on the problem of anti-gravity.' He sighed. 'You don't know Dr Fu Manchu, Pat—'

'Oh, but I do!' Pat burst out. 'He's horrible. I don't think he's quite human—'

Nayland Smith checked her words with upraised hand and boyish smile which belied his greying hair. 'I have often thought the same, Pat. You see, Dr Fu Manchu claims to have solved the puzzle of anti-gravity, though we still don't know whether that is true. I knew he would want to see Garfield's model. And so I flew home at the earliest possible moment. But I was too late.'

'What do you mean, Sir Denis, you were too late?'

'He means,' Bruce told her gently, 'that while he and I were at the reception, this flat was burgled. I discovered it on my return from the Mayflower and called you at once. There was no reply. Ten minutes' enquiry convinced me that you had disappeared from the moment you left the hotel with some unidentified man.'

'*I* have identified him,' Nayland Smith rapped. 'Dr Fu Manchu. Pat, the scale model of Garfield's interplanetary vehicle has been stolen. Only he and you knew where it was hidden. And you alone may be able to give us a clue leading to Fu Manchu's London base.'

Pat had got no further than her misty recollections of leaving the hotel when Nayland Smith broke in: 'You hadn't been gone an hour before your description was known to most of the Metropolitan Police.'

Pat looked up at Bruce and went ahead with her story. Her awakening in the silent room, the smell of incense, the complete inertia of brain and body, seemed to convey some message to Nayland Smith, for she saw him nod significantly to Bruce.

'As I thought, Garfield,' he said. 'And now, Pat, please be very detailed about your return from this place – if you can. Do you remember anything at all?'

Pat described the midnight drive, the narrow streets, the

Asiatic faces, the wide, deserted thoroughfare, the steamer whistles . . .

'The picture is clear. You agree, Inspector?'

'Entirely, Sir Denis. When your signal from Hong Kong reached us last week saying that Dr Fu Manchu had left for London, I got busy. Every known or suspected hideaway of Dr Fu Manchu was combed quietly. The only report that seemed at all warm came from K Division, Limehouse, as I have already told you. I have drawn a ring around a small area down there. I think the place where Miss Merton found herself tonight is inside that ring.'

'Then let's not waste a moment,' Nayland Smith said, getting to his feet. 'We may be too late, Inspector, but we'll have a go at capturing Fu Manchu. He has an inordinately high opinion of his hypnotic powers and may think himself quite safe. But my guess is that Pat came out of her trance sooner than he intended.'

As they drove toward Limehouse in a police car, Nayland Smith explained the rest of the story to Pat. 'Dr Fu Manchu had learned that you had a key to this flat, that you knew where the model was hidden. The door in the panelling which only you and Bruce know how to open is closed. But the model has gone. To be sure the plans are locked up in the War Office, but to a man of Fu Manchu's genius, the model would be enough. He brought you here from the Mayflower under hypnosis. You opened the panel and were taken to some hideaway where he could examine the model at leisure.'

'I'll never forgive myself,' Pat said sadly.

'Nonsense,' Bruce said quickly. 'There was nothing you could do about . . .'

Their police car raced on through the dark, still streets. Pat remembered the route, began to recognise certain landmarks. A man standing on the corner of a narrow street flashed a light three times as the car approached. 'We're inside the cordon,' Inspector Haredale reported.

And suddenly, 'I remember that alleyway!' Pat exclaimed.

'Pull in on the right here,' Haredale directed the driver. 'This is where the hard work begins.'

The car swung into a dead-end alley and, as they all got out, a man half hidden in its shadows saluted the inspector.

'Any movement, Elkin?'

'Not a thing, sir. If there was anybody in there, he's in there now.'

A riverside warehouse, boarded up and marked for demolition, was suspected to be secretly used by Dr Fu Manchu as a temporary base. One of K Division's detectives had found a way into it from a neighbouring building.

'We're in for some climbing, Pat,' Nayland Smith warned grimly. 'We need you or I wouldn't drag you along. Lead the way, Inspector.'

The way was through a building which had an exit on the blind alley. Pat found herself climbing a narrow stair, guided by the beam of a flashlight held by Inspector Haredale. The climb continued until they came to the seventh and final landing. Pat saw an iron ladder leading to a trap in the roof.

'I'll go first, miss,' the local detective told her. 'It's a darkish night, but I don't want to show a light.'

He went up, opened the trap, and stretched his hand down. Pat mounted, Bruce following, Nayland Smith and Haredale bringing up the rear. They stood in a narrow gutter, a sloping slate roof on one side and a sheer drop to the street on the other. An iron ladder to the top of a higher building adjoining led to a flat roof. A few yards away, in fleeting moonlight, Pat saw an oblong skylight.

'I must ask for silence now, sir,' Inspector Haredale said. 'Elkin, our guide, has managed to open a section of this skylight.'

Elkin hauled a rope-ladder from its hiding place, raised part of the skylight, hooked the ladder to the frame and climbed down. From below he flashed a light. 'I'm holding the ladder fast,' he whispered. 'Would you come next, Mr Garfield, and hang on to Miss Merton?'

The ladder was successfully negotiated, and the members

of the party found themselves in a stuffy loft impregnated with stifling exotic odours. The warehouse had belonged to a firm of spice importers.

Stairs led down to a series of galleries surrounding a lofty, echoing place where even their cautious footsteps sounded like the tramp of a platoon.

'No use going tiptoe,' snapped Nayland Smith. 'If there's anyone here, he knows we're here, too. The room you were in was on the ground floor, Pat. So let's get a move on. A little more light, Sergeant.'

They descended from gallery to gallery until they reached the bottom. Then they stood still, listening. There was no sound. The place had the odour of a perfume bazaar.

'It was your mention of incense, miss,' Inspector Haredale told Pat, 'that convinced me you had been here. Now, Elkin, what's the lay of the land?'

'There's an inner office, and a main office beyond which opens right on to the street.'

'Stand by for anything,' Nayland Smith directed. 'If we're lucky, Fu Manchu will be in there. If the door is locked, we'll break it down.'

The door was not locked. As it swung open, they saw a lighted room.

'Stay with Pat for a moment, Garfield,' Nayland Smith said tersely. 'I want to make sure what's ahead.'

He stepped in, followed by Haredale and Elkin. There was no one in the room. But as Pat strained forward to peer in, she saw a long couch illuminated by a tall pedestal lamp which shed a peculiar green light. 'This is the room I was in!' she cried out.

She and Bruce joined Nayland Smith and, 'Good God!' Bruce spoke almost in a whisper. 'Can it be true?'

On a table beside the couch a curious object lay gleaming in the rays of the lamp. It was composed of some silver-like metal moulded in the form of two saucers, one inverted above the other and upheld by four squat columns apparently of vulcanite.

'My model!' Bruce shouted, and sprang forward.

'One moment, sir!' Inspector Haredale grasped his arm. 'It may be booby-trapped. Elkin, make sure there's no wiring under that table.'

As the detective dropped to his knees and began searching, Nayland Smith stepped to the door of the main office. It was locked.

'No wires, sir,' Elkin reported. 'All clear.'

And almost before he had got to his feet Bruce had snatched up the model and was examining it.

'Bruce!' Pat spoke, breathless. 'Has it been tampered with?'

'I assure you, Miss Merton, it has not!' a sibilant, mocking voice replied.

'*Fu Manchu*!' Nayland Smith snapped. 'He's in the next room. Come on, Haredale. We have him!' He fired three revolver shots in quick order. It was the signal for the raid.

There came a quiet laugh. 'Ah, there you are, Sir Denis Nayland Smith. Before you start the raiding party, I have a few words to say. I assume that you are there, Mr Garfield? I could not resist the temptation of telling you myself that you have far to go in the field of gravity. After inspecting your model, I saw no harm in sharing a few facts. So I laid a trail, with the assistance of your charming friend, Miss Merton, which I felt sure you could easily follow.'

Bruce, feeling like a man in a dream, said, 'Very good of you!'

The wail of police whistles sounded, the roar of a racing engine, the screech as brakes were jammed on in the near-by street.

'Your model, Mr Garfield, is elementary,' the strangely sinister voice went on. 'But I was interested to examine it. You have advanced only a short way in the science of anti-gravity. But you are on the right route. Listen.' The sibilant voice droned on as Dr Fu Manchu became more explicit. Bruce listened, fascinated and rapidly made notes. Finally the voice concluded with this astonishing revelation.

'You may recall the sensation once created by the appearance of so-called flying saucers? Some of these – but not all – were test flights of my anti-gravity machine, which I have since perfected. The others, I assume, were from distant planets.'

The door of the outer office was being battered down. A voice shouted, 'Inspector Haredale! Are you there?'

'You may call off your raiders,' the calm voice continued. 'As I know you have already realised – I am not in the other office. I am fifty miles away. When you opened the door of the room in which you stand, you connected me with an amplifying device on a short-wave receiver, which, if you are patient, you may find in the main office. I installed it some time ago to enable me to give orders to subordinates assembled there.'

A crash announced the collapse of the street door. Men could be heard running down the stairs from the entrance on the roof. Pat was trembling. There were tears in her voice when she turned to Bruce, who was holding the model. 'Bruce, darling, is it true? Have you failed?'

Bruce put the model down, hugged Pat – and laughed. 'This is the first model I ever made, and I should have hated to lose it. I suppose I feel about it the way a sculptor feels about a rough clay study for a statue. But it doesn't tell Fu Manchu a thing. What's more, his boastfulness has made him tell *me* more than I think he meant to. But no one – not even you Pat – knows how far I have gone since that first model. Dr Fu Manchu isn't the only man who has solved the riddle of gravity. The other saucers he mentioned don't come from outer space. And so he's in for a surprise. One of the greatest firms in the world has financed, and is now flight-testing, my own anti-gravity machine. That is the real secret of the flying saucers!'

# The Funspot-Street Affair

## THOMAS BURKE

*Our tour of the capital's black spots now turns in the direction of the City by going down Commercial Road and then to Cable Street. Here in the maze of little roads which spread like veins from this seemingly endless thoroughfare that runs from Shadwell past the London Docks and on to the Tower of London, the author of this next story, Thomas Burke (1886–1945), found his inspiration. It is a curious tale of a man so absorbed in his dark and grim surroundings that his imagination begins to conjure up all kinds of crimes – until the terrible moment when fantasy becomes fact . . .*

*Burke is, of course, famous for the story of a serial killer on the loose in the East End, 'The Hands of Mr Ottermole', in which he described the activities of a newspaper reporter investigating the murders. First published in 1931, the mystery was described by the doyen of crime fiction, Ellery Queen, as 'the best detective story of all time' and apart from being anthologized countless times has been frequently broadcast on the radio and adapted for two of the most prestigious television series,* Suspense *and* Alfred Hitchcock Presents. *Burke's knowledge of the area of London described in both 'The Hands of Mr Ottermole' and 'The Funspot-Street Affair' had resulted from his childhood growing up in East London. Like Sax Rohmer, he found particular inspiration for many of his stories in Limehouse and several of the most memorable of these are to be found in his books,*

*Limehouse Nights (1916), More Limehouse Nights (1920) and A Tea-Shop in Limehouse (1931). One very poignant story, 'Broken Blossoms' about an interracial love affair between a Chinese youth and the daughter of a sadistic white boxer has been filmed twice: first in America in 1919 by D. W. Griffiths with Richard Barthelmass and Lillian Gish, and then in 1936 in Britain starring Emlyn Williams and Dolly Haas. Apart from its grim picture of the night streets of north-east London that the author knew so well, 'The Funspot-Street Affair' – originally written for the* Evening News *in 1938 – is unlike most of Burke's short stories in that it has never appeared in any of the collected editions of his work. This republication will surely be one that all his admirers will relish . . .*

ONCE A MONTH Morton passed that street. The business of the firm for which he worked as a collector took him once a month to an office just beyond the limits of the recent spread of the City; an office which called itself City; but was, indeed, North-East.

To reach that office from the Tube station he had to pass that street, and after passing it once a month for two years he found that it had grown upon him and become part of his imaginative life. Every time he passed it, its name, in conjunction with its dark, dishevelled aspect, struck him as bizarre.

After a while he was wanting to do something about it: write a song about it or a paragraph about it, or somehow get it into the news. He wished he knew some newspaper man, who could make it known. He wanted to see it in headlines; he thought it would look well – 'Funspot-street'. It seemed to him to cry for dramatization, and he wished it were possible for him to give it celebrity and immortality.

Funspot-street: he saw it on newspaper bills and he heard the radio announcer mentioning it in news-bulletins, and heard the giggles which the name would arouse in a million homes.

He wondered sometimes why it never had been in the

news. It was surely made for it. By the look of it, it was the sort of street whose people would be fairly regular guests of the police-courts, and whose name, when they gave it as an address, would give great chances to the men who write those facetious stories about other people's troubles, which have taken the place of serious police-court reporting.

Constantly thinking about it, and seeing it in many connections, comic and dramatic, he decided finally that it would look most apt in type as:

### THE FUNSPOT-STREET MURDER

He could see the sub-heads and cross-heads. Shocking Murder in Funspot-street . . . Early this morning the police were called to a house in Funspot-street . . . Detectives working on the Funspot-street tragedy are in possession of an important clue which is likely . . . Funspot Tragedy Arrest . . . No Reprieve for Funspot Murderer . . . And so on.

No; comedy wouldn't do. It called for tragedy, and the more squalid and grotesque the tragedy the more fitting. Something out of the inkwell of Baudelaire or Poe, or De Nerval. He could half see the kind of thing that would fit, and on each monthly visit to that district the fascination of the name and of fitting it with the right story provided him with entertainment for several evenings. He would add extra details to the half-formed idea in his mind, discarding those of last week in favour of some with a keener edge of the bizarre.

He wasn't a writer, and found it difficult to write two paragraphs in sequence, but the name of that street became almost a muse to him; a spur to do what he couldn't do, and write it into prominence.

He never did write it; but after long brooding there came a time when Funspot-street and its Horrible Tragedy were so clear in his mind that in abstracted moments he could hardly believe that it hadn't happened.

He could locate the house, the room, the time (it would be midnight, of course), and he could visualize the act itself as though he had been an eye-witness. He could see the room and its flimsy, shabby furniture. He could smell the stale, unopened reek of it. He could see the gas-bracket and its incandescent mantle, which would be broken and the flame spluttering.

He could see the violently flowered wallpaper, discoloured in places, and elsewhere peeling off. He could see the strip of cheap carpet, with holes at the points where feet had constantly rested. And he could see the man who had somehow, by some aberration, got into this squalid hole, away from his regular, decent surroundings: a slim, neatly-dressed fellow, something like himself.

And he could see the blowsy woman, the fitting châtelaine of such a house. He could hear the violent noises, and he could see the man turning in fury and disgust and striking the woman and rushing from the room.

And then the midday papers, with Funspot-street front-paged. And then the daily and hourly hunt for this decent young chap, just as it might be himself, who, for all his previous decency and integrity, would leave his name in certain records, and be exhibited at Madame Tussaud's as 'The Funspot-street Murderer'. Not even complete tragedy to mark his sudden fall, but tragedy streaked with the ridiculous . . . Funspot-street.

In building the story he attributed to the man, at the moment of walking to the scaffold, a burning grievance. Not at his fate, not at the irresponsible moment which had led him to his fate, or at his capture, when many men who have committed that act have escaped capture. But at the fact that it didn't happen in some other street – in Cavendish- street or Jermyn-street, or Kingsway. Over-riding remorse and resignation and the natural horror of the situation would stand this crowning indignity to a man's *finis* – Funspot-street. He felt that it was a good story, if only he could write it.

The salary which his firm considered an adequate balance to the services he rendered did not permit him much evening entertainment; a theatre or music-hall once a month, perhaps, and the movies once a week. Other evenings he spent in wandering about London, getting for nothing an entertainment superior to anything for which one pays money; the entertainment of the streets and the crowds.

On these walks, while observing the pageant, he let his mind play round his Funspot-street Tragedy, going over it again and again, detail for detail. He wished, whimsically, that somebody would put it into action; that there really would be a murder in Funspot-street, just like that, and that the evening-paper contents bills would flash it at him. But they never did.

It was on one of these walks, when he was wandering round the strange, lost byways of Islington, and playing with the trial in the Funspot-street Tragedy and the duel between prisoner and counsel, that something thick touched him softly on the forehead. For one moment he was aware that he was looking closely at a puddle in the road, and that above his head was the number-plate of a taxi and the wheels of a motor-bus. He was aware also of disturbed voices, and then of a babble; and then, through the babble, a firm voice which said: 'All right . . . we know him . . . we'll look after him.'

That was all he heard in that moment. Next moment, it seemed, he heard a voice saying, in a low growl: 'See if he's got the day's collection on him.' And then another voice saying: ' 'm! Here it is.'

His eyelids seemed of iron, but he managed to open them. They gave his eyes a sight of a strip of cheap carpet, with holes here and there. Above him he saw a gas-bracket, with the flame spluttering. Then he saw a violently flowered wall-paper, and places where it was peeling off.

Over him stood a large, heavy man. Just behind the man stood a blowsy woman wearing a flashy, stained frock which he thought he had seen before. In the woman's hands was a bundle of Treasury notes secured with a rubber band.

At the sight of them, and the memory of the words he had heard, his brain began to move. He realized that he had been robbed. The other details passed back into dream, but the fact that he had been robbed remained as a fact. Somehow or other he managed to scramble to his feet and to make a fierce lunge at the woman.

The midday papers of next afternoon had Funspot-street well on their bills and on their front pages. But Morton never saw them. The last thing he saw was a poker in the hand of the blowsy woman.

# The Girl Who Loved Graveyards

## P. D. JAMES

*Some of the blackest moments in London's history have been enacted within the forbidding walls of the Tower of London which our route takes us past and then via Tower Hill and alongside the Thames towards the City itself. Here the last vestiges of the East End give way to the business heart of the capital. And just by Southwark Bridge stands Queenhithe, an area steeped in the history of the city, which is also where London's best known fictional police officer, Commander Adam Dalgliesh, happens to have a flat. But it is not the shrewd and cultured police detective created in the novels by P. D. James – who has also recently been introduced to a whole new public on television through the urbane acting of Roy Marsden – that we are interested in. Instead, the next story is about crime in a typical East London suburb of the kind we have not long left behind. The kind of place that is full of huddled streets where evil might lurk behind any pair of chintz curtains, or a horrific murder might come to light behind any door. Alma Terrace, the setting of 'The Girl Who Loved Graveyards', is just such a location . . .*

*Baroness Phyllis Dorothy James (1920– ), who was made a Life Peer in 1990, has lived and worked in London for many years, and several of her distinctive and highly ingenious crime novels reveal her intimate knowledge of the capital. She herself began enjoying detective stories as a young girl growing up in a London suburb – Dorothy L. Sayers was her favourite author then – and her work in recent years has deservedly won her a place in the same rank as Sayers, Agatha Christie and Ruth Rendell. Though, curiously, P. D. James has written very few short stories, this next tale is as evocative and engrossing as the very best of her novels.*

SHE COULDN'T REMEMBER anything about the day in the hot August of 1956 when they first brought her to live with her Aunt Gladys and Uncle Victor in the small east London house at 49 Alma Terrace. She knew that it was three days after her tenth birthday and that she was to be cared for by her only living relations now that her father and grandmother were dead, killed by influenza within a week of each other. But those were just facts which someone, at some time, had briefly told her. She could remember nothing of her previous life. Those first ten years were a void, insubstantial as a dream which had faded but which had left on her mind a scar of unarticulated childish anxiety and fear. For her, memory and childhood both began with that moment when, waking in the small unfamiliar bedroom with the kitten, Sambo, still curled asleep on a towel at the foot of her bed, she had walked bare-foot to the window and drawn back the curtain.

And there, stretched beneath her, lay the cemetery, luminous and mysterious in the early morning light, bounded by iron railings and separated from the rear of Alma Terrace only by a narrow path. It was to be another warm day, and over the serried rows of headstones there lay a thin haze pierced by the occasional obelisk and by the wing tips of marble angels whose disembodied heads seemed to be floating on particles of shimmering light. And as she watched, motionless in an absorbed enchantment, the mist began to rise and the whole cemetery was revealed to her, a miracle of stone and marble, bright grass and summer-laden trees, flower-bedecked graves and intersection paths stretching as far as her eyes could see. In the far distance she could just make out the top of the Victorian chapel gleaming like the spire of some magical castle in a long-forgotten fairy tale. In those moments of growing wonder she found herself shivering with delight, an emotion so rare that it stole through her thin body like a pain. And it was then, on that first morning of her new life with the past a void and the future unknown and frightening, that she made the cemetery her own. Throughout her childhood and youth it was to remain a place of delight and mystery, her habitation and her solace.

It was a childhood without love, almost without affection. Her uncle Victor was her father's elder half-brother; that, too, she had been told. He and her aunt weren't really her relations. Their small capacity for love was expended on each other, and even here it was less a positive emotion than a pact of mutual support and comfort against the threatening world which lay outside the trim curtains of their small claustrophobic sitting room.

But they cared for her as dutifully as she cared for the cat Sambo. It was a fiction in the household that she adored Sambo, her own cat, brought with her when she arrived, her one link with the past, almost her only possession. Only she knew that she disliked and feared him. But she brushed and fed him with conscientious care as she did everything and in return he gave her a slavish allegiance, hardly ever leaving her side, slinking through the cemetery at her heels and only turning back when they reached the main gate. But he wasn't her friend. He didn't love her and he knew that she didn't love him. He was a fellow conspirator, gazing at her through slits of azure light, relishing some secret knowledge which was her knowledge too. He ate voraciously yet he never grew fat. Instead his sleek black body lengthened until, stretched in the sunlight along her window sill, his sharp nose turned always to the cemetery, he looked as sinister and unnatural as a furred reptile.

It was lucky for her that there was a side gate to the cemetery from Alma Terrace and that she could take a short cut to and from school across the graveyard avoiding the dangers of the main road. On her first morning her uncle had said doubtfully: 'I suppose it's all right. But it seems wrong some-how, a child walking every day through rows of the dead.'

Her aunt had replied: 'The dead can't rise from their graves. They lay quiet. She's safe enough from the dead.'

Her voice had been unnaturally gruff and loud. The words had sounded like an assertion, almost a defiance. But the child knew that she was right. She did feel safe with the dead, safe and at home.

The years in Alma Terrace slipped by, bland and dull as her aunt's blancmange, a sensation rather than a taste. Had she been happy? It wasn't a question which it had ever occurred to her to ask. She wasn't unpopular at school, being neither pretty nor intelligent enough to provoke much inter-est either from the children or the staff; an ordinary child, unusual only because she was an orphan but unable to capi-talize even on that sentimental advantage. Perhaps she might have found friends, quiet unenterprising children like herself who might have responded to her unthreatening mediocrity. But something about her repelled their timid advances, her self-sufficiency, the bland uncaring gaze, the refusal to give anything of herself even in casual friendship. She didn't need friends. She had the graveyard and its occupants.

She had her favourites. She knew them all, when they had died, how old they had been, sometimes how they had died. She knew their names and learned their memorials by heart. They were more real to her than the living, those rows of dearly loved wives and mothers, respected tradesmen, lamented fathers, deeply mourned children. The new graves hardly ever interested her although she would watch the funerals from a distance then creep up later to read the mourning cards. But what she liked best were the old neglected oblongs of mounded earth or chipped stones, the tilted crosses, the carved words almost erased by time. It was round the names of the long dead that she wove her childish fantasies.

Even the seasons of the year she experienced in and through the cemetery. The gold and purple spears of the first crocuses thrusting through the hard earth. April with its tossing daffodils. The whole graveyard *en fête* in yellow and white as mourners dressed the graves for Easter. The smell of mown grass and the earthy tang of high summer as if the dead were breathing the flower-scented air and exuding their own mysterious miasma. The glare of sunlight on stone and marble as the old women in their stained cotton dresses shuffled with their vases to fill them at the tap behind the chapel. Seeing the cemetery transformed by the first snow of winter, the marble angels grotesque in their high bonnets of glistening snow. Watching at her window for the thaw, hoping to catch that moment when the edifice would slip and the shrouded shapes become themselves again.

Only once had she asked about her father and then she had known as children do that this was a subject which, for some mysterious adult reason, it was better not to talk about. She had been sitting at the kitchen table with her homework while her aunt busied herself cooking supper. Looking up from her history book she had asked: 'Where is Daddy buried?'

The frying pan had clattered against the stove. The cooking fork dropped from her aunt's hand. It had taken her a long time to pick it up, wash it, clean the grease from the floor. The child had asked again: 'Where is Daddy buried?'

'Up north. At Creedon outside Nottingham with your mum and gran. Where else?'

'Can I go there? Can I visit him?'

'When you're older, maybe. No sense is there, hanging about graves. The dead aren't there.'

'Who looks after them?'

'The graves? The cemetery people. Now get on with your homework, do, child. I'll be wanting the table for supper.'

She hadn't asked about her mother, the mother who had died when she was born. That desertion had always seemed to her wilful, a source of secret guilt. 'You killed your mother.' Someone, some time, had spoken those words to her, had laid on her that burden. She wouldn't let herself think about her mother. But she knew that her father had stayed with her, had loved her, hadn't wanted to die and leave her. Some day, secretly, she would find his grave. She would visit it, not once but every week. She would tend it and plant flowers on it and clip the grass as the old ladies did in the cemetery. And if there wasn't a stone she would pay for one, not a cross but a gleaming obelisk, the tallest in the graveyard, bearing his name and an epitaph which she would choose. She would have to wait until she was older, until she could leave school and work, and save enough money. But one day she would find her father. She would have a grave of her own to visit and tend. There was a debt of love to be paid.

Four years after her arrival in Alma Terrace her aunt's only brother came to visit from Australia. Physically he and his sister were alike, the same stolid short-legged bodies, the same small eyes set in square pudgy faces. But Uncle Ned had a brash assurance, a cheerful geniality which was so alien to his sister's unconfident reserve that it was hard to believe that they were siblings. For the two weeks of his visit he dominated the little house with his strident alien voice and assertive masculinity. There were unfamiliar treats, dinners in the West End, a visit to a greyhound stadium, a show at Earls Court. He was kind to the child, tipping her lavishly, even walking through the cemetery with her one morning to buy his racing paper. And it was that evening, coming silently down the stairs to supper, that she overheard disjointed scraps of conversation, adult talk, incomprehensible at the time but taken into her mind and stored there.

First the harsh boom of her uncle's voice: 'We were looking at this grave stone together, see. Beloved husband and father. Taken from us suddenly on 14 March 1892. Something like that. Marble chips, cracked urn, bloody great angel pointing upwards. You know the kind of thing. Then the kid turned to me. "Daddy's death was sudden, too." That's what she said. Came out with it cool as you please. Now what in God's name made her say that? I mean, why then? Christ, it gave me a turn I can tell you. I didn't know where to put my face. And what a place to choose, the bloody cemetery. I'll say one thing for coming out to Sydney. You'll get a better view. I can promise you that.'

Creeping closer, she strained her ears vainly to catch the indistinct mutter of her aunt's reply.

Then came her uncle's voice again: 'That bitch never forgave him for getting Helen pregnant. No one was good enough for her precious only daughter. And then when Helen died having the kid she blamed him for that too. Poor sod, he bought a packet of trouble when he set eyes on that girl. Too soft, too romantic. That was always Martin's trouble.'

Again the murmur of indistinguishable voices, the sound of her aunt's footsteps moving from table to stove, the scrape of a chair. Then her Uncle Ned's voice again.

'Funny kid, isn't she? Old-fashioned. Morbid you might say. Seems to live in that bone yard, she and that damned cat. And the split image of her dad. Christ, it turned me up I can tell you. Looking at me with his eyes and then coming out with it. "Daddy's death was sudden, too." I'll say it was! Influenza? Well, it's as good a name for it as any if you can get away with it. Helps having such an ordinary name, I suppose. People don't catch on. How long ago is it now? Four years? It seems longer.'

Only one part of this half-heard, incomprehensible conversation had disturbed her. Uncle Ned was trying to persuade them to join him in Australia. She might be taken away from Alma Terrace, might never see the cemetery again, might have to wait for years before she could save enough money to return to England and find her father's grave. And how could she visit it regularly, how could she tend and care for it from the other side of the world? After Uncle Ned's visit ended it was months before she could see one of his rare letters with the Australian stamp drop through the letter box without the cold clutch of fear at the heart.

But she needn't have worried. It was October 1966 before they left England and they went alone. When they broke the news to her one Sunday morning at breakfast it was apparent that they had never even considered taking her with them. Dutiful as ever, they had waited to make their decision until she had left school and was earning her living as a shorthand typist with a local firm of estate agents. Her future was assured. They had done all that conscience required of them. Hesitant and a little shame-faced they justified their decision as if they believed that it was important to her, that she cared whether they left or stayed. Her aunt's arthritis was increasingly troublesome; they longed for the sun; Uncle Ned was their only close relation and none of them was getting any younger. Their plan, over which they had agonized for months in whispers behind closed doors, was to visit Sydney for six months and then, if they liked Australia, to apply to emigrate. The house in Alma Terrace was to be sold to pay the air fare. It was already on the market. But they had made provision for her. When they told her what had been arranged, she had to bend her face low over her plate in case the flood of joy should be too apparent. Mrs Morgan, three doors down, would be glad to take her as a lodger if she didn't mind having the small bedroom at the back overlooking the cemetery. In the surging tumult of relief she hardly heard her aunt's next words. There was one small problem. Everyone knew how Mrs Morgan was about cats. Sambo would have to be put down.

She was to move into 43 Alma Terrace on the afternoon of the day on which her aunt and uncle flew from Heathrow. Her two cases, holding all that she possessed in the world, were already packed. In her handbag she carefully stowed the meagre official confirmations of her existence: her birth certificate, her medical card, her Post Office savings book showing the £103 painstakingly saved towards the cost of her father's memorial. And, the next day, she would begin her search. But first she took Sambo to the vet to be destroyed. She made a cat box from two cartons fitted together, pierced it with holes, then sat patiently in the waiting room with the box at her feet. The cat made no sound and this patient resignation touched her, evoking for the first time a spasm of pity and affection. But there was nothing she could do to save him. They both knew it. But then, he had always known what she was thinking, what was past and what was to come. There was something they shared, some knowledge, some common experience which she couldn't remember and he couldn't express. Now with his destruction even that tenuous link with her first ten years would go for ever.

When it was her turn to go into the surgery she said: 'I want him put down.'

The vet passed his strong experienced hands over the sleek fur. 'Are you sure? He seems quite healthy still. He's old, of course, but he's in remarkably good condition.'

'I'm sure. I want him put down.'

And she left him there without a glance or another word.

She had thought that she would be glad to be free of the pretence of loving him, free of those slitted accusing eyes. But as she walked back to Alma Terrace she found herself crying; tears, unbidden and unstoppable, ran like rain down her face.

There was no difficulty in getting a week's leave from her job. She had been husbanding her holiday entitlement. Her work, as always, was up to date. She had calculated how much money she would need for her train and bus fares and for a week's stay in modest hotels. Her plans had been made. They had been made for years. She would begin her search with the address on her birth certificate, Cranstoun House, Creedon, Nottingham, the house where she had been born. The present owners might remember her and her father. If not, there would be neighbours or older inhabitants of the village who would be able to recall her father's death, where he was buried. If that failed she would try the local undertakers. It was, after all, only ten years ago. Someone locally would remember. Somewhere in Nottingham there would be a record of burials. She told Mrs Morgan that she was taking a week's holiday to visit her father's old home, packed a hold-all with overnight necessities and, next morning, caught the earliest-possible fast train from St Pancras to Nottingham.

It was during the bus ride from Nottingham to Creedon that she felt the first stirrings of anxiety and mistrust. Until then she had travelled in calm confidence, but strangely without excitement, as if this long-planned journey was as natural and inevitable as her daily walk to work, an inescapable pilgrimage ordained from that moment when a bare-footed child in her white nightdress had drawn back her bedroom curtains and seen her kingdom spread beneath her. But now her mood changed. As the bus lurched through the suburbs she found herself shifting in her seat as if mental unease were provoking physical discomfort. She had expected green countryside, small churches guarding neat domestic graveyards patterned with yew trees. These were graveyards she had visited on holidays, had loved almost as much as she loved the one she had made her own. Surely it was in such bird-loud sanctified peace that her father lay. But Nottingham had spread during the past ten years and Creedon was now little more than an urban village separated from the city by a ribbon development of brash new houses, petrol stations and parades of shops. Nothing in the journey was familiar, and yet she knew that she had travelled this road before and travelled it in anxiety and pain.

But when, thirty minutes later, the bus stopped at its terminus at Creedon she knew at once where she was. The Dog and Whistle still stood at one corner of the dusty litter-strewn village green with the same bus shelter outside it. And with the sight of its graffiti-scrawled walls memory returned as easily as if nothing had ever been forgotten. Here her father used to leave her when he brought her to pay her regular Sunday visits to her grandmother. Here her grandmother's elderly cook would be waiting for her. Here she would look back for a final wave and see her father patiently waiting for the bus to begin its return journey. Here she would be brought at six-thirty when he arrived to collect her. Cranstoun House was where her grandmother lived. She herself had been born there but it had never been her home.

She had no need to ask her way to the house. And when,

five minutes later, she stood gazing up at it in appalled fascination, no need to read the name painted on the shabby padlocked gate. It was a square built house of dark brick standing in incongruous and spurious grandeur at the end of a country lane. It was smaller than she now remembered, but it was still a dreadful house. How could she ever have forgotten those ornate overhanging gables, the high pitched roof, the secretive oriel windows, the single forbidding turret at the east end? There was an estate agent's board wired to the gate and it was apparent that the house was empty. The paint on the front door was peeling, the lawns were overgrown, the boughs of the rhododendron bushes were broken and the gravel path was studded with clumps of weed. There was no one here who could help her to find her father's grave. But she knew that she had to visit, had to make herself pass again through that intimidating front door. There was something the house knew and had to tell her, something that Sambo had known. She couldn't escape her next step. She must find the estate agent's office and get a permit to view.

She had missed the returning bus and by the time the next one had reached Nottingham it was after three o'clock. She had eaten nothing since her early breakfast but she was too driven now to be aware of hunger. But she knew that it would be a long day and that she ought to eat. She turned into a coffee bar and bought a toasted cheese sandwich and a mug of coffee, grudging the few minutes which it took to gulp them down. The coffee was hot but almost tasteless. Flavour would have been wasted on her, but she realised as the hot liquid stung her throat how much she had needed it.

The girl at the cash desk was able to direct her to the house agent's office. It seemed to her a happy augury that it was within ten minutes' walk. She was received by a sharp featured young man in an over-tailored pin-stripe suit who, in one practised glance at her old blue tweed coat, the cheap hold-all and bag of synthetic leather, placed her precisely in his private category of client from whom little can be expected and to whom less need be given. But he found the particulars for her and his curiosity sharpened as she merely glanced at them, then folded the paper away in her bag. Her request to view that afternoon was received, as she expected, with politeness but without enthusiasm. But this was familiar territory and she knew why. The house was unoccupied. She would have to be escorted. There was nothing in her respectable drabness to suggest that she was a likely purchaser. And when he briefly excused himself to consult a colleague and returned to say that he could drive her to Creedon at once she knew the reason for that too. The office wasn't particularly busy and it was time that someone from the firm checked up on the property.

Neither of them spoke during the drive. But when they reached Creedon and he turned down the lane to the house the apprehension she had felt on her first visit returned, but deeper and stronger. Yet now it was more than the memory of an old wretchedness. This was childish misery and fear relived, but intensified by a dreadful adult foreboding. As the house agent parked his Morris on the grass verge she looked up at the blind windows and was seized by a spasm of terror so acute that, momentarily, she was unable to speak or move. She was aware of the man holding open the car door for her, of the smell of beer on his breath, of his face, uncomfortably close, bending on her a look of exasperated patience. She wanted to say that she had changed her mind, that the house was totally wrong for her, that there would be no point in viewing it, that she would wait for him in the car. But she willed herself to rise from the warm seat and scrambled out under his supercilious eyes, despising herself for her gracelessness. She waited in silence as he unlocked the padlock and swung open the gate.

They passed together between the neglected lawns and the spreading rhododendron bushes towards the front door. And suddenly the feet shuffling the gravel beside her were different feet and she knew that she was walking with her father as she had walked in childhood. She had only to stretch out her hand to feel the grasp of his fingers. Her companion was saying something about the house but she didn't hear. The meaningless chatter faded and she heard a different voice, her father's voice, heard for the first time in over ten years.

'It won't be for always, darling. Just until I've found a job. And I'll visit you every Sunday for lunch. Then, afterwards, we'll be able to go for a walk together, just the two of us. Granny has promised that. And I'll buy you a kitten. I'll bring it next weekend. I'm sure Granny won't mind when she sees him. A black kitten. You've always wanted a black kitten. What shall we call him? Little black Sambo? He'll remind you of me. And then, when I've found a job, I'll be able to rent a little house and we'll be together again. I'll look after you, my darling. We'll look after each other.'

She dared not look up in case she should see again those desperately pleading eyes, begging her to understand, to make things easy for him, not to despise him. She knew now that she ought to have helped him, to have told him that she understood, that she didn't mind living with Granny for a month or so, that everything would be all right. But she hadn't managed so adult a response. She remembered tears, desperate clingings to his coat, her grandmother's old cook, tight-lipped, pulling her away from him and bearing her up to bed. And the last memory was of watching him from her room above the porch, of his drooping defeated figure making its way down the lane to the bus stop.

As they reached the front door she looked up. The window was still there. But, of course, it was. She knew every room in this dark house.

The garden was bathed in a mellow October sunlight, but the hall struck cold and dim. The heavy mahogany staircase led up from gloom to a darkness which hung above them like a pall. The estate agent felt along the wall for the light switch. But she didn't wait. She felt again the huge brass door knob which her childish fingers had hardly encompassed and moved unerringly into the drawing room.

The smell of the room was different. Then there had been

a scent of violets overlaid with furniture polish. Now the air smelt cold and musty. She stood in the darkness shivering but perfectly calm. It seemed to her that she had passed through a barrier of fear as a tortured victim might pass through a pain barrier into a kind of peace. She felt a shoulder brush against her as the man went across to the window and swung open the heavy curtains.

He said: 'The last owners have left it partly furnished. Looks better that way. Easier to get offers if the place looks lived in.'

'Has there been an offer?'

'Not yet. It's not everyone's cup of tea. Bit on the large size for a modern family. And then, there's the murder. Ten years ago, but people still talk in the neighbourhood. There's been four owners since then and none of them stayed long. It's bound to affect the price. No good thinking you can hush up murder.'

His voice was carefully nonchalant, but his gaze never left her face. Walking to the empty fire grate, he stretched one arm along the mantelpiece and followed her with his eyes as she moved as if in a trance about the room.

She heard herself asking: 'What murder?'

'A sixty-four-year-old woman. Battered to death by her son-in-law. The old cook came in from the back kitchen and found him with the poker in his hand. Come to think of it, it could have been one like that.'

He nodded down to a collection of brass fire-irons resting against the fender. He said: 'It happened right where you're standing now. She was sitting in that very chair.'

She said in a voice so gruff and harsh that she hardly recognized it: 'It wasn't this chair. It was bigger. Her chair had an embroidered seat and back and there were armrests edged with crochet and the feet were like lions' claws.

His gaze sharpened. Then he laughed warily. The watchful eyes grew puzzled, then the look changed into something else. Could it have been contempt?

'So you know about it. You're one of those.'

'One of those?'

'They aren't really in the market for a place. Couldn't afford one this size anyway. They just want a thrill, want to see where it happened. You get all sorts in this game and I can usually tell. I can give you all the gory details if you're interested. Not that there was much gore. The skull was smashed but most of the bleeding was internal. They say there was just a trickle falling down her forehead and dripping on to her hands.'

It came out so pat that she knew that he had told it all before, that he enjoyed telling it, this small recital of horror to titillate his clients and relieve the boredom of his day. She wished that she wasn't so cold. If only she could get warm again her voice wouldn't sound so strange.

She said through her dry and swollen lips: 'And the kitten. Tell me about the kitten.'

'Now that was something! That was a touch of horror if you like. The kitten was on her lap, licking up the blood. But then you know, don't you? You've heard all about it.'

'Yes,' she lied. 'I've heard all about it.'

But she had done more than that. She knew. She had seen it. She had been there.

And then the outline of the chair altered. An amorphous black shape swam before her eyes, then took form and substance. Her grandmother was sitting there, squat as a toad, dressed in her Sunday black for morning service, gloved and hatted, prayer book in her lap. She saw again the glob of phlegm at the corner of the mouth, the thread of broken veins at the side of the sharp nose. She was waiting to inspect her grandchild before church, turning on her again that look of querulous discontent. The witch was sitting there. The witch who hated her and her daddy, who had told her that he was useless and feckless and no better than her mother's murderer. The witch who was threatening to have Sambo put down because he had torn her chair, because Daddy had given him to her. The witch who was planning to keep her from Daddy for ever.

And then she saw something else. The poker was there, too, just as she remembered it, the long rod of polished brass with its heavy knob.

She seized it as she had seized it then and, with a high scream of hatred and terror, brought it down on her grandmother's head. Again and again she struck, hearing the brass thudding against the leather, blow on splitting blow. And still she screamed. The room rang with the terror of it. But it was only when the frenzy passed and the dreadful noise stopped that she knew from the pain of her torn throat that the screaming had been hers.

She stood shaking, gasping for breath. Beads of sweat stood out on her forehead and she felt the stinging drops seeping into her eyes. Looking up she was aware of the man's eyes, wide with terror, staring into hers, of a muttered curse, of footsteps running to the door. And then the poker slid from her moist hands and she heard it thud softly on the rug.

He had been right, there was no blood. Only the grotesque hat knocked forward over the dead face. But as she watched a sluggish line of deep red rolled from under the brim, zig-zagged down the forehead, trickled along the creases of the cheeks and began to drop steadily on to the gloved hands. And then she heard a soft mew. A ball of black fur crept from behind the chair and the ghost of Sambo, azure eyes frantic, leapt as he had leapt ten years earlier delicately up to that unmoving lap.

She looked at her hands. Where were the gloves, the white cotton gloves which the witch had always insisted must be worn to church? But these hands, no longer the hands of a nine-year-old child, were naked. And the chair was empty. There was nothing but the split leather, the burst of horsehair stuffing, a faint smell of violets fading on the quiet air.

She walked out of the front door without closing it behind her as she had left it then. She walked as she had walked then, gloved and unsullied, down the gravel path between the rhododendrons, out of the ironwork gate and up the lane towards the church. The bell had only just started ringing;

she would be in good time. In the distance she had glimpsed
her father climbing a stile from the water meadow into the
lane. So he must have set out early after breakfast and had
walked to Creedon. And why so early? Had he needed that
long walk to settle something in his mind? Had it been a
pathetic attempt to propitiate the witch by coming with
them to church? Or, blessed thought, had he come to take
her away, to see that her few belongings were packed and
ready by the time the service was over? Yes, that was what she
had thought at the time. She remembered it now, that foun-
tain of hope soaring and dancing into glorious certainty.
When she got home all would be ready. They would stand
there together and defy the witch, would tell her that they
were leaving together, the two of them and Sambo, that she
would never see them again. At the end of the road she
looked back and saw for the last time the beloved ghost
crossing the lane to the house towards that fatally open door.

   And after that? The vision was fading now. She could
remember nothing of the service except a blaze of red and
blue shifting like a kaleidoscope then fusing into a stained
glass window, the Good Shepherd gathering a lamb to his
bosom. And afterwards? Surely there had been strangers waiting in the porch, grave concerned faces, whispers and
sidelong glances, a woman in some kind of uniform, an
official car. And after that, nothing. Memory was a blank.

   But now, at last, she knew where her father was buried.
And she knew why she would never be able to visit him,
never make that pious pilgrimage to the place where he lay
because of her, the shameful place where she had put him.
There could be no flowers, no obelisk, no loving message
carved in marble for those who lay in quicklime behind a
prison wall. And then, unbidden, came the final memory.
She saw again the open church door, the trickle of the con-
gregation filing in, enquiring faces turning towards her as she
arrived alone in the porch. She heard again that high childish voice speaking the words which more than any others had
slipped that rope of hemp over his shrouded head.

'Granny? She isn't very well. She told me to come on my own. No, there's nothing to worry about. She's quite all right. Daddy's with her.'

# The Most Hated Man in London

## PATRICIA MOYES

*Less than a quarter of a mile from the River Thames stands Mansion House, the Bank of England and Cornhill, the financial heart of the City of London, and it is said that more crimes have been committed in this square mile of the capital than anywhere else in the entire country! Robbery, fraud, embezzlement, violence and even murder – the business institutions which control the nation's wealth have experienced all of these over the years. Indeed, all the shady dealers and crooked financiers to be found in works of fiction can hardly hold a candle to the real-life villains who have cheated the Stock Exchange and defrauded the Banks in the last two hundred years or so. It is certainly an area rich in material for the writer of crime fiction as Patricia Moyes demonstrates in her 'classic' story of 'The Most Hated Man in London'.*

*Patricia Moyes (1923–   ) led a very varied career before settling down as a writer of popular detective stories. She was a flight officer in the WAAF during the Second World War; served as secretary to Peter Ustinov between 1947 and 1953; and then became an assistant editor on* Vogue *in London. Her interest in high finance began during this period of her life and her insight has increased enormously since her marriage to John S. Hazard who works with the International Monetary Fund in Washington D.C. Combining crime with high finance began for Pat when she wrote the screenplay* School for Scoundrels *in*

*1960 and has since been seen at work in several of her novels about Chief Inspector Henry Tibbett, a quiet and self-effacing Scotland Yard detective who lives with his wife on the ground floor of a decaying Victorian house in London. Especially in Tibbett's cases of* Death on the Agenda *(about crime at an international conference, written in 1962),* Murder à la Mode *(which she wrote in 1963 and set in the offices of a fashion magazine) and* Black Widower *(featuring murder in diplomatic circles and published in 1975). The* Chicago Tribune, *recently reviewing Patricia Moyes' work, described her as having 'put back the "who" in "who-dunnit"' – and the story of the murder of Max Scotland, moneylender, 'The Most Hated Man in London' is one more example of her expertise at writing a crime story in the classic tradition . . .*

'IT ISN'T OFTEN,' said the Chief Inspector to his class of trainee-detectives, 'that you come across a case you can solve by pure logic; but the Max Scotland murder was a classic, and I'll give you a big hint. It was all a question of timing.

'If ever a man asked to be killed, Max did. He was officially a moneylender and unofficially a blackmailer. He conducted all his business, legitimate and otherwise, from an old-fashioned office in the City, where he made his "clients" call in person to hand over their money. Not all of his victims were rich. Max was democratic. He'd exploit even five bob's worth of human misery.

'Since he was probably the most hated man in London, I wasn't at all surprised to hear, one Saturday, that he'd been found in his office with his head bashed in. The alarm had been raised just before noon by Alfred Lightfoot, a young clerk from a nearby shipping firm, who'd had an appointment with Max, and found him dead.

'Now, here's the interesting part. The suite of offices where Max worked – if you can call it that – was guarded by a doorkeeper. An old soldier, very reliable. There was no way in or out except past the cubicle where this character, George Potts, was sitting all the morning.

'Potts told us that Max had arrived at ten o'clock. Nobody else was in, it being Saturday, but during the morning Max had three visitors. Sure enough, we found his engagement book on his desk, but it didn't help us much, because Max had used code names for his victims. He fancied himself as a scholar and always gave the poor devils classical names. A Mr Mars was expected at ten fifteen, and a Mrs Niobe at eleven o'clock. Mr Hermes – alias Lightfoot – was down for eleven thirty, but the entry had been altered in Max's writing to twelve o'clock.

'From the names I guessed that Mr Mars was involved with somebody else's wife, that Niobe's scandal had something to do with a child, and that young Alfred might have been better-named Lightfinger. Anyhow, it was obvious that each of them had a motive for murdering Max.

'George Potts knew Lightfoot and Niobe by sight. They were what he called "regulars" – came at the same time, first Saturday of every month. He didn't know their names, but he described Niobe as young, beautiful, and rich – she wore a mink coat. As for Mr Mars, he was a new client – middle-aged, stout, and extremely prosperous-looking.

'Mr Mars, George said, had arrived at ten fifteen prompt and spent ten minutes in Max's office. Then he'd come striding out, apparently very agitated, slamming the door behind him. Niobe had only been in the office for a minute or two. When she came out, she was crying – but she always was, according to George. Lightfoot had arrived at five to twelve. It hadn't struck midday before he came running out of the office, shouting murder.

'The next thing I did was to look at the office. It was bleak enough – two chairs, a desk, a filing cabinet, and a safe. The safe was open, and it was empty. The only cheerful thing about the room was the coal fire, and from the look of the ashes all the papers from the safe had been burnt in it.

'Max was lying on the floor between the desk and the safe. His head had been smashed in from behind with a heavy iron poker. There was less blood than I'd expected –

only a sluggish stream that had dried up just short of the doorway. There were no fingerprints except Max's, but there was a footprint. Just one, in the dried-up blood by the door. It was the print of a very fashionable ladies' shoe.

'We had one stroke of luck. Not all the papers in the grate were completely burnt, and we found several scraps with legible names on them – two of them women's. We got hold of photographs of these two ladies, and George Potts identified one of them as Niobe. She was Lady Elizabeth Carter-Johnson, daughter of an earl and wife of a rising politician. She was terribly distressed when I questioned her, begging me to keep her name out of the papers because of her husband's career. She didn't deny that she was being blackmailed, or that the footprint was hers. She'd arrived promptly at eleven, gone into the office and found Max lying there, dead. For a moment she'd been paralyzed with horror. Then she'd run away and not raised the alarm, for fear of being involved.

'Alfred Lightfoot said he'd telephoned at twenty to eleven, spoken to Max personally, and arranged to postpone his appointment. This was confirmed by Lightfoot's colleagues in his office. When he got there at five to twelve, he had found Max dead. Well, now . . .'

The Chief Inspector regarded his class quizzically. 'How many suspects have you eliminated so far?' There was dead silence.

'The first person in the clear,' the Chief Inspector went on, 'was Lightfoot. If he'd been the murderer, Lady Elizabeth would have found Max alive, and couldn't have described to me just how the body was lying, as she did. Then, the lady was saved by her own footprint. The doctor confirmed it would have taken about ten minutes for the stream of blood to reach the door. If she'd killed Max, she couldn't have left a footprint where she did.

'It began to look black for Mr Mars – in spite of the fact that Lightfoot's phone call apparently gave him a perfect alibi. You can imagine my surprise when Mr Mars telephoned Scotland Yard that afternoon, before the murder was reported in the papers. He was a businessman named Dacres, and the first of Max's victims to have the guts to report to the police. He swore he'd left Max alive and well at twenty-five past ten. You see my dilemma? Apparently, all three were telling the truth. Yet somebody was lying, and somebody had killed Max.

'I went and checked again with Potts. He was positive he'd got all the times right. People were always punctual for Mr Scotland, he said. Never kept *him* waiting. After that I went back to the Yard and thought it all out. And then I made my arrest.'

'You mean, you broke Dacres' alibi, sir?'

'No.'

'But—'

'The murderer,' said the Chief Inspector, 'was George Potts. I told you that Max didn't spurn the most humble of victims. After that second interrogation I knew Potts was lying. He insisted that all three visitors were punctual – but Lightfoot's usual appointment was for eleven thirty, and he didn't turn up until five to twelve. Potts must have known that the appointment had been changed – so he must have been *in Max's office* and seen the engagement book, *after* Lightfoot's phone call and *before* Lady Elizabeth arrived. And when Lady Elizabeth got there, Max had been dead for ten minutes. So, allowing three minutes for the phone call, George Potts must have killed him between seventeen and ten minutes to eleven. As I said, just a simple question of timing.'

# Flight From Fleet Street

## CARTER DICKSON

*It is a walk of only just over half a mile from the City to Fleet Street and another infamous black spot in London's criminal history. For here, in what used to be called 'The Street of Ink' before all the nation's leading newspapers moved out a few years ago to new premises on the banks of the Thames and in Docklands, lived the infamous Sweeney Todd, the 'Demon Barber of Fleet Street'. Arguments have raged for years as to whether Todd was actually a real person or the figment of a Penny Dreadful writer's imagination; whether he did, in fact, murder as many as 160 unsuspecting customers who sat in his revolving barber's chair and were then tumbled into a cellar below where their throats were cut, their valuables removed, and their corpses made into meat pies for sale by the barber's accomplice, a Mrs Lovett. Although the legend of Sweeney Todd was certainly first made famous in a weekly fictional serial called, rather prosaically, 'The String of Pearls' by Thomas Peckett Prest published in* The People's Periodical *in 1846 – later becoming the subject of a number of very popular theatrical melodramas – there is still strong evidence that he* did *live in Fleet Street about 150 years ago and perpetrated a reign of terror which has made him as infamous in London lore as Jack the Ripper and Dr Crippen. In one account of his life he has even been described as 'the greatest mass murderer in English history'.*

*For many years now, visitors have been coming to Fleet Street from all over the world looking for the whereabouts of his shop which was said to have been at number 186, near the site of the old Temple Bar. Among their number was John Dickson Carr (1906–1977), an American detective story writer who lived and worked in England for many years, and was also responsi-* ble for devising the well remembered Forties radio programme, Appointment With Fear, *in which Valentine Dyall as 'The Man in Black' introduced dramatized stories of horror and the supernatural. Carr also created a very popular London-based detective, Dr Gideon Fell (who appears in the second section of this book) as well as writing a number of first-rate mystery short stories under the pseudonym Carter Dickson. 'Flight From Fleet Street', his version of the Sweeney Todd legend which he described as an 'entertainment', was originally published in the* London Magazine *of February/March 1952 and is here mak-* ing *its first appearance in book form. It is one of the most surprising and ingenious tales of the Demon Barber that I have ever read.*

TABLEAU ONE

*THE SCENE IS London. The curtain rises on a private sitting-room in a small, old-fashioned, expensive hotel in a small, old-fashioned, expensive street that runs down to the Thames from the Strand. Fleet Street, lined with huge newspaper buildings and small shops, is close by, as you can partly see (when there isn't a fog) by crossing the road to stand by the statue of Dr Johnson in St Clement's churchyard. Hampden's Hotel is dingy, self-consciously dingy, like a certain famous shop in St James's. The carpets are old, but of the best quality, like the staff. Some of the staff have been there longer than the oldest regular visitor can remember. The atmosphere is redolent of friendly deference and easy courtesy. Even the lift is a vintage one. Without doubt, the oldest lift in London, it rises and descends so slowly, and with such creaks and tremblings, that it is no wonder rumour tells how it is pulled up and lowered by a mysterious boy turning a*

*windlass in the cellar. Two new patrons have just ascended to the
second floor of Hampden's and been shown to their rooms by an
ancient porter. They are Bill Leslie, an American, on his first
visit to London, and Brenda, his English wife. Bill is romantic
about London, and London, always polite, obligingly tried to
live up to Bill's notions of what it ought to be. As a start,
London provides him at once with that rarity, a thick fog, and
from the shrouded river the deep notes of ships' sirens sound
melancholy warnings. As the porter, well tipped, closes the door,
Brenda Leslie laughs delightedly.*

*Brenda:* Bill, darling, don't look so bewildered!

*Bill:* Was I looking bewildered, Brenda?

*Brenda:* I *know* the furniture is red plush and dates back to the eighteen-sixties! I know we can't get a private bathroom!

*Bill:* By George, the waiters look as old as the furniture!

*Brenda:* But if only we'd gone to Torridge's or the Hautboy, or—

*Bill:* Brenda, you don't understand.

*Brenda:* No?

*Bill:* Who the devil *wants* to go to those swank hotels? This is London!

*Brenda:* Bill, I'm afraid I still don't understand.

*Bill:* I've been in the Diplomatic Service for seven years. I've been stationed in three capitals.

But I've never been here.

*Brenda:* It's a lovely old town. It's – home.

*Bill:* It's home to me, too, in a way. It's put a spell on my imagination ever since I was a boy so-high. Sherlock Holmes! Dr Fu Manchu! Hansom-cabs rattling through the fog . . .

*Brenda:* Darling, you don't think we still ride about in hansoms?

*Bill:* No, but it's the spirit of the thing! Here! Look out of this window!

*Brenda:* Yes?

*Bill:* Grey-and-black buildings. A lovely fog. Night falling. And – yes! Listen!

*Brenda:* What? I don't hear anything.

*Bill:* It's one of your famous barrel-organs. What's the tune, Brenda? Do you know it?

*Brenda:* Something about, 'She's a lassie from Lancashire'. It's an old one.

*Bill:* But it's right, don't you see? Everything's right. And if I crane out of the window – sideways, like this – I can see down to the river. At least, I could except for this fog. That's where the bodies fall from the wharfs, and the police launches—

*Brenda:* Bill! Please listen to me!

*Bill:* Yes?

*Brenda:* I love you terribly, Bill. But of all the romantic Americans I've ever met, you have the most fantastic ideas about England. You don't really expect to find Scotland Yard men, in bowler hats, trailing your every step, do you?

*Bill:* That wasn't the point, Brenda! I only said—

*Brenda:* When you think about it, just remember that barrel-organ. Safe. Stodgy. Comfortable. That's London, Bill. Will you remember?

*As Bill gives his wife a friendly hug, the telephone rings. Bill, in mocking*

*tones, exclaims as he goes to answer it.*

*Bill:* So they've got telephones here! Hullo, Bill Leslie here. What's that? The police! Must be some mistake. What? Well, I guess you'd better send the gentleman upstairs. Thank you.

*Brenda:* What on earth's the matter, Bill?

*Bill:* Search me! A Scotland Yard man is on his way up to see me. What price safety and stodginess now, Brenda?

*Brenda:* You're joking, Bill. What can the police want with you?

*Bill:* About six hours in England, and—

*Brenda:* Oh, this is ridiculous! There must be some mistake!

*Bill:* There probably is. All the same, come to think of it, I don't feel very keen about facing one of these C.I.D. bowler hats in real life.

*As he speaks there is a rap on the door, a firm, official knock, not loud, but determined.*

Come in please, come in.

*The door opens, and Chief Inspector Radford enters. He is wearing a well-cut dark suit and carries a briefcase and the latest model in bowler hats. Yes, he has a neatly cropped black moustache. He has an affable manner and keen grey eyes. He bows slightly to Mrs Leslie. Then turns quickly to business.*

*Radford:* Mr William Leslie? Sorry to have to trouble you, sir. I'm a police-officer. Metropolitan C.I.D. Here's my warrant-card.
*Bill:* I see. 'Chief Inspector—'
*Radford:* Radford, sir. And I'm bound to tell you I'm here about a serious matter.
*Bill:* How delightful – I mean, how surprising. Please sit down, Inspector.
*Radford:* Thank you, sir. Now . . . don't mind my notebook. It's a mere formality . . . You and your wife arrived this morning by the *Maurevania*. Your wife is British, and carries her own passport. Correct?
*Bill:* Yes. That's correct . . .

*Radford:* A week from today you leave, by the same ship, for Lisbon. At Lisbon you take up a new diplomatic assignment at the American Embassy. Correct?
*Bill:* ⎤ Yes! But . . .
*Brenda:* ⎦ What's wrong?
*Radford:* Just a moment! I'd like you to look at this snapshot I have here . . . Who is it?
*Brenda:* But – it's Bill! No, it isn't. Look at that awful shirt and tie! It's your double, Bill!
*Bill:* So help me, I never had that picture taken. It must be my double. I never wore a shirt like that!
*Radford:* I know you didn't, Mr Leslie. That's Flash Morgan. Ever heard of him?
*Bill:* Never. Is he – *wanted* for something?
*Radford:* He's wanted for several murders. Also bank robbery. Also he's a ripper, if you know what that means. Uses a razor, and – likes it. Never has a gun. That's Flash in a flash, so to speak.
*Bill: Me?* The image of a murderer?
*Radford:* They don't look so different from the rest of us. Do you realize, sir, you can't

leave this hotel without being nabbed, as Morgan, by the first copper you meet? It isn't just a likeness, you'll agree. You're his double. You're the dead spit of him – as we say.

*Bill:* But I can prove who I am! I've got my papers!

*Radford:* You've got your papers. Right! Suppose Morgan gets 'em?

*Bill:* Morgan?

*Radford:* The *Maurevania* sails a week from today. Somebody called William Leslie, carrying diplomatic immunity, sails with her. What's to prove it's really you?

*Bill:* You mean he might—

*Radford:* I do.

*Bill:* That's impossible! He couldn't get away with it!

*Radford:* No, I don't think he could. But I'll give you ten to one he tries it. This is too small a country to hide in, and he can't get away. He's desperate. This is his last hope.

*Bill:* What about – Brenda here?

*Radford:* There are several things that might happen to Mrs Leslie. All unpleasant. There's just one more

matter I'm bound to warn you of. Morgan may try to get into this hotel.

*Bill:* But look here, Inspector! This ripper, or whatever he is, couldn't possibly know there's a man in town who looks just like him!

*Radford:* He couldn't, eh? Have you seen the evening papers?

*Bill:* No.

*Radford:* Some fool took a picture of you getting off the boat-train. It's been published, with comments on the resemblance, in all the evenings! You'll find Morgan's story in the *Evening News.* With pictures.

*Bill:* So I've made the front page at last!

*Brenda:* Don't laugh about it, Bill. But haven't you got any idea where this man is, Inspector?

*Radford:* No, ma'am; we haven't. He used to have a hangout at 996 Fleet Street, up over a barber's shop. But he won't go there now. He's loaded with money from the Whitehall Bank job. He's got a razor, and he's ready to use it. And now, if you'll excuse me, I must go.

But for your own sakes I want you to stay in this hotel, both of you, until that boat sails.

*Bill:* Cooped up here for a week? Just in case?

*Radford:* Yes, Mr Leslie. Just in case.

*Bill:* Suppose I do go out?

*Radford:* I can't stop you, sir. The guard I'm leaving here can't stop you. But I might send you some photographs of people with their throats cut. Sorry to have upset you. Good night.

*As the bowler-hatted representative of England's Criminal Investigation Department closes the door behind him, Bill and Brenda sit down on a sofa covered with red plush. For a few moments they simply stare at each other. From the street below the barrel-organ is playing 'The Lambeth Walk,' accompanied in the bass register by hoots and toots from the fog-covered Thames.*

*Bill:* Brenda! What price romantic London!

*Brenda:* Don't dear. This is serious. I'm scared, Bill.

*Bill:* What was the number of that address Radford gave us? Where Morgan used to hang out?

*Brenda:* I don't remember.

*Bill:* You mean, darling, you won't remember. Nine hundred and ninety-six, wasn't it? 996 Fleet Street?

*Brenda:* Why do you want to know?

*Bill:* Because I'm going there. And I'm going now.

*Brenda:* Yes. I thought that was it. Bill, you can't! You mustn't! You can't do anything there!

*Bill:* I know.

*Brenda:* Bill, come back here! You're not to go!

*Bill:* Where's my overcoat? Now, this address—

*Brenda:* If you go, I'm going with you.

*Bill:* Oh no. This isn't a woman's kind of dare; and you know it.

*Brenda:* It's as much my dare as yours!

*Bill:* 996 Fleet Street. Up over a barber-shop. How do I get there?

*Brenda:* I don't—

*Bill:* If you don't tell me, Brenda, I can easily find out.

*Brenda:* Oh, all right. I give up. It's not very far from here. You could walk it in ten minutes.

*Bill:* That's better! That's much better!

*Brenda:* What about your identification papers?

*Bill:* I'm throwing 'em out here on the bed. Morgan won't get *those*.

*Brenda:* But if you haven't got those papers, you won't be able to prove who you are!

*Bill:* I'll risk it, Brenda. I'll risk it. See you later!

*Brenda:* Bill, come back! It's idiotic! Don't leave me! Please come back! Please . . . If you don't, I'm coming, too . . .


TABLEAU TWO


*Fleet Street on a foggy October evening is not the easiest place in the world for a stranger to find a particular building. London street numbering is so eccentric that it seems arranged on purpose to puzzle, and Fleet Street is no exception. Bill Leslie has passed Temple Bar without seeing it, and is now stumbling across Fetter Lane. As he stares at the lighted windows of Peele's Coffee House (one of the street's noted taverns) the slow booming bell of St Paul's strikes seven, followed by the harsh clang of St Dunstan's. Bill bumps into someone as he reaches the narrow entrance to 'The Cheshire Cheese', and a cheerful Cockney voice shouts, 'Sorry, guv'nor.' Bill feels his throat apprehensively and begins to wish he had a Londoner as a guide. He mutters to himself:*


*Bill (soliloquizing):* Can't see the numbers. Those I can see seem to be in the wrong order. Fool stunt to come out alone in a fog. Wish I hadn't started. Supposing Morgan with his rip-throat razor is following me! But can't turn back now. Who's afraid? Mustn't be afraid. Might walk a little faster. No harm in walking a little faster. There! Number nine thirty-four. Can't be far off now. Was that a policeman's helmet? Doesn't matter. Police mean safety. Nobody can see my face. Another policeman's helmet! Swear to it! Over in that alley. A little faster . . . Take it easy, now; don't run. They can't possibly . . .

*Man's Voice:* You, there! Stop!

*Bill:* Mustn't get panicky. How do you stop panic? Got to find that address; got to justify myself; got to—

*Bill's soliloquy is interrupted by the shrill blast of a police whistle. As he begins to run, he stops abruptly. By a staircase open to the street Bill has noticed the number, 996. Then he sees a notice: 'Henry S. Todd, Barber'. As the police whistle blows again, he goes upstairs.*

### TABLEAU THREE

*Bill Leslie enters a large room, not too clean, with a cork floor giving back no sound. Facing him is a window. On his left is another door. On his right, a wall of mirrors with two white barber chairs and another door at the end. That is what Bill Leslie sees. What he can smell is the thick odour of hair-tonic. On a white stool sits a little old man with yellow-white hair and a reddish nose, peering up from an evening paper with Cockney friendliness . . .*

*Bill:* I – I beg your pardon. I didn't mean to crash in like this.

*Todd:* Not a bit of it, sir! Nobody 'ere, sir! Glad to 'ave you come up any way you like!

*Bill:* I've come about something important. I want – I want a shave, please. And I'll just close this door.

*Todd:* Shave, sir? *Very* good, sir! If you'll just come over 'ere . . . that's it . . . Your overcoat, sir; allow me . . . and in *this* chair, please. Now we'll just whip out the cloth and get busy.

*Bill:* Wait a minute! Don't tilt me backwards yet! Are *you* Mr Todd?

*Todd:* Me name *is* Todd, and

that's a fact. But mostly the gentlemen call me Old Scratch.

*Bill:* Old Scratch?

*Todd:* It's only their joke. If they call me Old Scratch, or as it might be Old Nick, it's 'cos they know I won't nick 'em. Never miss with a razor, *I* don't. There now! We'll just tip the chair back. And I'll bet this lather is as comfortable as – well, as going 'ome to tea and kippers on a night like this. It's remarkable, sir, 'ow comforting.

*In the mirror Bill Leslie is suddenly aware that his double has just slipped into the room and vanished again through the glass-panelled door on the left of the street door. The barber, busy with his razor, has seen and heard nothing.*

*Bill (whispering):* Mr Todd, listen carefully. Keep on lathering, and don't speak any louder than I do.

*Todd (whispering):* Wot is it, sir? Wot's up?'

*Bill:* Flash Morgan has just come in.

*Todd:* 'Oo?

*Bill:* Flash . . . Morgan.

*Todd:* Never 'eard of 'im.

*Bill:* He's a killer.

*Todd:* But there's nobody 'ere but you and me. Lift your 'ead up and look!

*Bill:* You didn't see him. You were looking at the shaving-mug. I saw him come in by the door from the stairs when you moved the chair. He went through the other door.

*Todd:* Swelpmearry!

*Bill:* He's a killer. Wanted by the police.

*Todd:* The police, 'ere now, are you—

*Bill (loudly):* Finished with the lather? Then start shaving, (*softly*) but make it quick. Get a razor! That's it. He didn't look at either of us. He didn't make a sound, I saw him in the mirror. I heard him bolt the street door on the inside. Look over and see if it isn't bolted.

*Todd:* Blimey – so it is!

*Bill:* He walked to that door there. Behind me. Where does it lead? Upstairs?

*Todd:* No, sir. there's no upstairs on this side of the 'ouse.

*Bill:* But there's got to be!

Morgan lives at 996!

*Todd:* Don't move your chin like that! Keep your 'ead where I put it! – if you was looking for nine-nine-six proper, you must 'a made a mistake.

*Bill:* What do you mean?

Todd: Nine-nine-six is under the arch and round the back, like a lot of these old 'ouses. This is nine-nine-six B.

*Bill:* Then where *does* the door lead?

*Todd:* Only to a cupboard, sir. A big cupboard. Blimey! And 'e is *'iding* there now.

*Bill:* That's right. Hiding there – with his razor.

*Todd (loudly):* That's the end of the shave, sir. 'Ot towel?

*Bill:* Yes, thanks. Hot and steaming. (*Softly.*) Hang on to your nerve, Old Scratch, and we'll get him in two minutes!

*Todd:* Towel satisfactory, sir? (*Softly.*) I'm a peaceful man, guv'nor. I don't want no trouble.

*Bill (whispering):* Now listen. When you take the towel off, go to the shelf under the mirrors and mess around with the bottles. Ask if I'd like some kind of lotion, and edge towards the glass door. When you get near it, run like blazes and yell for the police. The whole neighbourhood is full of cops. Morgan will come out fighting when he hears you run. I'll pick up that high stool and try to hold him off. The cops didn't find me, because I went to the wrong number . . .

*Todd (urgently):* Sir! That door behind you!

*Bill:* Well?

*Todd:* The knob's moving.

*Bill:* Then we'll have to do it when I count three.

*Todd:* I *can't*, sir. I just ain't up to it.

*Bill:* You can run, can't you? One! . . . Two! . . . Thr—

*The street door bursts open, and Inspector Radford enters, accompanied by a sergeant of City police and two constables.*

*Radford:* Better stay where you are. Both of you.

*Bill:* Well, well! Do I hear Chief Inspector Radford?

*Radford:* You do. Sorry to break the door, Old Scratch; but why is it bolted?

Bill: Inspector, don't you recognize me? I'm Bill Leslie!
Radford: Yes. You probably are. Where's Morgan?
Bill: He's in that cupboard over there. *I* don't want to handle him. Where's your gun?
Radford: We don't carry guns. Sergeant!
Sergeant: Yes, sir?

Radford: Guard that window. Constable, stay here. I'll take the wasp out of his nest. Coming out, Morgan? No? All right. Have it your own way. I'm turning the knob, and Lord Almighty! It's Morgan, all right. But he won't give any trouble. His throat's cut! . . .

TABLEAU FOUR

*The scene is Chief Inspector Radford's room at New Scotland Yard. The fog has penetrated even this official sanctum, which overlooks the invisible Thames. The river traffic is still hooting and tooting as it noses its way upstream or down. Big Ben, on the opposite side of Westminster Bridge, is striking eight o'clock as Chief Inspector Radford, flanked on one side by an official shorthand writer and on the other by two young policemen, continues his interrogation of Bill Leslie and the barber.*

Radford: Mr Leslie, why don't you tell us the truth?
Bill: Inspector, I have told you the truth. So has Old Scratch here.
Todd: Ah! Every word of it.
Radford: Let's face it, Mr Leslie. I suggest that you killed Morgan, and you don't seem to understand the law here.
Bill: How do you mean?
Radford: To kill a wanted man, even a murderer, is

just as bad as killing the Prime Minister. I can't help you if you say you didn't kill him! But I *can* if you admit you did it in self-defence.
Bill: Look, Inspector, I never set eyes on Morgan except when he walked through that shop. Scratch never saw him at all. I never stirred out of the chair for one second. Scratch never left me, never even took his

hands off me, for a second.
Neither of us did it.

*Radford:* Then who killed
Morgan?

*Bill:* I don't know!

*Radford:* I suggest that you
and Morgan met at the
barber's. There was a fight,
and you killed him,
unintentionally.

*Bill:* I killed him with what?

*Radford:* With his own
razor. We found it in the
cupboard. Then you bribed
Old Scratch to keep his
mouth shut.

*Todd:* 'Ere now, Inspector,
I—

*Radford:* Morgan was loaded
with money. Carried a
thousand quid in an oilskin
tobacco-pouch. It wasn't on
his body. If you gave it to
Scratch, and Scratch hid it
in the confusion after we
broke in—

*Bill:* You know, Inspector,
I've been wrong about this
whole thing.

*Radford:* That's better!

*Bill:* Not in the way you
mean! I thought my big
trouble would be to prove
my identity. But you don't
doubt my identity. Or do
you?

*Radford:* I don't, no. But

officially, until your wife
identifies you—

*Bill:* That's what I've been
asking all night; and you
won't answer! Where *is*
Brenda?

*Radford:* Well, sir. The fact
is—

*Bill:* You haven't got her
locked up somewhere?

*Radford:* No, of course not!
The fact is – we can't find
her.

*Bill:* Isn't she at the hotel?

*Radford:* No. Your wife left
the hotel just after you did.

*Bill:* Brenda left the . . .
Where did she go?

*Radford:* To 996 Fleet Street!

*Bill:* How do you know
that?

*Radford:* The real entrance
to 996 is at the back. Up a
flight of stairs past the
barber's window. One of our
men saw her there. Then
lost her.

*Bill:* You mean, Morgan
may have seen her before
he came into the shop and
attacked her. Brenda's
dead! That's what you're
saying! Don't start to
object. That's what you're
intimating! And if Brenda's
dead . . . I'm the cause of
it.

*There is a knock at the door and a sergeant enters.*

*Sergeant:* Chief Inspector!
*Radford:* Sergeant, keep out of here! I told you—
*Sergeant:* Yes, sir. But I couldn't help it. Mrs Leslie's here. She says she wants to give herself up. Here she is.
*Brenda:* Bill! Bill! Oh, Bill!
*Bill:* Brenda!
*Radford:* Please stay where you are, Mrs Leslie. You want to – give yourself up?
*Brenda:* Yes, I saw the murder.
*Radford:* You saw it? From where?
*Brenda:* From the back stairs, through the window. It was dark there but I could see into the lighted room quite easily. Bill, I got there before you did. You had to ask your way. I didn't. I – I saw you come in.
*Bill:* Into the barber-shop?
*Brenda:* Yes! But I think I'd have known what happened, even if I hadn't seen it.
*Radford:* Are you one of our women detectives, Mrs Leslie?
*Brenda:* Please! It's because I *am* a woman that I'd have noticed. You're too used to it. Bill *thinks* that . . . that man you call Old Scratch was never out of his sight for a moment. But he's forgotten something.
*Bill:* Forgotten what?
*Brenda:* You've forgotten there were thirty seconds when you had a hot towel over your face and eyes.
*Radford:* Sergeant! Grab our friend Scratch's arms! Quick!
*Brenda:* Keep him away from me! *Please* keep him—!
*Sergeant:* Got him safe, ma'am!
*Radford:* Go on, Mrs Leslie!
*Brenda:* He went to the cupboard. He opened the door only partly, and – and slashed inside and dropped the razor. He came back with an oilskin pouch. He put the money under a trap in the cork floor. It was done in seconds.
*Todd:* It's a pity I ain't got another razor. Old Scratch never misses with a razor.
*Radford:* Better put the cuffs on him, Sergeant!
*Brenda:* You see, I already guessed he was an accomplice of Morgan's . . .
*Bill:* You . . . *what?*

*Brenda:* Bill, you're so romantic you won't use common sense. He was reading an evening paper. With pictures of Morgan and you too on the front page. But he said he'd never heard of Morgan. You spoke first, so he knew you were the American. And he saw a way of killing Morgan for the money. If he just dropped that razor in the cupboard, the police would think it belonged to Morgan. I was so paralysed I couldn't even scream. Somebody chased me; maybe it was the police; and I fainted in some old woman's room. I – (*faltering*) Inspector, may I go to my husband now?

*Radford:* You may, Mrs Leslie. With the apologies of Scotland Yard.

[CURTAIN]

# Dangerous Game

## MICHAEL GILBERT

*At the top of Fleet Street, within sight of the spot once occupied by Sweeney Todd's shop, stand the huge and impressive buildings of the Royal Courts of Justice, the centre-point of London's legal world. Through these vaunted portals have passed some of the most wanted murderers and criminals in England's history, not to mention all of the nation's finest lawyers and barristers. The Law Courts seem to epitomise the ceaseless battle between crime and the law and no tour of London would be complete without at least a pause here. In fact, the next contributor climaxes his highly topical story of detection, action and retribution with a series of events in and around the famous old building.*

*Michael Gilbert (1912–   ), who is a practising lawyer as well as a superlative detective story writer, has just had his contribution to the crime story genre during the past 30 years acknowledged by the award of the Cartier Diamond Dagger – the highest honour bestowed by the prestigious Crime Writers' Association. This accolade underlines the claim made by Chris Steinbrunner and Otto Penzler in their* Encyclopedia of Mystery and Detection *(1976), that Gilbert is 'one of the finest of the post-World War II generation of detective story writers'. The nephew of Sir Maurice Gwyer, the Lord Chief Justice of India, he obtained his law degree in 1937 and later became a partner in a law firm based in the shadow of the Law Courts at Lincoln's Inn. Interestingly, he was for a time legal adviser to*

*Raymond Chandler, a factor which drew him towards crime fiction and has resulted in him writing hundreds of short stories as well as novels, books of non-fiction and plays for radio and television. Michael actually writes most of his work, he says, while commuting between Kent and his office. His day-to-day contact with the law through his profession has given him a unique source of information, much of which is to be found in his stories about series characters like Inspector Hazelrigg, Detective Sergeant Patrick Petrella, and his two counter-intelligence agents, Calder and Behrens, who made their debut in* Game Without Rules *published in 1967. Ellery Queen has called this book, 'after W. Somerset Maugham's* Ashenden, *the best volume of spy stories ever written'. Calder and Behrens also feature in 'Dangerous Game' which could hardly be more topical, dealing as it does with the IRA's appalling bombing campaign in the streets of London . . .*

'THEY BURNED HIM to death,' said Elfe. He said it without any attempt to soften the meaning of what he was saying. 'He was almost certainly alive when they dumped him in the car and set fire to it.'

Deputy Assistant Commissioner Elfe had a long sad face and grey hair. In the twenty years that he had been head of the Special Branch he had seen more brutality, more treachery, more fanaticism, more hatred than had any of his predecessors in war or in peace. Twice he had tried to retire, and twice had been persuaded to stay.

'He couldn't have put up much of a fight,' said Mr Calder, 'only having one arm and one and a half legs.'

They were talking about Michael Finnegan, whose charred carcass had been found in a burned-out stolen car in one of the lonelier parts of Hampstead Heath. Finnegan had been a lieutenant in the Marines until he had blown off his right arm and parts of his right leg while defusing a new type of anti-personnel mine. During his long convalescence his wife Sheilagh had held the home together, supplementing Michael's disability pension by working as a secretary. Then Finnegan had taught himself to write left-handed, and had gained a reputation and a reasonable amount of cash for his articles; first only in service journals, but later in the national press, where he had emerged as a commentator on men and affairs.

'It's odd,' as Mr Behrens once observed, 'you'd think that he'd be a militant chauvinist. Actually he seems to be a moderate and a pacifist. It was Finnegan who started arguing that we ought to withdraw our troops from Ireland. That was long before the I.R.A. made it one of the main planks in their platform.'

'You can never tell how a serious injury will affect a man,' said Mr Calder.

This was, of course, before he had become professionally involved with Michael Finnegan.

'For the last year you've been acting as his runner, haven't you?' said Elfe. 'You must have got to know him well.'

'Him and his wife,' said Mr Calder. 'They were a great couple.' He thought about the unremarkable house at Banstead with its tiny flower garden in front and its rather larger kitchen garden in the rear, both of which Michael Finnegan tended one-armed, hobbling down between times for a pint at the local. A respected man with many friends and acquaintances, none of whom knew he was playing a lonely, patient, dangerous game. His articles in the papers, his casual contacts, his letters to old friends in Ireland and conversations with new friends in the pub, all had been slanted toward a predetermined end.

The fact was that the shape of the I.R.A.'s activities was changing, a change which had been forced on them by the systematic penetration of their groups in England. Now, when an act of terrorism was planned, the operators came from Ireland to carry it out, departing as soon as it was done. They travelled a roundabout route, via Morocco or Tunis, entering England from France or Belgium and returning by the same way. Explosives, detonators, and other material for the job came separately, and in advance. Their one essential requirement was an operational base where materials could be stored and the operators could lodge for the few days needed for the job.

It was to hold out his house as such a safe base that every move in Michael Finnegan's life had been planned.

'We agreed,' said Mr. Calder, 'that as far as possible Michael should have no direct contacts of any sort with the security forces. What the Department did was to lease a house which had a good view, from its front windows, of Michael's back gate. They installed one of their pensioners in it, old Mrs Lovelock—'

'Minnie Lovelock?' said Elfe. 'She used to type for me forty years ago. I was terrified of her, even then.'

'All she had to do was to keep Michael's kitchen window sill under observation at certain hours. There was a simple code of signals. A flower pot meant the arrival of explosives or arms. One or more milk bottles signalled the arrival of that number of operators. And the house gave us one further advantage. Minnie put it about that she had sublet a room on the ground floor to a commercial gentleman who kept his samples there, and occasionally put up there for the night. For the last year the commercial gent was me. I was able to slip out, after dark, up the garden path and in at the back door of Michael's house. I tried to do it at least once a month. My ostensible job was to collect any information Michael might have for us. In fact, I believe my visits kept him sane. We used to talk for hours. He liked to hear the gossip, all about the interdepartmental feuds, and funny stories about the Minister.'

'And about the head of the Special Branch?'

'Oh, certainly. He particularly enjoyed the story of how two of your men tried to arrest each other.'

Elfe grunted, and said, 'Go on.'

'And there was one further advantage. Michael had a key to this room. In a serious emergency he could deposit a message – after dark, of course – or even use it as an escape hatch for Sheilagh and himself.'

'Did his wife know what he was up to?'

'She had to be told something, if only to explain my visits. Our cover story was that Michael was gathering information about subversion in the docks. This was plausible, as he'd done an Intelligence job in the Marines. She may have suspected that it was more than that. She never interfered. She's a grand girl.'

Elfe said, 'Yes,' and after a pause, 'Yes. That's really what I wanted to tell you. I've had a word with your chief. He agrees with me. This is a job we can't use you in.'

'Oh,' said Mr Calder coldly. 'Why not?'

'Because you'd feel yourself personally involved. You'd be unable to be sufficiently dispassionate about it. You knew Finnegan and his wife far too well.'

Mr Calder thought about that. If Fortescue had backed the prohibition it would be little use kicking. He said, 'I suppose we *are* doing something about it.'

'Of course. Superintendent Outram and Sergeant Fallows are handling it. They're both members of the A.T. squad, and very capable operators.'

'I know Tom Outram,' said Mr Calder. 'He's a sound man. I'll promise not to get under his feet. But I'm already marginally involved. If he wants to question Sheilagh he'll have to do it at my cottage. I moved her straight down there as soon as I heard the news. Gave her a strong sleeping pill and put her to bed.'

'They wondered where she'd disappeared to. I'll tell them she's living with you.'

'If you put it quite like that,' said Mr Calder, 'it might be misunderstood. She's being chaperoned, by Rasselas.'

'I think,' said Superintendent Outram, 'that we'd better see Mrs Finnegan alone. That is, if you don't mind.'

He and Sergeant Fallows had driven out to Mr Calder's cottage, which was built on a shoulder of the North Downs above Lamperdown in Kent.

'I don't mind,' said Mr Calder. 'But you'll have to look out for Rasselas.'

'Your dog?'

'Yes. Mrs Finnegan's still in a state of shock, and Rasselas is very worried about it. The postman said something sharp to her – not meaning any harm at all – and he went for him. Luckily I was there and I was able to stop him.'

'Couldn't we see her without Rasselas?'

'I wouldn't care to try and shift him.'

Outram thought about it. Then he said, 'Then I think you'd better sit in with us.'

'I think that might be wise,' said Mr Calder gravely.

Sheilagh Finnegan had black hair and a white face out of which looked eyes of startling Irish blue. Her mouth was thin and tight and angry. It was clear that she was under stress. When Outram and Fallows came in she took one look at them and jerked as though an electric shock had gone through her.

Rasselas, who was stretched out on the floor beside her, raised his head and regarded the two men thoughtfully.

'Just like he was measuring us for a coffin,' said Fallows afterward.

Mr Calder sat on the sofa, and put one hand on the dog's head.

It took Outram fifteen minutes of patient, low-keyed questioning to discover that Mrs Finnegan could tell him very little. Her husband, she said, had suggested that she needed a vacation, and had arranged for her to spend a week in a small private hotel at Folkestone. She wasn't sorry to agree because she hadn't had a real holiday in the last three or four years.

Outram nodded sympathetically. Had the holiday been fixed suddenly? Out of the blue, like? Sheilagh gave more attention to this than she had to some of the earlier questions. She said, 'We'd often talked about it before. Michael knew I had friends at Folkestone.'

'But on this occasion it was your husband who suggested it? How long before you left?'

'Two or three days.'

'Then it *was* fairly sudden.'

'Fairly sudden, yes.'

'Did he give any particular reason? Had he had an unexpected message? Something like that.'

'He didn't say anything about a message. I wouldn't have known about it, anyway. I was out at work all day.'

Outram said, 'Yes, of course.'

There was nothing much more she could tell them. A quarter of an hour later the two men drove off. As their car turned down the hill they passed Mr Behrens, who was walking up from Lamperdown. Mr Behrens waved to the Superintendent.

'Looks a genial old cove,' said Sergeant Fallows.

'That's what he looks like,' agreed Outram.

When Mr Behrens reached the cottage he found Mr Calder and Sheilagh making coffee in the kitchen. They added a third cup to the tray and carried it back to the sitting room where Rasselas was apparently asleep. By contrast with what had gone before it was a relaxed and peaceful scene.

Mr Calder tried the coffee, found it still too hot, put the cup carefully back on its saucer, and said, 'Why were you holding out on the Superintendent?'

'How did you know I was holding out?'

'Rasselas and I both knew it.'

Hearing his name the great dog opened one brown eye, as though to confirm what Mr Calder had said, and then shut it again.

'If I tell you about it,' said Sheilagh, 'you'll understand why I was holding out.'

'Then tell us at once,' said Mr Behrens.

'Of course I knew something was in the wind. I didn't know exactly what Michael was up to. He was careful not to tell me any details. But whatever it was he was doing, I realized it was coming to a head. That was why he sent me away. He said it shouldn't be more than two or three days. He'd get word to me as soon as he could. That was on the Friday. I had a miserable weekend, you can imagine. Monday came, and Tuesday, and still no word. By Wednesday I couldn't take it any longer. What I did was wrong, I know, but I couldn't help myself.'

'You went back,' said Mr Calder. He said it sympathetically.

'That's just what I did. I planned it all carefully. I wasn't going to barge in and upset all Michael's plans. I just wanted to see he was all right and go away again. He'd given me a key to that room in Mrs Lovelock's house. I got there after dark. There's a clear view from the window straight into our kitchen. The light was on and the curtains weren't drawn.'

As she talked she was living the scene. Mr Behrens pictured her, crouched in the dark, like an eager theatre-goer in the gallery staring down on to the lighted stage.

She said, 'I could see Michael. He was boiling a kettle on the stove and moving about, setting out cups and plates. There were two other people in the room. I could see the legs of a man who was sitting at the kitchen table. Once, when he leaned forward, I got a glimpse of him. All I could tell you was he was young and had black hair. The other was a girl. I saw her quite plainly. She was dark, too. Medium height and rather thin. The sort of girl who could dress as a man and get away with it.

'I got the impression, somehow, that they'd just arrived, and Michael was bustling about making them at home. The girl still had her outdoor coat on. Maybe that's what gave me the idea. Just then I saw another man coming. He was walking along the road which runs behind our kitchen garden, and when he stopped, he was right under the window where I was sitting. When he opened the gate I could see that he was taking a lot of trouble not to make any noise. He shut the gate very gently, and stood there for a moment, looking at the lighted kitchen window. Then he tiptoed up the garden path and stood, to one side of the kitchen window, looking in. That's when I saw his face clearly for the first time.'

Sheilagh was speaking more slowly now. Mr Calder was leaning forward with his hands on his knees. Rasselas was no longer pretending to be asleep. Mr Behrens could feel the tension without understanding it.

'Then he seemed to make up his mind. He went across to the kitchen door, opened it without knocking, and went in quickly, as though he was planning to surprise the people inside. Next moment someone had dragged the curtains across. From the moment I first saw that man I knew he meant harm to Michael. But once the curtains were shut I couldn't see what was happening.'

'You couldn't see,' said Mr Calder. 'But could you hear?'

'Nothing. On account of Mrs Lovelock's television set in the room just above me. She's deaf and keeps it on full strength. All I could do was sit and wait. It must have been nearly an hour later when I saw the back door open. All the lights in the house had been turned out and it was difficult to see, but Michael was between the two men. They seemed to be supporting him. The girl was walking behind. They came out and turned up the road. Then I noticed there was a car parked about twenty yards farther up. They all got into it. And I went on sitting there. I couldn't think what to do.'

There was a moment of silence. Neither of the men wanted to break it. Sheilagh said, 'I do realize now that I should have done something. I should have run down, screamed – anything to stop them taking Michael away like that. But I didn't know what was happening. Going with them might all have been part of his plan.'

'It was an impossible situation,' said Mr Calder.

'When you thought about it afterwards,' said Mr Behrens, 'am I right about this? You got the impression that things had been going smoothly until that other man arrived, and that he was the one who upset things.'

'He was the one who gave Michael away,' said Sheilagh. 'I'm sure of it.' There was a different note in her voice now. Something hard and very cold.

'I agree with Calder,' said Mr Behrens. 'You couldn't have done anything else at the time. But as soon as you knew that things had gone wrong for Michael, why didn't you tell the police everything that you've just told us? Time was vital. You could give a good description of two of the people involved. Surely there wasn't a moment to lose.'

Sheilagh said, 'I didn't go to the police because I recognized the man, the one who arrived on foot. I'd seen his photograph. Michael had pointed it out to me in the paper. I only saw him clearly as he stood outside the lighted window, but I was fairly certain I was right.' She paused, then added, 'Now I'm quite certain.'

Both men looked at her.

She said, 'It was Sergeant Fallows.'

The silence that followed was broken unexpectedly. Rasselas gave a growl at the back of his throat, got up, stalked to the door, pushed it open with his nose, and went out. They heard him settling down again outside.

'That's where he goes when he's on guard,' said Mr Calder.

There was another silence.

'I know what you're thinking,' said Sheilagh. 'You both think I'm crazy, but I'm not. It *was* Fallows.'

'Not an easy face to forget,' agreed Mr Calder, 'and it would explain something that has been puzzling me. We'd taken such tight precautions over Michael that I didn't see how they could suddenly have known that he was a plant. He might eventually have done something, or said something, which gave him away. They might have got suspicious. But not certain. Not straight away. It could only have happened like that if he was betrayed, and the only person who could have betrayed him was someone working in the Squad.'

Mr Behrens' mind had been moving on a different line. He said, 'When they got into the car, and turned the lights on, you'd have been able to see the number plate at the back, I take it.'

'That's right. I saw it and wrote it down. I've put it here. LKK 910 P.'

'Good girl. Now think back. When you were talking about the last man to arrive you called him 'the one who came on foot'. What made you say that?'

Sheilagh said, 'I'm not sure. I suppose because he came from the opposite direction to where the car was parked. So I assumed—'

'I'm not disputing it. In fact, I'm sure you were right. Fallows wouldn't have driven up in a police car. He wouldn't even have risked taking his own car. He'd have gone by bus or train to the nearest point and walked the rest of the way.'

Mr Calder said, 'Then the car belongs to the Irish couple. Of course they might have stolen it, like the one they left on the Heath.'

'They might. But why risk it? It would only draw attention to them, which was the last thing they wanted. My guess is that they hired it. Just for the time they were planning to be here.'

'If you're right,' said Mr Calder, 'there's a lot to do and not much time to do it. You'd better trace that car. And remember, we've been officially warned off, so you can't use the police computer.'

'LKK's a Kent number. I've got a friend in County Hall who'll help.'

'I'll look into the Fallows end of it. It'll mean leaving you alone here for a bit, Sheilagh, but if anyone should turn up and cause trouble, Rasselas will attend to him.'

'In case there might be two of them,' said Mr Behrens, 'you'd better take this. It's loaded. That's the safety catch. You push it down when you want to fire.'

The girl examined the gun with interest. She said, 'I've never used one, but I suppose, if I got quite close to the man, pointed it at his stomach, and pulled the trigger—'

'The results should be decisive,' said Mr Behrens.

Fallows was whistling softly to himself as he walked along the carpeted corridor to the door of his flat. It was on the top floor of a new block on the Regent's Park side of Albany Street and seemed an expensive pad for a detective sergeant. He opened the door, walked down the short hall into the living room, switched on the light, and stopped.

A middle-aged man, with greying hair and steel-rimmed glasses, was standing by the fireplace regarding him benevolently. Fallows recognized him, but had no time to be surprised. As he stepped forward something soft but heavy hit him on the back of the neck.

When he came round, about five minutes later, he was seated in a heavy chair. His arms had been attached to the arms of the chair and his legs to the chair's legs by yards of elastic bandage, wound round and round. Mr Behrens was examining the contents of an attaché case which he had brought with him. Mr Calder was watching him. Both men were in their shirtsleeves and were wearing surgical gloves.

'I think our patient is coming round,' said Mr Calder.

'What the bloody hell are you playing at?' said Fallows.

Mr Behrens said, 'First, I'm going to give you these pills. They're ordinary sleeping pills. I think four should be sufficient. We don't want him actually to go to sleep. Just to feel drowsy.'

'Bloody hell you will.'

'If you want me to wedge your mouth open, hold your nose, and hit you on the throat each time until you swallow, I'm quite prepared to do it, but it would be undignified and rather painful.'

Fallows glared at him, but there was an implacable look behind the steel spectacles which silenced him. He swallowed the pills.

Mr Behrens looked at his watch and said, 'We'll give them five minutes to start working. What we're trying' – he turned courteously back to Fallows – 'is an experiment which has often been suggested but never, I think, actually performed. We're going to give you successive doses of scopolamine dextrin to inhale, while we ask you some questions. In the ordinary way I have no doubt you would be strong enough to resist the scopolamine until you became unconscious. There are men who have sufficient resources of will power to do that. That's why we first weaken your resistance with a strong sedative. Provided we strike exactly the right balance, the results should be satisfactory. About ready now, I think.'

He took a capsule from a box on the table and broke it under Fallows' nose.

'The snag about this method,' Mr Behrens continued, in the same level tones of a professor addressing a class of students, 'is that the interreaction of the sedative and the stimulant would be so sharp that it might, if persisted with, affect the subject's heart. You'll appreciate therefore – head up, Sergeant – that by prolonging our dialogue you may be risking your own life. Now then. Let's start with your visit to Banstead—'

This produced a single, sharp obscenity.

Fifty minutes later Mr Behrens switched off his tape recorder. He said, 'I think he's gone. I did warn him that it might happen if he fought too hard.'

'And my God, did he fight,' said Mr Calder. He was sweating. 'We'd better set the scene. I think he'd look more convincing if we put him on his bed.'

He was unwinding the elastic bandages and was glad to see that, in spite of Fallows' struggles, they had left no mark. The nearly empty bottle of sleeping pills, a half-empty bottle of whiskey, and a tumbler were arranged on the bedside table. Mr Behrens closed Fallows' flaccid hand round the tumbler, then knocked it on to the floor.

'Leave the bedside light on,' said Mr Calder. 'No one commits suicide in the dark.'


'I've done a transcript of the tape for you,' said Sheilagh. 'I've cut out some of the swearing, but otherwise it's all there. There's no doubt now that he betrayed Michael, is there?'

'None at all,' said Mr Behrens. 'That was something he seemed almost proud of. The trouble was that when we edged up to one of the things we really wanted to know, an automatic defence mechanism seemed to take over, and when we fed him a little more scopolamine to break through it, he started to ramble.'

'All the same,' said Mr Calder, 'we know a good deal. We

know what they're planning to do, and roughly when. But not how.'

Mr Behrens was studying the neatly typed paper. He said, 'J. J. That's clear enough. Jumping Judas. It's their name for Mr Justice Jellicoe. That's their target, all right. They've been gunning for him ever since he sent down the Manchester bombers. I've traced their car. It was hired in Dover last Friday, for ten days. The man they hired it from told them he had another customer who wanted it on Monday afternoon. They said that suited them because they were planning to let him have it back by one o'clock that day, Monday. Which means that whatever they're going to do is timed to be done sometime on Monday morning, and they aim to be boarding a cross-Channel ferry by the time it happens.'

'They might have been lying to the man,' said Sheilagh.

'Yes. They might have been. But bear in mind that if they brought the car back on Saturday afternoon or Sunday the hire firm would be shut for the weekend and they'd have to leave the car standing about in the street, which would call attention to it. No. I think they've got a timetable, and they're sticking to it.'

'Which gives us three days to find out what it is,' said Mr Calder. 'If the payoff is on Monday there are two main possibilities. Jellicoe spends his weekends at his country house at Witham, in Essex. He's pretty safe there. He's got a permanent police guard and three boxer dogs that are devoted to him. He comes up to court on Monday by car, with a police driver. All right, that's one chance. They could arrange some sort of ambush. Detonate one of their favourite long-distance mines. Not easy, though, because there are three different routes the car can take. This isn't the Ulster border. They can't go round laying minefields all over Essex.'

'The alternative,' said Mr Behrens, 'is to try something in or around the Law Courts. We'll have to split this. You take the Witham end. Have a word with the bodyguard. They may not know that we've been warned off, so they'll probably cooperate. I'll tackle the London end.'

'Isn't there something I could do?' said Sheilagh.

'Yes,' said Mr Calder. 'There is. Play that tape over and over again. Twenty times. Until you know it by heart. There was something inside Fallows' muddled brain, something trying to get out. It may be a couple of words. Even a single word. If you can interpret it, it could be the key to the whole thing.'

So Friday was spent by Mr Calder at Witham, making friends with a police sergeant and a police constable; by Sheilagh Finnegan listening to the drug-induced ramblings of the man who had been responsible for her husband's death; and by Mr Behrens investigating the possibility of blowing up a judge in court.

As a first step Mr Behrens introduced himself to Major Haines. The Major, after service in the Royal Marines, had been given the job of supervising security at the Law Courts. He had known Michael Finnegan, and was more than willing to help.

He said, 'It's a rambling great building. I think the chap who designed it had a Ruritanian palace in mind. Narrow windows, heavy doors, battlements and turrets, and iron gratings. The judges have a private entrance, which is inside the car park. Everyone else, barristers, solicitors, visitors, all have to use the front door in the Strand, or the back door in Carey Street. They're both guarded, of course. Teams of security officers, good men. Mostly ex-policemen.'

'I was watching them for a time, first thing this morning,' said Mr Behrens. 'Most people had to open their bags and cases, but there were people carrying sort of blue-and-red washing bags. They let them through uninspected.'

'They'd be barristers, or barristers' clerks, and they'd let them through because they knew their faces. But I can assure you of one thing. When Mr Justice Jellicoe is on the premises everyone opens everything.'

'Which court will he be using?'

Major Haines consulted the printed list. 'On Monday he's in Court Number Two. That's one of the courts at the back. I'll show you.'

He led the way down the vast entrance hall. Mr Behrens saw what he meant when he described it as a palace. Marble columns, spiral staircases, interior balconies, and an elaborately tessellated floor.

'Up these stairs,' said Haines. 'That's Number Two Court. And there's the rear door, straight ahead of you. It leads out into Carey Street.'

'So that anyone making for Court Number Two would be likely to come this way.'

'Not if they were coming from the Strand.'

'True,' said Mr Behrens. 'I think I'll hang around for a bit and watch the form.'

He went back to the main hall and found himself a seat, which commanded the front entrance.

It was now ten o'clock and the flow of people coming in was continuous. They were channelled between desks placed lengthways, and three security guards were operating. They did their job thoroughly. Occasionally, when they recognized a face, a man was waved through. Otherwise everyone opened whatever they were carrying and placed it on top of the desk. Suitcases, briefcases, even women's handbags were carefully examined. The red-and-blue bags which, Mr Behrens decided, must contain law books, were sometimes looked into, sometimes not. But they would all be looked into on Monday morning.

'It looked pretty watertight to me,' said Mr Behrens to Sheilagh and Mr Calder, as they compared notes after supper. 'Enough explosive to be effective would be bulky and an elaborate timing device would add to the weight and bulk. They might take a chance and put the whole thing in the bottom of one of those book bags and hope it wouldn't be looked at, but they don't seem to me to be people who would take chances of that sort.'

'Could the stuff have been brought in during the weekend and left somewhere in the Court?'

'I put it to Haines. He said No. The building is shut on Friday evening and given a thorough going-over on Saturday.'

'Sheilagh and I have worked one thing out,' said Mr Behrens. 'There's a reference, towards the end, to "fields". In the transcript it's been reproduced as "in the fields", and the assumption was that the attempt was going to be made in the country, when Jellicoe was driving up to London. But if you listen very carefully it isn't 'in the fields'. It's "in fields" with the emphasis on the first word, and there's a sort of crackle in the tape before it which makes it difficult to be sure; but I think what he's saying is "Lincoln's Inn Fields".'

They listened once more to the tape.

Mr Calder said, 'I think you're right.'

'And it does explain one point,' said Mr Behrens. 'When I explored the area this morning it struck me how difficult it was to park a car. But Lincoln's Inn Fields could be ideal – there are parking spaces all down the South and East sides, and the South East corner is less than two hundred yards from the rear entrance to the Courts.'

'Likely enough,' said Mr Calder, 'but it still doesn't explain how they're going to get the stuff in. Did you get anything else out of the tape, Sheilagh?'

'I made a list of the words and expressions he used most often. Some were just swearing, but apart from that his mind seemed to be on the subject of time. He said "midday" and "twelve o'clock" a dozen times at least. And he talks about a "midday special". That seemed to be some sort of joke. He doesn't actually use the word "explosion", but he talks once or twice about a report, or reports.'

'Report?' said Mr Calder thoughtfully. 'That sounds more like a shot from a gun than a bomb.'

'It's usually in the plural. Reports.'

'Several guns.'

'Rather elaborate, surely. Hidden rifles, trained on the Bench, and timed to go off at midday?'

'And it still doesn't explain how he gets the stuff past the guards,' said Mr Behrens.

He took the problem down the hill with him to his house in Lamperdown village and carried it up to bed. He knew, from experience, that he would get little sleep until he had solved it. The irritating thing was that the answer was there. He was sure of it. He had only to remember what he had seen and connect it up with the words on the tape, and the solution would appear, as inevitably as the jackpot came out of the slot when you hit three lemons in a row.

Visualize the people, pouring through the entrance into the building, carrying briefcases, book bags, handbags. One man had had a camera slung over his shoulder. The guard had called his attention to a notice prohibiting the taking of photographs in Court. This little episode had held up the queue for a moment. The young man behind, a barrister's clerk Mr Behrens guessed, had been in a hurry, and had pushed past the camera owner. He had not been searched, because he hadn't been carrying a case. But he had been carrying *something*. When Mr Behrens reached this point he did, in fact, doze off, so that the solution must have reached him in his sleep.

Next morning, after breakfast, he telephoned his solicitor, catching him before he set out for the golf course. He said, 'When you go into Court and have to tell the judge what another judge said in another case—'

'Quote a precedent, you mean.'

'That's right. Well, do you take the book with you, or is it already in Court?'

'Both. There's a complete set of Reports in Court. Several sets, in fact. They're for the judges. And you bring your own with you.'

'That might mean lugging in a lot of books.'

'A trolleyful sometimes.'

'Suppose you had, say, five or six sets of Reports to carry. How would you manage?'

'I'd get my clerk to carry them.'

'All right,' said Mr Behrens patiently, 'how would he manage?'

'If it was just half a dozen books, he's got a sort of strap affair, with a handle.'

'That's what I thought I remembered seeing,' said Mr Behrens. 'Thank you very much.'

'I suppose you've got some reason for asking all these questions?'

'An excellent reason.'

His solicitor, who knew Mr Behrens well, said no more.

'We'll get there early,' said Mr Calder, 'and park as close as we can to the South East corner. There's plenty of cover in the garden and we can watch both lines of cars. As soon as one of us spots LKK 910P he tips off the others using one of these pocket radios. Quite easy, Sheilagh. Just press the button and talk. Then let it go, and listen.'

'That doesn't sound too difficult,' said Sheilagh. 'What then?'

'Then Henry gets busy.'

'Who's Henry?'

'An old friend of mine who'll be coming with us. His job is to unlock the boot of their car as soon as they're clear of it. By my reckoning he'll have ten minutes for the job, which will be nine and a half minutes more than he needs.'

The man and girl walked up Searle Street, not hurrying, but not wasting time, crossed Carey Street, climbed the five shallow steps, and pushed through the swing doors and into the Court building.

Mr Behrens had got there before them. He was standing on the far side of the barrier. A little queue had already formed and he had plenty of time to observe them.

They had dressed for the occasion with ritual care. The man in a dark suit, cream shirt, and dark red tie. The girl in the uniform of a female barrister, black dress, black shoes and stockings, with a single touch of colour, the collar points of a yellow shirt showing at the throat.

As he watched them edge forward to the barrier, Mr Behrens felt a prickle of superstitious dread. They may have been nervous, but they showed no sign of it. They looked serious and composed, like the young crusaders who, for the more thorough purging of the holy places, mutilated the living bodies of their pagan prisoners; like the novices who watched impassively at the auto-da-fé where men and women were burned to the greater glory of God.

Now they were at the barrier. The girl was carrying a book bag and a satchel. She opened them both. The search was thorough and took time. The man showed very slight signs of impatience.

Mr Behrens thought, they've rehearsed this very carefully.

When it came to the man's turn, he placed the six books, held together in a white strap, on the counter and opened his briefcase. The guard searched the briefcase, and nodded. The man picked up the books and the briefcase and walked down the short length of corridor to where the girl was standing. He ignored her, turned the corner, and made for Court Number 2.

Although it was not yet ten o'clock there were already a number of people in the courtroom. Two elderly barristers were standing by the front bench discussing something. Behind them a girl was arranging a pile of books and papers. The young man placed his six books, still strapped together, on the far end of the back bench, and went out as quietly as he had come in. No one took any notice of him.

A minute later Mr Behrens appeared, picked up the books, and left. No one took any notice of him either.

When the young man came out he joined the girl and they moved off together. Having come in by the back entrance it was evidently their intention to leave by the front. They had gone about ten paces when a man stopped them. He said, 'Excuse me, but have you got your cards?'

'Cards?' said the young man. He seemed unconcerned.

'We're issuing personal identity cards to all barristers using the court. Your clerk should have told you. If you'd come with me I'll give you yours.'

The girl looked at her companion, who nodded slightly, and they set off after their guide. He led the way down a long empty passage toward the western annex to the Courts.

The young man closed up behind the guide. He put his hand into a side pocket, pulled out a leather cosh, moved a step closer, and hit the man on the head. The guide fell forward on to his knees and rolled over on to his face.

The young man and the girl had swung round and were moving back the way they had come.

'Walk, don't run,' said the young man.

They turned a corner and went down a spiral staircase which led to the main hall and the front entrance.

When they were outside, and circling the Court building, the girl said, 'That man. Did you notice?'

'Notice what?'

'When you hit him. He was expecting it.'

'What do you mean?'

'He started to fall forward just before you hit him. It must have taken most of the force out of the blow.'

Without checking his pace the young man said, 'Do you think he was a plant? Holding us up so they could get to the car ahead of us?'

'I thought it might be.'

The young man put one hand on the shoulder holster inside his coat and said, 'If that's right, you'll see some fireworks.'

There was no one waiting for them by the car. The nearest person to the car was a small man, with a face like a friendly monkey, who was sitting on a bench inside the garden reading the *Daily Mirror*.

No one tried to stop them as they drove out of Lincoln's Inn Fields and turned south toward the Embankment. 'Twenty past ten,' said the young man, 'good timing.'

They were five miles short of Dover, on the bare escarpment over Bridge, before he spoke again. He said, 'Twelve o'clock. Any time now.'

Either his watch was fast or the timing mechanism was slow. It was fully five minutes later when their car went up in a searing sheet of white flame.

# Karmesin The Murderer

## GERALD KERSH

*From the Law Courts it is only about a mile across Kingsway through Covent Garden into Soho, the area renowned as a haven of crime and a part of the city where all kinds of rackets have flourished for years including gangsterism, vice, pornography and drugs. It is a district of narrow, garishly-lit streets and dark, litter-filled alleyways bounded by Oxford Street to the North and Piccadilly Circus to the south, which has also been described as one of the focal points of the London Underworld. Here, around such well-known thoroughfares as Brewer Street, Old Compton Street and Greek Street, can be found a world of strip joints and seedy night clubs which have recently been joined by numbers of tiny cinemas showing blue films and rows of buildings open to the street filled with slot machines and computer games. Despite its reputation, however, Soho remains a magnet for visitors from other parts of the United Kingdom as well as large numbers of tourists – and every night when darkness falls it takes on a character uniquely its own . . .*

*Of the many authors who have written about the underside of Soho life, few have possessed a more intimate knowledge of the place or its inhabitants than Gerald Kersh (1911–1968), the novelist and short story writer whom Simon Raven has described as, 'Rabelaisian, vigorous, readable, inventive and bizarre'. These qualities Kersh owed to his life in London as a baker, salesman, professional wrestler and night club bouncer – all of which occupations he followed before becoming a writer. For many years he was a familiar figure about Soho in his colourful suits and inevitable bow-tie, visiting the pubs and restaurants and conversing with the many characters who became his friends and the inspiration for a number of his stories. His reputation as a writer of crime and mystery tales was made with his book,* Night and the City, *a powerful novel of the London underworld published in 1938, and then through a whole range of post-war short stories, including a series about a crime reporter 'Swindle Sheet' Morris and the rogue known simply as Karmesin whom Ellery Queen has described as, 'A Falstaffian felon, a titanic transgressor – in a phrase, "the compleat criminal"'. He is, says Queen, either the greatest criminal or the greatest liar of our time! Karmesin actually lives in a flat in Soho and several of his best exploits occur in the area: in particular 'Karmesin the Murderer' in which a terrible revenge is threatened amidst the ranks of slot machines which never seem to stop . . .*

IT WAS ROUGH on my poor friend Karmesin. Finding a pound note in his possession for the first time in two months, he rushed out and bought a hundred cigarettes, and received a bad half-crown among the change.

Look,' he said, holding the coin in his fat, white fingers. He pressed: the half-crown bent. 'Lead!' said Karmesin. 'I could make better myself. Swindlers! Tramplers on the faces of the poor!'

'Take it back to the shop,' I suggested, 'and demand another coin.'

'How am I to prove that it was the shopkeeper who gave it to me?' asked Karmesin. Then he laughed, and said 'Bah. It is all in the game. That shopkeeper would probably spit on the name of a pickpocket, a forger, or an utterer of forged notes or coins. Yet let him receive a queer half-crown from a customer, and while that coin remains in his possession he is an enemy of society; his one desire is to pass it off on somebody else. This is the value of the popular conscience: you can buy it for a counterfeit coin. Bah, I say! Let him keep it. He thinks he is smart, but God will punish him. I tell you, my friend: the great wrongdoer who knows good from evil stands a better chance of paradise than the smug citizen who slinks behind the skirts of the law to do petty misdeeds. I could keep this half-crown and pass it to some other unfortunate person. But how am I to know what misery I might cause by so doing? A widow might ultimately receive it; or an old age pensioner. No.'

In spite of his fat and his age, Karmesin must have been as strong as an ox. He grunted, and tore the soft half-crown across, throwing the pieces out of the window.

'I heard a story,' he said, 'about a coin like that. Some men were playing cards. One of them lost everything, and borrowed a silver dollar for his fare home and his breakfast. On the way he was accosted by an unhappy girl in the last stages of despair. He was a good-hearted man, and was touched by her story. In short, he gave her the silver dollar and told her to go in peace. Next morning she was found drowned, a bad dollar clutched in her hand. That bad dollar, you understand, had been the last straw. If it had been a good one, she would have lived on until the dawn . . . and it is God's mercy, my friend, that the daylight always brings new strength. It is the depression of the small hours that kills men, my friend; the horrible seconds when you hear the clock strike three: then you are lost. You see: the man of whom I told you, he was a good man, but Providence used him for a tragic purpose.'

Karmesin became silent. I said, 'Have you ever wanted to commit suicide?'

'No,' said Karmesin. 'Only murder.'

'But I thought you disapproved of murder.'

'I do. Evil-doers should be left in the hands of their destiny, which always destroys them in the end. Nevertheless, I was responsible for the planning of the Perfect Murder.'

'How?'

'Come with me,' said Karmesin, jingling the remains of his pound. 'I have been your guest many times. Now you must be mine.'

He took me to Xavier's Bar and with an air of magnificence that sent the waiter skipping, ordered brandy.

'What is money?' said Karmesin. 'Dross, rubbish. Thank God I have always spent mine as fast as it came!'

He lumbered over to the slot machine in the corner, inserted a shilling, pulled the handle down. The numbered discs whirred round and thudded to a stop . . . 3, 3, 3. Ten shillings dropped out of the machine with a jingle.

'Observe,' said Karmesin. 'There is one thing in the world which no man can resist: the jingle of cash. See – every eye in the bar is upon us. Now, come and drink your brandy, and I will tell you about my murder . . .'

My scheme (said Karmesin) was not unconnected with a slot machine, in a club not unlike this, not many years ago. The victim was a man called Skobeleff, a man who richly deserved to die.

He was a criminal of the worst type, my friend: one who lives upon women. Skobeleff's speciality was blackmail. He had a genius for working his way into the affections of highly respectable women – women with highly placed husbands. You know how it sometimes happens with the wives of great men. Their husbands, preoccupied with affairs, neglect them. They yearn for attention, to be noticed. It is only natural. Then comes an intrigue, possibly an innocent intrigue – a friendship, quite often, with an unworthy man versed in the wiles of the woman-hunter.

Skobeleff was such a man. He moved in good circles; was tolerated, at least, as a friend of people who moved in good circles. Women found it difficult to resist him, for he had a handsome face, a fine Imperial Guardsman's figure, magnificent blue eyes, the flaxen hair of an angel, perfect self-confidence, a boundless experience of women, and a voice more melodious than harp-strings . . . together with a flow of conversation that could make the unhappy laugh, or bring a heartthrob to the bosom of the most nonchalant woman that ever lived.

He struck up friendships with several nice ladies of

uncertain age. Then one could see that he was becoming prosperous. He appeared, every day, in a new and elegant suit; marvellous shirts and ties; offered you rare cigars out of a platinum case. He was obviously doing well out of his friendships.

This was his line; he would profess love and the need for spiritual companionship; and then, by devious shifts, manage to get his victim to write him a tender note . . . you know, my friend, 'just to read when you are not here': it is an old trick. And it always worked. It always has and always will, for women are fools with their affection, just like men.

Having his note, he would begin to bleed the victim. She was, you understand, always the wife of a very great man; somebody who could not afford a scandal of any kind, even if she were utterly innocent. He had a heart of ice, that Skobeleff, and bled them dry. Apart from the money, he took a sadistic delight in the writhing of the victim. It was a hideous business.

And when he wanted to have a quiet drink, he always sat in the Maecenas Club near Piccadilly – an elegant drinking-den, with several slot machines in it, at which numerous idiots lost money enough to choke a hippopotamus.

Now it came to pass that I was approached one day by a woman for whom I entertained the deepest affection. I had better not tell you her name, but she was the wife of a very famous French politician. I liked her very much, in a quite platonic and brotherly way. Yes, brotherly is the word for it, for she was twenty years younger than me, and I had bought her an ivory teething-ring with golden bells on it when she was a mere liver-coloured handful of babe in long clothes. She approached me now and told me a sad story.

She was in terrible trouble. She had involved herself with Skobeleff, and had written him letters – which was worse. Now, he demanded twenty thousand pounds. Otherwise, he would place the letters in the hands of her husband's political opposition; ruin him, ruin her, ruin everything. Twenty thousand pounds was his price, and she had not got twenty thousand. By selling some jewels she could raise ten thousand, she told me, but Skobeleff would not take ten thousand. He said, 'Twenty or nothing. I can sell these letters for twenty thousand any way . . .'

Could I help? Could I lend her ten thousand pounds?

I said that I could do better than that: I could get back the letters.

I did so. It is a story of common burglary. I induced my friend to make up a bundle of money, meet Skobeleff at his apartment, and demand the letters in exchange. At a given moment I appeared, heavily disguised, with a large revolver, made him open his safe, took the entire contents of it, together with the letters my friend had written, and having knocked Skobeleff unconscious with the barrel of the gun, quietly made my departure. That was easy.

But when I came to examine the other papers I had taken, I was horrified. I, Karmesin, was disgusted! The man had made indexes and ledgers of dirty crime. He had a whole career of vile blackmail laid out. God knows what a trail of misery he was planning to leave in his wake. I only knew one thing: by stealing his papers, I had held him up only for a little while. Sooner or later he was certain to operate again.

The law could not touch him. If he left this country, he would operate elsewhere. I decided to take the law into my own hands; play God; kill him.

I approached him with a proposition.

I told him who I was, and he was impressed; he knew of the things Karmesin had done. Then I said, 'Do you know who lives in the flat above the Maecenas Club?'

'Yes,' said Skobeleff, 'old Lord Westerby.'

'Do you know what he keeps in his safe?' I asked.

'No, what?'

'The Westerby Collar.'

'The Westerby Collar!' said Skobeleff. 'A hundred and eighty priceless emeralds, and the Green Devil Emerald in the centre!'

'Yes. Well?'

'Well, what do you say?' he asked.

'You could help me get them. I have an immediate market. We can get at least two hundred thousand. Help me, and I'll split with you fifty-fifty.'

'But how?'

'Now, listen,' I said. 'I will do the work. I will get the emeralds. As for Westerby, leave him to me; I'll handle him.' I grinned ferociously. 'What I am going to suggest is this: I slip upstairs and get the jewels. A diversion is created that draws everybody in the Club into the slot machine room. You slip out on to the balcony in the room behind. That balcony stands directly underneath the servant's bedroom in the Westerby flat. We synchronize our watches. At midnight precisely, you step on to the balcony and I drop the jewels down into your hands. Then you rejoin the crowd in the next room, and nobody will ever know that you have not been there all the time. Next morning you meet me and give me the jewels.'

Even as I spoke to him I could see the idea of a double-cross entering his treacherous mind. I could see it in his eyes. What had he to lose? He had only to stand on a balcony. I was to do all the dirty work, take all the risks.

'But how will you get everybody into the slot machine room?' he asked.

'At ten minutes to twelve,' I said, 'a man will win the jackpot on every machine in the place.'

'If you can arrange that,' he said, 'you must be a wizard.'

'I am a wizard,' I said.

When I left him I looked up a man called Martin, a good little rogue who had had occasions to be thankful to me many a time, especially once when I supported his wife and three children while he spent a year in jail. He was something of a genius in engineering: I mean, very clever with wheels and springs. Would he help me? He would have gone through hell and high water for me. I promised him fifty pounds. His act was simple. At about eleven o'clock he had to come to the Club with a bag, showing the official card of the firm that manufactured the slot machines. Then he was to unlock each machine, and adjust it so that the next revolution of the wheels would bring the total to Three Bars, which wins the jackpot. That is a very simple matter for a man who knows how to handle machinery. Normally, of course, your slot machine engineer sends the wheels flying round six or seven times before leaving the thing, just to see that all is well. But Martin would not do this, of course, and nobody would notice.

I told you: nothing attracts people like the jingle of money. There must have been a dozen machines in the Club. The crash of a dozen jackpots at midnight would bring every member running from the next room: the floor would be knee-deep in silver. Everybody would be pulling handles, or stooping for fallen coins.

Then Skobeleff would come out on the balcony. He thought he ran no risk, for the secretary and commissionaire whom one had to pass before entering or leaving the Club could both swear that he had been in there all the time.

Only I was not going to be on the floor above with a priceless emerald collar. I was to be at the darkened window of the flat across the road. In my hands there was to be a rifle. I was a perfect shot, and still am. From that distance I could not miss. I should put a bullet in the centre of Skobeleff's forehead, and wipe his evil presence from the face of the earth. Martin was waiting in the street with a car. At ten seconds before twelve, as the theatre crowds filled the streets, he would jam the traffic; there would be a chaos of horns. He would make his engine backfire furiously. The sound of my shot would be unheard. It was perfect. And so it turned out.

A young fool called Poppins put a shilling in the slot machine and let out a deluge of coins. Others followed suit. The proprietor of the place came running, white in the face. The machines had gone mad! They were all paying out jackpots! The whole Club poured into the room, eager to put a shilling in, or to see money coming out. Simultaneously, a fearful uproar broke out in the street below. Cars jammed in a black mass, honking like fury. Martin's big automobile banged and thundered, giving out clouds of smoke.

I got Skobeleff's head in line, took a careful aim. He was outlined against the light. I could not miss – I who have knocked the head off a running antelope at five hundred yards. I pressed the trigger.

Skobeleff shrugged his shoulders and walked back into the club. Remembering everything, planning everything, organizing everything so perfectly, *I had forgotten to load my rifle!*

Karmesin laughed. 'Yet he deserved to die,' he said.

'Well?' I asked.

'Yes,' said Karmesin. 'It proves my point. Such men are always punished in the end. Nemesis is always upon them. They are never more than one jump ahead of vengeance.'

'But *Skobeleff?*

'Skobeleff,' said Karmesin. 'He stayed in the Club until one o'clock in the morning, then went home. Do you remember the big fire in the hosier's shop in Dublin Street, Piccadilly? Skobeleff lived above. He perished that very night. You see, in leaving that blank spot of forgetfulness in my brain, Fate was preserving Skobeleff for something even more terrible. A man cannot run away from his destiny.'

'But one thing more. How did you get into the flat exactly opposite the Club, when you meant to kill Skobeleff?'

'Ha!' said Karmesin. 'I got into it the same way as I got into it before: with a duplicate key. And I knew that the occupant would be on the balcony opposite. *It was Skobeleff's flat!*

'And the fire?'

'Inscrutable Providence,' said Karmesin dryly. 'Later that night I returned to Skobeleff's flat after he had gone to sleep. I took my cigar out of my mouth, and casually flipped it over my shoulder. "Let Providence proceed with the matter," I said. Providence! Fate! Skobeleff perished. It is right and proper that rubbish should be incinerated. So perish all rubbish! Another brandy?'

# The Day Lucky's Luck Ran Out

ALLAN PRIOR

*Escaping from the confines of Soho, the route to the next black spot takes us by way of the Haymarket, over Trafalgar Square, down Whitehall and along Victoria Street, past New Scotland Yard to reach Belgravia. For many years this area close beside Buckingham Palace has been regarded as one of the most fashionable residential areas in the capital – though like many another part there are dark secrets lurking down quite a few of its broad and palatial streets. It was in November 1974, in fact, that Belgravia, and in particular Lower Belgrave Street, made headlines around the world when Richard John Bingham, the seventh Earl of Lucan, a man well-known in London's gaming society as 'Lucky', disappeared after apparently attacking his wife and killing the family's nanny, 29-year-old Sandra Rivett. The events which made Lucan and Belgravia famous started reverberating when Lady Lucan, suffering from head wounds, staggered into a pub near their home screaming, 'He's murdered my nanny! My children, my children!' Despite an immediate and intensive police search in London which eventually spread throughout Great Britain and then further afield into Europe, the fugitive Earl has not been seen from that day to this, nor has anyone been able to discover any indication as to his ultimate fate. Twenty years on, this continuing mystery has not surprisingly earned Belgravia a special place in the history of London black spots.*

*The police, the press, even members of the public, have all advanced their own theories as to what might have driven Lucan to his crime – and where he might subsequently have gone. Some believe he committed suicide, others that he was spirited away by friends – but the only real fact is that the variety and ingenuity of these ideas would certainly fill a book on their own! Perhaps the most plausible, as well as being the most dramatic theory about his escape from justice is the one advanced in the following short story by Allan Prior (1922–   ), the thriller writer and TV playwright who was one of the guiding lights behind the hugely successful police series, Z-Cars. Allan's special knowledge of the working of crime detection has been shown in novels such as* One Away *(1961),* The Interrogators *(1965), and* Paradiso *(1972), and is present again in 'The Day Lucky's Luck Ran Out' which he wrote for the* Daily Mail *on the seventh anniversary of the earl's disappearance. The reader is invited to judge for himself whether it seems any more likely a supposition than all the rest . . .*

LUCKY SAT IN the darkened room over the little bistro on the Boulevard Helene and waited for the stitches to be taken out.

This had been the hardest part of all, the waiting. Almost two weeks of it. It seemed more like two years. Lucky could not sleep properly for he could not lie down in case the stitches pulled and split and had to be sewn back into his inflamed face once more. So he dozed upright on the hard chair and suffered.

It had been ten days since the German doctor had put them in, working silently with scalpel and needle. Only once had he spoken. 'You may not be quite so handsome, later. Do you mind that?'

Lucky had not replied. Handsome! It was the word everybody had always used about him. The handsomest man in the room, in the regiment, in the Casino.

Lucky would have grimaced if he could. Where had handsome got him except this dirty little room, his face and his hairline cut and clipped at by a man he couldn't see and whose name he didn't know? What did his face look like now? Something in a butcher's shop, he supposed.

Well, he thought grimly, he could live without his looks. In a way they had dictated all his actions. A man who looked as he did had to act as he did. Had to gamble as he did, raise hell as he did. Top stakes every time, let it ride and the hell with it. That had been his style, nobody could deny it.

Now, the Doctor had said, he would have to change all that. He would have to be cautious. Anyway, until he got there, until he was under the General's protection.

The General was looking forward to meeting him. If he did exactly as he was told and the luck ran his way, he had nothing to worry about.

Luck? He had lived with it, on it, by it, all his life.

'Be lucky, Guv,' the taxi-driver had said as he dropped him at Victoria, the night it all started, automatic cockney matiness, that was all, but Lucky had only just stopped himself over-tipping the man (that might be remembered) and had contented himself with a gruff, 'We all need that.'

Alone, on Victoria Station forecourt with some damnfool idea of getting a boat-train, he must have been mad! Every port, every airport would be watched by now surely? Well, his luck had held. Nobody had noticed the tall, lone figure. Not even in the public telephone box as, his head clearing a little from the frightful events of the night, he called the one man of all his friends he knew he could rely on. This friend knew everybody and everything.

He was another who played for high stakes. Another who understood. His friend had been in, lucky again, his voice had been cool, he had hardly sounded surprised. He had asked, 'Where's the car?' and when Lucky had told him he had said, 'I'll take care of that.' He had cut short Lucky's ramblings with a curt, 'Never mind that, old boy, the thing is to get you out.'

Out?

Lucky shifted on the hard chair in the darkened room

over the bistro. His fingers brushed his bare upper lip where the thick guardee's moustache had been. Out? The hours after Victoria had been blurred.

The dark limo that picked him up outside the nearby coffee bar, and his friend's arm around him in the leathery interior, the flash of brandy at his lips. All that was still vivid.

At the sand-dunes his friend had said good-bye, probably, Lucky supposed, for the last time. It was dark and wild that night and the sea boiled behind them. His friend's voice dropped: 'These people can be trusted. I've paid them and there's more when they get you there. Do as they say, they're professionals, usually they smuggle dope.'

He held both of Lucky's hands a long, long moment . . . 'Be Lucky'.

Lucky watched him until he was out of sight and turned to the three silent foreign-looking men in jeans and sailor caps. They gestured to a row-boat on the beach. 'Hope you're a good sailor, Sir,' said one, smiling. Lucky nodded but did not reply, and walked calmly towards the rowboat. Out at sea, beyond the shallows, he could see the dark shape of a motor yacht.

The French coast had been grey and grim in the dawn light. There had been a car waiting. He had waited in this room ever since. That had been (he did the sum again in his head) twelve days ago, no fourteen, he had forgotten the two days he had sat alone before the Doctor appeared. There had been food and drink in the room but the door had been locked. In the next room he could hear a tart plying her trade.

There were shutters across the windows and a note from his friend on the table. The message had been brief. *Do exactly as they say. Take care, Good luck.* There had also been a thousand pounds in mixed monies, French, German, Brazilian, Paraguayan.

The German doctor (Lucky supposed he was German, possibly Austrian, did it matter?) had been businesslike but not talkative. He said the news was good, the car had been found, the newspapers mostly thought he was dead. That had been four days ago.

Today, the stitches came out.

The Doctor took off his gloves and opened his case and laid out his instruments on the table, and shone the portable pencil-light on Lucky's face and took the bandages from Lucky's eyes and mouth very very slowly, hissing softly as he did so.

'So,' he said. 'Very good. Yes. I think so.'

'Don't you want to see your new self?' asked the Doctor, softly.

'I suppose so.' In truth he did not. He liked himself as he was. But that, he supposed, was all over. He nodded, and the Doctor, keeping the pencil-light on him, held up the small sharp mirror.

Lucky stared at the face. It was somebody else, somebody vaguely familiar. But not himself, not Lucky. Never in a million years.

The Doctor seemed to be waiting for something so Lucky said, 'Damn good, I must say.'

Even his voice seemed different.

He sat in the room another week, quite alone, the tart popping his day's supply of food in each morning, not looking at him, until the Doctor came again and examined his face, which had almost healed. 'We'll put some powder on,' said the Doctor, 'after I have cut your hair and so on.'

So Lucky's hair was now short and dyed grey and he was ten pounds lighter. Looking at himself in the mirror Lucky was shocked. It all seemed unreal. The Doctor brought him a suit, nothing like the kind of suit he was used to, the sort of suit he never expected to wear.

For one thing, somebody else had worn it and it smelled of tobacco and stale sweat.

The car ride to the airport scared Lucky, whom nothing had ever scared before. Goddammit, he thought, shaking. I'd be better off back *there*, facing it out. This isn't me. It's somebody else, shaking and sweating in this rotten old suit.

Steady. The Doctor's hand pressed his arm. 'Nothing to worry about. Soon we'll be on the plane. The odds are on our side.'

My God, his legs had turned to jelly as he stumbled towards the desk and the Doctor had explained, 'My friend is not too well but he's looking forward to his trip on the big bird,' and they had been all smiles at the desk as he had recovered (the bored security man did not even look his way) and nodded apologetically ('Don't speak, ever,' the Doctor had warned him) and then he was on Concorde.

Rio was a town he would once have taken delight in, have caroused and gambled wildly in, but his place in Rio was another small room in a small dingy hotel, while his passage further North was arranged. 'Too many bounty hunters in Rio,' said the Doctor. 'Once you are under the General's protection you will be safe.'

And now he was here. The series of fast cars had at last turned into a military jeep, there had been a bridge, a river, a crossing of a frontier.

Then he was in a villa of some sort and, the German doctor still at his elbow, smiling now. A door opened to a brightly lit room and blinking at the light, he saw across the splendid table there sat a middle-aged Germanic-looking man whom he instantly recognised, or anyway he knew who it must be, and Lucky knew that he was safe here, along with the concentration-camp murderers and the Gestapo men and anybody else who could pay the price and seemed the right sort.

Lucky also knew that nobody who came to this place ever left it. There was nowhere to go from here, except back to the avengers.

The General extended a meaty hand, smiling. 'My dear fellow, we have waited up to welcome you. We were beginning to wonder if your famous luck had run out?'

Lucky smiled back and took his hand.

'Not yet,' he said, knowing in his heart that it had.

# A Little Place off the Edgware Road

## GRAHAM GREENE

*From Belgravia, a walk around Hyde Park Corner and up Park Lane takes us to that rather bleak and almost endless stretch of road which disappears into the northern suburbs of the capital – the Edgware Road. In the past it was a notorious black spot that offered a fast escape route for criminals leaving the city while at the same time an ideal location for highwaymen to hold up unsuspecting travellers bound for the north. Today it still has a kind of strange remoteness that seems to descend upon it as soon as darkness falls. This feeling of emptiness so close to the heart of London is chillingly evoked in Graham Greene's story of 'A Little Place off the Edgware Road' which was brilliantly adapted for television in the 1975 Granada series,* Shades of Greene. *Dramatized by John Mortimer (the barrister and author of the* Rumpole of the Bailey *series) and directed by Philip Saville, it starred Tony Clavin as Craven and Michael Sheard as Inspector Tweedie.*

*Graham Greene (1904–1993) was fascinated by the subjects of crime and criminals throughout his working life – though more with the emotions and motivations of the law-breakers than their actions – and this is particularly evident in novels such as* A Gun For Sale *(1936),* Brighton Rock *(1938),* The Third Man *(1949) and* The Quiet American *(1958), all of which were, of course, filmed along with several other of his best-selling titles. Although he preferred to call these tales of crime and mystery 'entertainments', they are highly regarded by devotees of the detective story genre and their style of plotting and characterization have been widely imitated by later writers in the genre. Before becoming famous as a novelist, Greene worked on* The Times *newspaper for three years and was for a while a film reviewer. His interest in movies and his special ability to be able to weave a tale of murder and mystery in the prosaic surroundings of a little backstreet cinema make the next story compulsively readable. No London cinema may ever seem quite the same after the reader has experienced the events which occur one night in the little place off the Edgware Road . . .*

CRAVEN CAME UP past the Achilles statue in the thin summer rain. It was only just after lighting-up time, but already the cars were lined up all the way to the Marble Arch, and the sharp acquisitive faces peered out ready for a good time with anything possible which came along. Craven went bitterly by with the collar of his mackintosh tight round his throat: it was one of his bad days.

All the way up the Park he was reminded of passion, but you needed money for love. All that a poor man could get was lust. Love needed a good suit, a car, a flat somewhere, or a good hotel. It needed to be wrapped in cellophane. He was aware all the time of the stringy tie beneath the mackintosh, and the frayed sleeves: he carried his body about with him like something he hated. (There were moments of happiness in the British Museum reading-room, but the body called him back.) He bore, as his only sentiment, the memory of ugly deeds committed on park chairs. People talked as if the body died too soon – that wasn't the trouble, to Craven, at all. The body kept alive – and through the glittering tinselly rain, on his way to a rostrum, he passed a little man in a black suit carrying a banner, 'The Body shall rise again'. He remembered a dream from which three times he had woken trembling: he had been alone in the huge dark cavernous burying ground of all the world. Every grave was connected to another under the ground: the globe was honeycombed for the sake of the dead, and on each occasion of dreaming he had discovered anew the horrifying fact that the body doesn't decay. There are no worms and dissolution. Under the ground the world was littered with masses of dead flesh ready to rise again with their warts and boils and eruptions. He had lain in bed and remembered – as 'tidings of great joy' – that the body after all was corrupt.

He came up into the Edgware Road walking fast – the Guardsmen were out in couples, great languid elongated beasts – the bodies like worms in their tight trousers. He hated them, and hated his hatred because he knew what it was, envy. He was aware that every one of them had a better body than himself: indigestion creased his stomach: he felt sure that his breath was foul – but who could he ask? Sometimes he secretly touched himself here and there with scent: it was one of his ugliest secrets. Why should he be asked to believe in the resurrection of this body he wanted to forget? Sometimes he prayed at night (a hint of religious belief was lodged in his breast like a worm in a nut) that *his* body at any rate should never rise again.

He knew all the side streets round the Edgware Road only too well: when a mood was on, he simply walked until he tired, squinting at his own image in the windows of Salmon & Gluckstein and the A.B.C.s. So he noticed at once the posters outside the disused theatre in Culpar Road. They were not unusual, for sometimes Barclays Bank Dramatic Society would hire the place for an evening – or an obscure film would be trade-shown there. The theatre had been built in 1920 by an optimist who thought the cheapness of the site would more than counter-balance its disadvantage of lying a mile outside the conventional theatre zone. But no play had ever succeeded, and it was soon left to gather rat-holes and spider-webs. The covering of the seats was never renewed, and all that ever happened to the place was the temporary false life of an amateur play or a trade show.

Craven stopped and read – there were still optimists it appeared, even in 1939, for nobody but the blindest optimist could hope to make money out of the place as 'The Home of the Silent Film'. The first season of 'primitives' was announced (a high-brow phrase): there would never be a second. Well, the seats were cheap, and it was perhaps worth a shilling to him, now that he was tired, to get in somewhere out of the rain. Craven bought a ticket and went in to the darkness of the stalls.

In the dead darkness a piano tinkled something monotonous recalling Mendelssohn: he sat down in a gangway seat, and could immediately feel the emptiness all round him. No, there would never be another season. On the screen a large woman in a kind of toga wrung her hands, then wobbled with curious jerky movements towards a couch. There she sat and stared out like a sheep-dog distractedly through her loose and black and stringy hair. Sometimes she seemed to dissolve altogether into dots and flashes and wiggly lines. A sub-title said, 'Pompilia betrayed by her beloved Augustus seeks an end to her troubles.'

Craven began at last to see – a dim waste of stalls. There were not twenty people in the place – a few couples whispering with their heads touching, and a number of lonely men like himself, wearing the same uniform of the cheap mackintosh. They lay about at intervals like corpses – and again Craven's obsession returned: the tooth-ache of horror. He thought miserably – I am going mad: other people don't feel like this. Even a disused theatre reminded him of those interminable caverns where the bodies were waiting for resurrection.

'A slave to his passion Augustus calls for yet more wine.'

A gross middle-aged Teutonic actor lay on an elbow with his arm round a large woman in a shift. The Spring Song tinkled ineptly on, and the screen flickered like indigestion. Somebody felt his way through the darkness, scrabbling past Craven's knees – a small man: Craven experienced the unpleasant feeling of a large beard brushing his mouth. Then there was a long sigh as the newcomer found the next chair, and on the screen events had moved with such rapidity that Pompilia had already stabbed herself – or so Craven supposed – and lay still and buxom among her weeping slaves.

A low breathless voice sighed out close to Craven's ear, 'What's happened? Is she asleep ?'

'No. Dead.'

'Murdered ?' the voice asked with a keen interest.

'I don't think so. Stabbed herself.'

Nobody said 'Hush': nobody was enough interested to object to a voice. They drooped among the empty chairs in attitudes of weary inattention.

The film wasn't nearly over yet: there were children some-how to be considered: was it all going on to a second generation? But the small bearded man in the next seat seemed to be interested only in Pompilia's death. The fact that he had come in at that moment apparently fascinated him. Craven heard the word 'coincidence' twice, and he went on talking to himself about it in low out-of-breath tones. 'Absurd when you come to think of it,' and then 'no blood at all'. Craven didn't listen: he sat with his hands clasped between his knees, facing the fact as he had faced it so often before, that he was in danger of going mad. He had to pull himself up, take a holiday, see a doctor (God knew what infection moved in his veins). He became aware that his bearded neighbour had addressed him directly. 'What?' he asked impatiently, 'what did you say ?'

'There would be more blood than you can imagine.'

'What are you talking about?'

When the man spoke to him, he sprayed him with damp breath. There was a little bubble in his speech like an impedi-ment. He said, 'When you murder a man . . .'

'This was a woman,' Craven said impatiently.

'That wouldn't make any difference.'

'And it's got nothing to do with murder anyway.'

'That doesn't signify.' They seemed to have got into an absurd and meaningless wrangle in the dark.

'I know, you see,' the little bearded man said in a tone of enormous conceit.

'Know what?'

'About such things,' he said with guarded ambiguity.

Craven turned and tried to see him clearly. Was he mad ? Was this a warning of what he might become – babbling incomprehensibly to strangers in cinemas? He thought, By God, no, trying to see: I'll be sane yet. I *will* be sane. He could make out nothing but a small black hump of body. The man was talking to himself again. He said, 'Talk. Such talk. They'll say it was all for fifty pounds. But that's a lie. Reasons and reasons. They always take the first reason. Never look behind. Thirty years of reasons. Such simpletons,' he added again in that tone of breathless and unbounded conceit. So this was madness. So long as he could realize that, he must be sane himself – relatively speaking. Not so sane perhaps as the seekers in the park or the Guardsmen in the Edgware Road, but saner than this. It was like a message of encouragement as the piano tinkled on.

Then again the little man turned and sprayed him. 'Killed herself, you say ? But who's to know that? It's not a mere question of what hand holds the knife.' He laid a hand suddenly and confidingly on Craven's: it was damp and sticky: Craven said with horror as a possible meaning came to him, 'What are you talking about ?'

'I know,' the little man said. 'A man in my position gets to know almost everything.'

'What is your position?' Craven asked, feeling the sticky hand on his, trying to make up his mind whether he was being hysterical or not – after all, there were a dozen explanations – it might be treacle.

'A pretty desperate one *you'd* say.' Sometimes the voice almost died in the throat altogether. Something incomprehensible had happened on the screen – take your eyes from these early pictures for a moment and the plot had proceeded on at such a pace . . . Only the actors moved slowly and jerkily. A young woman in a nightdress seemed to be weeping in the arms of a Roman centurion: Craven hadn't seen either of them before. '*I am not afraid of death, Lucius – in your arms.*'

The little man began to titter – knowingly. He was talking

to himself again. It would have been easy to ignore him altogether if it had not been for those sticky hands which he now
removed: he seemed to be fumbling at the seat in front of
him. His head had a habit of lolling sideways – like an idiot
child's. He said distinctly and irrelevantly: 'Bayswater
Tragedy.'

'What was that?' Craven said. He had seen those words on
a poster before he entered the park.

'What?'

'About the tragedy.'

'To think they call Cullen Mews Bayswater.' Suddenly the
little man began to cough – turning his face towards Craven
and coughing right at him: it was like vindictiveness. The
voice said, 'Let me see. My umbrella.' He was getting up.

'You didn't have an umbrella.'

'My umbrella,' he repeated. 'My—' and seemed to lose the
word altogether. He went scrabbling out past Craven's knees.

Craven let him go, but before he had reached the billowy
dusty curtains of the Exit the screen went blank and bright –
the film had broken, and somebody immediately turned up
one dirt-choked chandelier above the circle. It shone down
just enough for Craven to see the smear on his hands. This
wasn't hysteria: this was a fact. He wasn't mad: he had sat
next to a madman who in some mews – what was the name,
Colon, Collin . . . Craven jumped up and made his own way
out: the black curtain flapped in his mouth. But he was too
late: the man had gone and there were three turnings to
choose from. He chose instead a telephone-box and dialled
with a sense odd for him of sanity and decision 999.

It didn't take two minutes to get the right department.
They were interested and very kind. Yes, there had been a
murder in a mews – Cullen Mews. A man's neck had been
cut from ear to ear with a bread knife – a horrid crime. He
began to tell them how he had sat next to the murderer in a
cinema: it couldn't be anyone else: there was blood on his
hands – and he remembered with repulsion as he spoke the
damp beard. There must have been a terrible lot of blood.

But the voice from the Yard interrupted him. 'Oh no,' it was saying, 'we have the murderer – no doubt of it at all. It's the body that's disappeared.'

Craven put down the receiver. He said to himself aloud, 'Why should this happen to *me*? Why to *me*?' He was back in the horror of his dream – the squalid darkening street outside was only one of the innumerable tunnels connecting grave to grave where the imperishable bodies lay. He said, 'It was a dream, a dream,' and leaning forward he saw in the mirror above the telephone his own face sprinkled by tiny drops of blood like dew from a scent-spray. He began to scream, 'I won't go mad. I won't go mad. I'm sane. I won't go mad.' Presently a little crowd began to collect, and soon a policeman came.

# People Don't Do Such Things

## RUTH RENDELL

*Bayswater Road, which adjoins the Edgware Road, provides the final black spot on our tour. The Bayswater area with its streets full of small hotels and old two- and three-storey houses converted into flats has sheltered two of London's most notorious twentieth-century murderers: John Reginald Halliday Christie and John George Haigh. Christie, the mass murderer and sexual psychopath who slaughtered at least six women, lived in the ground floor flat at 10 Rillington Place; while the handsome and charming Haigh who committed the horrendous 'Acid Bath Murders' resided at the Onslow Court Hotel and rented a 'workroom' at 79 Gloucester Road. As if these two were not enough to give the area a sinister reputation, the activities of another mass-murderer who killed and stripped naked the bodies of six prostitutes in the mid-sixties took place in nearby Hammersmith. The man, who has never been identified, has become known in popular folklore for obvious reasons as 'Jack the Stripper'. It comes as no surprise, therefore, to learn that Bayswater is regarded as London's 'Crimes of Passion' district – a factor which Ruth Rendell uses to particularly telling effect in the following pages.*

*In the last decade Ruth Rendell (1930–   ) has enjoyed a phenomenal success with her crime novels featuring Detective Chief Inspector Wexford – who has also been splendidly portrayed on television by George Baker – as well as her tales of psychological*

*horror under the hardly secret pen name of Barbara Vine.*
*Although by no means restricted to London for their settings, a*
*number of Ruth's novels and short stories do reveal a profound*
*knowledge of the city and its teeming population of ordinary*
*men and women as a result of her years spent living there – first*
*in a flat near Hampstead Heath and subsequently in a mews*
*house just off Baker Street. Recently, when she was being inter-*
*viewed at home by Helena de Bertodano of the* Sunday
Telegraph *about her depiction of the ways in which apparently*
*normal people could be driven to extremes, she admitted she*
*had puzzled for a long time about why people committed mur-*
*der, without being able to reach an answer. 'I've never wanted*
*to kill anyone myself,' she said, 'and I look around and I can't see*
*any of my friends wanting to kill. But who knows what our*
*unconscious is doing?' She continues to explore this theme in*
*this next story which also neatly completes the first half of our*
*journey around London after midnight . . .*

PEOPLE DON'T DO such things.

That's the last line of *Hedda Gabler*, and Ibsen makes this
chap say it out of a sort of bewilderment at finding truth
stranger than fiction. I know just how he felt. I say it myself
every time I come up against the hard reality that Reeve
Baker is serving fifteen years in prison for murdering my
wife, and that I played my part in it, and that it happened to
us three. People don't do such things. But they do.

Real life had never been stranger than fiction for me. It
had always been beautifully pedestrian and calm and pleasant, and all the people I knew jogged along in the same sort
of way. Except Reeve, that is. I suppose I made a friend of
Reeve and enjoyed his company so much because of the contrast between his manner of living and my own, and so that
when he had gone home I could say comfortably to
Gwendolen:

'How dull our lives must seem to Reeve!'

An acquaintance of mine had given him my name when

he had got into a mess with his finances and was having trouble with the Inland Revenue. As an accountant with a good many writers among my clients, I was used to their irresponsible attitude to money – the way they fall back on the excuse of artistic temperament for what is, in fact, calculated tax evasion – and I was able to sort things out for Reeve and show him how to keep more or less solvent. As a way, I suppose of showing his gratitude, Reeve took Gwendolen and me out to dinner, then we had him over at our place, and after that we became close friends.

Writers and the way they work hold a fascination for ordinary chaps like me. It's a mystery to me where they get their ideas from, apart from constructing the thing and creating characters and making their characters talk and so on. But Reeve could do it all right, and set the whole lot at the court of Louis Quinze or in medieval Italy or what not. I've read all nine of his historical novels and admired what you might call his virtuosity. But I only read them to please him really. Detective stories were what I preferred and I seldom bothered with any other form of fiction.

Gwendolen once said to me it was amazing Reeve could fill his books with so much drama when he was living drama all the time. You'd imagine he'd have got rid of it all on paper. I think the truth was that every one of his heroes was himself, only transformed into Cesare Borgia or Casanova. You could see Reeve in them all, tall, handsome and dashing as they were, and each a devil with the women. Reeve had got divorced from his wife a year or so before I'd met him, and since then he'd had a string of girl friends, models, actresses, girls in the fashion trade, secretaries, journalists, schoolteachers, high-powered lady executives and even a dentist. Once when we were over at his place he played us a record of an aria from *Don Giovanni* – another character Reeve identified with and wrote about. It was called the 'Catalogue Song' and it listed all the types of girls the Don had made love to, blonde, brunette, redhead, young, old, rich, poor, ending up with something about as long as she wears a petticoat you know what he does. Funny, I even remember the Italian for that bit, though it's the only Italian I know. *Purche porti la gonnella voi sapete quel che fa.* Then the singer laughed in an unpleasant way, laughed to music with a seducer's sneer, and Reeve laughed too, saying it gave him a fellow-feeling.

I'm old-fashioned, I know that. I'm conventional. Sex is for marriage, as far as I'm concerned, and what sex you have before marriage – I never had much – I can't help thinking of as a shameful secret thing. I never even believed that people did have much of it outside marriage. All talk and boasting, I thought. I really did think that. And I kidded myself that when Reeve talked of going out with a new girl he meant going out with. Taking out for a meal, I thought, and dancing with and taking home in a taxi and then maybe a good-night kiss on the doorstep. Until one Sunday morning, when Reeve was coming over for lunch, I phoned him to ask if he'd meet us in the pub for a pre-lunch drink. He sounded half-asleep and I could hear a girl giggling in the background. Then I heard him say:

'Get some clothes on, lovey, and make us a cup of tea, will you? My head's splitting.'

I told Gwendolen.

'What did you expect?' she said.

'I don't know,' I said. 'I thought you'd be shocked.'

'He's very good-looking and he's only thirty-seven. It's natural.' But she had blushed a little. 'I am rather shocked,' she said. 'We don't belong in his sort of life, do we?'

And yet we remained in it, on the edge of it. As we got to know Reeve better, he put aside those small prevarications he had employed to save our feelings. And he would tell us, without shyness, anecdotes of his amorous past and present. The one about the girl who was so possessive that even though he had broken with her, she had got into his flat in his absence and been lying naked in his bed when he brought his new girl home that night; the one about the married woman who had hidden him for two hours in her wardrobe until her husband had gone out; the girl who had come to borrow a pound of sugar and had stayed all night; fair girls, dark girls, plump, thin, rich, poor . . . *Purche porti la gonnella voi sapete quel che fa.*

'It's another world,' said Gwendolen.

And I said, 'How the other half lives.'

We were given to clichés of this sort. Our life was a cliché, the commonest sort of life led by middle-class people in the Western world. We had a nice detached house in one of the right suburbs, solid furniture and lifetime-lasting carpets. I had my car and she hers. I left for the office at half-past eight and returned at six. Gwendolen cleaned the house and went shopping and gave coffee mornings. In the evenings we liked to sit at home and watch television, generally going to bed at eleven. I think I was a good husband. I never forgot my wife's birthday or failed to send her roses on our anniversary or omitted to do my share of the dishwashing. And she was an excellent wife, romantically-inclined, not sensual. At any rate, she was never sensual with me.

She kept every birthday card I ever sent her, and the Valentines I sent her while we were engaged. Gwendolen was one of those women who hoard and cherish small mementoes. In a drawer of her dressing table she kept the menu card from the restaurant where we celebrated our engagement, a picture postcard of the hotel where we spent our honeymoon, every photograph of us that had ever been taken, our wedding pictures in a leather-bound album. Yes, she was an arch-romantic, and in her diffident way, with an air of daring, she would sometimes reproach Reeve for his callousness.

'But you can't do that to someone who loves you,' she said when he had announced his brutal intention of going off on holiday without telling his latest girl friend where he was going or even that he was going at all. 'You'll break her heart.'

'Gwendolen, my love, she hasn't got a heart. Women don't have them. She has another sort of machine, a combination of telescope, lie detector, scalpel and castrating device.'

'You're too cynical,' said my wife. 'You may fall in love yourself one day and then you'll know how it feels.'

'Not necessarily. As Shaw said –' Reeve was always quoting what other writers had said '– "Don't do unto others as you would have others do unto you, as we don't all have the same tastes."'

'We all have the same taste about not wanting to be ill-treated.'

'She should have thought of that before she tried to control my life. No, I shall quietly disappear for a while. I mightn't go away, in fact. I might just say I'm going away and lie low at home for a fortnight. Fill up the deep freeze, you know, and lay in a stock of liquor. I've done it before in this sort of situation. It's rather pleasant and I get a hell of a lot of work done.'

Gwendolen was silenced by this and, I must say, so was I. You may wonder, after these examples of his morality, just what it was I saw in Reeve. It's hard now for me to remember. Charm, perhaps, and a never-failing hospitality; a rueful way of talking about his own life as if it was all he could hope for, while mine was the ideal all men would aspire to; a helplessness about his financial affairs combined with an admiration for my grasp of them; a manner of talking to me as if we were equally men of the world, only I had chosen the better part. When invited to one of our dull modest gatherings, he would always be the exciting friend with the witty small talk, the reviver of a failing party, the industrious barman; above all, the one among our friends who wasn't an accountant, a bank manager, a solicitor, a general practitioner or a company executive. We had his books on our shelves. Our friends borrowed them and told their friends they'd met Reeve Baker at our house. He gave us a *cachet* that raised us enough centimetres above the level of the bourgeoisie to make us interesting.

Perhaps, in those days, I should have asked myself what it was he saw in us.

It was about a year ago that I first noticed a coolness between Gwendolen and Reeve. The banter they had gone in for, which had consisted in wry confessions or flirtatious compliments from him, and shy, somewhat maternal reproofs from her, stopped almost entirely. When we all three were together they talked to each other through me, as if I were their interpreter. I asked Gwendolen if he'd done something to upset her.

She looked extremely taken aback. 'What makes you ask?'

'You always seem a bit peeved with him.'

'I'm sorry,' she said. 'I'll try to be nicer. I didn't know I'd changed.'

She had changed to me too. She flinched sometimes when I touched her, and although she never refused me, there was an apathy about her love-making.

'What's the matter?' I asked her after a failure which disturbed me because it was so unprecedented.

She said it was nothing, and then, 'We're getting older. You can't expect things to be the same as when we were first married.'

'For God's sake,' I said. 'You're thirty-five and I'm thirty-nine. We're not in our dotage.'

She sighed and looked unhappy. She had become moody and difficult. Although she hardly opened her mouth in Reeve's presence, she talked about him a lot when he wasn't there, seizing upon almost any excuse to discuss him and speculate about his character. And she seemed inexplicably annoyed when, on our tenth wedding anniversary, a greetings card arrived addressed to us both from him. I, of course, had sent her roses. At the end of the week I missed a receipt for a bill I'd paid – as an accountant I'm naturally circumspect about these things – and I searched through our wastepaper basket, thinking I might have thrown it away. I found it, and I also found the anniversary card I'd sent Gwendolen to accompany the roses.

All these things I noticed. That was the trouble with me – I noticed things but I lacked the experience of life to add them up and make a significant total. I didn't have the worldly wisdom to guess why my wife was always out when

I phoned her in the afternoons, or why she was for ever buying new clothes. I noticed, I wondered, that was all.

I noticed things about Reeve too. For one thing, that he'd stopped talking about his girl friends.

'He's growing up at last,' I said to Gwendolen.

She reacted with warmth, with enthusiasm. 'I really think he is.'

But she was wrong. He had only three months of what I thought of as celibacy. And then when he talked of a new girl friend, it was to me alone. Confidentially, over a Friday night drink in the pub, he told me of this 'marvellous chick', twenty years old, he had met at a party the week before.

'It won't last, Reeve,' I said.

'I sincerely hope not. Who wants it to *last?*'

Not Gwendolen, certainly. When I told her she was incredulous, then aghast. And when I said I was sorry I'd told her since Reeve's backsliding upset her so much, she snapped at me that she didn't want to discuss him. She became even more snappy and nervous and depressed too. Whenever the phone rang she jumped. Once or twice I came home to find no wife, no dinner prepared; then she'd come in, looking haggard, to say she'd been out for a walk. I got her to see our doctor and he put her on tranquillizers which just made her more depressed.

I hadn't seen Reeve for ages. Then, out of the blue he phoned me at work to say he was off to the South of France for three weeks.

'In your state of financial health?' I said. I'd had a struggle getting him to pay the January instalment of his twice-yearly income tax, and I knew he was practically broke till he got the advance on his new book in May. 'The South of France is a bit pricey, isn't it?'

'I'll manage,' he said. 'My bank manager's one of my fans and he's let me have an overdraft.'

Gwendolen didn't seem very surprised to hear about Reeve's holiday. He'd told me he was going on his own – the 'marvellous chick' had long disappeared – and she said she thought he needed the rest, especially as there wouldn't be any of those girls to bother him, as she put it.

When I first met Reeve he'd been renting a flat but I persuaded him to buy one, for security and as an investment. The place was known euphemistically as a garden flat but it was in fact a basement, the lower ground floor of a big Victorian house in Bayswater. My usual route to work didn't take me along his street, but sometimes when the traffic was heavy I'd go through the back doubles and past his house. After he'd been away for about two weeks I happened to do this one morning and, of course, I glanced at Reeve's window. One always does glance at a friend's house, I think, when one is passing even if one knows that friend isn't at home. His bedroom was at the front, the top half of the window visible, the lower half concealed by the rise of lawn. I noticed that the curtains were drawn. Not particularly wise, I thought, an invitation to burglars, and then I forgot about it. But two mornings later I passed that way again, passed very slowly this time as there was a traffic hold-up, and again I glanced at Reeve's window. The curtains were no longer quite drawn. There was a gap about six inches wide between them. Now whatever a burglar may do, it's very unlikely he'll pull back drawn curtains. I didn't consider burglars this time. I thought Reeve must have come back early.

Telling myself I should be late for work anyway if I struggled along in this traffic jam, I parked the car as soon as I could at a meter. I'll knock on old Reeve's door, I thought, and get him to make me a cup of coffee. There was no answer. But as I looked once more at that window I was almost certain those curtains had been moved again, and in the past ten minutes. I rang the doorbell of the woman in the flat upstairs. She came down in her dressing gown.

'Sorry to disturb you,' I said. 'But do you happen to know if Mr Baker's come back?'

'He's not coming back till Saturday,' she said.

'Sure of that?'

'Of course I'm sure,' she said rather huffily. 'I put a note through his door Monday, and if he was back he'd have come straight up for this parcel I took in for him.'

'Did he take his car, d'you know?' I said, feeling like a detective in one of my favourite crime novels.

'Of course he did. What is this? What's he done?'

I said he'd done nothing, as far as I knew, and she banged the door in my face. So I went down the road to the row of lock-up garages. I couldn't see much through the little panes of frosted glass in the door of Reeve's garage, just enough to be certain the interior wasn't empty but that that greenish blur was the body of Reeve's Fiat. And then I knew for sure. He hadn't gone away at all. I chuckled to myself as I imagined him lying low for these three weeks in his flat, living off food from the deep freeze and spending most of his time in the back regions where, enclosed as those rooms were by a courtyard with high walls, he could show lights day and night with impunity. Just wait till Saturday, I thought, and I pictured myself asking him for details of his holiday, laying little traps for him, until even he with his writer's powers of invention would have to admit he'd never been away at all.

Gwendolen was laying the table for our evening meal when I got in. She, I'd decided, was the only person with whom I'd share this joke. I got all her attention the minute I mentioned Reeve's name, but when I reached the bit about his car being in the garage she stared at me and all the colour went out of her face. She sat down, letting the bunch of knives and forks she was holding fall into her lap. 'What on earth's the matter?' I said.

'How could he be so cruel? How could he do that to anyone?'

'Oh, my dear, Reeve's quite ruthless where women are concerned. You remember, he told us he'd done it before.'

'I'm going to phone him,' she said, and I saw that she was shivering. She dialled his number and I heard the ringing tone start.

'He won't answer,' I said. 'I wouldn't have told you if I'd thought it was going to upset you.'

She didn't say any more. There were things cooking on the stove and the table was half-laid, but she left all that and went into the hall. Almost immediately afterwards I heard the front door close.

I know I'm slow on the uptake in some ways but I'm not stupid. Even a husband who trusts his wife like I trusted mine – or, rather, never considered there was any need for trust – would know, after that, that something had been going on. Nothing much, though, I told myself. A crush perhaps on her part, hero-worship which his flattery and his confidences had fanned. Naturally, she'd feel let down, betrayed, when she discovered he'd deceived her as to his whereabouts when he'd led her to believe she was a special friend and privy to all his secrets. But I went upstairs just the same to reassure myself by looking in that dressing table drawer where she kept her souvenirs. Dishonourable? I don't think so. She had never locked it or tried to keep its contents private from me.

And all those little mementoes of our first meeting, our courtship, our marriage, were still there. Between a birthday card and a Valentine I saw a pressed rose. But there too, alone in a nest made out of a lace handkerchief I had given her, were a locket and a button. The locket was one her mother had left to her, but the photograph in it, that of some long-dead unidentifiable relative, had been replaced by a cut-out of Reeve from a snapshot. On the reverse side was a lock of hair. The button I recognized as coming from Reeve's blazer, though it hadn't, I noticed, been cut off. He must have lost it in our house and she'd picked it up. The hair was Reeve's, black, wavy, here and there with a thread of grey, but again it hadn't been cut off. On one of our visits to his flat she must have combed it out of his hairbrush and twisted it into a lock. Poor little Gwendolen . . . Briefly, I'd suspected Reeve. For one dreadful moment, sitting down there after she'd gone out, I'd asked myself, could he have . . .? Could my best friend have . . .? But, no. He hadn't even sent her a letter or a flower. It had been all on her side, and for that reason – I knew where she was bound for – I must stop her reaching him and humiliating herself.

I slipped the things into my pocket with some vague idea of using them to show her how childish she was being. She hadn't taken her car. Gwendolen always disliked driving in central London. I took mine and drove to the tube station I knew she'd go to.

She came out a quarter of an hour after I got there, walking fast and glancing nervously to the right and left of her. When she saw me she gave a little gasp and stood stock-still.

'Get in, darling,' I said gently. 'I want to talk to you.'

She got in but she didn't speak. I drove down to the Bayswater Road and into the Park. There, on the Ring, I parked under the plane trees, and because she still didn't utter a word, I said:

'You mustn't think I don't understand. We've been married ten years and I daresay I'm a dull sort of chap. Reeve's exciting and different and – well, maybe it's only natural for you to think you've fallen for him.'

She stared at me stonily. 'I love him and he loves me.'

'That's nonsense,' I said, but it wasn't the chill of the spring evening that made me shiver. 'Just because he's used that charm of his on you . . .'

She interrupted me. 'I want a divorce.'

'For heaven's sake,' I said. 'You hardly know Reeve. You've never been alone with him, have you?'

'Never been alone with him?' She gave a brittle, desperate laugh. 'He's been my lover for six months. And now I'm going to him. I'm going to tell him he doesn't have to hide from women any more because I'll be with him all the time.'

In the half-dark I gaped at her. 'I don't believe you,' I said, but I did. I did. 'You mean you along with all the rest . . .? My wife?'

'I'm going to be Reeve's wife. I'm the only one that understands him, the only one he can talk to. He told me that just before – before he went away.'

'Only he didn't go away.' There was a great redness in front of my eyes like a lake of blood. 'You fool,' I shouted at her. 'Don't you see it's you he's hiding from, *you*? He's done this to get away from you like he's got away from all the others. Love you? He never even gave you a present, not even a photograph. If you go there, he won't let you in. You're the last person he'd let in.'

'I'm going to him,' she cried, and she began to struggle with the car door. 'I'm going to him, to live with him, and I never want to see you again!'

In the end I drove home alone. Her wish came true and she never did see me again.

When she wasn't back by eleven I called the police. They asked me to go down to the police station and fill out a Missing Persons form, but they didn't take my fear very seriously. Apparently, when a woman of Gwendolen's age disappears they take it for granted she's gone off with a man. They took it seriously all right when a park keeper found her strangled body among some bushes in the morning.

That was on the Thursday. The police wanted to know where Gwendolen could have been going so far from her home. They wanted the names and addresses of all our friends. Was there anyone we knew in Kensington or Paddington or Bayswater, anywhere in the vicinity of the Park? I said there was no one. The next day they asked me again and I said, as if I'd just remembered:

'Only Reeve Baker. The novelist, you know.' I gave them his address. 'But he's away on holiday, has been for three weeks. He's not coming home till tomorrow.'

What happened after that I know from the evidence given at Reeve's trial, his trial for the murder of my wife. The police called on him on Saturday morning. I don't think they suspected him at all at first. My reading of crime fiction has taught me they would have asked him for any information he could give about our private life.

Unfortunately for him, they had already talked to some of

his neighbours. Reeve had led all these people to think he had really gone away. The milkman and the paper boy were both certain he had been away. So when the police questioned him about that, and he knew just why they were questioning him, he got into a panic. He didn't dare say he'd been in France. They could have shown that to be false without the least trouble. Instead, he told the truth and said he'd been lying low to escape the attentions of a woman. Which woman? He wouldn't say, but the woman in the flat upstairs would. Time and time again she had seen Gwendolen visit him in the afternoons, had heard them quarrelling, Gwendolen protesting her love for him and he shouting that he wouldn't be controlled, that he'd do anything to escape her possessiveness.

He had, of course, no alibi for the Wednesday night. But the judge and the jury could see he'd done his best to arrange one. Novelists are apt to let their imaginations run away with them; they don't realize how astute and thorough the police are. And there was firmer evidence of his guilt even than that. Three main exhibits were produced in the court: Reeve's blazer with a button missing from the sleeve; that very button; a cluster of his hairs. The button had been found by Gwendolen's body and the hairs on her coat . . .

My reading of detective stories hadn't been in vain, though I haven't read one since then. People don't, I suppose, after a thing like that.

# SECTION TWO
# CITY SLEUTHS

# The Elusive Bullet

## JOHN RHODE

*By coincidence it is only a stone's throw from the last of London's black spots on our tour to the home of one of the city's formidable group of private detectives who have dedicated their lives to solving crime. The first of them is Dr Lancelot Priestley who lives in Westbourne Terrace just beside Paddington Station. Priestley is a somewhat humourless and academic figure who was once a Professor of Mathematics at a leading English university which he left after a fierce disagreement with the authorities. Since then he has been able to use his private means to live quietly in Westbourne Terrace and devote himself to solving crime problems which involve the use of mathematics or, more particularly, pure logic. He has, though, poor eyesight, a dislike of the telephone, and generally relies on his cases being brought to him by Inspector Hanslet – which he prefers, if at all possible, to solve without leaving his room. The armchair detective personified! Priestley does, though, often require the help of his daughter, April, and Harold Merefield, who is both his son-in-law and secretary. The Professor made his debut in the appropriately titled* Paddington Mystery *(1925) in which he proved the innocence of Merefield and began their relationship, and thereafter built up a large readership for subsequent cases such as* The Murders in Praed Street *(1928),* Mystery at Olympia *(1935),* Death in Harley Street *(1946),* Domestic Agency *(1955),* The Vanishing Diary *(1961) and over 70 other novels and short stories. Dorothy L. Sayers was a particular admirer of the Dr Priestley stories and included several in her anthologies.*

*John Rhode (1884–1964) was almost as reclusive a figure as his creation: his real name was Cecil John Charles Street and he was a career army officer reaching the rank of major before his retirement. He was a prolific writer, too, and apart from the crime novels he also produced works of history, politics and biography as well as collaborating with Carter Dickson on* Drop To His Death *(1939) in which the murder took place in a lift. For many years Rhode was a member of the Detection Club in London. Although Dr Priestley was described by the American crime fiction historians, Jacques Barzun and Wendell Taylor, as 'one of the most impressive detectives in British mystery fiction' only one of the books has been filmed,* The Murders in Praed Street, *as* Twelve Good Men *by Warner Brothers in 1936 starring Henry Kendall. In 'The Elusive Bullet', written in 1936, John Rhode is able to draw on his army experiences of the use of weapons as Priestley sets about solving the case of a man who has been shot on a train . . .*

'BY THE WAY, professor, there's something in the evening papers that might interest you,' said Inspector Hanslet, handing over as he spoke the copy he had been holding in his hand. 'There you are, "Prominent City Merchant found dead". Read it, it sounds quite interesting.'

Dr Priestley adjusted his spectacles and began to read the paragraph. The professor and myself, Harold Merefield, who had been his secretary for a couple of years, had been sitting in the study of Dr Priestley's house in Westbourne Terrace, one fine June evening after dinner, when Inspector Hanslet had been announced. The inspector was an old friend of ours, who availed himself of the professor's hobby, which was the mathematical detection of crime, to discuss with him any investigations upon which he happened to be engaged. He had just finished giving the professor an outline of a recent burglary case, over which the police had confessed themselves puzzled, and had risen to go, when the item in the newspaper occurred to him.

'This does not appear to me to be particularly interesting,' said the professor. 'It merely states that on the arrival of the 3.20 train this afternoon at Tilbury station a porter, in examining the carriages, found the dead body of a man, since identified as a Mr Farquharson, lying in a corner of a first-class carriage. This Mr Farquharson appears to have met his death through a blow on the side of the head although no weapon capable of inflicting such a blow has so far been found. I can only suggest that if the facts are as reported, there are at least a dozen theories which could be made to fit in with them.'

'Such as?' inquired Hanslet tentatively.

The professor frowned. 'You know perfectly well, inspector, that I most strongly deprecate all conjecture,' he replied severely. 'Conjecture, unsupported by a thorough examination of facts, has been responsible for more than half the errors made by mankind throughout the ages. But, to demonstrate my meaning, I will outline a couple of theories which fit in with all the reported facts. Mr Farquharson may have been struck by an assailant who left the train before its arrival at Tilbury, and who disposed of the weapon in some way. On the other hand, he may have leant out of the window, and been struck by some object at the side of the line, or even by a passing train, if he was at the right-hand side of the carriage, looking in the direction in which the train was going. Of course, as I wish to emphasize, a knowledge of *all* the facts, not only those contained in this brief paragraph, would probably render both these theories untenable.'

Hanslet smiled. He knew well enough from experience the professor's passion for facts and his horror of conjecture.

'Well, I don't suppose the case will come my way,' he said as he turned towards the door. 'But if it does I'll let you know what transpires. I shouldn't wonder if we know the whole story in a day or two. It looks simple enough. Well good night, sir.'

The professor waited till the front door had closed behind him. 'I have always remarked that Hanslet's difficulties are comparatively easy of solution, but that what he calls simple problems completely baffle his powers of reasoning. I should not be surprised if we heard from him again very shortly.'

As usual, the professor was right. Hanslet's first visit had been on Saturday evening. On the following Tuesday, at about the same time, he called again, with a peculiarly triumphant expression on his face.

'You remember that Farquharson business, don't you, professor?' he began without preliminary. 'Well, it did come my way, after all. The Essex police called Scotland Yard in, and I was put on to it. I've solved the whole thing in under forty-eight hours. Not a bad piece of work eh? Mr Farquharson was murdered by—'

Dr Priestley held up his hand protestingly. 'My dear inspector, I am not the least concerned with the murderer of this Mr Farquharson. As I have repeatedly told you my interest in these matters is purely theoretical, and confined to the processes of deduction. You are beginning your story at the wrong end. If you wish me to listen to it, you must first tell me the full facts, then explain the course of your investigations, step by step.'

'Very well, sir,' replied Hanslet, somewhat crestfallen. 'The first fact I learnt was how Farquharson was killed. It appeared at first sight that he had been struck a terrific blow by some weapon like a pole-axe. There was a wound about two inches across on the right side of his head. But, at the post-mortem, this was found to have been caused by a bullet from an ordinary service rifle, which was found embedded in his brain.'

'Ah!' remarked the professor. 'A somewhat unusual instrument of murder, surely? What position did the body occupy in the carriage when it was found?'

'Oh, in the right-hand corner, facing the engine, I believe,' replied Hanslet impatiently. ' But that's of no importance, as you'll see. The next step, obviously, was to find out something about Farquharson, and why any one should want to murder him. The discovery of a motive is a very great help in an investigation like this. Farquharson lived with his daughter in a biggish house near a place called Stanford-le-Hope, on the line between Tilbury and Southend. On Saturday last he left his office, which is close to Fenchurch Street station, about one o'clock. He lunched at a restaurant near by, and caught the 2.15 at Fenchurch Street. As this was the train in which his dead body was found, I need hardly detail the inquiries by which I discovered these facts.'

The professor nodded. 'I am prepared to take your word for them,' he said.

'Very well, now let us come to the motive,' continued Hanslet. 'Farquharson was in business with his nephew, a rather wild young fellow named Robert Halliday. It seems that this young man's mother, Farquharson's sister, had a good deal of money in the business, and was very anxious that her son should carry it on after Farquharson's death. She died a couple of years ago, leaving rather a curious will, by which all her money was to remain in her brother's business, and was to revert to her son only at her brother's death.'

The professor rubbed his hands. 'Ah, the indispensable motive begins to appear!' he exclaimed with a sarcastic smile. 'I am sure that you feel that no further facts are necessary, inspector. It follows, of course, that young Halliday murdered his uncle to secure the money. You described him as a wild young man, I think? Really, the evidence is most damning!'

'It's all very well for you to laugh at me, professor,' replied Hanslet indignantly. 'I'll admit that you've given me a line on things that I couldn't find for myself often enough. But in this case there's no possible shadow of doubt about what happened. What would you say if I told you that Halliday actually travelled in the very train in which his uncle's body was found?'

'Speaking without a full knowledge of the facts, I should say that this rather tended to establish his innocence,' said the professor gravely.

Hanslet winked knowingly. ' Ah, but that's by no means all,' he replied. 'Halliday is a Territorial, and he left London on Saturday afternoon in uniform, and carrying a rifle. It seems that, although he's very keen, he's a shocking bad marksman, and a member of a sort of awkward squad which goes down occasionally to Purfleet ranges to practise. Purfleet is a station between London and Tilbury. Halliday got out there, fired a number of rounds, and returned to London in the evening.'

'Dear, dear, I'm sorry for that young man,' remarked the professor. 'First we have a motive, then an opportunity. Of course, he travelled in the same carriage as his uncle, levelled his musket at his head, inflicted a fearful wound, and decamped. Why, there's hardly a weak link in the whole chain.'

'It wasn't quite as simple as that,' replied Hanslet patiently. 'He certainly didn't travel in the same carriage as his uncle, since that very morning they had quarrelled violently. Farquharson, who was rather a strict old boy, didn't approve of his nephew's ways. Not that I can find out much against him, but he's a bit of a young blood, and his uncle didn't like it. He travelled third class, and swears that he didn't know his uncle was on the train.'

'Oh, you have interviewed him already, have you?' said the professor quietly.

'I have,' replied Hanslet. 'His story is that he nearly missed the train, jumped into it at the last moment, in fact. Somewhere after Barking he found himself alone, and that's all he told me. When I asked him what he was doing scrambling along the footboard outside the train between Dagenham and Rainham, he became very confused, and explained that on putting his head out of the window he had seen another member of the awkward squad a few carriages away, and made up his mind to join him. He gave me the man's name, and when I saw him he confirmed Halliday's story.'

'Really, inspector, your methods are masterly,' said the

professor. 'How did you know that he had been on the footboard?'

'A man working on the line had seen a soldier in uniform, with a rifle slung over his back, in this position,' replied Hanslet triumphantly.

'And you immediately concluded that this man must be Halliday,' commented the professor. 'Well, guesses must hit the truth sometimes, I suppose. What exactly is your theory of the crime?'

'It seems plain enough,' replied Hanslet. 'Halliday had watched his uncle enter the train, then jumped into a carriage close to his. At a predetermined spot he clambered along with his loaded rifle, shot him through the window, then, to avert suspicion, joined his friend, whom he had also seen enter the train, a little further on. It's as plain as a pikestaff to me.'

'So it appears,' remarked the professor dryly. 'What steps do you propose to take in the matter?'

'I propose to arrest Halliday at the termination of the inquest,' replied Hanslet complacently.

The professor made no reply to this for several seconds. 'I think it would be to everybody's advantage if you consulted me again before doing so,' he said at last.

A cloud passed for an instant over Hanslet's face. 'I will, if you think it would do any good,' he replied. 'But you must see for yourself that I have enough evidence to secure a conviction from any jury.'

'That is just what disquiets me,' returned the professor quickly. 'You cannot expect the average juryman to have an intelligence superior to yours, you know. I have your promise?'

'Certainly, if you wish it,' replied Hanslet rather huffily. He changed the subject abruptly, and a few minutes later he rose and left the house.

In the course of our normal routine I forgot the death of Mr Farquharson entirely. It was not until the following afternoon, when Mary the parlourmaid entered the study with the announcement that a Miss Farquharson had called and begged that she might see the professor immediately, that the matter recurred to me.

'Miss Farquharson!' I exclaimed. 'Why, that must be the daughter of the fellow who was murdered the other day. Hanslet said he had a daughter, you remember.'

'The balance of probability would appear to favour that theory,' replied the professor acidly. 'Yes, I'll see her. Show Miss Farquharson in, please, Mary.'

Miss Farquharson came in, and the professor greeted her with his usual courtesy. 'To what do I owe the pleasure of this visit?' he inquired.

Miss Farquharson hesitated a moment or two before she replied. She was tall and fair, dressed in deep mourning with an elusive prettiness which I, at least, found most attractive. And even before she spoke, I guessed something of the truth from the flush which suffused her face at the professor's question.

'I'm afraid you may think this an unpardonable intrusion,' she said at last. ' The truth is that Bob – Mr Halliday – who is my cousin, has heard of you and begged me to come and see you.'

The professor frowned. He hated his name becoming known in connection with any of the investigations which he undertook, but in spite of all his efforts, many people had come to know of his hobby. Miss Farquharson took his frown for a sign of disapproval, and continued with an irresistible tone of pleading in her voice.

'It was only as a last hope I came to you,' she said. 'It's all so awful that I feel desperate. I expect you know that my father was found dead last Saturday in a train at Tilbury, while he was on his way home?'

The professor nodded. 'I am aware of some of the facts,' he replied non-committally. 'I need not trouble you to repeat them. But in what way can I be of assistance to you?'

'It's too terrible!' she exclaimed with a sob. 'The police suspect Bob of having murdered him. They haven't said so, but they have been asking him all sorts of dreadful questions. Bob thought perhaps you might be able to do something—'

Her voice tailed away hopelessly under the professor's unwinking gaze.

'My dear young lady, I am not a magician,' he replied. 'I may as well tell you that I have seen Inspector Hanslet who has what he considers a convincing case against your cousin.'

'But you don't believe it, do you, Doctor Priestley?' interrupted Miss Farquharson eagerly.

'I can only accept the inspector's statements as he gave them to me,' replied the professor. 'I know nothing of the case beyond what he has told me. Perhaps you would allow me to ask you a few questions?'

'Of course!' she exclaimed. 'I'll tell you everything I can.'

The professor inclined his head with a gesture of thanks. 'Was your father in the habit of travelling by the 2.15 train from Fenchurch Street on Saturday afternoons?'

'No,' replied Miss Farquharson with decision. 'Only when he was kept later than usual at the office. His usual custom was to come home to a late lunch.'

'I see. Now, can you tell me the reason for the quarrel between him and your cousin?'

This time Miss Farquharson's reply was not so prompt. She lowered her head so that we could not see her face, and kept silence for a moment. Then, as though she had made up her mind, she spoke suddenly.

'I see no harm in telling you. As a matter of fact, Bob and I have been in love with one another for a long time, and Bob decided to tell my father on Saturday morning. Father was rather old-fashioned, and he didn't altogether approve of Bob. Not that there was any harm in anything he did, but father couldn't understand that a young man liked to amuse himself. There was quite a scene when Bob told him, and father refused to hear anything about it until Bob had reformed, as he put it. But I know that Bob didn't kill him,' she concluded entreatingly. 'It's impossible for anybody who knew him to believe he could. You don't believe it, do you?'

'No, I do not believe it,' replied the professor slowly. 'If it is any consolation to you and Mr Halliday, I may tell you in confidence that I never have believed it. When is the inquest to be?'

A look of deep thankfulness overspread her features. 'I am more grateful to you than I can say, Doctor Priestley,' she said earnestly. ' The inquest? On Saturday morning. Will you be there?'

The professor shook his head. 'No, I shall not be there,' he replied. 'You see, it is not my business. But I shall take steps before then to make certain inquiries. I do not wish to raise your hopes unduly, but it is possible that I may be able to divert suspicion from Mr Halliday. More than that I cannot say.'

Tears of thankfulness came to her eyes. 'I can't tell you what this means to Bob and me,' she said. 'He has been terribly distressed. He quite understands that things look very black against him, and he cannot suggest who could have wanted to kill my father. Father hadn't an enemy in the world, poor dear.'

'You are sure of that?' remarked the professor.

'Quite,' she replied positively. 'I knew every detail of his life, he never hid the smallest thing from me.'

And after a further short and unimportant conversation she took her leave of us.

The professor sat silent for some minutes after her departure. 'Poor girl!' he said at last. 'To lose her father so tragically, and then to see the man she loves accused of his murder! We must see what we can do to help her, Harold. Get me the one-inch map of the country between London and Tilbury, and a time-table of the Southend trains.'

I hastened to obey him, and for an hour or more he pored over the map, working upon it with a rule and a protractor. At the end of this period he looked up and spoke abruptly.

'This is remarkably interesting, more so than I imagined at first it would be. Run out and buy me the sheets of the six-inch survey which cover Rainham and Purfleet. I think we shall need them.'

I bought the maps he required and returned with them. For the rest of the day he busied himself with these, and it was not until late in the evening that he spoke to me again.

'Really, my boy, this problem is beginning to interest me,' he said. 'There are many points about it which are distinctly baffling. We must examine the country on the spot. There is a train to Purfleet, I see, at 10.30 tomorrow morning.'

'Have you formed any theory, sir?' I inquired eagerly. The vision of Miss Farquharson, and her conviction of her cousin's innocence, had impressed me in her favour.

The professor scowled at me. 'How often am I to tell you that facts are all that matter?' he replied. 'Our journey tomorrow will be for the purpose of ascertaining facts. Until we know these, it would be waste of time to indulge in conjecture.'

He did not mention the subject again until the next morning, when we were seated in the train to Purfleet. He had chosen an empty first-class carriage, and himself took the right-hand corner facing the engine. He said nothing until the train was travelling at a good speed, and then he addressed me suddenly.

'You are a good shot with a rifle, are you not?' he inquired.

'I used to be pretty fair,' I replied in astonishment. 'But I don't think I've had a rifle in my hand since the war.'

'Well, take my stick, and hold it as you would a rifle. Now go to the far end of the carriage and lean against the door. That's right. Point your stick at my right eye, as though you were going to shoot at it. Stand like that a minute. Thank you, that will do.'

He turned away from me, took a pair of field-glasses from a case he was carrying, and began to survey the country through the window on his side. This he continued to do until the train drew up at Purfleet and we dismounted on to the platform.

'Ah, a lovely day!' he exclaimed. 'Not too warm for a little walking. We will make our first call at Purfleet ranges. This was where young Halliday came to do his shooting, you remember.'

We made our way to the ranges, and were lucky enough to

find the warden at home. Dr Priestley had, when he chose, a most ingratiating way with him, and he and the warden were very shortly engaged in an animated conversation.

'By the way,' inquired the professor earnestly, 'was there any firing going on here between half-past two and three on Saturday last?'

The range-warden scratched his head with a thoughtful expression on his face. 'Let me see, now, last Saturday afternoon? We had a squad of Territorials here on Saturday afternoon, but they didn't arrive till after three. Lord, they was queer hands with a rifle, some of them. Much as they could do to hit the target at all at three hundred. They won't never make marksmen, however hard they try.'

'Isn't it rather dangerous to allow such wild shots to fire at all?' suggested the professor.

'God bless your heart, sir, it's safe enough,' replied the range-warden. 'There's never been an accident the whole time I've been here. They can't very well miss the butts, and even if they did, there's nobody allowed on the marshes when firing's going on.'

'That is comforting, certainly,' said the professor. 'Apart from this squad, you had nobody else?'

The range-warden shook his head. 'No, sir, they was the only people on the range that day.'

'I suppose it is part of your duty to issue ammunition?' inquired the professor.

'As a rule, sir. But, as it happens, this particular squad always brings their own with them.'

The professor continued his conversation for a little longer, then prepared to depart.

'I'm sure I'm very much obliged to you,' he said as he shook hands. 'By the way, I believe there are other ranges about here somewhere?'

'That's right, sir,' replied the range-warden. 'Over yonder, beyond the butts. Rainham ranges, they're called.'

'Is there any objection to my walking across the marshes to them?'

'Not a bit, sir. There's no firing today. Just keep straight on past the butts, and you'll come to them.'

The professor and I started on our tramp, the professor pausing every hundred yards or so to look about him through his field-glasses and to verify his position on the map. We reached the Rainham ranges at last, discovered the warden, who fell under the influence of the professor's charm as readily as his colleague at Purfleet had done, and opened the conversation with him in much the same style.

'On Saturday afternoon last, between half-past two and three?' replied the warden to the professor's inquiry. 'Well, sir, not what you might call any shooting. There was a party from Woolwich, with a new sort of light machine-gun, something like a Lewis. But they wasn't shooting, only testing.'

'What is the difference?' asked the professor.

'Well, sir, by testing I mean they had the thing held in a clamp, so that it couldn't move. The idea is to keep it pointing in exactly the same direction, instead of wobbling about as it might if a man was holding it. They use a special target, and measure up the distance between the various bullet-holes on it when they've finished.'

'I see,' replied the professor. 'I wonder if you would mind showing me where they were firing from?'

'Certainly, sir, it's close handy.' The range-warden led us to a firing-point near by, and pointed out the spot on which the stand had been erected.

'That's the place, sir. They were firing at number 10 target over yonder. A thousand yards it is, and wonderful accurate the new gun seemed. Shot the target to pieces they did.'

The professor made no reply, but took out his map and drew a line upon it from the firing-point to the butts. The line, when extended, led over a tract of desolate marshes until it met the river.

'There is very little danger on these ranges, it appears,' remarked the professor, with a note of annoyance in his voice. 'If a shot missed the butts altogether, it could only fall into the river, far away from any frequented spot.'

'That's what they were laid out for,' replied the range-warden. 'You see, on the other side there's a house or two, to say nothing of the road and the railway. It wouldn't do to have any stray rounds falling among them.'

'It certainly would not,' replied the professor absently. 'I see by the map that Rainham station is not far beyond the end of the ranges. Is there any objection to my walking to it past the butts?'

'None at all, sir, it's the best way to get there when there's no firing on. Thank you, sir, it's been no trouble at all.'

We started to walk down the ranges, a puzzled frown on the professor's face. Every few yards he stopped and examined the country through his glasses, or pulled out the map and stared at it with an absorbed expression. We had reached the butts before he said a word, and then it was not until we had climbed to the top of them that he spoke.

'Very puzzling, very!' he muttered. 'There must, of course, be some explanation. A mathematical deduction from facts can never be false. But I wish I could discover the explanation.'

He was looking through his field-glasses as he spoke, and suddenly his attention became riveted upon an object in front of him. Without waiting for me he hurried down the steep sides of the butts, and almost ran towards a flagstaff standing a couple of hundred yards on the far side of them. When he arrived at the base of it, he drew a couple of lines on the map, walked half round the flagstaff and gazed intently through his glasses. By the time I had caught up with him he had put the glasses back in their case, and was smiling benevolently.

'We can return to town by the next train, my boy,' he said cheerfully. 'I have ascertained everything I wished to know.'

He refused to say a word until our train was running into Fenchurch Street station. Then suddenly he turned to me.

'I am going to the War Office,' he said curtly. 'Will you go to Scotland Yard, see Inspector Hanslet, and ask him to come to Westbourne Terrace as soon as he can?'

I found Hanslet, after some little trouble, and gave him the professor's message.

'Something to do with the Farquharson business, I suppose?' he replied. ' Well, I'll come if the professor wants to see me. But I've got it all fixed up without his help.'

He turned up, true to his promise, and the professor greeted him with a pleasant smile.

'Good evening, inspector, I'm glad you were able to come. Will you be particularly busy tomorrow morning?'

'I don't think so, professor,' replied Hanslet in a puzzled voice. 'Do you want me to do anything?'

'Well, if you can spare the time, I should like to introduce you to the murderer of Mr Farquharson,' said the professor casually.

Hanslet lay back in his chair and laughed. 'Thanks very much, professor, but I've met him already,' he replied. 'It would be a waste of your time, I'm afraid.'

'Never mind,' said the professor, with a tolerant smile. ' I assure you that it will be worth your while to spend the morning with me. Will you meet me by the bookstall at Charing Cross at half-past ten?'

Hanslet reflected for a moment. The professor had never yet led him on a wild-goose chase, and it might be worth while to humour him.

'All right,' he replied reluctantly. 'I'll come. But I warn you it's no good.'

The professor smiled, but said nothing. Hanslet took his leave of us, and the professor appeared to put all thought of the Farquharson case out of his head.

We met again at Charing Cross the next day. The professor had taken tickets to Woolwich, and we got out of the train there and walked to the gates of the arsenal. The professor took an official letter out of his pocket, which he gave to the porter. In a few minutes we were led to an office, where a young officer rose to greet us.

'Good morning, Doctor Priestley,' he said. 'Colonel Conyngham rang me up to say that you were coming. You want to see the stand we use for testing the new automatic rifle? It happens to be in the yard below, being repaired.'

'Being repaired?' repeated the professor quickly. 'May I ask what is the matter with it?'

'Oh, nothing serious. We used it at Rainham the other day, and the clamp broke just as we were finishing a series. We had fired ninety-nine rounds out of a hundred, when the muzzle of the gun slipped up. I don't know what happened to the round. I suppose it went into the river somewhere. Beastly nuisance, we shall have to go down and start all over again.'

'Ah!' exclaimed the professor, in a satisfied tone. 'That explains it. But I wouldn't use number 10 target again, if I were you. Can we see this stand?'

'Certainly,' replied the officer. 'Come along.'

He led us into the yard, where a sort of tripod with a clamp at the head of it was standing. The professor looked at it earnestly for some moments, then turned to Hanslet.

'There you see the murderer of Mr Farquharson,' he said quietly.

Of course Hanslet, the officer, and myself bombarded him with questions, which he refused to answer until we had returned to London and were seated in his study. Then, fixing his eyes upon the ceiling and putting the tips of his fingers together, he began.

'It was, to any intelligent man, perfectly obvious that there are half a dozen reasons why young Halliday could not have shot his uncle. In the first place, he must have fired at very close range, from one side or other of the carriage, and a rifle bullet fired at such a range, although it very often makes a very extensive wound of entry, does not stay in a man's brain. It travels right through his head, with very slightly diminished velocity. Next, if Halliday fired at his uncle at all, it must have been from the left-hand side of the carriage. Had he fired from the right-hand side, the muzzle of the weapon would have been almost touching his victim, and there would have been signs of burning or blackening round the wound. Do you admit this, inspector?'

'Of course,' replied Hanslet. 'My theory always has been that he fired from the left-hand side.'

'Very well,' said the professor quickly. 'Now Halliday is notoriously a very bad shot, hence his journey to Purfleet. Harold, on the contrary, is a good shot. Yet, during our expedition of yesterday, I asked him to aim at my right eye with a stick while the train was in motion. I found that never for an instant could he point the stick at it. I find it impossible to believe that a bad shot, firing from the footboard and therefore compelled to use one hand at least to retain his hold, could shoot a man on the far side of the carriage exactly on the temple.'

The professor paused, and Hanslet looked at him doubtfully.

'It all sounds very plausible, professor, but until you can produce a better explanation I shall continue to believe that my own is the correct one.'

'Exactly. It was to verify a theory which I had formed that I carried out my investigations. It was perfectly obvious to me, from your description of the wound, that it had been inflicted by a bullet very near the end of its flight, and therefore possessing only enough velocity to penetrate the skull without passing through it. This meant that it had been fired from a considerable distance away. Upon consulting the map, I discovered that there were two rifle ranges near the railway between London and Tilbury. I could not help feeling that the source of the bullet was probably one of these ranges. It was, at all events, a possibility worth investigating.

'But at the outset I was faced with what seemed an insuperable objection. I deduced from the map, a deduction subsequently verified by examination of the ground, that a round fired at any of the targets on either range would take a direction away from the railway. I also discovered that the only rounds fired while the train in which Mr Farquharson's body was found was passing the ranges were by an experimental party from the arsenal. This party employed a special device which eliminated any inaccuracy due to the human element. At this point it occurred to me that my theory was incapable of proof, although I still adhered to my view that it was correct.'

The professor paused and Hanslet ventured to remark:

'I still do not see how you can prove that the breakage of the clamp could have been responsible,' he said. 'The direction of the bullet remained the same, and only its elevation was affected. By your own showing, the last shot fired from the machine must have landed in the marshes or the river.'

'I knew very well that notwithstanding the apparent impossibility, this must have been the bullet which killed Mr Farquharson,' replied the professor equably. 'I climbed the butts behind the target at which the arsenal party had been firing, and while there I made an interesting discovery which solved the difficulty at once. Directly in line with number 10 target and some distance behind it was a flagstaff. Further, upon examination of this flagstaff I discovered that it was made of steel.

'Now the map had told me that there was only a short stretch of line upon which a train could he struck by a bullet deflected by this flagstaff. If this had indeed been the case, I knew exactly where to look for traces, and at my first inspection I found them. High up on the staff is a scar where the paint has recently been removed. To my mind the cause of Mr Farquharson's death is adequately explained.'

Hanslet whistled softly. ' By Jove, there's something in it!' he exclaimed. 'Your theory, I take it, is that Farquharson was struck by a bullet deflected by the flagstaff?'

'Of course,' replied the professor. 'He was sitting on the right-hand side of the carriage, facing the engine. He was struck on the right side of the head, which supports the theory of a bullet coming through the open window. A bullet deflected in this way usually turns over and over for the rest of its flight, which accounts for the size of the wound. Have you any objection to offer?'

'Not at the moment,' said Hanslet cautiously. 'I shall have to verify all these facts, of course. For one thing, I must take the bullet to the arsenal and see if it is one of the same type as the experimental party were using.'

'Verify everything you can, certainly,' replied the professor.' But remember that facts, not conjecture, are what should guide you.'

Hanslet nodded. 'I'll remember, professor,' he said. And with that he left us.

Two days later Mary announced Miss Farquharson and Mr Halliday. They entered the room, and Halliday walked straight up to the professor and grasped his hand.

'You have rendered me the greatest service one man can render to another, sir!' he exclaimed. ' Inspector Hanslet tells me that all suspicion that I murdered my uncle has been cleared away, and that this is due entirely to your efforts.'

Before the professor could reply, Miss Farquharson ran up to him and kissed him impulsively. 'Doctor Priestley, you're a darling!' she exclaimed.

The professor beamed at her through his spectacles. 'Really, my dear, you make me feel quite sorry that you are going to marry this young man,' he said.

# The Adventure of the Worst
# Man in London

## SIR ARTHUR CONAN DOYLE

*From Westbourne Grove, the walk to the address of the most
famous detective of all is almost exactly a mile along Harrow
Road and Marylebone Road to a turning within sight of the
Planetarium and Madame Tussaud's Exhibition. Here, at 221B
Baker Street, Sherlock Holmes – 'consulting detective' according
to his visiting card -- lived and received those in trouble who
came to enlist his extraordinary powers of observation and
deduction. Almost invariably his close friend and companion,
Doctor Watson, would be in attendance as well as their long-suf-
fering housekeeper, Mrs Hudson. Although the site of 221B is
generally thought to be that now occupied by the Abbey National
Building Society, according to Edgar Wallace who once walked
the length of Baker Street with Holmes' creator, Sir Arthur
Conan Doyle (1859–1930), Doyle indicated he envisaged it on
the opposite side of the road near the corner formed with George
Street. (Interestingly, Granada Television also opted for this position when building their impressive reconstruction of Baker
Street for the series of Sherlock Holmes adventures starring the
late Jeremy Brett which ran for ten years.)*

*There is, of course, no doubt about Holmes himself: his image
was set by Sidney Paget in the* Strand *magazine, and all his
attributes and foibles – from a predilection for drugs to a retirement plan rearing bees – have not only been carefully recorded
by Dr Watson in the novels and short stories, but studied and*

*argued over endlessly by Sherlockians all over the world. The sleuth of Baker Street is without doubt one of the world's immortals and so real is he to some people that the Abbey National employs a secretary to answer the mail which arrives each day addressed to 'Sherlock Holmes Esq' requesting his assistance in every kind of problem from the loss of a pet to the whereabouts of buried treasure! No mean accolade to a detective who never lived.*

*This story about Holmes is not, as some keen-eyed Sherlockians might think, a lost adventure because of the unfamiliar title, but the account of the detective's confrontation with another of his great adversaries, Charles Augustus Milverton. The reason for this title change is that it is the original one Conan Doyle wrote on his manuscript in 1904 and then crossed out to insert the more familiar 'Adventure of Charles Augustus Milverton'. I have this on the authority of the Holmesian expert Edgar W. Smith who owns the original holograph manuscript: 'On page one of this MS, Dr Doyle first wrote "The Adventure of the Worst Man in London" then (how much later I do not know) he crossed this out and substituted the title eventually used for publication. I think this was definitely a change for the worse!' Most people would agree, and whether Doyle made the change of his own volition or on the instructions of the Editor of the* Strand, *I have no hesitation in restoring the original here. Milverton, whom Holmes described unequivocally as the 'worst man in London', lived in some style in Hampstead from where he exercised his power as the king of blackmailers. He had extorted thousands of pounds from unfortunate victims without the law being able to lay a finger on him – that is until Holmes was brought into the case. The story has been filmed several times, but undoubtedly the best version was the two-hour adaptation by Granada in 1992 with Robert Hardy as an evil, malevolent Milverton. It was also unique in that Jeremy Brett's Holmes was called upon to kiss a servant girl as part of his ploy to wheedle information from her – a scene which made newspaper stories worldwide! The story itself is all the more intriguing because Doyle admitted he based Milverton on a notorious*

*Victorian blackmailer named Charles Augustus Howell who had earlier been found murdered in Chelsea – a fact which probably spared the author receiving the same treatment Howell's other victims had suffered!*

IT IS YEARS since the incidents of which I speak took place, and yet it is with diffidence that I allude to them. For a long time, even with the utmost discretion and reticence, it would have been impossible to make the facts public; but now the principal person concerned is beyond the reach of human law, and with due suppression the story may be told in such fashion as to injure no one. It records an absolutely unique experience in the career both of Mr Sherlock Holmes and of myself. The reader will excuse me if I conceal the date or any other fact by which he might trace the actual occurrence.

We had been out for one of our evening rambles, Holmes and I, and had returned about six o'clock on a cold, frosty winter's evening. As Holmes turned up the lamp the light fell upon a card on the table. He glanced at it, and then, with an ejaculation of disgust, threw it on the floor. I picked it up and read:

> CHARLES AUGUSTUS MILVERTON,
> APPLEDORE TOWERS,
> HAMPSTEAD.
> *Agent.*

'Who is he?' I asked.

'The worst man in London,' Holmes answered, as he sat down and stretched his legs before the fire. 'Is anything on the back of the card?'

I turned it over.

'Will call at 6.30 – C.A.M.,' I read.

'Hum! He's about due. Do you feel a creeping, shrinking sensation, Watson, when you stand before the serpents in the Zoo and see the slithery, gliding, venomous creatures, with their deadly eyes and wicked, flattened faces? Well, that's how

Milverton impresses me. I've had to do with fifty murderers in my career, but the worst of them never gave me the repulsion which I have for this fellow. And yet I can't get out of doing business with him – indeed, he is here at my invitation.'

'But who is he?'

'I'll tell you, Watson. He is the king of all the blackmailers. Heaven help the man, and still more the woman, whose secret and reputation come into the power of Milverton. With a smiling face and a heart of marble he will squeeze and squeeze until he has drained them dry. The fellow is a genius in his way, and would have made his mark in some more savoury trade. His method is as follows: He allows it to be known that he is prepared to pay very high sums for letters which compromise people of wealth or position. He receives these wares not only from treacherous valets or maids, but frequently from genteel ruffians who have gained the confidence and affection of trusting women. He deals with no niggard hand. I happen to know that he paid seven hundred pounds to a footman for a note two lines in length, and that the ruin of a noble family was the result. Everything which is in the market goes to Milverton, and there are hundreds in this great city who turn white at his name. No one knows where his grip may fall, for he is far too rich and far too cunning to work from hand to mouth. He will hold a card back for years in order to play it at the moment when the stake is best worth winning. I have said that he is the worst man in London, and I would ask you how could one compare the ruffian who in hot blood bludgeons his mate with this man, who methodically and at his leisure tortures the soul and wrings the nerves in order to add to his already swollen money-bags?'

I had seldom heard my friend speak with such intensity of feeling.

'But surely,' said I, 'the fellow must be within the grasp of the law?'

'Technically, no doubt, but practically not. What would it profit a woman, for example, to get him a few months' imprisonment if her own ruin must immediately follow? His victims dare not hit back. If ever he blackmailed an innocent person, then, indeed, we should have him; but he is as cunning as the Evil One. No, no; we must find other ways to fight him.'

'And why is he here?'

'Because an illustrious client has placed her piteous case in my hands. It is the Lady Eva Brackwell, the most beautiful *débutante* of last season. She is to be married in a fortnight to the Earl of Dovercourt. This fiend has several imprudent letters – imprudent, Watson, nothing worse – which were written to an impecunious young squire in the country. They would suffice to break off the match. Milverton will send the letters to the earl unless a large sum of money is paid him. I have been commissioned to meet him, and – to make the best terms I can.'

At that instant there was a clatter and a rattle in the street below. Looking down I saw a stately carriage and pair, the brilliant lamps gleaming on the glossy haunches of the noble chestnuts. A footman opened the door, and a small, stout man in a shaggy astrachan overcoat descended. A minute later he was in the room.

Charles Augustus Milverton was a man of fifty, with a large, intellectual head, a round, plump, hairless face, a perpetual frozen smile, and two keen grey eyes, which gleamed brightly from behind broad, golden-rimmed glasses. There was something of Mr Pickwick's benevolence in his appearance, marred only by the insincerity of the fixed smile and by the hard glitter of those restless and penetrating eyes. His voice was as smooth and suave as his countenance, as he advanced with a plump little hand extended, murmuring his regret for having missed us at his first visit.

Holmes disregarded the outstretched hand and looked at him with a face of granite. Milverton's smile broadened; he shrugged his shoulders, removed his overcoat, folded it with great deliberation over the back of a chair, and then took a seat.

'This gentleman,' said he, with a wave in my direction. 'Is it discreet? Is it right?'

'Dr Watson is my friend and partner.'

'Very good, Mr Holmes. It is only in your client's interests that I protested. The matter is so very delicate—'

'Dr Watson has already heard of it.'

'Then we can proceed to business. You say that you are acting for Lady Eva. Has she empowered you to accept my terms?'

'What are your terms?'

'Seven thousand pounds.'

'And the alternative?'

'My dear sir, it is painful to me to discuss it; but if the money is not paid on the fourteenth there certainly will be no marriage on the eighteenth.' His insufferable smile was more complacent than ever. Holmes thought for a little.

'You appear to me,' he said at last, 'to be taking matters too much for granted. I am, of course, familiar with the contents of these letters. My client will certainly do what I may advise. I shall counsel her to tell her future husband the whole story and to trust to his generosity.'

Milverton chuckled.

'You evidently do not know the earl,' said he.

From the baffled look upon Holmes' face I could clearly see that he did.

'What harm is there in the letters?' he asked.

'They are sprightly – very sprightly,' Milverton answered. 'The lady was a charming correspondent. But I can assure you that the Earl of Dovercourt would fail to appreciate them. However, since you think otherwise, we will let it rest at that. It is purely a matter of business. If you think that it is in the best interests of your client that these letters should be placed in the hands of the earl, then you would indeed be foolish to pay so large a sum of money to regain them.' He rose and seized his astrachan coat.

Holmes was grey with anger and mortification.

'Wait a little,' he said. 'You go too fast. We would certainly make every effort to avoid scandal in so delicate a matter.'

Milverton relapsed into his chair.

'I was sure that you would see it in that light,' he purred.

'At the same time,' Holmes continued, 'Lady Eva is not a wealthy woman. I assure you that two thousand pounds would be a drain upon her resources, and that the sum you name is utterly beyond her power. I beg, therefore, that you will moderate your demands, and that you will return the letters at the price I indicate, which is, I assure you, the highest that you can get.'

Milverton's smile broadened and his eyes twinkled humorously.

'I am aware that what you say is true about the lady's resources,' said he. 'At the same time, you must admit that the occasion of a lady's marriage is a very suitable time for her friends and relatives to make some little effort upon her behalf. They may hesitate as to an acceptable wedding present. Let me assure them that this little bundle of letters would give more joy than all the candelabra and butter-dishes in London.'

'It is impossible,' said Holmes.

'Dear me, dear me, how unfortunate!' cried Milverton, taking out a bulky pocket-book. 'I cannot help thinking that ladies are ill-advised in not making an effort. Look at this!' He held up a little note with a coat-of- arms upon the envelope. ' That belongs to – well, perhaps it is hardly fair to tell the name until tomorrow morning. But at that time it will be in the hands of the lady's husband. And all because she will not find a beggarly sum which she could get in an hour by turning her diamonds into paste. It *is* such a pity. Now, you remember the sudden end of the engagement between the Honourable Miss Miles and Colonel Dorking? Only two days before the wedding there was a paragraph in the *Morning Post* to say that it was all off. And why? It is almost incredible, but the absurd sum of twelve hundred pounds would have settled the whole question. Is it not pitiful? And there I find you, a man of sense, boggling about terms when your client's future and honour are at stake. You surprise me, Mr Holmes.'

'What I say is true,' Holmes answered. 'The money cannot be found. Surely it is better for you to take the substantial sum which I offer than to ruin this woman's career, which can profit you in no way?'

'There you make a mistake, Mr Holmes. An exposure would profit me indirectly to a considerable extent. I have eight or ten similar cases maturing. If it was circulated among them that I had made a severe example of the Lady Eva I should find all of them much more open to reason. You see my point?'

Holmes sprang from his chair.

'Get behind him, Watson. Don't let him out! Now, sir, let us see the contents of that notebook.'

Milverton had glided as quick as a rat to the side of the room, and stood with his back against the wall.

'Mr Holmes, Mr Holmes!' he said, turning the front of his coat and exhibiting the butt of a large revolver, which projected from the inside pocket. 'I have been expecting you to do something original. This has been done so often, and what good has ever come from it? I assure you that I am armed to the teeth, and I am perfectly prepared to use my weapon, knowing that the law will support me. Besides, your supposition that I would bring the letters here in a notebook is entirely mistaken. I would do nothing so foolish. And now, gentlemen, I have one or two little interviews this evening, and it is a long drive to Hampstead.' He stepped forward, took up his coat, laid his hand on his revolver, and turned to the door. I picked up a chair, but Holmes shook his head, and I laid it down again. With a bow, a smile, and a twinkle Milverton was out of the room, and a few moments after we heard the slam of the carriage door and the rattle of the wheels as he drove away. Holmes sat motionless by the fire, his hands buried deep in his trouser pockets, his chin sunk upon his breast, his eyes fixed upon the glowing embers. For half an hour he was silent and still. Then, with the gesture of a man who has taken his decision, he sprang to his feet and passed into his bedroom. A little later a rakish young workman with a goatee beard and a swagger lit his clay pipe at the lamp before descending into the street. 'I'll be back some time, Watson,' said he, and vanished into the night. I understood that he had opened his campaign against Charles Augustus Milverton; but I little dreamed the strange shape which that campaign was destined to take.

For some days Holmes came and went at all hours in this attire, but beyond a remark that his time was spent at Hampstead, and that it was not wasted, I knew nothing of what he was doing. At last, however, on a wild, tempestuous evening, when the wind screamed and rattled against the windows, he returned from his last expedition, and, having removed his disguise, he sat before the fire and laughed heartily in his silent, inward fashion.

'You would not call me a marrying man, Watson?'

'No, indeed!'

'You will be interested to hear that I am engaged.'

'My dear fellow! I congrat—'

'To Milverton's housemaid.'

'Good heavens, Holmes!'

'I wanted information, Watson.'

'Surely you have gone too far?'

'It was a most necessary step. I am a plumber with a rising business, Escott by name. I have walked out with her each evening, and I have talked with her. Good heavens, those talks! However, I have got all I wanted. I know Milverton's house as I know the palm of my hand.'

'But the girl, Holmes?'

He shrugged his shoulders.

'You can't help it, my dear Watson. You must play your cards as best you can when such a stake is on the table. However, I rejoice to say that I have a hated rival who will certainly cut me out the instant that my back is turned. What a splendid night it is!'

'You like this weather?'

'It suits my purpose. Watson, I mean to burgle Milverton's house tonight.'

I had a catching of the breath, and my skin went cold at the words, which were slowly uttered in a tone of concentrated resolution. As a flash of lightning in the night shows up in an instant every detail of a wide landscape, so at one glance I seemed to see every possible result of such an action – the detection, the capture, the honoured career ending in irreparable failure and disgrace, my friend himself lying at the mercy of the odious Milverton.

'For Heaven's sake, Holmes, think what you are doing!' I cried.

'My dear fellow, I have given it every consideration. I am never precipitate in my actions, nor would I adopt so energetic and indeed so dangerous a course if any other were possible. Let us look at the matter clearly and fairly. I suppose that you will admit that the action is morally justifiable, though technically criminal. To burgle his house is no more than to forcibly take his pocket-book – an action in which you were prepared to aid me.'

I turned it over in my mind.

'Yes,' I said, 'it is morally justifiable so long as our object is to take no articles save those which are used for an illegal purpose.'

'Exactly. Since it is morally justifiable, I have only to consider the question of personal risk. Surely a gentleman should not lay much stress upon this when a lady is in most desperate need of his help?'

'You will be in such a false position.'

'Well, that is part of the risk. There is no other possible way of regaining these letters. The unfortunate lady has not the money, and there are none of her people in whom she could confide. Tomorrow is the last day of grace, and unless we can get the letters tonight this villain will be as good as his word, and will bring about her ruin. I must, therefore, abandon my client to her fate, or I must play this last card. Between ourselves, Watson, it's a sporting duel between this fellow Milverton and me. He had, as you saw, the best of the first exchanges; but my self-respect and my reputation are concerned to fight it to a finish.'

'Well, I don't like it; but I suppose it must be,' said I. 'When do we start?'

'You are not coming.'

'Then you are not going,' said I. 'I give you my word of honour – and I never broke it in my life – that I will take a cab straight to the police-station and give you away unless you let me share this adventure with you.'

'You can't help me.'

'How do you know that? You can't tell what may happen. Anyway, my resolution is taken. Other people besides you have self-respect and even reputations.'

Holmes had looked annoyed, but his brow cleared, and he clapped me on the shoulder.

'Well, well, my dear fellow, be it so. We have shared the same room for some years, and it would be amusing if we ended by sharing the same cell. You know, Watson, I don't mind confessing to you that I have always had an idea that I would have made a highly efficient criminal. This is the chance of my lifetime in that direction. See here!' He took a neat little leather case out of a drawer, and opening it he exhibited a number of shining instruments. 'This is a first-class, up-to-date burgling kit, with nickel-plated jemmy, diamond-tipped glass cutter, adaptable keys, and every modern improvement which the march of civilization demands. Here, too, is my dark lantern. Everything is in order. Have you a pair of silent shoes?'

'I have rubber-soled tennis shoes.'

'Excellent. And a mask?'

'I can make a couple out of black silk.'

'I can see that you have a strong natural turn for this sort of thing. Very good; do you make the masks. We shall have some cold supper before we start. It is now nine-thirty. At eleven we shall drive as far as Church Row. It is a quarter of an hour's walk from there to Appledore Towers. We shall be at work before midnight. Milverton is a heavy sleeper, and retires punctually at ten-thirty. With any luck we should be back here by two, with the Lady Eva's letters in my pocket.'

Holmes and I put on our dress-clothes, so that we might appear to be two theatre-goers homeward bound. In Oxford Street we picked up a hansom and drove to an address in Hampstead. Here we paid off our cab, and with our great-coats buttoned up – for it was bitterly cold, and the wind seemed to blow through us – we walked along the edge of the Heath.

'It's a business that needs delicate treatment,' said Holmes. 'These documents are contained in a safe in the fellow's study, and the study is the ante-room of his bedchamber. On the other hand, like all these stout, little men who do them-selves well, he is a plethoric sleeper. Agatha – that's my fiancée – says it is a joke in the servants' hall that it's impos-sible to wake the master. He has a secretary who is devoted to his interests, and never budges from the study all day. That's why we are going at night. Then he has a beast of a dog which roams the garden. I met Agatha late the last two evenings, and she locks the brute up so as to give me a clear run. This is the house, this big one in its own grounds. Through the gate – now to the right among the laurels. We might put on our masks here, I think. You see, there is not a glimmer of light in any of the windows, and everything is working splendidly.'

With our black silk face-coverings, which turned us into two of the most truculent figures in London, we stole up to the silent, gloomy house. A sort of tiled veranda extended along one side of it, lined by several windows and two doors.

'That's his bedroom,' Holmes whispered. 'This door opens straight into the study. It would suit us best, but it is bolted as well as locked, and we should make too much noise get-ting in. Come round here. There's a greenhouse which opens into the drawing-room.'

The place was locked, but Holmes removed a circle of glass and turned the key from the inside. An instant afterwards he had closed the door behind us, and we had become felons in the eyes of the law. The thick warm air of the conservatory and the rich, choking fragrance of exotic plants took us by the throat. He seized my hand in the darkness and led me swiftly past banks of shrubs which brushed against our faces. Holmes had remarkable powers, carefully cultivated, of seeing in the dark. Still holding my hand in one of his, he opened a door, and I was vaguely conscious that we had entered a large room in which a cigar had been smoked not long before. He felt his way among the furniture, opened another door, and closed it behind us. Putting out my hand I felt several coats hanging from the wall, and I understood that I was in a passage. We passed along it, and Holmes very gently opened a door upon the right-hand side. Something rushed out at us, and my heart sprang into my mouth, but I could have laughed when I realized that it was the cat. A fire was burning in this new room, and again the air was heavy with tobacco smoke. Holmes entered on tiptoe, waited for me to follow, and then very gently closed the door. We were in Milverton's study, and a *portière* at the farther side showed the entrance to his bedroom.

It was a good fire, and the room was illuminated by it. Near the door I saw the gleam of an electric switch, but it was unnecessary, even if it had been safe, to turn it on. At one side of the fireplace was a heavy curtain, which covered the bay window we had seen from outside. On the other side was the door which communicated with the veranda. A desk stood in the centre, with a turning chair of shining red leather. Opposite was a large bookcase, with a marble bust of Athene on the top. In the corner between the bookcase and the wall there stood a tall green safe, the firelight flashing back from the polished brass knobs upon its face. Holmes stole across and looked at it. Then he crept to the door of the bedroom, and stood with slanting head listening intently. No sound came from within. Meanwhile it had struck me that it would be wise to secure our retreat through the outer door, so I examined it. To my amazement it was neither locked nor bolted! I touched Holmes on the arm, and he turned his masked face in that direction. I saw him start, and he was evidently as surprised as I.

'I don't like it,' he whispered, putting his lips to my very ear. 'I can't quite make it out. Anyhow, we have no time to lose.'

'Can I do anything?'

'Yes; stand by the door. If you hear anyone come, bolt it on the inside, and we can get away as we came. If they come the other way, we can get through the door if our job is done, or hide behind these window curtains if it is not. Do you understand?'

I nodded and stood by the door. My first feeling of fear had passed away, and I thrilled now with a keener zest than I had ever enjoyed when we were the defenders of the law instead of its defiers. The high object of our mission, the consciousness that it was unselfish and chivalrous, the villainous character of our opponent, all added to the sporting interest of the adventure. Far from feeling guilty, I rejoiced and exulted in our dangers. With a glow of admiration I watched Holmes unrolling his case of instruments and choosing his tool with the calm, scientific accuracy of a surgeon who performs a delicate operation. I knew that the opening of safes was a particular hobby with him, and I understood the joy which it gave him to be confronted with this green and gold monster, the dragon which held in its maw the reputations of many fair ladies. Turning up the cuffs of his dress-coat – he had placed his overcoat on a chair – Holmes laid out two drills, a jemmy, and several skeleton keys. I stood at the centre door with my eyes glancing at each of the others, ready for any emergency; though, indeed, my plans were somewhat vague as to what I should do if we were interrupted. For half an hour Holmes worked with concentrated energy, laying down one tool, picking up another, handling each with the strength and delicacy of the trained mechanic. Finally I heard a click, the broad green door swung open, and inside I had a glimpse of a number of paper packets, each tied, sealed, and inscribed. Holmes picked one out, but it was hard to read by the flickering fire, and he drew out his little dark lantern, for it was too dangerous, with Milverton in the next room, to switch on the electric light. Suddenly I saw him halt, listen intently, and then in an instant he had swung the door of the safe to, picked up his coat, stuffed his tools into the pockets, and darted behind the window curtain, motioning me to do the same.

It was only when I had joined him there that I heard what had alarmed his quicker senses. There was a noise somewhere within the house. A door slammed in the distance. Then a confused, dull murmur broke itself into the measured thud of heavy footsteps rapidly approaching. They were in the passage outside the room. They paused at the door. The door opened. There was a sharp snick as the electric light was turned on. The door closed once more, and the pungent reek of a strong cigar was borne to our nostrils. Then the footsteps continued backwards and forwards, backwards and forwards, within a few yards of us. Finally, there was a creak from a chair, and the footsteps ceased. Then a key clicked in a lock, and I heard the rustle of papers. So far I had not dared to look out, but now I gently parted the division of the curtains in front of me and peeped through. From the pressure of Holmes' shoulder against mine I knew that he was sharing my observations. Right in front of us, and almost within our reach, was the broad, rounded back of Milverton. It was evident that we had entirely miscalculated his movements, that he had never been to his bedroom, but that he had been sitting up in some smoking- or billiard-room in the farther wing of the house, the windows of which we had not seen. His broad, grizzled head, with its shining patch of baldness, was in the immediate foreground of our vision. He was leaning far back in the red leather chair, his legs outstretched, a long black cigar projecting at an angle from his mouth. He wore a semi-military smoking-jacket, claret-coloured, with a black velvet collar. In his hand he held a long legal document, which he was reading in an indolent fashion, blowing rings of tobacco smoke from his lip as he did so. There was no promise of a speedy departure in his composed bearing and his comfortable attitude.

I felt Holmes' hand steal into mine and give me a reassuring shake, as if to say that the situation was within his powers, and that he was easy in his mind. I was not sure whether he had seen what was only too obvious from my position – that the door of the safe was imperfectly closed, and that Milverton might at any moment observe it. In my own mind I had determined that if I were sure, from the rigidity of his gaze, that it had caught his eye, I would at once spring out, throw my greatcoat over his head, pinion him, and leave the rest to Holmes. But Milverton never looked up. He was languidly interested by the papers in his hand, and page after page was turned as he followed the argument of the lawyer. At least, I thought, when he has finished the document and the cigar he will go to his room; but before he had reached the end of either there came a remarkable development which turned our thoughts into quite another channel.

Several times I had observed that Milverton looked at his watch, and once he had risen and sat down again, with a gesture of impatience. The idea, however, that he might have an appointment at so strange an hour never occurred to me until a faint sound reached my ears from the veranda outside. Milverton dropped his papers and sat rigid in his chair. The sound was repeated, and then there came a gentle tap at the door. Milverton rose and opened it.

'Well,' said he curtly, 'you are nearly half an hour late.'

So this was the explanation of the unlocked door and of the nocturnal vigil of Milverton. There was the gentle rustle of a woman's dress. I had closed the slit between the curtains as Milverton's face turned in our direction, but now I ventured very carefully to open it once more. He had resumed his seat, the cigar still projecting at an insolent angle from the corner of his mouth. In front of him, in the full glare of the electric light, there stood a tall, slim, dark woman, a veil over her face, a mantle drawn round her chin. Her breath came quick and fast, and every inch of the lithe figure was quivering with strong emotion.

'Well,' said Milverton, 'you've made me lose a good night's rest, my dear. I hope you'll prove worth it. You couldn't come any other time – eh?'

The woman shook her head.

'Well, if you couldn't you couldn't. If the countess is a hard mistress you have your chance to get level with her now. Bless the girl, what are you shivering about? That's right! Pull yourself together! Now, let us get down to business.' He took a note from the drawer of his desk. 'You say that you have five letters which compromise the Countess d'Albert. You want to sell them. I want to buy them. So far so good. It only remains to fix a price. I should want to inspect the letters, of course. If they are really good specimens — Great heavens, is it you?'

The woman without a word had raised her veil and dropped the mantle from her chin. It was a dark, handsome, clear-cut face which confronted Milverton, a face with a curved nose, strong, dark eyebrows, shading hard, glittering eyes, and a straight, thin-lipped mouth set in a dangerous smile.

'It is I,' she said, 'the woman whose life you have ruined.'

Milverton laughed, but fear vibrated in his voice. 'You were so very obstinate,' said he. 'Why did you drive me to such extremities? I assure you I wouldn't hurt a fly of my own accord, but every man has his business, and what was I to do? I put the price well within your means. You would not pay.'

'So you sent the letters to my husband, and he – the noblest gentleman that ever lived, a man whose boots I was never worthy to lace – he broke his gallant heart and died. You remember that last night when I came through that door I begged and prayed you for mercy, and you laughed in my face as you are trying to laugh now, only your coward heart cannot keep your lips from twitching? Yes; you never thought to see me here again, but it was that night which taught me how I could meet you face to face, and alone. Well, Charles Milverton, what have you to say?'

'Don't imagine that you can bully me,' said he, rising to his feet. 'I have only to raise my voice, and I could call my servants and have you arrested. But I will make allowance for your natural anger. Leave the room at once as you came, and I will say no more.'

The woman stood with her hand buried in her bosom, and the same deadly smile on her thin lips.

'You will ruin no more lives as you ruined mine. You will wring no more hearts as you wrung mine. I will free the world of a poisonous thing. Take that, you hound, and that! – and that! – and that! – and that!'

She had drawn a little gleaming revolver, and emptied barrel after barrel into Milverton's body, the muzzle within two feet of his shirt-front. He shrank away, and then fell forward upon the table, coughing furiously and clawing among the papers. Then he staggered to his feet, received another shot, and rolled upon the floor. 'You've done me,' he cried, and lay still. The woman looked at him intently and ground her heel into his upturned face. She looked again, but there was no sound or movement. I heard a sharp rustle, the night air blew into the heated room, and the avenger was gone.

No interference upon our part could have saved the man from his fate; but as the woman poured bullet after bullet into Milverton's shrinking body, I was about to spring out, when I felt Holmes' cold, strong grasp upon my wrist. I understood the whole argument of that firm, restraining grip – that it was no affair of ours; that justice had overtaken a villain; that we had our own duties and our own objects which were not to be lost sight of. But hardly had the woman rushed from the room when Holmes, with swift, silent steps, was over at the other door. He turned the key in the lock. At the same instant we heard voices in the house and the sound of hurrying feet. The revolver shots had roused the household. With perfect coolness Holmes slipped across to the safe, filled his two arms with bundles of letters, and poured them all into the fire. Again and again he did it, until the safe was empty. Someone turned the handle and beat upon the outside of the door. Holmes looked swiftly round. The letter which had been the messenger of death for Milverton lay, all mottled with his blood, upon the table. Holmes tossed it in among the blazing papers. Then he drew the key from the outer door, passed through after me, and locked it on the outside. 'This way, Watson,' said he, 'we can scale the garden wall in this direction.'

I could not have believed that an alarm could have spread so swiftly. Looking back, the huge house was one blaze of light. The front door was open, and figures were rushing down the drive. The whole garden was alive with people, and one fellow raised a view-halloa as we emerged from the veranda and followed hard at our heels. Holmes seemed to know the ground perfectly, and he threaded his way swiftly among a plantation of small trees, I close at his heels, and our foremost pursuer panting behind us. It was a six-foot wall which barred our path, but he sprang to the top and over. As I did the same I felt the hand of the man behind me grab at my ankle; but I kicked myself free, and scrambled over a glass-strewn coping. I fell upon my face among some bushes; but Holmes had me on my feet in an instant, and together we dashed away across the huge expanse of Hampstead Heath. We had run two miles, I suppose, before Holmes at last halted and listened intently. All was absolutely silence behind us. We had shaken off our pursuers, and were safe.

We had breakfasted and were smoking our morning pipe, on the day after the remarkable experience which I have recorded, when Mr Lestrade, of Scotland Yard, very solemn and impressive, was ushered into our modest sitting-room.

'Good morning, Mr Holmes,' said he, 'good morning. May I ask if you are very busy just now?'

'Not too busy to listen to you.'

'I thought that, perhaps, if you had nothing particular on

hand, you might care to assist us in a most remarkable case which occurred only last night at Hampstead.'

'Dear me!' said Holmes. 'What was that?'

'A murder – a most dramatic and remarkable murder. I know how keen you are upon these things, and I would take it as a great favour if you would step down to Appledore Towers and give us the benefit of your advice. It is no ordinary crime. We have had our eyes upon this Mr Milverton for some time, and, between ourselves, he was a bit of a villain. He is known to have held papers which he used for blackmailing purposes. These papers have all been burned by the murderers. No article of value was taken, as it is probable that the criminals were men of good position, whose sole object was to prevent social exposure.'

'Criminals!' exclaimed Holmes. 'Plural!'

'Yes, there were two of them. They were, as nearly as possible, captured red-handed. We have their footmarks, we have their description; it's ten to one that we trace them. The first fellow was a bit too active, but the second was caught by the under-gardener, and only got away after a struggle. He was a middle-sized, strongly built man – square jaw, thick neck, moustache, a mask over his eyes.'

'That's rather vague,' said Sherlock Holmes. 'Why, it might be a description of Watson.'

'It's true,' said the Inspector, with much amusement. 'It might be a description of Watson.'

'Well, I am afraid I can't help you, Lestrade,' said Holmes. 'The fact is that I knew this fellow Milverton, that I considered him one of the most dangerous men in London, and that I think there are certain crimes which the law cannot touch, and which therefore, to some extent, justify private revenge. No, it's no use arguing. I have made up my mind. My sympathies are with the criminals rather than with the victim, and I will not handle this case.'

Holmes had not said one word to me about the tragedy which we had witnessed, but I observed all the morning that he was in the most thoughtful mood, and he gave me the impression, from his vacant eyes and his abstracted manner, of a man who is striving to recall something to his memory. We were in the middle of our lunch, when he suddenly sprang to his feet. 'By Jove, Watson! I've got it!' he cried. 'Take your hat! Come with me!' He hurried at his top speed down Baker Street and along Oxford Street, until we had almost reached Regent Circus. Here on the left hand there stands a shop window filled with photographs of the celebrities and beauties of the day. Holmes' eyes fixed themselves upon one of them, and following his gaze I saw the picture of a regal and stately lady in Court dress, with a high diamond tiara upon her noble head. I looked at that delicately curved nose, at the marked eyebrows, at the straight mouth, and the strong little chin beneath it. Then I caught my breath as I read the time-honoured title of the great nobleman and statesman whose wife she had been. My eyes met those of Holmes, and he put his finger to his lips as we turned away from the window.

# The Bottle Party

## H. C. BAILEY

*Only a few minutes walk from the junction of Baker Street
and George Street lies Wimpole Street, another of the famous
old London thoroughfares steeped in history. It is also where
Reginald Fortune, the 'specialist in the surgery of crime', lives
in a flat in Montmorency House. Although he is not often
referred to as 'Doctor', Reggie Fortune is actually a practising
physician and surgeon whose special knowledge of medicine
and the human anatomy – particularly where violence or murder may have been used upon it – has resulted in his
appointment as a special adviser to Scotland Yard.
Notwithstanding this, he more often than not has to take a
philosophical attitude when some of his triumphs are treated
with resentment in certain police quarters. A Londoner by
birth, Reggie qualified as a general practitioner, but when two
criminal cases were brought to his attention in quick succession
he found himself set on a career for life. Something of a
gourmet, his gentle manner belies a tough physique and a
painstaking method of sifting evidence. His usual associates
from the Yard are the chief of the C.I.D., Stanley Lomas, and
his assistant, Superintendent Bell. When he does not feel it will
appear too ostentatious, Reggie likes nothing better than driving his Rolls-Royce around London. Over twenty books recount
his cases from* Call Mr Fortune *(1920) to* Saving A Rope
*(1948), which have inspired historian Otto Penzler to declare*

*that he was 'probably the most popular sleuth in England between the two world wars'.*

*Fortune's creator, Henry Christopher Bailey (1878–1961), was also born in London and received a classical education at Oxford. He joined the staff of the* Daily Telegraph *where he worked as a drama critic, leader writer and war correspondent before achieving popular fame with the stories of his doctor-detective in the twenties. 'The Bottle Party' (1940) reveals Fortune at his most astute when the arrest of a drunken young man leads first to hints of drug-taking and then the discovery of the body of a young woman in a car nearby . . .*

FEW ARE THE cases which have given Mr Fortune so pure a pleasure.

When Carteret Square was built on a swamp, our ancient aristocracy bid against each other for its mansions and put their horses and carriages into a foul mews on the eastern side. The square is now a colossal quadrangle of flats inhabited by the new rich. The stables of the mews have been rebuilt to make garages for some of them and little houses for those who live upon them and renamed, to preserve the dignity of all, Carteret Place.

It is a narrow, prim street, empty, when the children of the chauffeurs dwelling over the garages have been put to bed, unless some knowing creature has left a car parked in one of the bulges provided to give a turning circle for the chariots of the past. But behind the curtains of the neat houses there is often some noise at night, and policemen stroll by from hour to hour.

About eleven on a misty autumn night a constable was pacing along Carteret Place from the southern end when he heard a police whistle blow at the other. He ran upon the sound and, reaching the northern end, found another breathless officer who had heard the whistle, but no one else. They hunted highways and byways in vain. The neighbourhood is prolific in bright young things who delight to take a rise out of the police.

About one o'clock he came down Carteret Place again. The little houses were quieter than usual. But by one of them a man bumped into him and when rebuked knocked his helmet off. They had a scuffle, the man fell, the constable picked him up and dragged him off, wambling in his walk, to the station, and charged him with assault. The man seemed dazed or drunk. With difficulty the inspector got a name out of him, which was Antony Cray, put him in a cell and sent for a doctor.

At nine o'clock next morning Mr Fortune was, as usual, in his bath. Mrs Fortune opened the door and exhorted him to come out. 'Why?' He sank deeper into the water. 'Why are wives?' She turned on the cold shower. 'Not for that, no,' he moaned.

'A lady has called to see you,' she said severely.

'My dear girl! Have a heart. Not before breakfast.'

'Parker says she wouldn't go away. And she's been here nearly an hour. Her name is Valerie Milburn.'

'Not guilty. Means nothing in my young life.'

'You've seen her. She plays the blondes that gentlemen prefer.'

'An actress? Before nine a.m.? Oh no, Joan.'

'I didn't say she could act,' said Mrs Fortune.

The secret of his eminence, he likes to explain, is a capacity to dress quicker than any man, thus making time for higher things. He ate half a cold partridge before he went to his consulting-room and yet half-past nine had not struck when Valerie Milburn sat down in front of him.

The silly, pretty face of the enchantress of light comedy was not at its best. Without make-up her fair complexion looked insipid. She tried her popular, yearning glance, but the smile on the pale lips was a spasm.

'Oh, Mr Fortune, how kind you are!' She used the drawl of allure with which she spoke all her parts, though her voice could put no life into it.

'Not kind, no. Only curious. Who sent you to me, Miss Milburn?'

'Nobody. I came of myself.'

'Oh! Had a bad night?'

She laughed, rather too long. 'There's nothing the matter with me. It's someone else, Tony Cray, Antony Cray, you know, he's the nephew of Lord Frome.'

'I don't. Is he ill?'

'I believe he is, Mr Fortune. It's like this. I live in Carteret Place, you know the dinky little houses there. I had a bottle party last night, starting ten o'clock. Tony – Mr Cray was there on the dot. I'm sure he shouldn't have come at all. You can back him to be on top of the world at any show, but last night nobody could get a rise out of him. He just sat and gloomed. He owned up, about one, he didn't feel too good, he'd go home. Then the ghastly thing happened. Just outside my door a policeman barged into him, the silly brute, got rough with him, said he was drunk and ran him in. They've kept him at the station, they're going to charge him this morning. But he wasn't drunk, Mr Fortune. He couldn't have been. He wouldn't have a spot. He was sickly sober. But you know what the police are. If they get him convicted it'll break him. He hasn't a bean, except what he gets from Lord Frome. The old man was just going to wangle a Foreign Office job for him. That's right off, suppose Tony's in the news for drunk and scragging policemen. You see?'

'I wonder,' said Mr Fortune.

'You could stop it, you could, couldn't you?' she panted. 'He wasn't drunk, he's never violent. Do help him, do save him.'

'The police won't stop for me. Mustn't count on me to save anybody, Miss Milburn. Feeling this rather a lot, aren't you? However. Curious case. Interestin' case. As you put it. I'll see if they'll let me look it over.'

'Oh, thank you so much,' she started up and ran round the table to clutch his hands.

'Don't do that,' Mr Fortune withdrew them and rang the bell. 'Don't hope too much.' Valerie was shown out gurgling laughter and tears.

Mr Fortune rang up the Chief of the Criminal Investigation Department. 'Fortune speakin', Lomas. Most improperly. To foul the springs of justice. Any objection?'

'I've been pining to catch you at it for years, Reginald. Go on.'

'The woman tempted me. One Valerie Milburn.' He paused for a reply. None came. 'Know her?'

'Not officially,' said Lomas. 'On the stage, yes. The delight of callow youth and aged rips. I thought you had better taste. When did she tempt you? And how? If it's fit for my ears.'

'When? She's only just gone.'

'Good God! Are you talking in your sleep? It's very early for temptation – and for you to be up.'

'I've been up an hour.'

'And fallen for a pretty lady already. Fie!'

'Didn't say fallen. Miss Milburn was woe on the top note. But points did emerge. Her trouble is one Antony Cray. Ever heard of him?'

Again the answer was delayed for some moments. Then Lomas repeated. 'Cray? Do you mean a nephew of old Lord Frome?'

'That's the fellow. Miss Milburn says you've pinched him for drunk and assaulting the constabulary which you didn't ought.' Reggie related precisely all that Valerie had told him. . . .

'Do you believe her, Reginald?'

'What the lady said isn't evidence. However. Statement could be true.'

'Quite,' Lomas admitted. 'Some of these cases are the devil. It's hard measure to ruin a young fellow's career because he had a rough and tumble with the police. And if this fellow was seedy!'

'As you say,' Reggie murmured, but he contemplated the telephone with a small, satiric smile. 'Very fair, Lomas. Very human. May I look the case over?'

'By all means,' Lomas said heartily. 'You'd like to see the boy before he's charged?'

'Yes, please. And the police doctor. And the policeman.'

'I agree. I'll send Bell to meet you at the police station.' Lomas rang off.

'Well, well,' Reggie sighed to the dead telephone. '"Barkis is willin'."'

Ten minutes later he entered the station and met the solid form of Superintendent Bell. 'This swift attention from the higher powers is gratifyin',' he returned thanks. 'Are you going to tell me things?'

'I don't know any more about the case than you do,' said Bell stolidly. 'But it wants checking up. This way, please.' Reggie was taken to the cell which contained Antony Cray.

He was dirty and tousled and of a yellow pallor, his eyes red rimmed and swollen, his shaking, twitching hands had bled from the knuckles. Yet reason for Valerie's interest in him could be detected. In good condition he might have been a fine fellow, at least a woman's man. He had long legs and a good pair of shoulders, the blurred features of the sickly face were well cut by nature.

'Sorry about this, Mr Cray,' said Reggie. 'I'm a doctor.'

'What do you want?' Cray's voice was hoarse. 'I'm not drunk. I wasn't drunk. The policeman did this,' he held out his damaged hands.

'No drink taken last night?'

'A small whisky at dinner. That's all.'

'Anything besides drink?'

'Yes. I had a splitting headache. I took some phenacetin tablets. They made me all the worse. I couldn't stand the row of the party. When I went out I was dizzy, and stumbled into the policeman, and he said I was drunk and beat me up.'

'Oh. Phenacetin. Often use that?'

'When I get a head.'

Reggie felt his pulse, murmuring: 'Any sickness? No? Rather depressed, what? Did you see things normal last night?'

'With a sick headache? Who does?'

Reggie looked into the swollen eyes and with his fingers on the chin tilted the head back.

Cray jerked it aside. 'Look out! My head's devilish sore.'

'Yes. It would be. That's all, Mr, Cray.' Reggie left the cell.

The police doctor, he found, had been told the same tale, and sardonically pronounced it a good story.

'You don't believe it?'

'I never believe 'em. The young rascal wasn't drunk when I saw him, but he smelt of drink. He'd had more than one.'

'That could be, yes. But something else also, what?'

'I dare say. Certainly, I thought him rather down than up.'

'Still is. Not a drunk. No. Nerves all wrong.'

'Well, of course, your opinion is decisive, Mr Fortune,' the doctor was quick to answer. 'If I say neuralgic condition and an overdose of some sedative, that would be about right, I take it?'

'Yes. As near as we can get,' Reggie sighed.

The doctor bustled out.

'Everybody loves me,' Reggie complained to the empty room.

Bell entered. 'The doctor tells me, sir, you and him are agreed Cray was a sick man?'

'Why this kindly joy, Bell?'

'No joy from me one way or the other. I just want things straight.'

'What about the assaulted constable?'

'You want to talk to him, sir? Very good.'

An uncomfortable policeman was brought in. 'This Mr Cray,' Reggie asked, 'How did he collide with you?'

'Sort of staggered into me, sir. But I have to own he wasn't noisy. He caught hold of me, I reproached him. Then he got excited and hit out wild and I had to take him along.'

'Did him proud, didn't you?'

'Sir?' The policeman was aggrieved.

'Bruise under the chin?'

'Then it must have come from his falling down, sir. He did fall heavy. He barked his knuckles proper.'

'Well, well. Nothing more, thanks.'

The constable departed and Bell asked: 'Is that all right, Mr Fortune?'

'My dear Bell. Splendid. Great force, the police force. However. I'd like to see this through.'

'Very good, sir. Come along into court. Cray's case'll be on any minute.'

It went with a rush. The policeman was mild, the doctor masterfully sympathetic. Reggie had just made out the wan face of Valerie watching Cray tell his tale of headache and phenacetin before the magistrate dismissed the charge with soft, paternal words.

'Sort of thing that makes England what she is,' Reggie murmured to Bell as they went out.

'We do know how to be fair,' Bell answered. 'Now would you come along with me? There's a big case turned up.'

Reggie looked up with wide, plaintive eyes. 'Big? What is big? Murder?'

'I want your opinion on that. There's a woman dead.'

'Where?'

'In the Westminster mortuary. Only five minutes' walk.'

'Walk?' Reggie's voice went up. 'My car's here.'

It brought them into the yard of the mortuary. A smaller car stood there, a coupé of class. 'She's inside that,' said Bell.

Reggie gave one glance within and turned. 'Why is she?' he complained.

'I couldn't say, sir.'

'Cautious fellow. Couldn't say whether it was murder! Look again.'

'I leave it to you, Mr Fortune,' Bell recoiled.

The woman's body lay huddled between the seat and the instrument board. Under that her head lolled back, the cheeks, the closed eyes bulged, the nose and lips spread flat. All the face was livid but for purple and yellow marks of bruising. A squirrel coat covered her from bent knees to chin. Reggie drew back its collar. Round the full neck bruises were black to the knot of red bronze hair behind.

He opened the coat wider. Beneath it was a green evening

dress. He contemplated that with a pensive gaze which slowly extended to survey the whole of the car's interior before he turned to Bell.

'You don't want to look at her again? Not a cheerin' sight. Not a perfect world. Get your fellows to take her into the mortuary. When she's gone you might bear to look into the car. The higher intelligence could work out a fact or so.'

Bell glowered at him. 'I reckon I'll finish with the car before you're through. If you come back to the station I'll be there.'

Some hours later Reggie entered the bleak room where Bell sat writing, subsided on the only other chair and lit a pipe. 'Not to spoil the story,' he murmured and blew smoke rings. 'Dead woman was forty or so, in good health, well preserved. Married woman as per wedding ring. Cause of death, asphyxia. From throttling with human hands. She died hard. Fought it out.'

'Ah. Clear case of murder,' Bell grunted.

'Oh yes. Not a nice murderer – or murderers. Things are what they seemed. On that point. Hands were almost clenched. Between the fingers of right hand light yellow hairs, from bobbed or shingled woman. On her teeth some scraps of human skin, colour indeterminate, bitten off assailant. Dress and other clothes not torn, not pulled about, but body and legs heavily bruised. She was on her back and somebody knelt on her to kill her. Murder therefore was not committed in the car. Time of murder indefinitely before midnight. That's the medical evidence. How do you like it?'

'Not so bad, Mr Fortune.'

'Always happy to gratify the higher powers. What is the story you're composin'?'

'I was just putting things together in order.'

'Order is a felt want. Yes. Got it?'

'Well, sir, fairly clearly. That car was found at three-fifteen this morning in Carteret Place.'

'Oh! Where Valerie Milburn gave her bottle party. Where Cray had his scrap with the policeman.'

'That's right. At least in a manner of speaking. The car wasn't at Miss Milburn's house but some way up the street, in a little sort of dead end. The constable who arrested Cray says it wasn't there when he went up Carteret Place at eleven p.m. We can fix the time it was left between eleven and three.'

'As near as that! Better than me.'

'Ah! We might get nearer yet,' said Bell. 'At three another constable spotted the car. He didn't bother with it, being no obstruction. He came back about five and it was still there. Thinking that queer he looked in and saw the woman.'

'Oh my Bell!' Reggie protested. 'You haven't put things in order. How did it begin? Who is she?'

'Yes, sir. She's been identified. She's Mrs Arundel, a lady living just by where the car was found, and it's her car.'

Reggie blew one smoke ring inside another. 'Who is Mrs Arundel? What is she, that someone strangles her and dumps her in her own car by her own house? Is there a Mr Arundel?'

'Not to my knowledge,' said Bell solemnly, 'but she has had three real husbands.'

'Rather careless with spouses, what?'

'She was no better than she should be, Mr Fortune. A fast woman, half in society, more than half out.'

'The lady's – friends?' Reggie drawled. 'Are they known to the police?'

'She lived in a rackety crowd.'

Reggie smiled. 'Yes, Bell, Carteret Place was having frequent visits from the police at night – eleven, one, three, five. Why?'

'We don't like that street, sir. We have nothing hard, but there is reason to believe it has snow falls. Cocaine, you know.'

'I do. Yes. Though not mentioned when I was introduced to your friend Cray. So Mrs Arundel was suspect of dope dealing?'

'We had her in view. But there have been other reasons for watching Carteret Place, complaints of rowdy parties there and spots of trouble in the neighbourhood. Only last night there was one.' He related the vain pursuit of a police whistle by the eleven o'clock constable.

Reggie sat up. His round face was plaintive and reproachful. 'My Bell! Oh my Bell! Is this puttin' things in order? No. Carteret Place was deprived of the eleven o'clock police inspection. Curious and interestin' fact. Yet I had to pull it out of you with forceps.'

'I'm sorry, sir. It don't signify. The constable went right along the street at eleven and he swears no car was in it. I told you.'

'But he left the street clear. So the car could have been brought along. The woman may have been killed some time before. He didn't come back till one and then he got busy arrestin' Cray. So we don't know whether she and the car were there then. Pity.'

'I grant you there is a look of tricks,' Bell frowned. 'But whistling to get a rise out of the police is a common game with the bright young things round there. I am giving you all the facts, Mr Fortune. When I went over the car I found this –' He displayed a scrap of pale blue silk. 'It was caught on the edge of the door the driver's side. From a woman's dress and not Mrs Arundel's dress. Hers was green.'

'As you say,' Reggie murmured. 'Not her colour. Dress probably worn by a blonde. Same like the hair in the fingers of the deceased. And Valerie of the bottle party is a blonde. Did you get her to look at Mrs Arundel?'

'Why no, sir. Mrs Arundel was recognised by the constable and then identified by her servant – she kept a house man, no maid, that was her style. I have no reason to think Miss Milburn was a special friend.'

'Till this,' Reggie held up the blue silk. 'Further conversation with Miss Milburn is required.'

'I was going to,' said Bell.

'My dear chap, we do agree beautiful.' Reggie stood up and looked at his watch. 'Help! Have you got a car? Mine has to go home.' He strolled out and, with brief instructions, sent his chauffeur away.

Bell joined him. 'We can walk it as quick as drive, sir.'

'Not me,' Reggie protested, hailing a taxi. But he stopped it at the beginning of Carteret Place. 'Walkin' is only justified when you can't get what is wanted otherwise. As now. In this nasty, neat little street. Where you have to show me things. Mrs Arundel's house. Dead end in which Mrs Arundel's car stood. After that, house of Miss Milburn.'

At that hour of the afternoon, the narrow street was a playground and a mixed club. Children of the chauffeurs who lodged over its garages sported across the roadway, chauffeurs and their wives clustered about the garage doors in gossip.

'That's where the car was found.' Bell glanced at a bulge in the roadway which went up between two houses to a blank wall. 'Used to be a turning circle when this was a mews, often used for parking.'

'Handy,' Reggie murmured, 'yet out of the way. Good and dark after dark.'

'That's right,' Bell nodded. 'Now the next house but one is Mrs Arundel's.'

It had an emerald green door and russet window frames and curtains of brown netting. 'Suits her complexion,' Reggie murmured. 'By the way, when did she leave the house yesterday?'

'Ah! You're asking something,' Bell grunted. 'Her man servant don't know. He was taking his weekly day off yesterday, and had leave for the night, he says. He went out at two o'clock, went to see his old dad at Kingston and didn't get back till eight this morning.'

'Do you believe him?'

'I have no reason not to. He hasn't been with Mrs Arundel long – only a month – and he's given us a story we can easily check.'

'Will aged father say son was with him at time of murder? Some check! However. Let's try Miss Milburn.'

'There's her house,' Bell pointed. It was some fifty yards from Mrs Arundel's on the same side, a little larger, double fronted, its door, and everything else that could be painted, white. All the windows had boxes of white flowers, geraniums and petunias.

The door was opened by an oldish maid who glared.

'If you please.' Bell stepped into the hall. 'Tell Miss Milburn I want to see her at once.' He held out his card.

'Madam's not at home.' The maid was shrill.

'Do as you're told,' Bell growled, and she slunk away into a room on the right and slammed the door, came out again looking malice sideways and went upstairs. She was not gone long. From the landing she beckoned them.

They were taken into a small room on the first floor, which was entirely white and cream but for two people in it. Valerie shimmered silver grey as she glided to meet them. The man behind her had put his lumpy form into bright blue tweeds and a honey-coloured beard and side whiskers grew on his large pink face.

Valerie was flushed out of insipidity. 'Superintendent Bell?' she smiled and the upward glance of allure had a gleam in it.

'Me too, Miss Milburn,' said Reggie.

'Oh, Mr Fortune. How too kind of you. It was splendid about poor old Tony.'

'Has he been here?'

'No, did you want him?'

'I wonder. Let's see. About your party last night, Miss Milburn—' Reggie stopped and glanced at the bearded man.

'I was here, sir.' The man's voice was high.

'You don't know each other,' Valerie giggled. 'How futile! On the left Mr Fortune, on the right Ned Patten.'

'Friend of Mr Cray's?' Reggie asked.

'I think so,' the man answered.

'Seen him since?'

'Since the party? No.'

'Mr Fortune ! ' Valerie cried. 'Has something happened to Tony?'

'What could happen? Charge dismissed. Revertin' to the party—' Valerie was staring at the stolid menace of Bell. 'Please—' Reggie waved her to a chair and sat down beside her. 'You told me it began at ten. When did Cray arrive?'

'With the first bunch,' Patten answered. 'So did I.'

'Many bunches? Lot of people?'

'Quite a crush,' said Patten.

'All in here?' Reggie looked round the little room.

'Heavens no,' Valerie giggled. 'The state apartments are beneath.'

'Oh! Do you mind – like to look at actual scene.'

'Why?' Valerie gasped.

'Want to make sure where Cray was all the time.'

'But – but Tony's out now. You just said so.'

'Yes. He is. However.' Reggie moved to the door.

Valerie sprang up, slid past him downstairs and flung open the doors on either side the hall. Through one was a narrow dining-room of different gold shades, the other opened upon a lounge, with walls, carpet and furniture all white.

'There you are,' she cried. 'Now you know the worst, Mr Fortune. The lily house. Décor by Ned. Spirit by me.' She made him a curtsey, looking up under her eyelashes.

'Charmin' harmony. Yes.' Reggie glanced at the gold room and went into the white lounge. 'Bottle party buzzed about; what? But the main body here. Were you here all the time, Patten?'

'In and out from the gold room. That's where the drinks were.'

'And you, Miss Milburn?'

'I was here in the lounge from start to finish.'

'Where was Cray?'

'Down and dumb in the corner over there,' Patten pointed.

'Poor old Tony,' said Valerie. 'He was sick and hating himself for it.'

'Yet he stayed. Stayed from ten till one.'

'I couldn't shift him,' Valerie cried.

'Silly dam' fool,' said Patten. ' I tried to push him off.'

Reggie looked from one to the other. 'Who else was here?'

Valerie broke out laughing. 'Who wasn't? Hordes! Half my crowd.'

'Mrs Arundel among 'em?' Reggie asked.

That froze them both. Patten spoke first. 'Mrs Arundel was here hours.'

'It seemed like years,' said Valerie. 'She didn't go till after Tony's row with the policeman.'

'Oh. She was still here when he'd been arrested? Quite sure?' Reggie's eyes were set on Valerie.

'Absolutely.' Valerie stared back unflinching. 'She ragged us about it.'

Reggie strolled across the room to a settee. Its rough silk cover showed marks at one end as if it had been scraped by something hard. He bent over it, Bell came to look, they exchanged a glance. Valerie met them as they turned and gasped: 'What, what's the matter?'

'When did she go?' Reggie drawled.

'Mrs Arundel? Some time after Tony.'

'About ten past one,' said Patten.

'How?'

'What do you mean?' Patten scowled at him.

'On her own legs?'

'Of course,' Valerie gasped. 'She didn't have a car. Her house is only a few doors off.'

'I've seen it. So you say Mrs Arundel walked out of your house soon after one. Cray bein' then in the hands of the police. Who remained here?'

Valerie and Patten consulted together with their eyes. 'I did,' said Patten.

'Nobody else?'

'Me of course,' Valerie cried. 'Only me.'

'And then?'

'Then I sat some time with Val and went home,' Patten answered.

'Which way?'

Patten was silent for a moment and grew pale before he answered: 'I live up the street.'

'Beyond Mrs Arundel's house. So you passed it. When did you know Mrs Arundel had been killed?'

'My housekeeper told me this morning.'

'Oh yes. Yes. But passin' Mrs Arundel's house last night, didn't you give an eye to her car?'

'I didn't see any car.'

'Of course we didn't,' Valerie giggled. 'We were only seeing ourselves.'

'Oh. You were with him?'

The giggle faded in a languishing smile. 'It is so hard to say good night. Hasn't anyone ever told you that, Mr Fortune? Give them a chance.'

'I have,' Reggie sighed. 'Good night, Miss Milburn.' He went out.

'You'll be required to make a further statement miss, and you, sir,' Bell told them. 'I warn you what you have said will be tested.'

Reggie had shut the door behind him, and when Bell emerged came from the inner recesses of the hall. 'This bein' thus,' he murmured. 'Passed to you.'

Bell did not answer till they were in the street. 'A pretty couple!'

'As you say.' Reggie stopped and contemplated the house.

'That minx with her goo-goo eyes!'

'Cloyin' damsel. Yes. Cloyin' house. All overdone.' Reggie made a weary gesture. 'Even the side door white.'

'Ah, overdone is right,' Bell chuckled. 'Such silly lying, they didn't know where to stop.'

Reggie looked up at him with pensive wonder. 'That is so. We do agree, Bell.'

'Ah! You got 'em over the car. They knew all about it.'

'One or both. Yes. Lies not so good on that. Smash the rest and all is gas and gaiters. Check the beastly bottle party.' Reggie hailed a taxi and drove off in it.

That night the Chief of the Criminal Investigation Department found him solitary at supper in one of their sprightlier clubs. A bottle of champagne was on his table, he was eating marrow bones.

'Reginald!' Lomas rebuked him. 'And you a married man! Is this domestic virtue?'

'No. Debauch. To preserve sanity. Sufferin' from a public dinner. Mass production food and speeches. On top of your distressful case. The mind was hysterical.'

Lomas sat down with him and ordered a devilled sole and brandy and soda.

Reggie sipped his champagne. 'You may be right. Both equally coarse. Only a wine in name. What's your trouble?'

'Nothing but fatigue. We've done very well. We roped in some of the bottle party and got out of 'em it was an uncomfortable show. Valerie and Mrs Arundel on the edge of a flare up all the time. They've always been cats to each other, but last night well above themselves. They've had Cray in common for a boy friend and he funked both women hard. Mrs Arundel fed the party brimstone scandal about Valerie and Patten. When Cray left he looked dead to the world. On his scrap with the policeman the party broke up. The last of Mrs Arundel comes from a fellow who heard her ragging Valerie and Valerie scolding back. Not too clean, he says. So there's the motive. Then we have the damage to the settee. If the woman was thrown down and strangled there, her heels would have made marks like that.'

'As you say,' Reggie sighed. 'Strikin' and suggestive, the double scrape. Any more evidence?'

'That hair in Mrs Arundel's fingers matches Valerie's. The scrap of pale blue silk in the car was torn from the dress Valerie wore last night. We found finger-prints on the door and window of the car and they're Patten's.'

'Careless animal. Futile liar. So you've taken his prints and searched her lily house. Charged 'em?'

'Not yet,' Lomas smiled. 'We got their prints on statements we handed them to sign. They are detained for enquiries. They'll be charged tomorrow.'

Reggie drank up his champagne. 'End of a perfect day,' he murmured. 'Began by gettin' one rackety fool off a twopenny crime, went on to lag two lying fools for murder. In sweet

agreement with the higher intelligence.' He gazed at Lomas
with heavy eyes. 'Pleasant dreams. Do you dream? I never
could.' He wandered out.

Before eleven next morning Lomas heard his voice again.
It came over the telephone. 'I want Bell,' it said. 'Bell in a fast
car. With another hefty man or so. At the Oval tube station.
Now.'

'Good Gad!' Lomas exclaimed. 'What—'

'I said now,' said Reggie, and rang off.

But when the car stopped by the Oval station, he was not
there. Bell fumed for some minutes before a taxi crossed all
the traffic lanes and Reggie sprang from it, ran to the police
car, slammed the door which Bell opened and thrust himself
between the driver and the other man in front. 'Camberwell
Road. Let her out.' Between buses and trams the driver did
wonders, but Reggie fidgeted and lifted up his voice. 'I asked
for a fast car.' The driver flushed and scared all traffic over
three busy miles.

Then he was directed into a glum, suburban avenue.
'Slow. Stop,' Reggie ordered. Bell frowned at rows of small
houses, each asserting that it was different from the other but
of a blinding uniformity.

A man loitering by the corner of a side street turned to
look and went on looking.

'Come along, Bell,' Reggie jumped out.

Bell caught him up before he reached the corner, and
received a wink from the man standing there. 'My oath!' he
muttered, for he knew the man as Reggie's chauffeur. 'What's
the idea, Mr Fortune?'

'All present and correct,' said the chauffeur out of the
corner of his mouth.

'To see Killarney,' said Reggie. 'Leave your men here.' He
turned down the side street.

The houses there were of still bleaker gentility and
detached. Scrawny hedges of privet, laurel and aucuba
protected each from neighbours and the vulgar world.

Killarney had its name in gold on a red gate. Inside that a

monkey puzzler rose over straggling rhododendrons through which a curving path led to the lurid stained glass of the front door. Some noise came out of the house, petulant voices talking together. On a sudden both fell to silence. Reggie took Bell's arm and drew him from the door to a window beyond.

They looked in round aspidistras, upon a dowdy drawing-room and a woman and a man standing close together. Reggie pushed up the window. 'Thanks very much, Cray,' he laughed.

Cray shrank and sagged and stumbled away from the woman. She stood fast. Her purple dress suited the maroon drawing-room, came near matching the mottled flush of her cheeks, but made a cruel discord with the bronze red hair above. She looked from Cray to Reggie and Bell, and they saw her eyes gleam dark.

'Good morning, Mrs Arundel,' Reggie cried, 'this is a pleasure.'

Bell thrust head and shoulders through the window. She clutched the table beside her, a table on which lay some woollen knitting. She looked again at Cray, who was white and dumb.

'Yes, kind of Cray to bring us along,' said Reggie. 'Superintendent Bell did want you.'

She picked up the knitting, she turned and flung herself at Cray and drove the needles into his face, into his throat.

Bell shouted; Bell clambered into the room. Cray had fallen and she was upon him, stabbing at him with the bestial strength of frenzy.

Bell dragged her off. She kicked and bit, till his men came through the window and mastered her. Reggie was kneeling by Cray. 'Don't be rough,' he said over his shoulder. Handcuffs were put on her, her legs were tied.

'She has done you proud,' he said to Cray, whose throat was welling blood. 'However.' He rose and came to Mrs Arundel. 'Allow me.' He drew her long sleeves back from the handcuffs. On the right arm the skin had been torn and dents showed red. 'Oh yes. Where sister bit you,' he murmured, and the woman shrieked. 'Take her away. Me for the other victim.'

That afternoon he came into Lomas's room dreamy and benign. 'One of your larger cigars is indicated.' He helped himself and sank down in the easiest chair. 'Pleasin' case.'

Lomas took up his telephone. 'Come along, Bell. Mr Fortune's here at last.'

'My dear old thing!' Reggie protested. 'Only paused for a simple lunch.'

'Till half-past three,' Lomas rebuked him.

Bell strode in. 'What about Cray, Mr Fortune? Is he going to come through?'

'He thinks not. I didn't tell him he was wrong.'

'My oath!' Bell muttered.

'Had a confession from him?'

'Yes, sir. Him believing he wouldn't live.'

'Last dying speech,' Reggie smiled. 'Anything like the truth?'

'It's a queer story. He says Mrs Arundel was in the dope business, and broke him down teaching him to take snow. She told him the dead woman was her sister and lived on her, passed her the dope and blackmailed her over it. The trade was bad lately. Money ran short and this sister turned nasty, threatened she'd give the whole game away. She came to Mrs Arundel's house day before yesterday. Mrs Arundel 'phoned him, and when he got there the woman was dead. Mrs Arundel said she'd had to kill her, the only way to stop her mouth; she was going to split on 'em both, but it would be all right if he helped get the body taken for Mrs Arundel's, she'd go off and pass as her sister. But he wouldn't stand for it; he wouldn't do a thing, and he quit. Then this morning he had a telegram: 'Come Killarney,' and he didn't dare not go for fear of her.'

'Fearful fellow. Yes. That's why he's such a brute. He helped to strangle the sister. Hence the bruise under his chin. Any confession from Mrs Arundel?'

'Not a word.'

'There will be. When she hears his. However. Don't matter. Been over Mrs Arundel's house yet?'

'We have, sir. What are you thinking of?'

'Oh my Bell. Settee, divan or bed. Scratches thereon, same like the white settee of Valerie.'

'That's pretty good.' Bell smiled grimly. 'We didn't find anything scratched. But Mrs Arundel's house man says there's an old Persian rug gone from the couch in the drawing-room.'

'Splendid,' Reggie purred. 'Pleasin' case. Subtle female, Mrs Arundel. All clear.'

'Clear!' Lomas exclaimed. 'You flatter yourself, Reginald.'

'Not myself. No.' Reggie sank down in his chair. 'Do I flatter you? Surely not.'

'We can convict these two beauties now, but we don't know how the thing was worked.'

'Oh my Lomas. Think again. Believe the evidence. Cray and the Arundel strangled Mrs Jones and she left her mark on both of 'em, some time before ten. I told you she died earlier than midnight. Cray went off to Valerie's party at ten. The Arundel stripped dead sister and put on the body clothes of her own, evenin' dress matchin' the one she wore herself at the bottle party. Not a nice job. Not a nice woman. Twisted some of Valerie's hair in the dead fingers. Next event. Eleven o'clock constable called out of Carteret Place by a police whistle. No doubt Mrs Arundel blew that from her car. Him being gone, Cray slunk out of Valerie's lily house – I showed you the side door, Bell, it opens on a passage where the cloak room is. The Arundel brought her car round, Cray helped her put the body in the car, covered it with the missin' rug, so it wouldn't show and came back to party via side door and cloak room. The Arundel then arrived by the front door. Either of 'em could easily get a bit torn off Valerie's blue dress to shove in the car, easily scratch the settee like the heels of the woman scratched the rug when they murdered her. When the one o'clock constable was due Cray barged out and got himself arrested, thus fakin' a perfect alibi for the murder of Mrs Arundel, then alive. After puttin' up a row with Valerie to make more evidence against her, the Arundel went off, dressed herself in dead sister's clothes, removed the rug from the body, proceeded to Killarney and became the sister. She is just like sister – to those who haven't had close ups of both. Cray was sweetly confident Valerie would swear he'd never left the party and Patten would back her through hell. Kindly nature, Cray's. Perfect trust in his friends. Patten took his good night walk with Valerie. They saw the car, knew it was Mrs Arundel's. They looked inside, Patten leavin' his fool prints on the door, and saw a dead woman. I should say he didn't recognise her. Not easy to see in the dark, not nice to investigate that face. They wouldn't think of it being Mrs Arundel as she'd only just left 'em. But there was a very dead woman in her car. Cray had behaved queer at the party, funking Valerie, lurking. They knew he might have slunk out and done the kill. They hated Mrs Arundel, they liked him, they knew she had him on a string. All they cared for was to save him. They left the woman for somebody else to find, and fixed up they'd give Cray his alibi, and Valerie came round bright and early to rub it in on me he was a poor, sick fellow under her eye all the time till arrested. Dear fools, Valerie and her Ned. Made for each other. Must have hit 'em cruel hard when they heard the dead woman was Mrs Arundel. And yet they stuck to their story. Very good effort. Bless 'em. Nice people. Hope you haven't charged 'em, Lomas?' Reggie smiled.

'We have not,' said Lomas with dignity. 'They were let go this morning.'

'Splendid. Not a blot on the official scutcheon. Now. I have my uses, Lomas.'

'Confound your impudence.' Lomas made a grimace. 'How did you know the Arundel woman had a sister?'

'By believin' evidence. Try sometime. I told you the dead woman was in good health, well preserved. Too good, too well for a woman who'd led a nasty life, as alleged of the

Arundel. She shows wear and tear. Dead face so distorted, identification could only be from general likeness, hair, clothes and what not, and the identification was not made by intimates. So I wondered. I sent my chauffeur, Sam, to browse among the children of Carteret Place. Observant animals girl children. They told him Mrs Arundel wasn't always smart, quite shabby when she went on the buses. Some of 'em spotted her the day before descendin' from a Lewisham bus. Not the first time. Sam tried the Lewisham bus conductors, and heard of a lady like the Arundel who got on in those parts and got off at the stop by Carteret Square. Then the local milkman and postman gave him the glad news she was Mrs Jones, of Killarney. Quite the lady, kept herself to herself, most respectable, though only using a charwoman two days a week. Sam called as a tout and looked her over. Me too, from the adjacent aucubas. On which I 'phoned for the higher powers. There you are. All clear, as I said.'

'Is it?' Lomas put up his eyeglass. 'Why did Cray go to her?'

'My dear old thing!' Reggie stared back with large reproachful eyes. 'Use the evidence. Cray told you in his confession. He got a telegram: "Come Killarney." The Arundel had the wind up. Probably failed to like Sam's face. He will grin.'

'Failed to like Cray when he came,' Lomas answered. 'That's what broke her.'

'It could be,' Reggie murmured. 'Don't suppose he was comfortin'.'

'Who sent the telegram?' Lomas demanded.

'Oh my Lomas! Futile question. Answer obvious. Mrs Arundel.'

'She'll deny it.'

Over Reggie's face came a pensive smile. 'She may, yes. Nobody'll believe her.'

'Why should she telegraph? She was on the telephone.'

'Yet she couldn't get Cray? Nor Cray her? Only wrong numbers. Too bad.'

'The line's broken on the wall of the house, Reginald. Who did that?'

'Take the goods the gods provide. Telegram's all right. Pleasin' case.'

# Aces High

## PETER CHEYNEY

*At the end of Wimpole Street, our route takes us across Oxford Street and into the imposing Mayfair landmark, Berkeley Square, where the nightingale was once reputed to have sung and which is now home to some of London's premier gambling clubs. There are quite a number of company offices here, too, and among them is to be found the rather less grandiose suite belonging to Slim Callaghan, described as 'fiction's most ruthless detective'. Callaghan is forty years old, sophisticated and ironic, and very tough. He likes a drink ('three or four fingers of whisky'), often starts the day nursing a hangover, and smokes cigarettes endlessly. He employs a young, attractive secretary, Effie Thompson, who is inclined to be cynical about her boss, and Windermere 'Windy' Nikolls, a Canadian-born assistant, who has an eye for 'the dames' and a wise crack forever ready on his lips. Slim Callaghan operates in and around the clubs of London's West End and is very* au fait *with the tricks of gambling and the traffic in illegal drugs and sex. Some of his cases, which began with* The Urgent Hangman *(1938), were attacked by the critics for their excessive cruelty and violence, but this did nothing to halt Cheyney's huge sales on both sides of the Atlantic. A number of films were also made from the books including* Uneasy Terms *(1948) with Michael Rennie as Callaghan,* Meet Mr Callaghan *(1954) starring Derrick de Marney, and* Diplomatic Courier *in which the American actor Tyrone Power made the detective less of a tough guy and more a handsome charmer.*

*Peter Cheyney (1896–1951) was born in London and became familiar with the West End he was to depict so colourfully when he was still a boy by wandering all over Mayfair and the surrounding districts. Peter actually trained to be a lawyer, but soon grew tired of office routine and after a period of army service and some months as a special constable in Victoria, he opted for the life of a freelance journalist and writer. For a while he even owned and ran a detective agency, Cheyney Research and Investigations which, it is said, provided him with a lot of the raw material for his Slim Callaghan stories. 'Aces High' is typical of Callaghan at work in the surroundings he knows best when he is hired to help an aristocratic gambler who has got into debt and is now being threatened with scandal . . .*

LORD PRIORTON – A perfect replica of the stage nobleman – rose from the desk and advanced to meet Callaghan. His face was long, lean, distinguished; his drooping but well-trimmed grey moustache gave him the appearance, Callaghan thought, of an unhappy seal.

He said: 'Sit down please, Mr Callaghan.' He opened a silver box of cigarettes, handed it to Callaghan. He went on: 'Like most other people of my class, Mr Callaghan, I've very little money. In fact I've nothing except this house, my cottage in the country, and, when I've paid my taxes, a few hundreds a year to live on. But I have one thing – my pride. And I'm afraid it has received a severe shock.'

Callaghan said: 'That's too bad! And you think I can do something to help about it?'

The peer nodded. 'It's not only a matter of pride, but of reputation,' he said, 'and also –' he paused for a second – 'of some money.'

'I see,' said Callaghan. 'Supposing you tell me about it.'

Priorton said: 'As you probably know, Mr Callaghan, I used to be a great gambler. Well, I still gamble a little. From time to time I have a few friends in here, give them dinner and we play cards. Such a party was held here last week.' He sighed. 'Little did I realize when I arranged it,' he went on, 'what the results were to be.'

Callaghan said: 'So the results weren't so good, hey? I suppose you knew the people you were playing cards with?'

Lord Priorton nodded. 'I know them all very well,' he said. 'The party consisted of two men, a woman and myself. We were playing poker. One of the men was a rich American – George Vandeler – who is over here on business; the other man – a young man of thirty – Eustace Willhaven, the eldest son of my old friend Hubert Willhaven; the lady, a charming widow – Mrs Melody Vazeley – is the sister of another good friend of mine, Charles Venning. Last, there was, of course, myself. In other words,' continued the peer gloomily, 'there was no one who is not very well known to me. You understand?'

'I understand perfectly,' said Callaghan. 'Go on, Lord Priorton. And who did what to who?'

The other nodded. He said: 'Exactly! You've put it very succinctly, Mr Callaghan. Who did what to who! To cut a long story short, I was very lucky, and when the settlement came I had won just over three thousand pounds. The upshot of it was that Eustace Willhaven owed me three thousand five hundred – a very nice sum.'

'Did he mind losing the money?' asked Callaghan.

'Good heavens, no,' said Priorton. 'Anyway, he knew his father would pay – his father always does pay. He's a rich man and even if he does keep Eustace short of money he's only too glad to settle his gambling debts when he loses and even more delighted when his son wins.'

Callaghan asked: 'And did Eustace settle?'

'Not then,' said Priorton. 'He said laughingly that he couldn't give me a cheque on his own bank because he'd only a few pounds in his account, but that if I wouldn't mind he would arrange things with his father and send a cheque round to me in the course of the next day. Well . . . he did so.'

'I see. And what happened?' asked Callaghan.

Priorton took a cigarette from the silver box on the table. He lit it. Callaghan noticed that the hand that held the lighter was shaking a little.

Priorton said: 'The cheque was an open cheque. I went round to Eustace's bank to cash it. Well, they wouldn't cash it. They marked it "Orders not to pay" and gave it back to me.'

Callaghan nodded. 'Not so good,' he said. 'So Eustace Willhaven had stopped payment of the cheque. Why?'

Priorton shook his head. 'I don't know,' he said gloomily.

Callaghan asked: 'I suppose Eustace's father – Hubert Willhaven – isn't hard up?'

Priorton smiled. 'Don't worry about that,' he said. 'Willhaven is practically a millionaire. Three thousand five hundred means nothing to him. That's what I can't understand.'

Callaghan said: 'I see. You mean that Eustace must have a really serious reason for stopping payment of this cheque?'

'Precisely,' said Priorton.

Callaghan drew on his cigarette. He said: 'It's odd, isn't it? I suppose Willhaven knew his son had been playing cards here?'

'Good heavens, yes,' said Priorton. 'Young Willhaven plays here at least once a month. Several times his father's been here and played with him, or stood by and watched the game.'

Callaghan said: 'What do you want me to do?'

'First of all,' said the peer. 'I'm fearfully worried about Willhaven having stopped that cheque. Quite obviously, he or his father must *think* they've got a good reason for doing so. They may think that I'm going to tell people that Eustace stopped payment of a cheque for a debt of honour, and he'll naturally want to defend himself against such an accusation. He may say things that will react against my character.

'Secondly, I want the money, Mr Callaghan. Three thousand five hundred pounds is a lot to me.'

Callaghan asked casually: 'Lord Priorton, did it ever occur

to you to ring up Eustace Willhaven and ask him why he'd stopped payment of that cheque?'

Priorton nodded his head. 'It did occur to me,' he said. 'I rang up Eustace, and he said that he was fearfully sorry about it, but that he did it because his father *ordered* him to stop payment – he didn't know why.'

'I see,' said Callaghan. 'You didn't speak to the father?'

'No,' said Priorton. 'I think it's his business to explain his action to *me*.'

Callaghan said: 'You're quite right.' He got up. 'Well, I'll do my best,' he said.

Priorton asked: 'What are you going to do, Mr Callaghan?'

Callaghan grinned. He said: 'Perhaps it would be better if I didn't tell you. What people don't know can't hurt 'em.'

Priorton nodded. He said: 'About your fee. You know I'm pretty hard up.'

Callaghan said: 'I'll take a chance on you, Lord Priorton. I think you've told me the truth. If I get that cheque paid, I'll take the odd five hundred. If I don't, I'll charge you nothing. How's that?'

'Very sportin'!' said the peer.

Callaghan stopped Eustace Willhaven on his way out of the Berkeley Buttery. He said: 'Excuse me, Mr Willhaven, my name's Callaghan. I'm a private detective. I'm trying to clear up a small point that's worrying a client of mine – Lord Priorton. It's about that cheque you gave him in settlement of your gambling losses.'

Eustace Willhaven said: 'Well, really! Do you think this is a good place to discuss it?'

'It's as good as any other, isn't it?' retorted Callaghan. 'Do you know why your father told you to stop that cheque?'

Willhaven adjusted his eyeglass. He looked seriously at Callaghan. He said: 'To tell you the truth, Mr Callaghan, I don't. I don't know why my father told me to stop that cheque. But if you knew anything about my father, you'd know he's not likely to do a thing like that without good reason. Good-day to you!'

Hubert Willhaven – tall, distinguished, ascetic looking – listened attentively to what Callaghan had to say. When the detective had finished talking, Willhaven smoked silently for a few seconds. Then he said: 'What you have to say interests me very much, Mr Callaghan. And I appreciate your explanation as to why Lord Priorton should have employed you to try and settle this matter.' Callaghan said: 'Let's not become confused about the issues at stake, Mr Willhaven. The position, to my mind, is quite simple.'

Willhaven raised his eyebrows. 'Is it?' he queried.

Callaghan said: 'To my mind, yes. A settlement was arrived at when this poker game was over – a general settlement. On this general settlement your son had to pay three thousand five hundred pounds to Lord Priorton. Quite obviously, when he left that house he intended to pay that debt. The proof of that is that he asked you for the money. The fact that *you* thought he owed it is proved by you having given him the money to put into his bank so that he could send a cheque to Lord Priorton.' Callaghan grinned. 'After that, of course,' he said, 'there's a snag.'

Willhaven smiled. He thought that Callaghan's grin was infectious.

'The snag being that I told Eustace to stop the cheque. Perhaps you can tell me something about that too, Mr Callaghan,' he suggested.

Callaghan said: 'I think I can. To my mind there is only one reason why you should have done that. There *could* only be one reason; that is that one of the other people who took part in that game besides Lord Priorton and your son have influenced you to have the payment of that cheque stopped. Lord Priorton *wanted* to receive the money. You *intended* it should be paid. Something made you alter your mind. My guess is, it was one of those two other people, and I'm going to find out. Either you tell me or I'll find some means of making them talk.'

Willhaven said: 'They might not *want* to talk, Mr Callaghan.'

Callaghan said: 'Whenever I want somebody to talk I find a means of making 'em talk.' He grinned. 'You'd be surprised,' he said.

Willhaven said: 'I probably shouldn't be. But I'll save them the inconvenience. You're quite right in your supposition, because one of the other parties who took part in that game gave me some information which merited the payment being stopped.'

Callaghan said: 'One of the other parties? That would be Mr Vandeler or Mrs Vazeley.'

'Exactly,' said Willhaven. 'Mrs Vazeley wrote me a note and informed me that in her opinion the game had been crooked from start to finish.'

Callaghan said: 'Do you know Mrs Vazeley well?'

Willhaven shook his had. 'Not *very* well,' he said. 'I've met her.'

Callaghan nodded. 'You were prepared to accept this accusation from a woman who is merely an acquaintance, against the reputation of a man – Lord Priorton – whom you've known for years?'

Willhaven said: 'The point doesn't arise, Mr Callaghan. She was able to prove what she said!'

Mrs Vazeley was a delightful woman of about thirty-eight. Her clothes were simple but marvellous. She had *chic* and an extraordinary allure. Callaghan thought he could fall for Mrs Vazeley very easily. He said: 'You know, Mrs Vazeley, you're in rather a jam.'

She said airily: 'Am I, Mr Callaghan? How exciting! My life is so uneventful that the idea of being in a jam almost appeals to me. Another thing, I ought to tell you that I'm absolutely *thrilled* at meeting a private detective. Please have a cigarette. And would you like a drink?'

Callaghan said he would. Whilst he was drinking the brandy and soda, she said:

'Do tell me about the jam I'm in. I think I ought to know, don't you?'

Callaghan said: 'You wrote a note to Hubert Willhaven, and you afterwards talked to him, either personally or on the telephone, and told him that the poker game at Lord Priorton's house was crooked. Quite obviously, as Willhaven told his son to stop payment of the cheque after that conversation with you, the suggestion was that Lord Priorton was the crook. Have you ever heard of the law of libel and slander, Mrs Vazeley? If you can't prove that Lord Priorton was responsible for that game being crooked you will be in a jam, and it might cost you a lot of money.'

She said: 'I know. I knew that when I told Mr Willhaven. But what else could I do? You see I *knew* that game was crooked, Mr Callaghan.'

Callaghan said: 'May I know how you knew?'

She said: 'It's fearfully simple. *I* had no reason to complain about the game. I won about fifty pounds. I won fifty pounds from Mr Vandeler, and he settled that in bank-notes before the general settlement was made between the others. So you'll agree that I've no cause for complaint.'

Callaghan said: 'That's agreed. But how can you prove that that game was crooked and that Priorton was responsible?'

She said: 'I'll tell you. I was rather elated at winning fifty pounds, and when the game broke up I left my cigarette case behind. It's rather a valuable case. I'd left it on a little table by the side of my chair whilst I was playing. Next morning I had a very early appointment to leave London for Bangor on a train at seven-twenty, and I thought that on my way to the station I'd call in at Lord Priorton's house – I thought that possibly the servants would be up – and get my cigarette case. When I arrived at the house, the boot-boy let me in. I told him what I wanted and he said he'd go and look for my cigarette case. He seemed a rather stupid boy, so I told him not to bother but to go on with his work and I'd go and get the cigarette case because I knew exactly where it was. So I went up to the room on the first floor where we'd played, and there was my cigarette case. I picked it up. The card table was just as we'd left it the night before with the cards still lying on the table.

'The early morning sunlight was coming through the windows. It reflected on the glazed backs of the cards, and I saw something that gave me rather a shock.'

Callaghan asked: 'What did you see?'

'Every one of those cards was marked,' said Mrs Vazeley. 'They'd been beautifully marked – cleverly marked – with a pin. Once you knew where to look you could see the little tiny pin-points, and if you were dealing you could tell the value of the card by the touch. Needless to say I was shocked. But I wanted to make quite certain. I examined all the cards. They were all marked. I took three or four of them and I showed them to Mr Willhaven when I talked to him about it. If that isn't proof, what is?'

Callaghan said: 'It looks as if there isn't a great deal of argument.' He picked up his hat. 'I'm afraid you won't have to worry about that action for slander.'

She said: 'No, I didn't think I should. Must you be going, Mr Callaghan?

Hubert Willhaven put down his newspaper as Callaghan was shown into the room. He said: 'Good morning, Mr Callaghan. What can I do for you?'

Callaghan lit a cigarette. He said casually: 'I think the easiest thing for you to do, Willhaven, would be to give me a cheque for three thousand five hundred pounds, and we'll call this business quits.'

Willhaven said: 'You're being funny, aren't you? I'm not in a frame of mind for humour this morning.'

Callaghan said: 'I'm not being funny. Just listen to me for a moment. When I'm handling a case I never look for clues. I leave that to the detectives in fiction. Usually I'm only interested in people. If I can find that somebody in a case has done something that seems to me incongruous, I wonder why.' Callaghan grinned. 'It usually gets me somewhere,' he said.

Willhaven said: 'It would have to be a hell of an incongruity to get you three thousand five hundred pounds from me, Callaghan.'

'I'll get it all right,' said Callaghan. 'Because it was a hell of an incongruity. Listen. I wondered why it was that Mrs Vazeley had to telephone *you* and tell *you* that that game was crooked. Why didn't she telephone your son? She knows him. He's a man. He's thirty years of age. The obvious thing for her to have done was to have telephoned to *him*. She didn't do it.'

Willhaven said: 'I don't see the point.'

'Of course you don't,' said Callaghan. 'I'll tell you what the point was. It was necessary for the success of your son's little plot that there should seem to be no connection between Mrs Vazeley and himself. That's why she telephoned you.'

Willhaven said: 'Are you suggesting that this is a put-up job between my son and Mrs Vazeley?'

'I'm not suggesting anything. I'm *telling* you,' said Callaghan. 'Lord Priorton told me that you'd paid your son's gambling debts before. You're a rich man and you aren't going to have people saying that his debts of honour are unpaid. But quite obviously your son is often short of money – you keep him so because of his extravagance – otherwise he wouldn't have to go to you to pay money into his bank in order to give a cheque that would be met for a gambling debt.' He grinned. 'Not only has he been doing it on the people that he and Mrs Vazeley have played cards with, but he's also been doing it on *you.*'

Willhaven said: 'I think you're talking nonsense. I still don't understand what you mean.'

Callaghan said: 'I'll tell you what I mean. Your son and Mrs Vazeley went into that poker game at Lord Priorton's as partners. If they both won, it was going to be all right, but on this occasion Mrs Vazeley won fifty pounds, and your son dropped three thousand five hundred. So Mrs Vazeley leaves her cigarette case behind. The next morning, before anybody's up, she goes round to the house, rings the bell and asks for her cigarette case. She says she knows where she's left it. She probably tells the boot-boy to get on with his business and not bother to take her upstairs. While she was up there she very quickly marked the cards with a pin. That was easy. She's used to doing it, and it would take her five or six minutes. Then she went off, taking four or five of the cards with her. She rang you up. She knew you'd tell your son; that he'd stop the cheque. And she also knew, as *he* knew, that you wouldn't ask him to return the three thousand five hundred pounds. Get it?'

Willhaven said: 'I see. You might be wrong, mightn't you?'

Callaghan said: 'I *might* be. But unfortunately for herself Mrs Vazeley told me that she got up early that morning in order to catch a train for Bangor in North Wales – the seven-twenty. Well, there wasn't a seven-twenty. That substantiates it a little bit, doesn't it?'

Willhaven nodded.

'The other thing is this,' said Callaghan, 'I understand from Lord Priorton that the last person to shuffle and deal the cards was your son. Therefore his thumb-prints should have been superimposed on practically every card in the pack. But that wasn't so. The most recent thumb-prints on every card in the pack were Mrs Vazeley's.' Callaghan grinned. 'I think that clinches it, don't you?' he said.

Willhaven said: 'I'm not going to argue. Anyway, I'll give you the cheque.'

He went to the desk, got his cheque book.

Lord Priorton handed Callaghan a large whisky and soda. He said: 'Very nice work, Mr Callaghan. I shall be delighted to pay you your fee. I congratulate you on your brilliant idea of checking the finger-prints on the back of the cards. I didn't know you had done that. That really was first class.'

Callaghan said: 'You can save your congratulations. I didn't check *any* finger-prints on *any* cards. I had a hunch and I played it.'

# Yellow Iris

## AGATHA CHRISTIE

*Mayfair is also home territory to a detective very different to Slim Callaghan: the short, egocentric, rather effete but nevertheless brilliant former Belgian Sûreté police officer, Hercule Poirot. According to the accounts of his cases, Poirot initially shared a home with his friend and associate, Captain Arthur Hastings, at 14, Farraway Street, but after the Captain's marriage moved to Whitehaven Mansions, a modern block of flats near Park Lane. Here an efficient secretary, Miss Lemon, caters to his mercurial moods and receives his steady stream of clients and visitors – among whom is Mrs Ariadne Oliver, a detective novelist with a habit of stumbling across real-life crimes. Poirot with his egg-shaped head, fastidious tastes in food and clothes – not to mention his waxed and pointed moustache – is famous for his expression about using his 'little grey cells' to solve any problem. To millions of readers he is one of the most celebrated detectives in English crime fiction, though novelist and historian H. R. F. Keating says somewhat tongue-in-cheek that Poirot's taste for a tisane of thick sweet chocolate in preference to a cup of tea 'made him at one bound the detective all Englishmen loved to hate'.*

*Arriving in England in 1914 after the German invasion of his homeland had forced him to flee, Poirot's first case,* The Mysterious Affair at Styles *(1920) made him and his authoress famous. His subsequent appearance in 33 novels and*

*ten collections of short stories guaranteed an enduring fame*
*which was underlined when the cases were later adapted for the*
*stage, cinema and television, starring such distinguished actors as*
*Charles Laughton, Francis L. Sullivan, Tony Randall, Albert*
*Finney, Peter Ustinov, Ian Holm and, arguably the definitive*
*portrayal, by David Suchet in the current LWT series.*

*Dame Agatha Christie (1890—1976) is one of the Queens of*
*Crime Fiction and her books have probably sold more copies*
*than any other author of the twentieth century. Her inspiration*
*for Poirot may well have been Hercules Popeau, a short, vain,*
*but shrewd and intuitive retired French detective living in*
*England who appeared in several novels and short stories writ-*
*ten by Marie Belloc Lowndes prior to 1920. All Agatha*
*admitted was that she had chosen to make Poirot a Belgian*
*after being deeply moved by the plight of some First World War*
*refugees from that country who lived near her home in Torquay.*
*'Yellow Iris', written in the mid-Thirties, is an intriguing Poirot*
*case combining his love of food with solving a seemingly unsolv-*
*able case of poisoning. Agatha Christie also re-wrote the basic*
*idea into one of the most successful of all her novel-length Poirot*
*cases,* Sparkling Cyanide, *published in 1945.*

HERCULE POIROT STRETCHED out his feet towards the electric radiator set in the wall. Its neat arrangement of red-hot
bars pleased his orderly mind.

'A coal fire,' he mused to himself, 'was always shapeless and
haphazard! Never did it achieve the symmetry.'

The telephone bell rang. Poirot rose, glancing at his watch
as he did so. The time was close on half-past eleven. He
wondered who was ringing him up at this hour. It might, of
course, be a wrong number.

'And it might,' he murmured to himself with a whimsical
smile, 'be a millionaire newspaper proprietor, found dead in
the library of his country house, with a spotted orchid
clasped in his left hand and a page torn from a cookery book
pinned to his breast.'

Smiling at the pleasing conceit, he lifted the receiver.

Immediately a voice spoke – a soft husky woman's voice with a kind of desperate urgency about it.

'*Is that M. Hercule Poirot? Is that M. Hercule Poirot?*'

'Hercule Poirot speaks.'

'*M. Poirot – can you come at once – at once – I'm in danger – in great danger – I know it . . .*'

Poirot said sharply,

'Who are you? Where are you speaking from?'

The voice came more faintly but with an even greater urgency.

'*At once . . . it's life or death . . . The Jardin des Cygnes . . . at once . . . table with yellow irises . . .*'

There was a pause – a queer kind of gasp – the line went dead.

Hercule Poirot hung up. His face was puzzled. He murmured between his teeth:

'There is something here very curious.'

In the doorway of the Jardin des Cygnes, fat Luigi hurried forward.

'Buona sera, M. Poirot. You desire a table – yes?'

'No, no, my good Luigi. I seek here for some friends. I will look round – perhaps they are not here yet. Ah, let me see, that table there in the corner with the yellow irises – a little question by the way, if it is not indiscreet. On all the other tables there are tulips – pink tulips – why on that one table do you have yellow iris?'

Luigi shrugged his expressive shoulders.

'A command, Monsieur! A special order! Without doubt, the favourite flowers of one of the ladies. That table, it is the table of Mr Barton Russell – an American – immensely rich.'

'Aha, one must study the whims of the ladies, must one not, Luigi?'

'Monsieur has said it,' said Luigi.

'I see at that table an acquaintance of mine. I must go and speak to him.'

Poirot skirted his way delicately round the dancing floor

on which couples were revolving. The table in question was set for six, but it had at the moment only one occupant, a young man who was thoughtfully, and it seemed pessimistically, drinking champagne.

He was not at all the person that Poirot had expected to see. It seemed impossible to associate the idea of danger or melodrama with any party of which Tony Chapell was a member.

Poirot paused delicately by the table.

'Ah, it is, is it not, my friend Anthony Chapell?'

'By all that's wonderful – Poirot the police hound!' cried the young man. 'Not Anthony, my dear fellow – Tony to friends!'

He drew out a chair.

'Come, sit with me. Let us discourse of crime! Let us go further and drink to crime.' He poured champagne into an empty glass. 'But what are you doing in this haunt of song and dance and merriment, my dear Poirot? We have no bodies here, positively not a single body to offer you.'

Poirot sipped the champagne.

'You seem very gay, *mon cher*?'

'Gay? I am steeped in misery – wallowing in gloom. Tell me, you hear this tune they are playing. You recognize it?'

Poirot hazarded cautiously:

'Something perhaps to do with your baby having left you?'

'Not a bad guess,' said the young man, 'but wrong for once. "There's nothing like love for making you miserable!" That's what it's called.'

'Aha?'

'My favourite tune,' said Tony Chapell mournfully. 'And my favourite restaurant and my favourite band – and my favourite girl's here and she's dancing it with somebody else.'

'Hence the melancholy?' said Poirot.

'Exactly. Pauline and I, you see, have had what the vulgar call words. That is to say, she's had ninety-five words to five of mine out of every hundred. My five are: '*But, darling – I can explain.*' Then she starts in on her ninety-five again and we get no further. I think,' added Tony sadly, 'that I shall poison myself.'

'Pauline?' murmured Poirot.

'Pauline Weatherby. Barton Russell's young sister-in-law. Young, lovely, disgustingly rich. Tonight Barton Russell gives a party. You know him? Big Business, clean-shaven American – full of pep and personality. His wife was Pauline's sister.'

'And who else is there at this party?'

'You'll meet 'em in a minute when the music stops. There's Lola Valdez – you know, the South American dancer in the new show at the Metropole, and there's Stephen Carter. D'you know Carter – he's in the diplomatic service. Very hush-hush. Known as silent Stephen. Sort of man who says, "*I am not at liberty to state, etc., etc.*" Hullo, here they come.'

Poirot rose. He was introduced to Barton Russell, to Stephen Carter, to Señora Lola Valdez, a dark and luscious creature, and to Pauline Weatherby, very young, very fair, with eyes like cornflowers.

Barton Russell said:

'What, is this the great M. Hercule Poirot? I am indeed pleased to meet you, sir. Won't you sit down and join us? That is, unless—'

Tony Chapell broke in.

'He's got an appointment with a body, I believe, or is it an absconding financier, or the Rajah of Borrioboolagah's great ruby?'

'Ah, my friend, do you think I am never off duty? Can I not, for once, seek only to amuse myself?'

'Perhaps you've got an appointment with Carter here. The latest from Geneva. International situation now acute. The stolen plans *must* be found or war will be declared tomorrow!'

Pauline Weatherby said cuttingly:

'Must you be so *completely* idiotic, Tony?'

'Sorry, Pauline.'

Tony Chapell relapsed into crestfallen silence.

'How severe you are, Mademoiselle.'

'I hate people who play the fool all the time!'

'I must be careful, I see. I must converse only of serious matters.'

'Oh, no, M. Poirot. I didn't mean you.'

She turned a smiling face to him and asked:

'Are you really a kind of Sherlock Holmes and do wonderful deductions?'

'Ah, the deductions – they are not so easy in real life. But shall I try? Now then, I deduce – that yellow irises are your favourite flowers?'

'Quite wrong, M. Poirot. Lilies of the valley or roses.'

Poirot sighed.

'A failure. I will try once more. This evening, not very long ago, you telephoned to someone.'

Pauline laughed and clapped her hands.

'Quite right.'

'It was not long after you arrived here?'

'Right again. I telephoned the minute I got inside the doors.'

'Ah – that is not so good. You telephoned *before* you came to this table?'

'Yes.'

'Decidedly very bad.'

'Oh, no, I think it was very clever of you. How did you know I had telephoned?'

'That, Mademoiselle, is the great detective's secret. And the person to whom you telephoned – does the name begin with a P – or perhaps with an H?'

Pauline laughed.

'Quite wrong. I telephoned to my maid to post some frightfully important letters that I'd never sent off. Her name's Louise.'

'I am confused – quite confused.'

The music began again.

'What about it, Pauline?' asked Tony.

'I don't think I want to dance again so soon, Tony.'

'Isn't that too bad?' said Tony bitterly to the world at large.

Poirot murmured to the South American girl on his other side:

'Señora, I would not dare to ask you to dance with me. I am too much of the antique.'

Lola Valdez said:

'Ah, it ees nonsense that you talk there! You are steel young. Your hair, eet is still black!'

Poirot winced slightly.

'Pauline, as your brother-in-law and your guardian,' Barton Russell spoke heavily, 'I'm just going to force you on to the floor! This one's a waltz and a waltz is about the only dance I really can do.'

'Why, of course, Barton, we'll take the floor right away.'

'Good girl, Pauline, that's swell of you.'

They went off together. Tony tipped back his chair. Then he looked at Stephen Carter.

'Talkative little fellow, aren't you, Carter?' he remarked. 'Help to make a party go with your merry chatter, eh, what?'

'Really, Chapell, I don't know what you mean?'

'Oh, you don't – don't you?' Tony mimicked him.

'My dear fellow.'

'Drink, man, drink, if you won't talk.'

'No, thanks.'

'Then I will.'

Stephen Carter shrugged his shoulders.

'Excuse me, must just speak to a fellow I know over there. Fellow I was with at Eton.'

Stephen Carter got up and walked to a table a few places away.

Tony said gloomily:

'Somebody ought to drown old Etonians at birth.'

Hercule Poirot was still being gallant to the dark beauty beside him.

He murmured:

'I wonder, may I ask, what are the favourite flowers of Mademoiselle?'

'Ah, now, why ees eet you want to know?'

Lola was arch.

'Mademoiselle, if I send flowers to a lady, I am particular that they should be flowers she likes.'

'That ees very charming of you, M. Poirot. I weel tell you – I adore the big dark red carnations – or the dark red roses.'

'Superb – yes, superb! You do not, then, like yellow flowers – yellow irises?'

'Yellow flowers – no – they do not accord with my temperament.'

'How wise . . . Tell me, Mademoiselle, did you ring up a friend tonight, since you arrived here?'

'I? Ring up a friend? No, what a curious question!'

'Ah, but I, I am a very curious man.'

'I'm sure you are.' She rolled her dark eyes at him. 'A vairy *dan*gerous man.'

'No, no, not dangerous; say, a man who may be useful – in danger! You understand?'

Lola giggled. She showed white even teeth.

'No, no,' she laughed. 'You are dangerous.'

Hercule Poirot sighed.

'I see that you do not understand. All this is very strange.'

Tony came out of a fit of abstraction and said suddenly:

'Lola, what about a spot of swoop and dip? Come along.'

'I weel come – yes. Since M. Poirot ees not brave enough!'

Tony put an arm round her and remarked over his shoulder to Poirot as they glided off:

'You can meditate on crime yet to come, old boy!'

Poirot said: 'It is profound what you say there. Yes, it is profound . . .'

He sat meditatively for a minute or two, then he raised a finger. Luigi came promptly, his wide Italian face wreathed in smiles.

'*Mon vieux*,' said Poirot. 'I need some information.'

'Always at your service, Monsieur.'

'I desire to know how many of these people at this table here have used the telephone tonight?'

'I can tell you, Monsieur. The young lady, the one in white, she telephoned at once when she got here. Then she went to leave her cloak and while she was doing that the other lady came out of the cloakroom and went into the telephone box.'

'So the Señora *did* telephone! Was that *before* she came into the restaurant?'

'Yes, Monsieur.'

'Anyone else?'

'No, Monsieur.'

'All this, Luigi, gives me furiously to think!'

'Indeed, Monsieur.'

'Yes. I think, Luigi, that *tonight of all nights*, I must have my wits about me! *Something* is going to happen, Luigi, and I am not at all sure what it is.'

'Anything I can do, Monsieur—'

Poirot made a sign. Luigi slipped discreetly away. Stephen Carter was returning to the table.

'We are still deserted, Mr Carter,' said Poirot.

'Oh – er – quite,' said the other.

'You know Mr Barton Russell well?'

'Yes, known him a good while.'

'His sister-in-law, little Miss Weatherby, is very charming.'

'Yes, pretty girl.'

'You know her well, too?'

'Quite.'

'Oh, quite, quite,' said Poirot.

Carter stared at him.

The music stopped and the others returned.

Barton Russell said to a waiter:

'Another bottle of champagne – quickly.'

Then he raised his glass.

'See here, folks. I'm going to ask you to drink a toast. To tell you the truth, there's an idea back of this little party tonight. As you know, I'd ordered a table for six. There were only five of us. That gave us an empty place. Then, by a very strange coincidence, M. Hercule Poirot happened to pass by and I asked him to join our party.

'You don't know yet what an apt coincidence that was. You see that empty seat tonight represents a lady – the lady in whose memory this party is being given. This party, ladies and gentlemen, is being held in memory of my dear wife – Iris – who died exactly four years ago on this very date!'

There was a startled movement round the table. Barton Russell, his face quietly impassive, raised his glass.

'I'll ask you to drink to her memory. *Iris!*'

'Iris?' said Poirot sharply.

He looked at the flowers. Barton Russell caught his glance and gently nodded his head.

There were little murmurs round the table.

'Iris – Iris . . .'

Everyone looked startled and uncomfortable.

Barton Russell went on, speaking with his slow monotonous American intonation, each word coming out weightily.

'It may seem odd to you all that I should celebrate the anniversary of a death in this way – by a supper party in a fashionable restaurant. But I have a reason – yes, I have a reason. For M. Poirot's benefit, I'll explain.'

He turned his head towards Poirot.

'Four years ago tonight, M. Poirot, there was a supper party held in New York. At it were my wife and myself, Mr Stephen Carter who was attached to the Embassy in Washington, Mr Anthony Chapell who had been a guest in our house for some weeks, and Señora Valdez who was at that time enchanting New York City with her dancing. Little Pauline here' – he patted her shoulder – 'was only sixteen but she came to the supper party as a special treat. You remember, Pauline?'

'I remember – yes.' Her voice shook a little.

'M. Poirot, on that night a tragedy happened. There was a roll of drums and the cabaret started. The lights went down – all but a spotlight in the middle of the floor. When the lights went up again, M. Poirot, my wife was seen to have fallen forward on the table. She was dead – stone dead. There was potassium cyanide found in the dregs of her wine-glass, and the remains of the packet was discovered in her handbag.'

'She had committed suicide?' said Poirot.

'That was the accepted verdict . . . It broke me up, M. Poirot. There was, perhaps, a possible reason for such an action – the police thought so. I accepted their decision.'

He pounded suddenly on the table.

'But I was not satisfied . . . No, for four years I've been thinking and brooding – and I'm not satisfied: I don't believe Iris killed herself. I believe, M. Poirot, that she was murdered – by one of those people at the table.'

'Look here, sir—'

Tony Chapell half sprung to his feet.

'Be quiet, Tony,' said Russell. 'I haven't finished. One of them did it – I'm sure of that now. Someone who, under cover of the darkness, slipped the half emptied packet of cyanide into her handbag. I think I know which of them it was. I mean to know the truth—'

Lola's voice rose sharply.

'You are mad – crazee – who would have harmed her? No, you are mad. Me, I will not stay—'

She broke off. There was a roll of drums.

Barton Russell said:

'The cabaret. Afterwards we will go on with this. Stay where you are, all of you. I've got to go and speak to the dance band. Little arrangement I've made with them.'

He got up and left the table.

'Extraordinary business,' commented Carter. 'Man's mad.'

'He ees crazee, yes,' said Lola.

The lights were lowered.

'For two pins I'd clear out,' said Tony.

'No!' Pauline spoke sharply. Then she murmured, 'Oh, dear – oh, dear—'

'What is it, Mademoiselle?' murmured Poirot.

She answered almost in a whisper. 'It's horrible! It's just like it was that night—'

'Sh! Sh!' said several people.

Poirot lowered his voice.

'A little word in your ear.' He whispered, then patted her shoulder. 'All will be well,' he assured her.

'My God, listen,' cried Lola.

'What is it, Señora?'

'*It's the same tune* – the same song that they played that night in New York. Barton Russell must have fixed it. I don't like this.'

'Courage – courage—'

There was a fresh hush.

A girl walked out into the middle of the floor, a coal black girl with rolling eyeballs and white glistening teeth. She began to sing in a deep hoarse voice – a voice that was curiously moving.

I've forgotten you
I never think of you
The way you walked
The way you talked
The things you used to say
I've forgotten you
I never think of you
I couldn't say
For sure today
Whether your eyes were blue or grey
I've forgotten you
I never think of you.

I'm through
Thinking of you
I tell you I'm through
Thinking of you . . .
You . . . you . . . you . . .

The sobbing tune, the deep golden negro voice had a powerful effect. It hypnotized – cast a spell. Even the waiters felt it. The whole room stared at her, hypnotized by the thick cloying emotion she distilled.

A waiter passed softly round the table filling up glasses, murmuring 'champagne' in an undertone but all attention was on the one glowing spot of light – the black woman whose ancestors came from Africa, singing in her deep voice:

I've forgotten you
I never think of you
Oh, what a lie
I shall think of you, think of you, think of you

Till I die . . .

The applause broke out frenziedly. The lights went up. Barton Russell came back and slipped into his seat.

'She's great, that girl—' cried Tony.

But his words were cut short by a low cry from Lola.

'*Look – look . . .*'

And then they all saw. Pauline Weatherby dropped forward on to the table.

Lola cried:

'She's dead – just like Iris – like Iris in New York.'

Poirot sprang from his seat, signing to the others to keep back. He bent over the huddled form, very gently lifted a limp hand and felt for a pulse.

His face was white and stern. The others watched him. They were paralyzed, held in a trance.

Slowly, Poirot nodded his head.

'Yes, she is dead – *la pauvre petite*. And I sitting by her! Ah! but this time the murderer shall not escape.'

Barton Russell, his face grey, muttered:

'Just like Iris . . . She saw something – Pauline saw something that night – Only she wasn't sure – she told me she wasn't sure . . . We must get the police . . . Oh, God, little Pauline.'

Poirot said:

'Where is her glass?' He raised it to his nose. 'Yes, I can smell the cyanide. A smell of bitter almonds . . . the same method, the same poison . . .'

He picked up her handbag.

'Let us look in her handbag.'

Barton Russell cried out:

'You don't believe this is suicide, too? Not on your life.'

'Wait,' Poirot commanded. 'No, there is nothing here. The lights went up, you see, too quickly, the murderer had not time. Therefore, the poison is still on him.'

'Or her,' said Carter.

He was looking at Lola Valdez.

She spat out:

'What do you mean – what do you say? That I killed her – eet is not true – not true – why should I do such a thing!'

'You had rather a fancy for Barton Russell yourself in New York. That's the gossip I heard. Argentine beauties are notoriously jealous.'

'That ees a pack of lies. And I do not come from the Argentine. I come from Peru. Ah – I spit upon you. I—' She relapsed into Spanish.

'I demand silence,' cried Poirot. 'It is for me to speak.'

Barton Russell said heavily:

'Everyone must be searched.'

Poirot said calmly:

'*Non, non,* it is not necessary.'

'What d'you mean, not necessary?'

'I, Hercule Poirot, know. I see with the eyes of the mind. And I will speak! M. Carter, *will you show us the packet in your breast pocket?*'

'There's nothing in my pocket. What the hell—'

'Tony, my good friend, if you will be so obliging.'

Carter cried out:

'Damn you—'

Tony flipped the packet neatly out before Carter could defend himself.

'There you are, M. Poirot, just as you said!'

'It's a damned lie,' cried Carter.

Poirot picked up the packet, read the label.

'Cyanide of potassium. The case is complete.'

Barton Russell's voice came thickly.

'Carter! I always thought so. Iris was in love with you. She wanted to go away with you. You didn't want a scandal for the sake of your precious career so you poisoned her. You'll hang for this, you dirty dog.'

'Silence!' Poirot's voice rang out, firm and authoritative. 'This is not finished yet. I, Hercule Poirot, have something to say. My friend here, Tony Chapell, he says to me when I arrive, that I have come in search of crime. That, it is partly true. There *was* crime in my mind – but it was to prevent a crime that I came. And I have prevented it. The murderer, he planned well – but Hercule Poirot he was one move ahead. He had to think fast, and to whisper quickly in Mademoiselle's ear when the lights went down. She is very quick and clever, Mademoiselle Pauline, she played her part well. Mademoiselle, will you be so kind as to show us that you are not dead after all?'

Pauline sat up. She gave an unsteady laugh.

'Resurrection of Pauline,' she said.

'Pauline – darling.'

'Tony!'

'My sweet.'

'Angel.'

Barton Russell gasped.

'I – I don't understand . . .'

'I will help you to understand, Mr Barton Russell. Your plan has miscarried.'

'My plan?'

'Yes, your plan. Who was the only man who had an *alibi* during the darkness. The man who left the table – you, Mr Barton Russell. But you returned to it under cover of the darkness, circling round it, with a champagne bottle, filling up glasses, putting cyanide in Pauline's glass and dropping the half empty packet in Carter's pocket as you bent over him to remove a glass. Oh, yes, it is easy to play the part of a waiter in darkness when the attention of everyone is elsewhere. That was the real reason for your party tonight. The safest place to commit a murder is in the middle of a crowd.'

'What the – why the hell should I want to kill Pauline?'

'It might be, perhaps, a question of money. Your wife left you guardian to her sister. You mentioned that fact tonight. Pauline is twenty. At twenty-one or on her marriage you would have to render an account of your stewardship. I suggest that you could not do that. You have speculated with it. I do not know, Mr Barton Russell, whether you killed your wife in the same way, or whether her suicide suggested the idea of this crime to you, but I do know that tonight you have been guilty of attempted murder. It rests with Miss Pauline whether you are prosecuted for that.'

'No,' said Pauline. 'He can get out of my sight and out of this country. I don't want a scandal.'

'You had better go quickly, Mr Barton Russell, and I advise you to be careful in future.'

Barton Russell got up, his face working.

'To hell with you, you interfering little Belgian jackanapes.'

He strode out angrily.

Pauline sighed.

'M. Poirot, you've been wonderful . . .'

'You, Mademoiselle, you have been the marvellous one. To pour away the champagne, to act the dead body so prettily.'

'Ugh,' she shivered, 'you give me the creeps.'

He said gently:

'It was you who telephoned me, was it not?'

'Yes.'

'Why?'

'I don't know. I was worried and – frightened without knowing quite why I was frightened. Barton told me he was having this party to commemorate Iris' death. I realized he had some scheme on – but he wouldn't tell me what it was. He looked so – so queer and so excited that I felt something terrible might happen – only of course I never dreamed that he meant to – to get rid of *me*.'

'And so, Mademoiselle?'

'I'd heard people talking about you. I thought if I could only get you here perhaps it would stop anything happening. I thought that being a – a foreigner – if I rang up and pretended to be in danger and – and made it sound mysterious—'

'You thought the melodrama, it would attract me? That is what puzzled me. The message itself – definitely it was what you call 'bogus' – it did not ring true. But the fear in the voice – that was real. Then I came – and you denied very categorically having sent me a message.'

'I had to. Besides, I didn't want you to know it was me.'

'Ah, but I was fairly sure of that! Not at first. But I soon realized that the only two people who could know about the yellow irises on the table were you or Mr Barton Russell.'

Pauline nodded.

'I heard him ordering them to be put on the table,' she explained. 'That, and his ordering a table for six when I knew only five were coming, made me suspect—'

She stopped, biting her lip.

'What did you suspect, Mademoiselle?'

She said slowly:

'I was afraid – of something happening – to Mr Carter.'

Stephen Carter cleared his throat. Unhurriedly but quite decisively he rose from the table.

'Er – h'm – I have to – er – thank you, Mr Poirot. I owe you a great deal. You'll excuse me, I'm sure, if I leave you. Tonight's happenings have been rather upsetting.'

Looking after his retreating figure, Pauline said violently:

'I hate him. I've always thought it was – because of him that Iris killed herself. Or perhaps – Barton killed her. Oh, it's all so hateful . . .'

Poirot said gently:

'Forget, Mademoiselle . . . forget . . . Let the past go . . . Think only of the present . . .'

Pauline murmured, 'Yes – you're right . . .'

Poirot turned to Lola Valdez.

'Señora, as the evening advances I become more brave. If you would dance with me now—'

'Oh, yes, indeed. You are! – you are ze cat's whiskers, M. Poirot. I inseest on dancing with you.'

'You are too kind, Señora.'

Tony and Pauline were left. They leant towards each other across the table.

'Darling Pauline.'

'Oh, Tony, I've been such a nasty spiteful spitfiring little cat to you all day. Can you ever forgive me?'

'Angel! This is Our Tune again. Let's dance.'

They danced off, smiling at each other and humming softly:

There's nothing like Love for making you miserable
There's nothing like Love for making you blue
Depressed
Possessed
Sentimental
Temperamental
There's nothing like Love
For getting you down.

There's nothing like Love for driving you crazy
There's nothing like Love for making you mad
Abusive
Allusive
Suicidal
Homicidal
There's nothing like Love
There's nothing like Love . . .

# Trent and the Fool-proof Lift

## E. C. BENTLEY

*Walking all the way down Park Lane, along Knightsbridge, and down Sloane Street brings us to Cadogan Place, the home of journalist, artist and amateur detective Philip Trent whom H. R. F. Keating has referred to as 'the first of the ungreat detectives – the human ones'. The first appearance of the detective was, curiously, in* Trent's Last Case, *published in 1913, but the book which was evidently a satire on detective fiction in general was such a success that the public were soon demanding more cases about the friendly, tactful and quietly humorous man of many talents. Trent is a tall, gangly figure, concerned and fallible, but respected both for his artistic talents and his skill as a journalist, and more often than not he is sent to investigate a case by his Fleet Street employers, the* Record. *Similarly, stories about him have also become widely admired – the critic Charles Shibuk called* Trent's Last Case, *'one of the ten best mystery novels of all time', while Dorothy L. Sayers admitted that her detective, Lord Peter Wimsey, owed a number of his characteristics and attitudes towards crime to Trent.*

*Edmund Clerihew Bentley (1875–1956) was born in Shepherd's Bush, and qualified as a lawyer, but instead chose to work as a journalist on the* Daily Telegraph, *where he remained for over twenty years. Bentley confessed that he set out quite deliberately to write his first book as an exposure of what he saw as the 'sterility and artificiality of the contemporary detective story'. Initially he could find no one willing to publish his manuscript – his original title,* Philip Gasket's Last Case *may well not have enhanced his chances! – and it took the instincts of an American editor who happened to be visiting London to suggest that a new name for the sleuth and a new title for the book might make all the difference. It did.* The New York Times *at once called the story, 'one of the few classics of detective fiction', and its later success caused another critic, John Carter, to hail Bentley as 'the father of the contemporary detective story'. In the years which followed it was also filmed no less than three times: in 1920 starring Gregory Scott as Trent; then with Raymond Griffith in 1929 and once more in 1953 with Michael Wilding as a rather more attractive sleuth than his predecessors. In the following story, all three elements of Trent's persona are featured – the artist, the reporter and the curious amateur detective – as he endeavours to solve a particularly baffling crime in a most unusual location.*

ONE OF THE commonest forms of fatal accident in the life of the town is falling down a lift shaft. Every coroner of large urban experience has dealt with cases by the score, whether due to short-sight, negligence, faulty construction, or defective safety mechanism. And there is another possibility.

One perfect day in June M. Armand Binet-Gailly, who held an important agency in the wine trade, left his office in Jermyn Street rather earlier than usual, and strolled homewards through the Parks to his bachelor flat at 42 Rigby Street. This was a tall old house, 'converted' from the errors of its pre-Victorian youth. There were five flats, and M. Binet-Gailly's was the second above the ground level. About 5.30 – so went his statement to the police – he entered by the front door which always stood open during the daytime, and went to the lift at the end of the hall. The lift was not at the ground floor, as he could see through the lattice gate, and he pressed the button which should bring it down. But nothing happened.

M. Binet-Gailly was very much annoyed. A portly man,

he did not relish the prospect of climbing two flights of stairs on a warm day when he had paid for lift service. He aimlessly seized and shook the handle of the lattice gate. To his amazement, the gate slid aside as if the lift were in place. It should, of course, have been impossible to move it unless the lift were there. The whole system was out of order, he thought. He put his head into the shaft and looked upwards. There was the lift, so far as he could judge, at the top floor. Then, as he drew back his head, his eye was caught by something at the bottom of the shallow well in which the lift-shaft ended. There was a strong electric ceiling lamp always alight at this dark end of the hall, and it showed M. Binet-Gailly quite enough.

Like most of his countrymen, he had served in arms, and things of this kind did not upset him. Plump though he was, he began to clamber down into the well; then he bethought himself. Certainly there could be no life in that crumpled bundle of humanity. The thing to do was to leave it untouched until the arrival of the police. M. Binet-Gailly went to the door communicating with the basement and bellowed downstairs for Pimblett, the caretaker. 42 Rigby Street, though distant by little more than the breadth of Oxford Street from the elegance of Mayfair, did not rise to the luxury of a uniformed porter, and neither Pimblett nor his wife was usually to be seen after the morning job of cleaning the hall and staircase was done.

Pimblett, who also had served in arms, and had seen more dirty work than had M. Binet-Gailly, took in the situation at a glance. Wasting no words, he strode to the hall telephone and rang up the police station. Both men then mounted the stairs to find which gate it was through which the unknown – for the face of the corpse could not be seen – had plunged to his death. On the floor immediately above M. Binet-Gailly's they found the gate drawn back. On this floor was the flat occupied by Mr Anthony Villiers Maxwell – a young man of sporting tastes – and his valet. M. Binet-Gailly proposed ringing the bell of the flat to make inquiries, but

Pimblett remarked that the police would prefer to have all that left to them.

An hour later M. Binet-Gailly, sipping a glass of Campari in his own rooms, discussed with his servant, by name Aristide, what he had just learnt of this mysterious affair. The dead man had turned out to be his own landlord, Mr Stephen Havelock Hermon, who had bought the house a few years before, and had installed his nephew, Anthony Maxwell, in the flat above-stairs on its falling vacant soon afterwards. There had been some slight lack of sympathy between M. Binet-Gailly and Mr Hermon, owing to the fact that Mr Hermon had among his eccentricities a passionate hatred of liquor in every form, and when he purchased the place had not concealed his chagrin on finding that one of the sitting tenants was engaged in the wine trade, which Mr Hermon preferred to call the drink-traffic.

No one in the building had seen Mr Hermon enter it that afternoon. No one had seen him at all before the finding of his body. No one had known of his intention to come to the house. Mr Clayton Haggett, the famous surgeon, who had the top flat, had not been at home; his housekeeper had heard no ring. Anthony Maxwell also had been out, and his valet had had the afternoon 'off'. Aristide could vouch for it, as he had already informed the police that no one had called at M. Binet-Gailly's. Mr Lucian Corderoy, the eminent dress designer, and his wife had both been at his shop in Malyon Street, and their 'daily' servant was never in the place after twelve noon. As for Sir George Stower, the Keeper of Phoenician Antiquities at the British Museum, he was enjoying a hard-earned holiday at Margate, and his flat on the ground floor had been shut up for some days past.

'But naturally,' remarked Aristide, fingering a swarthy chin, 'the old gentleman wished to call upon his nephew.'

'It is very probable,' M. Binet-Gailly agreed. 'He was devoted to that young animal, and they say he had no other relative living. The nephew will be his heir, no doubt, and he will make the money roll a little faster than the uncle ever did.'

'Ah! when one is young,' observed Aristide sentimentally.

'And when one is a waster by nature,' M. Binet-Gailly added. 'Well, Aristide, it is time for me to dress.'

Philip Trent, in his first outline of the case for the readers of the *Record*, had given these facts about the other tenants of the building. 'It is naturally assumed [he wrote] that Mr Hermon had called, as he often did, to see his nephew, to whom he is said to have been much attached. His ringing at the door had been resultless, and he had turned away to go down by the way he had come. He had opened the gate, believing the lift to be in position there – and stepped out into emptiness. He was known to be extremely short-sighted. His neck, so says the police surgeon, was broken, and there were other injuries that must have been immediately fatal. When his body was found he had been dead not more than an hour.

'This is very simple, but it leaves all the important questions unanswered.

'Why was not the lift where he expected it to be? He had only just left it; and according to the information gathered by the police there had been no one leaving or entering any of the flats since the early afternoon, when Mr Clayton Haggett and Mr Maxwell went out.

'Why was it at the top floor?

'How was it that he had been able to open the gate, which should have been locked automatically the moment the lift moved from that floor?

'Why was the gate on the ground floor unlocked? Why indeed? Conceivably the mechanism of the upstairs gate had gone wrong, so that Mr Hermon could open it; but the gate at the bottom could not be opened by a dead man.

'Why were all the other gates in working order – the top gate, where the lift was, unlocked; the other two locked?

'On this very vital point I have had some conversation with the expert who was sent to investigate by the firm which built and installed the lift. The mechanism, he told me, was tested by the makers at monthly intervals, and had been in perfect order at the last examination, ten days before. The system was as nearly fool-proof as it could be. "But," he added, "it isn't tool-proof. Any engineer could see with half an eye that both those locks had been forced."

'Here are the elements of a very sinister mystery. Some one who was not Mr Hermon forced the ground-floor gate. Presumably he forced the other. The only persons known to have been in the house from three o'clock onwards were the caretaker in the basement, the French manservant in M. Binet-Gailly's flat, and the housekeeper in Mr Haggett's. Did some one enter the house before Mr Hermon; or did some one accompany him? To this point the inquiries of the police are being directed – so far, I believe, without result.

'If Mr Hermon was a victim of violence, it is hard to think that any feeling of ill-will could have been at work. It is true that he was a man of strong opinions, often violently expressed in public controversy – the hard knocks exchanged between him and his tenant, Mr Clayton Haggett, in their dispute over vivisection last year will be remembered. But he was always a fair and even a chivalrous fighter, on the friend-liest footing with opponents to whom he was personally known. His nature was kindly and generous, his great wealth was largely devoted to works of benevolence; the hospital endowments made by him as memorials to his late wife are but a part of his service to humanity.'

Trent did not try to intrude on the sorrow of Anthony Maxwell, but he had from the young man's valet, Joseph Weaver, some material information. He learnt that the nephew felt his loss very deeply indeed; that he did not look like the same man. He had, Weaver said, a feeling heart. A little wild he might have been – young gentlemen would be young gentlemen – but he had what they call a nice nature. He owed everything to Mr Hermon, who had been a father to him after his parents died when he was a child. Naturally he was very much upset.

Trent reflected privately on the deceitfulness of appearances; for he knew Anthony Maxwell by sight, and would
not have said that either his eye, his mouth, or his bearing
proclaimed the niceness of his nature. Perhaps Weaver was
being loyal to his employer. He did not look particularly
loyal; but then he did not look anything to speak of. He had
the expressionlessness of his calling. His quiet voice, neat
clothes, and sleek black hair suggested nothing but discretion. Trent asked a question.

Mr Hermon, Weaver said, came up fairly often on business from his place in Surrey, and when he did so, always
visited his nephew. Sometimes he came on purpose to see
him. No; Mr Maxwell had not been expecting him on the
day of the accident; he had given no notice that he was coming. If he had done so, Mr Maxwell would naturally have
been at home. Weaver thought it unlikely that Mr Hermon
had been intending to call on any of the other tenants. He
did do so from time to time, to talk about some matters of
repairs or other landlord's business; but that would always be
by appointment, and not during the working day. All the
tenants, Weaver pointed out, were busy men, with the exception of Mr Maxwell; they would seldom be at home until the
evening.

Yes; Mr Hermon attended personally to the management
of all his house property in the West End. There was a good
deal of it, and it gave him occupation. No; he was not what
they call a hard landlord; quite the contrary, Weaver would
say. Mr Hermon liked to do things for people, being a very
generous man, as Weaver had good reason to know.

'You mean that he was generous to you,' Trent suggested.
'A present for you when he called here – that sort of thing?'

'Mr Hermon always behaved like a gentleman,' Weaver
said demurely. 'But I meant more than that, sir. You see, I
was two years in his service before I came to Mr Maxwell;
that is how I came to know so much about his habits, and to
appreciate his kindness. Then when Mr Hermon went on a
tour round the world, he suggested I should go to Mr

Maxwell, who was not satisfied with the valet he had then; and I have remained in his service since then – about nine months ago it would be.

When Trent went to talk it over with his friend Chief-Inspector Bligh, he found that officer cheerfully interested in what he described as a very nice case.

'There's nothing easy,' he said, 'about it so far. Of course, it's a murder – that's certain. You have heard what the lift company's man says. And, of course, it was meant to look as if it might be an accident.'

'Then how about the ground-floor gate being forced as well as the other? That doesn't look like an accident.'

'Well, what does it look like?' Mr Bligh wanted to know.

'It looks to me as it looks to you, I suppose. When the old man had been pushed into the lift-shaft, the murderer realized that something had gone wrong with his plan. Hermon had had something on him that might give the murderer away if it was found on the body. The only thing for him to do was to run downstairs, prise open the bottom gate, and take what he wanted off the body. If Pimblett or anybody appeared while he was doing so, he could say he had seen the old man open the gate and fall down the shaft, and had rushed down and forced the gate to see if he was still alive.'

The inspector nodded. 'Yes; that's the idea. And he did get what he wanted, presumably; and nobody did see him. Of course, it's the sort of place where nobody is about most of the time, and the man who did the job knew that.'

'Well, how about the people who live here? Are they all above suspicion?'

'There is no such thing,' Mr Bligh declared, 'as being above suspicion – not if I do the suspecting. And it just happens that most of them haven't an alibi. The Museum man has, of course; his flat was shut up, and is still. And the Corderoys were at their dress shop till after six. But the Frenchman was alone when he came in and reported having found the body; and his story of how he found it, and what time he entered the house, is quite unsupported. Maxwell says he lunched at his flat, went out immediately afterwards, and spent all the afternoon at Lord's watching Lancashire take a licking from Middlesex; then went to his club with some other bright boys, had drinks, and came home to dress for dinner. But Lord's is a place you can dodge out of and return to later, and it's no distance for a car to Rigby Street. Then there's Clayton Haggett, the surgeon. He had lunch in his flat too, after a morning at the hospital; went down to his car at two-thirty, had an operation at a nursing-home and another at a private house; finished by four-fifteen, had a cup of tea, and then spent two hours driving about down Richmond way – just to take the air, and nobody with him all that time, which is a pity.'

'He didn't like Hermon,' Trent remarked. 'He was very bitter in that tussle they had over vivisection.'

'Yes, and he's got a naughty temper when he's crossed. Loses his self-control. He had to resign from the Hunter Club for knocking a man down in the smoking-room. Nobody would have anything to do with him if he wasn't such a wizard with the knife.'

'And what about the servants in the building? Do they come into the picture at all?'

'All I can tell you is that none of their stories can be checked. Pimblett says he was in the basement all the afternoon until the Frenchman shouted for him; his wife was away calling on her sister in Highbury. The French manservant and Haggett's housekeeper say they never opened the doors of their flats until the police looked them up after the finding of the body. Maxwell's man says he had the afternoon off, went out after his master had gone, and sat through the cinema programme at the Byzantine, getting back a little before Anthony did. Well, what good's that? Like the other three, he can't prove anything at all about where he was for some hours before the police were called in.'

'Any of them ever been in trouble?'

'Nothing known against any of them. Ex-Sergeant

Pimblett – excellent record. Mrs Hargreaves, the house-keeper – ditto. Weaver used to be employed at Harding's the big barber shop in Duke Street, where old Hermon used to go when he was in town. He always had Weaver to attend to him, and at last he took him on as his valet. Afterwards—'

'Yes, he told me; he was switched on to Anthony. Perfectly respectable. And the French domestic?'

'All I know about Aristide Recot is that he has a wooden face and side-whiskers, and doesn't mind being seen in an apron. What I'm told by his master is that he has been with him for some years, and given every satisfaction. But what's the use? We had to consider the servants, of course; but what motive could any of them have had? It's a different thing when you come to their employers. Haggett, for instance.'

Trent looked the inspector in the eyes. 'You were talking about motive,' he said gently. 'Is Haggett's resentment really the strongest you can think of? I don't like being teased.'

'All right; I was coming to it,' Mr Bligh responded with a faint grin. 'Yes, I suppose the expectation of coming into the greater part of a very large fortune might operate as a motive. That is what Maxwell will do, according to our information. Unless something happens to him. His uncle made him a very generous allowance, and he lived rent free, and Weaver's wages were paid by the old man. Maxwell ought to have been grateful, and perhaps he was; but there you are – he's a vicious young brute, and always in debt; and though Hermon wasn't strong, he might have lived to any old age. Now then! Will that do for you?'

'Something of the sort had crossed my mind,' Trent admitted. 'Certainly it will do – until something better comes along.'

Mr Bligh raised an impressive finger. 'And now,' he said, 'I'll tell you something that hadn't crossed your mind. It's information received. If it's right, the coroner will hear it at a later stage, but at present we would rather the murderer didn't know about it. You remember I mentioned that Clayton Haggett left his flat at two-thirty that afternoon.

Well, he had more to tell us than that. He went down by the lift, he said. It's rather a slow-motion lift. As it passed down by the floor below – Anthony's floor – Haggett heard some words spoken. He could see as he passed that the door of the flat was just being opened from inside, and as it opened he heard a loud bullying voice call out, ' You do what I say, and look sharp about it. If you get on the wrong side of me, you know what to expect.' That is as near as Haggett can go to the actual words he heard – I asked him to be particular.'

Trent stared at the inspector with kindling eyes. 'You do like saving up the best bit to the last, don't you? And you had this – this! – simply handed to you. On a plate.'

'With parsley round it,' added Mr Bligh unashamed.

'I have heard you use that phrase before,' Trent said thoughtfully. 'It meant, I think, that you were rather mistrustful of good things that came so easily. But now, what about this remarkable addition to the record? Did Haggett recognize the voice? Did he see anybody?'

'No. Haggett says it might have been Maxwell he heard talking; but he only knows Maxwell by sight, has never spoken to him, and has no idea what his voice would sound like if it was raised. And, of course, it might have been anybody else in the world. Then I asked him what class of voice it was – like a curate's, or a dustman's, or what. All he could tell me was that it was not a coarse voice, and not a refined one; just middling. Very useful! But that isn't all. As the lift got to the bottom he heard a door above slam violently, which he assumed to be the one he had just seen being opened; and as he was getting into his car, Maxwell came out of the street door, with his hat on, looking furiously angry and very red in the face, and walked away rapidly.'

Trent considered this. 'So that is Haggett's information. And what does Maxwell say about it?'

'He hasn't been asked – yet. He is being given a little more time to make mistakes. But, of course, it may all be a lie. Yes, you may look surprised; but Haggett isn't out of it yet, as I told you. There's another piece of news I've got for you which certainly isn't a lie. When Jackson did the post mortem he found something that wants a lot of explaining.'

'What! Another thing you are keeping dark?'

'For the present. He noticed that the finger nails of the right hand looked as if they had been scratching hard at something, and there was a very faint odour that he couldn't place; so he took some scrapings from the nails to be analyzed. They found some tiny scraps of human skin; also traces of some things with hydrocarbo scientific names that don't seem to tell you much, and one thing that I have heard of quite often before.'

'Yes. What?'

'Chloroform.'

Thinking it over in his studio, Trent could make no more of this at first than Mr Bligh and he had made between them. If there had been a struggle, and if chloroform had been used, it did seem to point to the one resident in the house who might be presumed to know all about chloroform and what could be done with it. And Haggett was known to be violent tempered and a good hater, as well as a very able and successful professional man – not an unknown combination of qualities. But Trent found it hard to believe in such a character expressing its dislike in murder done by tricky and treacherous means. A quarrel; yes. An assault; possibly. An assault with a fatal result, legally a murder; such things did happen. But a planned and cold-blooded crime, with the murderer scheming to avoid detection by means of a trumped-up tale – Trent did not see it. In his experience, trained faculties, high responsibility, and professional distinction did not go with dirty actions and circumstantial lying.

But if Haggett's story of what he had heard and seen was true, how could it be fitted to the known facts? Maxwell's own statement about the time at which he had left the building agreed with Haggett's. Weaver's statement was that he had, as was natural, gone out a little later. Both of them had said nothing of this loud-voiced unknown who had used threatening language in Maxwell's flat. It might have been Maxwell himself. Could it have been Hermon? But Hermon had been fond, even foolishly fond, of his nephew. Unless – and here opened a new vista of ugliness – both Maxwell and his servant had been concealing the truth on that point, building up the fiction of a generous benefactor whom for worlds Maxwell would not have injured. There might be purpose enough in their doing so. The inspector had not thought of that; at least (Trent reflected with a wry smile) he had not mentioned it. Hermon's visit, by the way, had been a surprise visit according to Weaver.

Trent, at this point in his meditations, rose and began to pace the studio. Soon he went across to the model's dressing-room and examined his appearance in the mirror there. His hair had been cut fairly recently, but another trimming would not upset the balance of nature, he thought. Within the hour he was one of a dozen sheeted forms, sitting in a strange chair before a tall mirror, and had met the attendant's opening comment on the warmth of the day with the due rejoinder that it looked like rain later on.

Trent, like many other men, found his thoughts the clearer for being written down, and would often prepare for the drafting of a dispatch that could be published by a private memorandum, including all that could not. That evening he sat at his bureau, and did not rise until the account of what he had discovered, and the conclusions drawn, was complete in black and white.

'Starting with the belief that Haggett's story was true [he wrote], I had to make out who the person in Maxwell's flat was who gave some order, in offensive words, coupled with a vague threat; and who the person ordered about and threatened was. As Bligh said, it might have been any one who used those words; some one who had not as yet come into view in the case. But it was as well to consider first those who were known to have been in the place; and one of these was Hermon. But the accounts we had of Hermon made this seem unlikely; and they were not only the accounts given by Maxwell and his valet. Hermon's general reputation was that of a man who would be the last in the world to bully and threaten. As for the others who had been in the other flats, there was no visible shadow of a reason for suspecting any one of them.

'There remained Maxwell and his valet.

'Maxwell might be capable of bullying and threatening. He is not a nice young man. Could he have been the speaker, and either Hermon or Weaver the man spoken to?

'Well, is it likely? Maxwell is not a lunatic. No man in his senses would talk like that to his rich uncle whose fortune he expected to inherit; nor to his valet unless he was prepared for the man leaving him on the spot, and for being obliged to do his own valeting and cooking and housework until he could get another servant. Unless, of course, he had got either of them under his thumb in some way. Has Hermon, or Weaver, a guilty past, known to Maxwell?

'I had got as far as this when a new point occurred to me. Weaver, when I saw him, had told me that Maxwell had not been expecting his uncle's visit. As this looked very much like a plain lie, I thought some attention paid to Weaver might be worth the trouble; and so I went and had my hair cut at Harding's.

'The man who cut it was as ready for conversation as barbers usually are. I spoke of the fatal accident to Mr Hermon, and the barber, who may have been reading my own remarks on the subject, said that it was a funny sort of accident, giving his reasons for that view. Then I mentioned that I knew Mr Hermon's former valet had once had a job at Harding's. The man remembered both of them very well. He only wished he had the chance of bettering himself as Weaver had done. He had not known that Weaver had become Mr Maxwell's valet, but he had known that Weaver had done very well for himself. Besides that, Weaver had come into a bit of money of his own; he had mentioned it confidential. He was quite the gentleman now, especially in the last six months. He had taken to having his hair done at Harding's once a fortnight, probably just to show off a bit among his old pals. Gold wrist-watch, diamond tie-pin, quite the swell. Liked to do himself well, too, in his time off; and why not if you could run to it? Sometimes he would have my barber and other friends from Harding's to meet him after hours, and would stand drinks like a lord; and you could always see he had had a few beforehand.

'So far, my visit to Harding's had yielded more than I had any right to expect. But this was not all. My man came at length to that stage of the proceedings at which it is usual for the barber to hint delicately that the condition of one's scalp is not all that could be wished, and that this could be remedied by the use of some sort of hair-wash. With a flash of inspiration I asked what Weaver was in the habit of buying for himself. The best hair tonic there is, said my barber with enthusiasm; Harding's own preparation, Capillax – just the thing for me; and I would understand that Weaver knew, as a hairdresser, how excellent it was. I thought, when I was told the price of it, that Weaver also knew how impressively costly it was. I was shown a bottle of Capillax; a green fluted bottle, with NOT TO BE TAKEN stamped in the glass. Why, I asked my barber, should I be forbidden to take Capillax if I should choose to buy Capillax?

'He turned the bottle over, and showed me on the back a tiny pasted label. It read:

This preparation, containing among other valuable ingredients a small amount of Chloroform, is, in accordance with the Pharmacy Act, hereby labelled POISON.

'I ordered a bottle, of course. I thought my barber had earned his commission on the sale. And I asked him if he could tell me why chloroform should be used in a tonic for the hair, because I had thought it was for putting people to sleep. He said yes, but that was only the vapour of chloroform; in solution it acted as a stimulant to the skin, and had cleansing properties.

'My reconstruction of this crime is that Weaver planned the murder of Hermon. He had found out something that Maxwell did not dare have known about himself; he put the screw on him and bled him for every shilling he could raise. A servant who knows too much about his employer is a figure common enough in the odorous annals of blackmail. Weaver had 'come into money' indeed! Probably he got rid of a lot of it by betting. Anyhow, the more he got, the more he wanted. He had tasted easy money; he could not do without it; and there was no more in sight. But he knew that Maxwell, when his uncle died, would be a rich man. Weaver thought it over; and he formed a plan, to be carried out the first time that opportunity offered.

'On the morning of Hermon's death Maxwell heard, by letter or telephone, that his uncle intended to call that afternoon. Weaver's tale, that the old man had given no notice of his coming, was hardly credible. It was the height of summer, and it was utterly unlikely that Maxwell would be staying indoors that afternoon unless he was expecting a visitor. Hermon would certainly have let him know he was coming. This was what Weaver had been waiting for. After lunch he told Maxwell to leave the flat, go somewhere where he could mix with friends, and stay away until dinner-time. I do not believe Maxwell knew what was intended, because Haggett's story makes it plain that he protested against this. He did not see why he should deliberately absent himself when his uncle had asked him to be at home; why should he affront the old man? Weaver then went to the door of the flat, and as he opened it he raised his voice in the bullying words that Haggett caught as the lift went down. Maxwell, in a furious temper, did as he was told.

'When Hermon arrived, coming up by the lift, Weaver opened the door to him. He framed some lie to account for Maxwell's absence, and asked him to come in, perhaps for a rest and a cup of tea. Hermon did so; and while he was alone in the sitting-room, Weaver slipped out, took the lift to the floor above, and forced the lift gate on Maxwell's floor. When the old man went, Weaver saw him to the lift, opened the gate, and thrust him into the empty shaft. He knew better than most people how bad Hermon's sight was, and how little strength he had for a struggle. And here the plan went wrong. Hermon realized at the last instant that the lift was not there, and grabbed at Weaver as he felt the push given him. His right hand clutched Weaver's hair, tearing some of it out as he fell to his death, and lacerating the man's scalp.

'Weaver had seen instantly that if hair was found in the dead man's hand there would be an end of the theory that he had met with an accident. The police would be looking for a man with black hair and a scratched head; and they would not have far to look. There was only one thing for it. Weaver ran down to the ground floor, forced the gate there, stepped into the well, and carefully removed the hair he found in the dead man's grasp. There was nothing else he could do. He must simply stick to the story he had already made up, and trust to luck. After all, as far as he knew, there had been no witness whatever to anything that had passed.'

It was late by the time Trent had finished his memorandum. He read and re-read it, then slipped it into an envelope, addressed it to Mr Bligh at Scotland Yard, went out and registered it at the district post office.

Trent was at work in his studio next morning when the telephone bell called him.

Mr Bligh, not an effusive man by nature, said that Trent's report had reached him. 'There's no doubt but what you're right,' he went on. 'It's a pity, though, that we shall never hear what it was Weaver knew about Maxwell. It might very well have been a job for us.'

'Well, you called him a vicious young brute,' Trent said. 'With my morbid imagination and your fund of horrid experience, we ought to be able to guess a few of the things that it might have been. But why do you say you will never know? If you bring the murder home to Weaver, he will probably give Maxwell away, having no further use for his secret. It would be just like him.'

'Weaver won't do that.' There was a note of grimness in the inspector's voice. 'At eight fifteen last night Weaver was on his way down Coventry Street. He had been drinking, and couldn't walk straight. A dozen people saw him stumble off the kerb and into the road, right under a passing bus. He was killed instantly. His injuries—'

'Thanks, I don't want to hear about his injuries.' Trent wiped his brow. 'They were fatal – that's enough for me.'

'Yes, but there were some that weren't fatal. On the head, concealed by the hair, there were four deep scratches, not completely healed, and the signs of some hair having been torn out by the roots. I thought you'd like to know.'

# The Cave of Ali Baba

## DOROTHY L. SAYERS

*Appropriately, by walking across Belgravia, over Grosvenor Place and round Hyde Park Corner, we are soon at the doorway of the next of London's celebrated detectives – the man who was said to have been inspired by Philip Trent – the aristocratic Lord Peter Wimsey. Another of the immortals of the genre, Wimsey lives at 110 Piccadilly (a flat believed by members of the Dorothy L. Sayers Society to be on the site of the Park Lane Hotel), with his 'gentleman's gentleman', Bunter, who was his sergeant during the First World War. The younger son of the 15th Duke of Denver, Wimsey has an eclectic variety of hobbies including rare books, history, fine wines, music and cricket, but above all a passion for criminology which has made him, according to certain experts, the leading amateur detective in the capital. His aristocratic bearing fostered at Eton and Oxford is re-emphasized by his dandified appearance, man-about-town manners, and monocle. Among his associates are Inspector Charles Parker from Scotland Yard, and Harriet Vane, a mystery writer, with whom he fell in love and finally married after a tortuous courtship. The first of his cases,* Whose Body?, *appeared in 1923, and it was not until fifty years later that his final adventure, 'Tallboys' was published. Lord Peter has appeared on the stage, on radio and in films and television, played by such skilled actors as Peter Haddon (in the first movie,* The Silent Passenger, *in 1935), Robert Montgomery, Edward Petherbridge and Ian Carmichael who remains most viewers' ideal impersonation. H. R. F. Keating has called Wimsey, 'a person one can thoroughly believe in, like, and even love as many women readers do, or hate, as some male readers do'.*

*Dorothy Leigh Sayers (1893–1957) never made any bones about the fact that she created Lord Peter to make money. Fascinated by religious literature and a dedicated poet, she had to work in an advertising agency to earn her living and it was there that the idea for her detective sprang into her mind and subsequently made her fortune. Unashamedly as she admitted her motives for writing crime fiction, Dorothy also attempted to make her stories literary as well as exciting and is consequently regarded as a trend-setter in this particular aspect of the history of the detective story. In the thirties she revealed her wide knowledge of the genre by editing three landmark anthologies of crime fiction for her publisher, Victor Gollancz, which are still held up today as models of their kind – not to mention being much prized by collectors. 'The Adventurous Exploit of The Cave of Ali Baba' (to give this tale its original title) is a fascinating Wimsey exploit in which disguise and deception are required to unmask another of London's master criminals . . .*

IN THE FRONT room of a grim and narrow house in Lambeth a man sat eating kippers and glancing through the *Morning Post*. He was smallish and spare, with brown hair rather too regularly waved and a strong, brown beard, cut to a point. His double-breasted suit of navy-blue and his socks, tie, and handkerchief, all scrupulously matched, were a trifle more point-device than the best taste approves, and his boots were slightly too bright a brown. He did not look a gentleman, not even a gentleman's gentleman, yet there was something about his appearance which suggested that he was accustomed to the manner of life in good families. The breakfast-table, which he had set with his own hands, was arrayed with the attention to detail which is exacted of good-class servants. His action, as he walked over to a little side-table and carved himself a plate of ham, was the action of a superior butler; yet he was not old enough to be a retired butler; a footman, perhaps, who had come into a legacy.

He finished the ham with good appetite, and, as he sipped his coffee, read through attentively a paragraph which he had already noticed and put aside for consideration.

'LORD PETER WIMSEY'S WILL
BEQUEST TO VALET
£10,000 TO CHARITIES

'The will of Lord Peter Wimsey, who was killed last December while shooting big game in Tanganyika, was proved yesterday at £500,000. A sum of £10,000 was left to various charities, including [here followed a list of bequests]. To his valet, Mervyn Bunter, was left an annuity of £500 and the lease of the testator's flat in Piccadilly. [Then followed a number of personal bequests.] The remainder of the estate, including the valuable collection of books and pictures at 110a Piccadilly, was left to the testator's mother, the Dowager Duchess of Denver.

'Lord Peter Wimsey was thirty-seven at the time of his death. He was the younger brother of the present Duke of Denver, who is the wealthiest peer in the United Kingdom. Lord Peter was distinguished as a criminologist and took an active part in the solution of several famous mysteries. He was a well-known book collector and man-about-town.'

The man gave a sigh of relief.

'No doubt about that,' he said aloud. 'People don't give their money away if they're going to come back again. The blighter's dead and buried right enough. I'm free.'

He finished his coffee, cleared the table, and washed up the crockery, took his bowler hat from the hall-stand, and went out.

A bus took him to Bermondsey. He alighted, and plunged into a network of gloomy streets, arriving after a quarter of an hour's walk at a seedy-looking public-house in a low quarter. He entered and called for a double whisky.

The house had only just opened, but a number of customers, who had apparently been waiting on the doorstep for this desirable event, were already clustered about the bar. The man who might have been a footman reached for his glass, and in doing so jostled the elbow of a flash person in a check suit and regrettable tie.

'Here!' expostulated the flash person, 'what d'yer mean by it? We don't want your sort here. Get out!'

He emphasized his remarks with a few highly coloured words, and a violent push in the chest.

'Bar's free to everybody, isn't it?' said the other, returning the shove with interest.

'Now then!' said the barmaid, 'none o' that. The gentleman didn't do it intentional, Mr Jukes.'

'Didn't he?' said Mr Jukes. 'Well, I *did*.'

'And you ought to be ashamed of yourself,' retorted the young lady, with a toss of the head. 'I'll have no quarrelling in my bar – not this time in the morning.'

'It was quite an accident,' said the man from Lambeth. 'I'm not one to make a disturbance, having always been used to the best houses. But if any gentleman *wants* to make trouble—'

'All right, all right,' said Mr Jukes, more pacifically. 'I'm not keen to give you a new face. Not but what any alteration wouldn't be for the better. Mind your manners another time, that's all. What'll you have?'

'No, no,' protested the other, 'this one must be on me. Sorry I pushed you. I didn't mean it. But I didn't like to be taken up so short.'

'Say no more about it,' said Mr Jukes generously. 'I'm standing this. Another double whisky, miss, and one of the usual. Come over here where there isn't so much of a crowd, or you'll be getting yourself into trouble again.'

He led the way to a small table in the corner of the room.

'That's all right,' said Mr Jukes. 'Very nicely done. I don't think there's any danger here, but you can't be too careful. Now, what about it, Rogers? Have you made up your mind to come in with us?'

'Yes,' said Rogers, with a glance over his shoulder, 'yes, I have. That is, mind you, if everything seems all right. I'm not looking for trouble, and I don't want to get let in for any dangerous games. I don't mind giving you information, but it's understood as I take no active part in whatever goes on. Is that straight?'

'You wouldn't be allowed to take an active part if you wanted to,' said Mr Jukes. 'Why, you poor fish, Number One wouldn't have anybody but experts on his jobs. All you have to do is to let us know where the stuff is and how to get it. The Society does the rest. It's some organization, I can tell you. You won't even know who's doing it, or how it's done. You won't know anybody, and nobody will know you – accept Number One, of course. He knows everybody.'

'And you,' said Rogers.

'And me, of course. But I shall be transferred to another district. We shan't meet again after today, except at the general meetings, and then we shall all be masked.'

'Go on!' said Rogers incredulously.

'Fact. You'll be taken to Number One – he'll see you, but you won't see him. Then, if he thinks you're any good, you'll be put on the roll, and after that you'll be told where to make your reports to. There is a divisional meeting called once a fortnight, and every three months there's a general meeting and share-out. Each member is called up by number and has his whack handed over to him. That's all.'

'Well, but suppose two members are put on the same job together?'

'If it's a daylight job, they'll be so disguised their mothers wouldn't know 'em. But it's mostly night work.'

'I see. But, look here – what's to prevent somebody following me home and giving me away to the police?'

'Nothing, of course. Only I wouldn't advise him to try it, that's all. The last man who had that bright idea was fished out of the river down Rotherhithe way, before he had time to get his precious report in. Number One knows everybody, you see.'

'Oh! – and who is this Number One?'

'There's lots of people would give a good bit to know that.'

'Does nobody know?'

'Nobody. He's a fair marvel, is Number One. He's a gentleman, I can tell you that, and a pretty high-up one, from his ways. *And* he's got eyes all round his head. *And* he's got an arm as long as from here to Australia. *But* nobody knows anything about him, unless it's Number Two, and I'm not even sure about her.'

'There are women in it, then?'

'You can bet your boots there are. You can't do a job without 'em nowadays. But that needn't worry you. The women are safe enough. They don't want to come to a sticky end, no more than you and me.'

'But, look here, Jukes – how about the money? It's a big risk to take. Is it worth it?'

'Worth it?' Jukes leant across the little marble-topped table and whispered.

'Coo!' gasped Rogers. 'And how much of that would I get, now?'

'You'd share and share alike with the rest, whether you'd been in that particular job or not. There's fifty members, and you'd get one-fiftieth, same as Number One and same as me.'

'Really? No kidding?'

'See that wet, see that dry!' Jukes laughed. 'Say, can you beat it? There's never been anything like it. It's the biggest thing ever been known. He's a great man, is Number One.'

'And do you pull off many jobs?'

'Many? Listen. You remember the Carruthers necklace, and the Gorleston Bank robbery? And the Faversham burglary? And the big Rubens that disappeared from the National Gallery? And the Frensham pearls? All done by the Society. And never one of them cleared up.'

Rogers licked his lips.

'But now, look here,' he said cautiously. 'Supposing I was a spy as you might say, and supposing I was to go straight off and tell the police about what you've been saying?'

'Ah!' said Jukes, 'suppose you did, eh? Well, supposing something nasty didn't happen to you on the way there – which I wouldn't answer for, mind—'

'Do you mean to say you've got me watched?'

'You can bet your sweet life we have. Yes. Well, *supposing* nothing happened on the way there, and you was to bring the slops to this pub, looking for yours truly—'

'Yes?'

'You wouldn't find me, that's all. I should have gone to Number Five.'

'Who's Number Five?'

'Ah! I don't know. But he's the man that makes you a new face while you wait. Plastic surgery, they call it. And new fin-ger-prints. New everything. We go in for up-to-date methods in our show.'

Rogers whistled.

'Well, how about it?' asked Jukes, eyeing his acquaintance over the rim of his tumbler.

'Look here – you've told me a lot of things. Shall I be safe if I say "no"?'

'Oh, yes – if you behave yourself and don't make trouble for us.'

'H'm, I see. And if I say "yes"?'

'Then you'll be a rich man in less than no time, with money in your pocket to live like a gentleman. And nothing to do for it, except to tell us what you know about the houses you've been to when you were in service. It's money foɪ jam if you act straight by the Society.'

Rogers was silent, thinking it over.

'I'll do it!' he said at last.

'Good for you, Miss! The same again, please. Here's to it, Rogers! I knew you were one of the right sort the minute I set eyes on you. Here's to money for jam, and take care of

Number One! Talking of Number One, you'd better come round and see him to-night. No time like the present.'

'Right you are. Where'll I come to? Here?'

'Nix. No more of this little pub for us. It's a pity, because it's nice and comfortable, but it can't be helped. Now, what you've got to do is this. At ten o'clock tonight exactly, you walk north across Lambeth Bridge' (Rogers winced at this intimation that his abode was known), 'and you'll see a yellow taxi standing there, with the driver doing something to his engine. You'll say to him, "Is your bus fit to go?" and he'll say, "Depends where you want to go to." And you'll say, "Take me to Number One, London." There's a shop called that, by the way, but he won't take you there. You won't know where he s taking you, because the taxi-windows will be covered up, but you mustn't mind that. It's the rule for the first visit. Afterwards, when you're regularly one of us, you'll be told the name of the place. And when you get there, do as you're told and speak the truth, because, if you don't, Number One will deal with you. See?'

'I see.'

'Are you game? You're not afraid?'

'Of course I'm not afraid.'

'Good man! Well, we'd better be moving now. And I'll say good-bye, because we shan't see each other again. Good-bye – and good luck!'

'Good-bye.'

They passed through the swing-doors, and out into the mean and dirty street.

The two years subsequent to the enrolment of the ex-footman Rogers in a crook society were marked by a number of startling and successful raids on the houses of distinguished people. There was the theft of the great diamond tiara from the Dowager Duchess of Denver; the burglary at the flat formerly occupied by the late Lord Peter Wimsey, resulting in the disappearance of £7,000 worth of silver and gold plate; the burglary at the country mansion of Theodore Winthrop, the

millionaire – which, incidentally, exposed that thriving gentleman as a confirmed Society blackmailer and caused a
reverberating scandal in Mayfair; and the snatching of the
famous eight-string necklace of pearls from the neck of the
Marchioness of Dinglewood during the singing of the Jewel
Song in *Faust* at Covent Garden. It is true that the pearls
turned out to be imitation, the original string having been
pawned by the noble lady under circumstances highly painful
to the Marquis, but the coup was nevertheless a sensational
one.

On a Saturday afternoon in January, Rogers was sitting in
his room in Lambeth, when a slight noise at the front door
caught his ear. He sprang up almost before it had ceased,
dashed through the small hallway, and flung the door open.
The street was deserted. Nevertheless, as he turned back to
the sitting-room, he saw an envelope lying on the hat-stand.
It was addressed briefly to 'Number Twenty-one'.
Accustomed by this time to the somewhat dramatic methods
used by the Society to deliver its correspondence, he merely
shrugged his shoulders, and opened the note.

It was written in cipher, and, when transcribed, ran thus:

'Number Twenty-one – An Extraordinary General
Meeting will be held tonight at the house of Number
One at 11.30. You will be absent at your peril. The
word is FINALITY.'

Rogers stood for a little time considering this. Then he made
his way to a room at the back of the house, in which there
was a tall safe, built into the wall. He manipulated the combination and walked into the safe, which ran back for some
distance, forming, indeed, a small strong-room. He pulled
out a drawer marked 'Correspondence', and added the paper
he had just received to the contents.

After a few moments he emerged, re-set the lock to a new
combination, and returned to the sitting-room.

'Finality,' he said. 'Yes – I think so.' He stretched out his hand to the telephone – then appeared to alter his mind.

He went upstairs to an attic, and thence climbed into a loft close under the roof. Crawling among the rafters, he made his way into the farthest corner; then carefully pressed a knot on the timber-work. A concealed trap-door swung open. He crept through it, and found himself in the corresponding loft of the next house. A soft cooing noise greeted him as he entered. Under the skylight stood three cages, each containing a carrier pigeon.

He glanced cautiously out of the skylight, which looked out upon a high blank wall at the back of some factory or other. There was nobody in the dim little courtyard, and no window within sight. He drew his head in again, and, taking a small fragment of thin paper from his pocket-book, wrote a few letters and numbers upon it. Going to the nearest cage, he took out the pigeon and attached the message to its wing. Then he carefully set the bird on the window-ledge. It hesitated a moment, shifted its pink feet a few times, lifted its wings, and was gone. He saw it tower up into the already darkening sky over the factory roof and vanish into the distance.

He glanced at his watch and returned downstairs. An hour later he released the second pigeon, and in another hour the third. Then he sat down to wait.

At half-past nine he went up to the attic again. It was dark, but a few frosty stars were shining, and a cold air blew through the open window. Something pale gleamed faintly on the floor. He picked it up – it was warm and feathery. The answer had come.

He ruffled the soft plumes and found the paper. Before reading it, he fed the pigeon and put it into one of the cages. As he was about to fasten the door, he checked himself.

'If anything happens to me,' he said, 'there's no need for you to starve to death, my child.'

He pushed the window a little wider open and went downstairs again. The paper in his hand bore only the two letters, 'OK'. It seemed to have been written hurriedly, for there was a long smear of ink in the upper left-hand corner.

He noted this with a smile, put the paper in the fire, and, going out into the kitchen, prepared and ate a hearty meal of eggs and corned beef from a new tin. He ate it without bread, though there was a loaf on the shelf near at hand, and washed it down with water from the tap, which he let run for some time before venturing to drink it. Even then he carefully wiped the tap, both inside and outside, before drinking.

When he had finished, he took a revolver from a locked drawer, inspecting the mechanism with attention to see that it was in working order, and loaded it with new cartridges from an unbroken packet. Then he sat down to wait again.

At a quarter before eleven, he rose and went out into the street. He walked briskly, keeping well away from the wall, till he came out into a well-lighted thoroughfare. Here he took a bus, securing the corner seat next the conductor, from which he could see everybody who got on and off. A succession of buses eventually brought him to a respectable residential quarter of Hampstead. Here he alighted and, still keeping well away from the walls, made his way up to the Heath.

The night was moonless, but not altogether black, and, as he crossed a deserted part of the Heath, he observed one or two other dark forms closing in upon him from various directions. He paused in the shelter of a large tree, and adjusted to his face a black velvet mask, which covered him from brow to chin. At its base the number 21 was clearly embroidered in white thread.

At length a slight dip in the ground disclosed one of those agreeable villas which stand, somewhat isolated, among the rural surroundings of the Heath. One of the windows was lighted. As he made his way to the door, other dark figures, masked like himself, pressed forward and surrounded him. He counted six of them.

The foremost man knocked on the door of the solitary house. After a moment, it was opened slightly. The man advanced his head to the opening; there was a murmur, and the door opened wide. The man stepped in, and the door was shut.

When three of the men had entered, Rogers found himself to be the next in turn. He knocked, three times loudly, then twice faintly. The door opened to the extent of two or three inches, and an ear was presented to the chink. Rogers whispered, 'Finality.' The ear was withdrawn, the door opened, and he passed in.

Without any further word of greeting, Number Twenty-one passed into a small room on the left, which was furnished like an office, with a desk, a safe, and a couple of chairs. At the desk sat a massive man in evening dress, with a ledger before him. The new arrival shut the door carefully after him; it clicked to, on a spring lock. Advancing to the desk, he announced, 'Number Twenty-one, sir,' and stood respectfully waiting. The big man looked up, showing the number 1 startlingly white on his velvet mask. His eyes, of a curious hard blue, scanned Rogers attentively. At a sign from him, Rogers removed his mask. Having verified his identity with care, the President said, 'Very well, Number Twenty-one,' and made an entry in the ledger. The voice was hard and metallic, like his eyes. The close scrutiny from behind the immovable black mask seemed to make Rogers uneasy; he shifted his feet, and his eyes fell. Number One made a sign of dismissal, and Rogers, with a faint sigh as though of relief, replaced his mask and left the room. As he came out, the next comer passed in in his place.

The room in which the Society met was a large one, made by knocking the two largest of the first-floor rooms into one. It was furnished in the standardised taste of twentieth-century suburbia and brilliantly lighted. A gramophone in one corner blared out a jazz tune, to which about ten couples of masked men and women were dancing, some in evening dress and others in tweeds and jumpers.

In one corner of the room was an American bar. Rogers went up and asked the masked man in charge for a double whisky. He consumed it slowly, leaning on the bar. The room filled. Presently somebody moved across to the gramophone and stopped it. He looked round. Number One had appeared on the threshold. A tall woman in black stood beside him. The mask, embroidered with a white 2, covered hair and face completely; only her fine bearing and her white arms and bosom and the dark eyes shining through the eye-slits proclaimed her a woman of power and physical attraction.

'Ladies and gentlemen.' Number One was standing at the upper end of the room. The woman sat beside him; her eyes were cast down and betrayed nothing, but her hands were clenched on the arms of the chair and her whole figure seemed tensely aware.

'Ladies and gentlemen. Our numbers are two short tonight.' The masks moved; eyes were turned, seeking and counting. 'I need not inform you of the disastrous failure of our plan for securing the plans of the Court-Windlesham helicopter. Our courageous and devoted comrades, Number Fifteen and Number Forty-eight, were betrayed and taken by the police.'

An uneasy murmur arose among the company.

'It may have occurred to some of you that even the well-known steadfastness of these comrades might give way under examination. There is no cause for alarm. The usual orders have been issued, and I have this evening received the report that their tongues have been effectually silenced. You will, I am sure, be glad to know that these two brave men have been spared the ordeal of so great a temptation to dishonour, and that they will not be called upon to face a public trial and the rigours of a long imprisonment.'

A hiss of intaken breath moved across the assembled members like the wind over a barley-field.

'Their dependants will be discreetly compensated in the usual manner. I call upon Numbers Twelve and Thirty-four to undertake this agreeable task. They will attend me in my office for their instructions after the meeting. Will the Numbers I have named kindly signify that they are able and willing to perform this duty?'

Two hands were raised in salute. The President continued, looking at his watch:

'Ladies and gentlemen, please take your partners for the next dance.'

The gramophone struck up again. Rogers turned to a girl near him in a red dress. She nodded, and they slipped into the movement of a fox-trot. The couples gyrated solemnly and in silence. Their shadows were flung against the blinds as they turned and stepped to and fro.

'What has happened?' breathed the girl in a whisper, scarcely moving her lips. 'I'm frightened, aren't you? I feel as if something awful was going to happen.'

'It does take one a bit short, the President's way of doing things,' agreed Roger, 'but it's safer like that.'

'Those poor men—'

A dancer, turning and following on their heels, touched Rogers on the shoulder.

'No talking, please,' he said. His eyes gleamed sternly; he twirled his partner into the middle of the crowd and was gone. The girl shuddered.

The gramophone stopped. There was a burst of clapping. The dancers again clustered before the President's seat.

'Ladies and gentlemen. You may wonder why this extraordinary meeting has been called. The reason is a serious one. The failure of our recent attempt was no accident. The police were not on the premises that night by chance. We have a traitor among us.'

Partners who had been standing close together fell distrustfully apart. Each member seemed to shrink, as a snail shrinks from the touch of a finger.

'You will remember the disappointing outcome of the Dinglewood affair,' went on the President, in his harsh voice. 'You may recall other smaller matters which have not turned out satisfactorily. All these troubles have been traced to their origin. I am happy to say that our minds can now be easy. The offender has been discovered and will be removed. There will be no more mistakes. The misguided member who introduced the traitor to our Society will be placed in a position where his lack of caution will have no further ill-effects. There is no cause for alarm.'

Every eye roved about the company, searching for the traitor and his unfortunate sponsor. Somewhere beneath the black masks a face must have turned white; somewhere under the stifling velvet there must have been a brow sweating, not with the heat of the dance. But the masks hid everything.

'Ladies and gentlemen, please take your partners for the next dance.'

The gramophone struck into an old and half-forgotten tune: 'There ain't nobody loves me'. The girl in red was claimed by a tall mask in evening dress. A hand laid on Rogers's arm made him start. A small, plump woman in a green jumper slipped a cold hand into his. The dance went on.

When it stopped, amid the usual applause, everyone stood, detached, stiffened in expectation. The President's voice was raised again.

'Ladies and gentlemen, please behave naturally. This is a dance, not a public meeting.'

Rogers led his partner to a chair and fetched her an ice. As he stooped over her, he noticed the hurried rise and fall of her bosom.

'Ladies and gentlemen.' The endless interval was over. 'You will no doubt wish to be immediately relieved from suspense. I will name the persons involved. Number Thirty seven!'

A man sprang up with a fearful, strangled cry.

'Silence!'

The wretch choked and gasped.

'I never – I swear I never – I'm innocent.'

'Silence. You have failed in discretion. You will be dealt with. If you have anything to say in defence of your folly, I will hear it later. Sit down.'

Number Thirty-seven sank down upon a chair. He pushed his handkerchief under the mask to wipe his face. Two tall men closed in upon him. The rest fell back, feeling the recoil of humanity from one stricken by mortal disease.

The gramophone struck up.

'Ladies and gentlemen, I will now name the traitor. Number Twenty-one, stand forward.'

Rogers stepped forward. The concentrated fear and loathing of forty-eight pairs of eyes burned upon him. The miserable Jukes set up a fresh wail.

'Oh, my God! Oh, my God!'

'Silence! Number Twenty-one, take off your mask.'

The traitor pulled the thick covering from his face. The intense hatred of the eyes devoured him.

'Number Thirty-seven, this man was introduced here by you, under the name of Joseph Rogers, formerly second footman in the service of the Duke of Denver, dismissed for pilfering. Did you take steps to verify that statement?'

'I did – I did! As God's my witness, it was all straight. I had him identified by two of the servants. I made enquiries. The tale was straight – I'll swear it was.'

The President consulted a paper before him, then he looked at his watch again.

'Ladies and gentlemen, please take your partners . . .'

Number Twenty-one, his arms twisted behind him and bound, and his wrists handcuffed, stood motionless, while the dance of doom circled about him. The clapping, as it ended, sounded like the clapping of the men and women who sat, thirsty-lipped beneath the guillotine.

'Number Twenty-one, your name has been given as Joseph Rogers, footman, dismissed for theft. Is that your real name?'

'No.'

'What is your name?'

'Peter Death Bredon Wimsey.'

'We thought you were dead.'

'Naturally. You were intended to think so.'

'What has become of the genuine Joseph Rogers?'

'He died abroad. I took his place. I may say that no real

blame attaches to your people for not having realized who I was. I not only took Rogers's place; I *was* Rogers. Even when I was alone, I walked like Rogers, I sat like Rogers, I read Rogers's books, and wore Rogers's clothes. In the end, I almost thought Rogers's thoughts. The only way to keep up a successful impersonation is never to relax.'

'I see. The robbery of your own flat was arranged?'

'Obviously.'

'The robbery of the Dowager Duchess, your mother, was connived at by you?'

'It was. It was a very ugly tiara – no real loss to anybody with decent taste. May I smoke, by the way?'

'You may not. Ladies and gentlemen . . .'

The dance was like the mechanical jigging of puppets. Limbs jerked, feet faltered. The prisoner watched with an air of critical detachment.

'Numbers Fifteen, Twenty-two, and Forty-nine. You have watched the prisoner. Has he made any attempts to communicate with anybody?'

'None.' Number Twenty-two was the spokesman. 'His letters and parcels have been opened, his telephone tapped, and his movements followed. His water-pipes have been under observation for Morse signals.'

'You are sure of what you say?'

'Absolutely.'

'Prisoner, have you been alone in this adventure? Speak the truth, or things will be made somewhat more unpleasant for you than they might otherwise be.'

'I have been alone. I have taken no unnecessary risks.'

'It may be so. It will, however, be as well that steps should be taken to silence the man at Scotland Yard – what is his name? – Parker. Also the prisoner's manservant, Mervyn Bunter, and possibly also his mother and sister. The brother is a stupid oaf, and not, I think, likely to have been taken into the prisoner's confidence. A precautionary watch will, I think, meet the necessities of his case.'

The prisoner appeared, for the first time, to be moved.

'Sir, I assure you that my mother and sister know nothing which could possibly bring danger on the Society.'

'You should have thought of their situation earlier. Ladies and gentlemen, please take—'

'No – no!' Flesh and blood could endure the mockery no longer. 'No! Finish with him. Get it over. Break up the meeting. It's dangerous. The police—'

'Silence!'

The President glanced round at the crowd. It had a dangerous look about it. He gave way. 'Very well. Take the prisoner away and silence him. He will receive Number four treatment. And be sure you explain it to him carefully first.'

'Ah!'

The eyes expressed a wolfish satisfaction. Strong hands gripped Wimsey's arms.

'One moment – for God's sake let me die decently.'

'You should have thought this over earlier. Take him away. Ladies and gentlemen, be satisfied – he will not die quickly.'

'Stop! Wait!' cried Wimsey desperately. 'I have something to say. I don't ask for life – only for a quick death. I – I have something to sell.'

'To sell?'

'Yes.'

'We make no bargains with traitors.'

'No – but listen! Do you think I have not thought of this? I am not so mad. I have left a letter.'

'Ah! now it is coming. A letter. To whom?'

'To the police. If I do not return tomorrow—'

'Well?'

'The letter will be opened.'

'Sir,' broke in Number Fifteen. 'This is bluff. The prisoner has not sent any letter. He has been strictly watched for many months.'

'Ah! but listen. I left the letter before I came to Lambeth.'

'Then it can contain no information of value.'

'Oh, but it does.'

'What?'

'The combination of my safe.'

'Indeed? Has this man's safe been searched?'

'Yes, sir.'

'What did it contain?

'No information of importance, sir. An outline of our organisation – the name of this house – nothing that cannot be altered and covered before morning.'

Wimsey smiled. 'Did you investigate the inner compartment of the safe?'

There was a pause.

'You hear what he says,' snapped the President sharply. 'Did you find this inner compartment?'

'There was no inner compartment, sir. He is trying to bluff.'

'I hate to contradict you,' said Wimsey, with an effort at his ordinary pleasant tone, 'but I really think you must have overlooked the inner compartment.'

'Well,' said the President, 'and what do you say is in this inner compartment, if it does exist?'

'The names of every member of this Society, with their addresses, photographs, and finger-prints.'

'What?'

The eyes round him now were ugly with fear. Wimsey kept his face steadily turned towards the President.

'How do you say you have contrived to get this information?'

'Well, I have been doing a little detective work on my own, you know.'

'But you have been watched.'

'True. The finger-prints of my watchers adorn the first page of the collection.'

'This statement can be proved?'

'Certainly. I will prove it. The name of Number Fifty, for example—'

'Stop!'

A fierce muttering arose. The President silenced it with a gesture.

'If you mention names here, you will certainly have no hope of mercy. There is a fifth treatment – kept specially for people who mention names. Bring the prisoner to my office. Keep the dance going.'

The President took an automatic from his hip-pocket and faced his tightly fettered prisoner across the desk.

'Now speak!' he said.

'I should put that thing away, if I were you,' said Wimsey contemptuously. 'It would be a much pleasanter form of death than treatment Number five, and I might be tempted to ask for it.'

'Ingenious,' said the President, 'but a little too ingenious. Now, be quick; tell me what you know.'

'Will you spare me if I tell you?'

'I make no promises. Be quick.'

Wimsey shrugged his bound and aching shoulders.

'Certainly. I will tell you what I know. Stop me when you have heard enough.'

He leaned forward and spoke low. Overhead the noise of the gramophone and the shuffling of feet bore witness that the dance was going on. Stray passers-by crossing the Heath noted that the people in the lonely house were making a night of it again.

'Well,' said Wimsey, 'am I to go on?'

From beneath the mask the President's voice sounded as though he were grimly smiling.

'My lord,' he said, 'your story fills me with regret that you are not, in fact, a member of our Society. Wit, courage, and industry are valuable to an association like ours. I fear I cannot persuade you? No – I supposed not.'

He touched a bell on his desk.

'Ask the members kindly to proceed to the supper-room,' he said to the mask who entered.

The 'supper-room' was on the ground-floor, shuttered and curtained. Down its centre ran a long, bare table, with chairs set about it.

'A Barmecide feast, I see,' said Wimsey pleasantly. It was the first time he had seen this room. At the far end, a trap-door in the floor gaped ominously.

The President took the head of the table.

'Ladies and gentlemen,' he began, as usual – and the foolish courtesy had never sounded so sinister – 'I will not conceal from you the seriousness of the situation. The prisoner has recited to me more than twenty names and addresses which were thought to be unknown, except to their owners and to me. There has been great carelessness' – his voice rang harshly – 'which will have to be looked into. Finger-prints have been obtained – he has shown me the photographs of some of them. How our investigators came to overlook the inner door of this safe is a matter which calls for enquiry.'

'Don't blame them,' put in Wimsey. 'It was meant to be overlooked, you know. I made it like that on purpose.'

The President went on, without seeming to notice the interruption.

'The prisoner informs me that the book with the names and addresses is to be found in this inner compartment, together with certain letters and papers stolen from the houses of members, and numerous objects bearing authentic finger-prints. I believe him to be telling the truth. He offers the combination of the safe in exchange for a quick death. I think the offer should be accepted. What is your opinion, ladies and gentlemen?'

'The combination is known already,' said Number Twenty-two.

'Imbecile! This man has told us, and has proved to me, that he is Lord Peter Wimsey. Do you think he will have forgotten to alter the combination? And then there is the secret of the inner door. If he disappears tonight and the police enter his house—'

'I say,' said a woman's rich voice, 'that the promise should, be given and the information used – and quickly. Time is getting short.'

A murmur of agreement went round the table.

'You hear,' said the President, addressing Wimsey. 'The Society offers you the privilege of a quick death in return for the combination of the safe and the secret of the inner door.'

'I have your word for it?'

'You have.'

'Thank you. And my mother and sister?'

'If you in your turn will give us your word – you are a man of honour – that these women know nothing that could harm us, they shall be spared.'

'Thank you, sir. You may rest assured, upon my honour, that they know nothing. I should not think of burdening any woman with such dangerous secrets – particularly those who are dear to me.'

'Very well. It is agreed – yes?'

The murmur of assent was given, though with less readiness than before.

'Then I am willing to give you the information you want. The word of the combination is UNRELIABILITY.'

'And the inner door?'

'In anticipation of the visit of the police – the inner door – which might have presented difficulties – is open.'

'Good! You understand that if the police interfere with our messenger—'

'That would not help me, would it?'

'It is a risk,' said the President thoughtfully, 'but a risk which I think we must take. Carry the prisoner down to the cellar. He can amuse himself by contemplating apparatus Number five. In the meantime, Numbers Twelve and Forty-six—'

'No, no!'

A sullen mutter of dissent arose and swelled threateningly.

'No,' said a tall man with a voice like treacle. 'No – why should any members be put in possession of this evidence? We have found one traitor among us tonight and more than one fool. How are we to know that Numbers Twelve and Forty-six are not fools and traitors also?'

The two men turned savagely upon the speaker, but a girl's voice struck into the discussion, high and agitated.

'Hear, hear! That's right, I say. How about us? We ain't going to have our names read by somebody we don't know nothing about. I've had enough of this. They might sell the 'ole lot of us to the narks.'

'I agree,' said another member. 'Nobody ought to be trusted, nobody at all.'

The President shrugged his shoulders.

'Then what, ladies and gentlemen, do you suggest?'

There was a pause. Then the same girl shrilled out again:

'I say Mr President oughter go himself. He's the only one as knows all the names. It won't be no cop to him. Why should we take all the risk and trouble and him sit at home and collar the money? Let him go himself, that's what I say.'

A long rustle of approbation went round the table.

'I second that motion,' said a stout man who wore a bunch of gold seals at his fob. Wimsey smiled as he looked at the seals; it was that trifling vanity which had led him directly to the name and address of the stout man, and he felt a certain affection for the trinkets on that account.

The President looked round.

'It is the wish of the meeting, then, that I should go? 'he said, in an ominous voice.

Forty-five hands were raised in approbation. Only the woman known as Number Two remained motionless and silent, her strong white hands clenched on the arm of the chair.

The President rolled his eyes slowly round the threatening ring till they rested upon her.

'Am I to take it that this vote is unanimous?' he enquired.

The woman raised her head.

'Don't go,' she gasped faintly.

'You hear,' said the President, in a faintly derisive tone. 'This lady says, don't go.'

'I submit that what Number Two says is neither here nor there,' said the man with the treacly voice. 'Our own ladies might not like us to be going, if they were in madam's privileged position.' His voice was an insult.

'Hear, hear!' cried another man. 'This is a democratic society, this is. We don't want no privileged classes.'

'Very well,' said the President. 'You hear, Number Two. The feeling of the meeting is against you. Have you any reasons to put forward in favour of your opinion?'

'A hundred. The President is the head and soul of our Society. If anything should happen to him – where should we be? You' – she swept the company magnificently with her eyes – 'you have all blundered. We have your carelessness to thank for all this. Do you think we should be safe for five minutes if the President were not here to repair your follies?'

'Something in that,' said a man who had not hitherto spoken.

'Pardon my suggesting,' said Wimsey maliciously, 'that, as the lady appears to be in a position peculiarly favourable for the reception of the President's confidences, the contents of my modest volume will probably be no news to her. Why should not Number Two go herself?'

'Because I say she must not,' said the President sternly, checking the quick reply that rose to his companion's lips. 'If it is the will of the meeting, I will go. Give me the key of the house.'

One of the men extracted it from Wimsey's jacket-pocket and handed it over.

'Is the house watched?' he demanded of Wimsey.

'No.'

'That is the truth?'

'It is the truth.'

The President turned at the door.

'If I have not returned in two hours' time,' he said, 'act for the best to save yourselves, and do what you like with the prisoner. Number Two will give orders in my absence.'

He left the room. Number Two rose from her seat with a gesture of command.

'Ladies and gentlemen. Supper is now considered over. Start the dancing again.'

Down in the cellar the time passed slowly, in the contemplation of apparatus Number five. The miserable Jukes, alternately wailing and raving, at length shrieked himself into exhaustion. The four members guarding the prisoners whispered together from time to time.

'An hour and a half since the President left,' said one.

Wimsey glanced up. Then he returned to his examination of the room. There were many curious things in it, which he wanted to memorize.

Presently the trap-door was flung open. 'Bring him up!' cried a voice. Wimsey rose immediately, and his face was rather pale.

The members of the gang were again seated round the table. Number Two occupied the President's chair, and her eyes fastened on Wimsey's face with a tigerish fury, but when she spoke it was with a self-control which roused his admiration.

'The President has been two hours gone,' she said. 'What has happened to him? Traitor twice over – what has happened to him?'

'How should I know?' said Wimsey. 'Perhaps he has looked after Number One and gone while the going was good!'

She sprang up with a little cry of rage, and came close to him.

'Beast! liar!' she said, and struck him on the mouth. 'You know he would never do that. He is faithful to his friends. What have you done with him? Speak – or I will make you speak. You two, there – bring the irons. He *shall* speak!'

'I can only form a guess, madame,' replied Wimsey, 'and I shall not guess any the better for being stimulated with hot irons, like Pantaloon at the circus. Calm yourself, and I will tell you what I think. I think – indeed, I greatly fear – that Monsieur le Président in his hurry to examine the interesting exhibits in my safe may, quite inadvertently, no doubt, have let the door of the inner compartment close behind him. In which case—'

He raised his eyebrows, his shoulders being too sore for shrugging, and gazed at her with a limpid and innocent regret.

'What do you mean?'

Wimsey glanced round the circle. 'I think,' he said, 'I had better begin from the beginning by explaining to you the mechanism of my safe. It is rather a nice safe,' he added plaintively. 'I invented the idea myself – not the principle of its working, of course; that is a matter for scientists – but just the idea of the thing.

'The combination I gave you is perfectly correct as far as it goes. It is a three-alphabet thirteen-letter lock by Bunn & Fishett – a very good one of its kind. It opens the outer door, leading into the ordinary strong-room, where I keep my cash and my Froth Blower's cuff-links and all that. But there is an inner compartment with two doors, which open in a quite different manner. The outermost of these two inner doors is merely a thin steel skin, painted to look like the back of the safe and fitting closely, so as not to betray any join. It lies in the same plane as the wall of the room, you understand, so that if you were to measure the outside and the inside of the safe you would discover no discrepancy. It opens outwards with an ordinary key, and, as I truly assured the President, it was left open when I quitted my flat.'

'Do you think,' said the woman sneeringly, 'that the President is so simple as to be caught in a so obvious trap? He will have wedged open that inner door undoubtedly.'

'Undoubtedly, madame. But the sole purpose of that outer inner door, if I may so express myself, is to appear to be the only inner door. But hidden behind the hinge of that door is another door, a sliding panel, set so closely in the thickness of the wall that you would hardly see it unless you knew it was there. This door was also left open. Our revered Number One had nothing to do but to walk straight through into the inner compartment of the safe, which, by the way, is built into the chimney of the old basement kitchen, which runs up the house at that point. I hope I make myself clear?'

'Yes, yes – get on. Make your story short.'

Wimsey bowed, and, speaking with even greater deliberation than ever, resumed:

'Now, this interesting list of the Society's activities, which I have had the honour of compiling, is written in a very large book – bigger, even, than Monsieur le Président's ledger which he uses downstairs. (I trust, by the way, madame, that you have borne in mind the necessity of putting that ledger in a safe place. Apart from the risk of investigation by some officious policeman, it would be inadvisable that any junior member of the Society should get hold of it. The feeling of the meeting would, I fancy, be opposed to such an occurrence.)'

'It is secure,' she answered hastily. '*Mon dieu!* get on with your story.'

'Thank you – you have relieved my mind. Very good. This big book lies on a steel shelf at the back of the inner compartment. Just a moment. I have not described this inner compartment to you. It is six feet high, three feet wide, and three feet deep. One can stand up in it quite comfortably, unless one is very tall. It suits me nicely – as you may see, I am not more than five feet eight and a half. The President has the advantage of me in height; he might be a little cramped, but there would be room for him to squat if he grew tired of standing. By the way, I don't know if you know it, but you have tied me up rather tightly.'

'I would have you tied till your bones were locked together. Beat him, you! He is trying to gain time.'

'If you beat me,' said Wimsey, 'I'm damned if I'll speak at all. Control yourself, madame; it does not do to move hastily when your king is in check.'

'Get on!' she cried again, stamping with rage.

'Where was I? Ah! the inner compartment. As I say, it is a little snug – the more so that it is not ventilated in any way. Did I mention that the book lay on a steel shelf?'

'You did.'

'Yes. The steel shelf is balanced on a very delicate concealed spring. When the weight of the book – a heavy one, as I said – is lifted, the shelf rises almost imperceptibly. In rising it makes an electrical contact. Imagine to yourself, madame; our revered President steps in – propping the false door open behind him – he sees the book – quickly he snatches it up. To make sure that it is the right one, he opens it – he studies the pages. He looks about for the other objects I have mentioned, which bear the marks of fingerprints. And silently, but very, very quickly – you can imagine it, can you not? – the secret panel, released by the rising of the shelf, leaps across like a panther behind him. Rather a trite simile, but apt, don't you think?'

'My God! oh, my God!' Her hand went up as though to tear the choking mask from her face. 'You – you devil – devil! What is the word that opens the inner door? Quick! I will have it torn out of you – the word!'

'It is not a hard word to remember, madame – though it has been forgotten before now. Do you recollect, when you were a child, being told the tale of *Ali Baba and the Forty Thieves?* When I had that door made, my mind reverted, with rather a pretty touch of sentimentality, in my opinion, to the happy hours of my childhood. The words that open the door are – "Open Sesame".'

'Ah! How long can a man live in this devil's trap of yours?'

'Oh,' said Wimsey cheerfully, 'I should think he might hold out a few hours if he kept cool and didn't use up the available oxygen by shouting and hammering. If we went there at once, I dare say we should find him fairly all right.'

'I shall go myself. Take this man and – do your worst with him. Don't finish him till I come back. I want to see him die!'

'One moment,' said Wimsey, unmoved by this amiable wish. 'I think you had better take me with you.'

'Why – why?'

'Because, you see, I'm the only person who can open the door.'

'But you have given me the word. Was that a lie?'

'No – the word's all right. But, you see, it's one of these new-style electric doors. In fact, it's really the very latest thing in doors. I'm rather proud of it. It opens to the words "Open Sesame" all right – *but to my voice only.*'

'Your voice? I will choke your voice with my own hands. What do you mean – your voice only?'

'Just what I say. Don't clutch my throat like that, or you may alter my voice so that the door won't recognize it. That's better. It's apt to be rather pernickety about voices. It got stuck up for a week once, when I had a cold and could only implore it in a hoarse whisper. Even in the ordinary way, I sometimes have to try several times before I hit on the exact right intonation.'

She turned and appealed to a short, thick-set man standing beside her.

'Is this true? Is it possible?'

'Perfectly, ma'am, I'm afraid,' said the man civilly. From his voice Wimsey took him to be a superior workman of some kind – probably an engineer.

'Is it an electrical device? Do you understand it?'

'Yes, ma'am. It will have a microphone arrangement somewhere, which converts the sound into a series of vibrations controlling an electric needle. When the needle has traced the correct pattern, the circuit is completed and the door opens. The same thing can be done by light vibrations equally easily.'

'Couldn't you open it with tools?'

'In time, yes, ma'am. But only by smashing the mechanism, which is probably well protected.'

'You may take that for granted,' interjected Wimsey reassuringly.

She put her hands to her head.

'I'm afraid we're done in,' said the engineer, with a kind of respect in his tone for a good job of work.

'No – wait! Somebody must know – the workmen who made this thing?'

'In Germany,' said Wimsey briefly.

'Or – yes, yes, I have it – a gramophone. This – this – *he* – shall be made to say the word for us. Quick – how can it be done?'

'Not possible, ma'am. Where should we get the apparatus at half-past three on a Sunday morning? The poor gentleman would be dead long before . . .'

There was a silence, during which the sounds of the awakening day came through the shuttered windows. A motor-horn sounded distantly.

'I give in,' she said. 'We must let him go. Take the ropes off him. You will free him, won't you?' she went on, turning piteously to Wimsey. 'Devil as you are, you are not such a devil as that! You will go straight back and save him!'

'Let him go, nothing!' broke in one of the men. 'He doesn't go to peach to the police, my lady, don't you think it. The President's done in, that's all, and we'd all better make tracks while we can. It's all up, boys. Chuck this fellow down the cellar and fasten him in, so he can't make a row and wake the place up. I'm going to destroy the ledgers. You can see it done if you don't trust me. And you, Thirty, you know where the switch is. Give us a quarter of an hour to clear, and then you can blow the place to glory.'

'No! You can't go – you can't leave him to die – your President – your leader – my – I won't let it happen. Set this devil free. Help me, one of you, with the ropes—'

'None of that, now,' said the man who had spoken before. He caught her by the wrists, and she twisted, shrieking, in his arms, biting and struggling to get free.

'Think, think,' said the man with the treacly voice. 'It's getting on to morning. It'll be light in an hour or two. The police may be here any minute.'

'The police!' She seemed to control herself by a violent effort. 'Yes, yes, you are right. We must not imperil the safety of all for the sake of one man. *He* himself would not wish it. That is so. We will put this carrion in the cellar where it cannot harm us, and depart, every one to his own place, while there is time.'

'And the other prisoner?'

'He? Poor fool – he can do no harm. He knows nothing. Let him go,' she answered contemptuously.

In a few minutes' time Wimsey found himself bundled unceremoniously into the depths of the cellar. He was a little puzzled. That they should refuse to let him go, even at the price of Number One's life, he could understand. He had taken the risk with his eyes open. But that they should leave him as a witness against them seemed incredible.

The men who had taken him down strapped his ankles together and departed, switching the lights out as they went.

'Hi! Kamerad!' said Wimsey. 'It's a bit lonely sitting here. You might leave the light on.'

'It's all right, my friend,' was the reply. 'You will not be in the dark long. They have set the time-fuse.'

The other man laughed with rich enjoyment, and they went out together. So that was it. He was to be blown up with the house. In that case the President would certainly be dead before he was extricated. This worried Wimsey; he would rather have been able to bring the big crook to justice. After all, Scotland Yard had been waiting six years to break up this gang.

He waited, straining his ears. It seemed to him that he heard footsteps over his head. The gang had all crept out by this time . . .

There was certainly a creak. The trap-door had opened; he felt, rather than heard, somebody creeping into the cellar.

'Hush!' said a voice in his ear. Soft hands passed over his face, and went fumbling about his body. There came the cold touch of steel on his wrists. The ropes slackened and dropped off. A key clicked in the handcuffs. The strap about his ankles was unbuckled.

'Quick! quick! they have set the time-switch. The house is mined. Follow me as fast as you can. I stole back – I said I had left my jewellery. It was true. I left it on purpose. *He* must be saved – only you can do it. Make haste!'

Wimsey, staggering with pain, as the blood rushed back

into his bound and numbed arms, crawled after her into the room above. A moment, and she had flung back the shutters and thrown the window open.

'Now go! Release him! You promise?'

'I promise. And I warn you, madame, that this house is surrounded. When my safe-door closed it gave a signal which sent my servant to Scotland Yard. Your friends are all taken—'

'Ah! But you go – never mind me – quick! The time is almost up.'

'Come away from this!'

He caught her by the arm, and they went running and stumbling across the little garden. An electric torch shone suddenly in the bushes.

That you, Parker?' cried Wimsey. 'Get your fellows away. Quick! the house is going up in a minute.'

The garden seemed suddenly full of shouting, hurrying men. Wimsey, floundering in the darkness, was brought up violently against the wall. He made a leap at the coping, caught it, and hoisted himself up. His hands groped for the woman; he swung her up beside him. They jumped; everyone was jumping; the woman caught her foot and fell with a gasping cry. Wimsey tried to stop himself, tripped over a stone, and came down headlong. Then, with a flash and a roar, the night went up in fire.

Wimsey picked himself painfully out from among the débris of the garden wall. A faint moaning near him proclaimed that his companion was still alive. A lantern was turned suddenly upon them.

'Here you are!' said a cheerful voice. 'Are you all right, old thing? Good lord! what a hairy monster!'

'All right,' said Wimsey. 'Only a bit winded. Is the lady safe? H'm – arm broken, apparently – otherwise sound. What's happened?'

'About half a dozen of 'em got blown up; the rest we've bagged.' Wimsey became aware of a circle of dark forms in the wintry dawn. 'Good Lord, what a day! What a come-back for a public character! You old stinker – to let us go on for two years thinking you were dead! I bought a bit of black for an arm-band. I did, really. Did anybody know, besides Bunter?'

'Only my mother and sister. I put it in a secret trust – you know, the thing you send to executors and people. We shall have an awful time with the lawyers, I'm afraid, proving I'm me. Hullo! Is that friend Sugg?'

'Yes, my lord,' said Inspector Sugg, grinning and nearly weeping with excitement. 'Damned glad to see your lordship again. Fine piece of work, your lordship. They're all wanting to shake hands with you, sir.'

'Oh, Lord! I wish I could get washed and shaved first. Awfully glad to see you all again, after two years' exile in Lambeth. Been a good little show, hasn't it?'

'Is he safe?'

Wimsey started at the agonized cry.

'Good Lord!' he cried. 'I forgot the gentleman in the safe. Here, fetch a car, quickly. I've got the great big top Moriarty of the whole bunch quietly asphyxiating at home. Here – hop in, and put the lady in too. I promised we'd get back and save him – though' (he finished the sentence in Parker's ear) 'there may be murder charges too, and I wouldn't give much for his chance at the Old Bailey. Whack her up. He can't last much longer shut up there. He's the bloke you've been wanting, the man at the back of the Morrison case and the Hope-Wilmington case, and hundreds of others.'

The cold morning had turned the streets grey when they drew up before the door of the house in Lambeth. Wimsey took the woman by the arm and helped her out. The mask was off now, and showed her face, haggard and desperate, and white with fear and pain.

'Russian, eh?' whispered Parker in Wimsey's ear.

'Something of the sort. Damn! the front door's blown shut, and the blighter's got the key with him in the safe. Hop through the window, will you?'

Parker bundled obligingly in, and in a few seconds threw

open the door to them. The house seemed very still. Wimsey led the way to the back room, where the strong-room stood. The outer door and the second door stood propped open with chairs. The inner door faced them like a blank green wall.

'Only hope he hasn't upset the adjustment with thumping at it,' muttered Wimsey. The anxious hand on his arm clutched feverishly. He pulled himself together, forcing his tone to one of cheerful commonplace.

'Come on, old thing,' he said, addressing himself conversationally to the door. 'Show us your paces. Open Sesame, confound you. Open Sesame!'

The green door slid suddenly away into the wall. The woman sprang forward and caught in her arms the humped and senseless thing that rolled out from the safe. Its clothes were torn to ribbons, and its battered hands dripped blood.

'It's all right,' said Wimsey, 'it's all right! He'll live – to stand his trial.'

# The Border-line Case

## MARGERY ALLINGHAM

*Further along Piccadilly – not far from famous Piccadilly Circus – in a little cul-de-sac called Bottle Street lives another of the city's aristocratic detectives, Albert Campion, with his indefatigable Cockney manservant, Magersfontein Lugg. Art collector, wine connoisseur and clubman, Campion was a confirmed bachelor for a considerable portion of his career until he met Lady Amanda Fitton, an energetic and shrewd young woman with a passion for mechanics and engineering. Much of the detective's early life is shrouded in mystery – certainly his noble birth and given name of 'Rudolph' are hardly mentioned along with his occupation until he returned from intelligence work during the Second World War and moved into a bachelor flat at 17a Bottle Street, which is located above a police station. His valet, Lugg, is a reformed burglar who brings to Campion's aid an insider's knowledge of the criminal mind plus unswerving devotion. The detective himself has a well-developed skill at seeming a bit stupid in order to fool his criminal adversaries and is an expert at disguise – having solved one early case in drag! Following his debut in* The Crime at Black Dudley *(1929), Campion ages gradually in the later stories, becoming less frenetic and more serious, his fair hair turning a distinguished white and the eyes behind his large horn-rimmed glasses appearing more perceptive and sympathetic to the victims of crime. His cases have ranged from international criminal conspiracies to helping young society girls in trouble. He is even described in one adventure as having all the hall-marks of a 'universal uncle'. Campion's most constant associate among the forces of law and order is Inspector Stanislaus Oates.*

*Margery Allingham (1904–1966) was born in London into a family of writers and published her first book, a novel about smuggling, when she was still a teenager. After her marriage to another author, Philip Youngman Carter in 1927, she began to produce the series of novels about Albert Campion which would make her famous – writing either at the couple's flat in Great Russell Street or their retreat at Tolleshunt d'Arcy, a remote hamlet on the Essex coast. The first of her books to be filmed was* Tiger in the Smoke *(1956), an action-packed adventure about a manhunt in the London underworld with Donald Sinden; and in 1988 Campion was adapted for BBC television starring Peter Davison, Brian Glover as Lugg and Andrew Burt as Inspector Oates. In 'The Border-line Case' (published in 1969) Campion finds himself in a sticky situation both literally and figuratively when, one hot summer night, he is drawn into a case of a London gangland killing . . .*

IT WAS SO hot in London that night that we slept with the wide skylight in our city studio open and let the soot-blacks fall in on us willingly, so long as they brought with them a single stirring breath to move the stifling air. Heat hung on the dark horizons and beneath our particular bowl of sky the city fidgeted, breathless and uncomfortable.

The early editions of the evening papers carried the story of the murder. I read it when they came along about three o'clock on the following afternoon. My mind took in the details lazily, for my eyelids were sticky and the printed words seemed remote and unrelated to reality.

It was a straightforward little incident, or so I thought it, and when I had read the guarded half-column I threw the paper over to Albert Campion, who had drifted in to lunch and stayed to sit quietly in a corner, blinking behind his spectacles, existing merely, in the sweltering day.

The newspapers called the murder the 'Coal Court Shooting Case', and the facts were simple.

At one o'clock in the morning, when Vacation Street, N.E., had been a deserted lane of odoriferous heat, a policeman on the beat had seen a man stumble and fall to the pavement. The intense discomfort of the night being uppermost in his mind, he had not unnaturally diagnosed a case of ordinary collapse and, after loosening the stranger's collar, had summoned the ambulance.

When the authorities arrived, however, the man was pronounced to be dead and the body was taken to the mortuary, where it was discovered that death had been due to a bullet wound neatly placed between the shoulder-blades. The bullet had made a small blue hole and, after perforating the left lung, had furrowed the heart itself, finally coming to rest in the body structure of the chest.

Since this was so, and the fact that the police constable had heard no untoward sound, it had been reasonable to believe that the shot had been fired at some little distance from a gun with a silencer.

Mr Campion was only politely interested. The afternoon certainly was hot and the story, as it then appeared, was hardly original or exciting. He sat on the floor reading it patiently, his long thin legs stretched out in front of him.

'Someone died at any rate,' he remarked at last and added after a pause: 'Poor chap! Out of the frying-pan . . . Dear me, I suppose it's the locality which predisposes one to think of that. Ever seen Vacation Street, Margery?'

I did not answer him. I was thinking how odd it was that a general irritant like the heat should make the dozens of situations arising all round one in the great city seem suddenly almost personal. I found I was desperately sorry for the man who had been shot, whoever he was.

It was Stanislaus Oates who told us the real story behind the half-column in the evening paper. He came in just after four, looking for Campion. He was a Detective-Inspector in those days and had just begun to develop the habit of chatting over his problems with the pale young man in the horn-rimmed spectacles. Theirs was an odd relationship. It was certainly not a case of the clever amateur and the humble policeman: rather the irritable and pugnacious policeman taking it out on the inoffensive, friendly representative of the general public.

On this occasion Oates was rattled.

'It's a case right down your street,' he said briefly to Campion as he sat down. 'Seems to be impossible, for one thing.'

He explained after a while, having salved his conscience by pointing out that he had no business to discuss the case and excusing himself most illogically on grounds of the heat.

'It's "low-class" crime,' he went on briskly. 'Practically gang-shooting. And probably quite uninteresting to all of you who like romance in your crimes. However, it's got me right down on two counts: the first because the man who shot the fellow who died couldn't possibly have done so, and second because I was wrong about the girl. They're so true to type, these girls, that you can't even rely on the proverbial exception.'

He sighed as if the discovery had really grieved him.

We heard the story of Josephine as we sat round in the paralysingly hot studio and, although I never saw the girl then or afterwards, I shall not forget the scene; the three of us listening, breathing rather heavily, while the Inspector talked.

She had been Donovan's girl, so Oates said, and he painted a picture of her for us: slender and flat-chested, with black hair and eyes like a Russian madonna's in a transparent face. She wore blouses, he said, with lace on them and gold ornaments, little chains and crosses and frail brooches whose security was reinforced by gilt safety-pins. She was only twenty, Oates said, and added enigmatically that he would have betted on her, but that it served him right and showed him there was no fool like an old one.

He went on to talk about Donovan, who, it seemed, was

thirty-five and had spent ten years of his life in gaol. The Inspector did not seem to think any the less of him for that. The fact seemed to put the man in a definite category in his mind and that was all.

'Robbery with violence and the R.O. boys,' he said with a wave of his hand and smiled contentedly as though he had made everything clear. 'She was sixteen when he found her and he's given her hell ever since.'

While he still held our interest he mentioned Johnny Gilchick. Johnny Gilchick was the man who was dead.

Oates, who was never more sentimental than was strictly reasonable in the circumstances, let himself go about Josephine and Johnny Gilchick. It was love, he said – love, sudden, painful and ludicrous; and he admitted that he liked to see it.

'I had an aunt once who used to talk about the Real Thing,' he explained, 'and embarrassingly silly the old lady sounded, but after seeing those two youngsters meet and flame and go on until they were a single fiery entity – youngsters who were pretty ordinary tawdry material without it – I find myself sympathizing with her if not condoning the phrase.'

He hesitated and his smooth grey face cracked into a deprecating smile.

'Well, we were both wrong, anyway,' he murmured, 'my aunt and I. Josephine let her Johnny down just as you'd expect her to and after he had got what was coming to him and was lying in the mortuary he was born to lie in she upped and perjured her immortal soul to swear his murderer an alibi. Not that her testimony is of much value as evidence. That's beside the point. The fact remains that she's certainly done her best. You may think me sentimental, but it depresses me. I thought that girl was genuine and my judgement was out.'

Mr Campion stirred.

'Could we have the details?' he asked politely. 'We've only seen the evening paper. It wasn't very helpful.'

Oates glared at him balefully.

'Frankly, the facts are exasperating,' he said. 'There's a little catch in them somewhere. It must be something so simple that I missed it altogether. That's really why I've come to look for you. I thought you might care to come along and take a glance at the place. What about it?'

There was no general movement. It was too hot to stir. Finally the Inspector took up a piece of chalk and sketched a rough diagram on the bare boards of the model's throne.

'This is Vacation Street,' he said, edging the chalk along a crack. 'It's the best part of a mile long. Up this end, here by the chair, it's nearly all wholesale houses. This sandbin I'm sketching in now marks the boundary of two police divisions. Well, here, ten yards to the left, is the entrance to Coal Court, which is a cul-de-sac composed of two blank backs of ware-house buildings and a café at the far end. The café is open all night. It serves the printers from the two big presses farther down the road. That's its legitimate trade. But it is also a sort of unofficial headquarters for Donovan's mob. Josephine sits at the desk downstairs and keeps an eye on the door. God knows what hours she keeps. She always seems to be there.'

He paused and there came into my mind a recollection of the breathless night through which we had all passed, and I could imagine the girl sitting there in the stuffy shop with her thin chest and her great black eyes.

The Inspector was still speaking.

'Now,' he said, 'there's an upstairs room in the café. It's on the second floor. That's where our friend Donovan spent most of his evening. I expect he had a good few friends with him and we shall locate them all in time.'

He bent over the diagram.

'Johnny Gilchick died here,' he said, drawing a circle about a foot beyond the square which indicated the sandbin. 'Although the bobby was right down the road, he saw him pause under the lamp post, stagger and fall. He called the Constable from the other division and they got the ambulance. All that is plain sailing. There's just one difficulty. Where was Donovan when he fired the shot? There were two policemen in the street at the time, remember. At the moment of the actual shooting one of them, the Never Street man, was making a round of a warehouse yard, but the other, the Phyllis Court chap, was there on the spot, not forty yards away, and it was he who actually saw Johnny Gilchick fall, although he heard no shot. Now I tell you, Campion, there's not an ounce of cover in the whole of that street. How did Donovan get out of the café, where did he stand to shoot Johnny neatly through the back, and how did he get back again without being seen? The side walls of the cul-de-sac are solid concrete backs of warehouses, there is no way round from the back of the café, nor could he possibly have gone over the roofs. The warehouses tower over the café like liners over a tug. Had he come out down the road one or other of the bobbies must have been certain to have seen him. How did he do it?'

'Perhaps Donovan didn't do it,' I ventured and received a pitying glance for my temerity.

'That's the one fact,' said the Inspector heavily. 'That's the one thing I do know. I know Donovan. He's one of the few English mob boys who carry guns. He served five years with the gangs in New York and has the misfortune to take his liquor in bouts. After each bout he has a period of black depression, during which he may do anything. Johnny Gilchick used to be one of Donovan's mob and when Johnny fell for the girl he turned in the gang, which was adding insult to injury where Donovan was concerned.'

He paused and smiled.

'Donovan was bound to get Johnny in the end,' he said. 'It was never anything but a question of time. The whole mob expected it. The neighbourhood was waiting for it. Donovan had said openly that the next time Johnny dropped into the café would be his final appearance there. Johnny called last night, was ordered out of the place by the terrified girl, and finally walked out of the cul-de-sac. He turned the corner and strolled down the road. Then he was shot by Donovan. There's no way round it, Campion. The doctors say that death was as near instantaneous as may be. Johnny Gilchick could not have walked three paces with the bullet in his back. As for the gun, that was pretty obviously Donovan's too. We haven't actually picked it up yet, but we know he had one of the type we are after. It's a clear case, a straightforward case, if only we knew where Donovan stood when he fired the shot.'

Mr Campion looked up. His eyes were thoughtful behind his spectacles.

'The girl gave Donovan an alibi?' he inquired.

Oates shrugged his shoulders. 'Rather,' he said. 'She was passionate about it. He was there the whole time, every minute of the time, never left the upper room once in the whole evening. I could kill her and she would not alter her story; she'd take her dying oath on it and so on. It didn't mean anything either way. Still, I was sorry to see her doing it, with her boy friend barely cold. She was sucking up to the mob, of course; probably had excellent reasons for doing so. Yet, as I say, I was sorry to hear her volunteering the alibi before she was asked.'

'Ah! she volunteered it, did she?' Campion was interested.

Oates nodded and his small eyes widened expressively.

'Forced it on us. Came roaring round to the police station with it. Threw it off her chest as if she were doing something fine. I'm not usually squeamish about that sort of thing, but it gave me a distinct sense of distaste, I don't mind telling you. Frankly, I gave her a piece of my mind. Told her to go and look at the body, for one thing.'

'Not kind of you,' observed Mr Campion mildly. 'And what did she do?'

'Oh, blubbered herself sick, like the rest of 'em.' Oates was still disgruntled. 'Still, that's not of interest. What girls like Josephine do or don't do doesn't really matter. She was saving her own skin. If she hadn't been so enthusiastic about it I'd have forgiven her. It's Donovan who is important. Where was Donovan when he fired?'

The shrill chatter of the telephone answered him and he glanced at me apologetically.

'I'm afraid that's mine,' he said. 'You don't mind, do you? I left the number with the Sergeant.'

He took off the receiver and as he bent his head to listen his face changed. We watched him with an interest it was far too hot to dissemble.

'Oh,' he said flatly after a long pause. 'Really? Well, it doesn't matter either way, does it? . . . Still, what did she do it for? . . . What? . . . I suppose so . . . Yes? . . . Really?'

He seemed suddenly astounded as his informant at the other end of the wire evidently came out with a second piece of information more important than the first.

'You can't be certain . . . you are? . . . What?'

The faraway voice explained busily. We could hear its steady drone. Inspector Oates's exasperation grew.

'Oh, all right, all right,' he said at last. 'I'm crackers . . . we're all crackers . . . have it your own damned way.'

With which vulgar outburst he rang off.

'Alibi sustained?' inquired Mr Campion.

'Yes.' The Inspector grunted out the word. 'A couple of printers who were in the downstairs room swear he did not go through the shop all the evening. They're sound fellows. Make good witnesses. Yet Donovan shot Johnny. I'm certain of it. He shot him clean through the concrete angle of a piano warehouse as far as I can see.' He turned to Campion almost angrily. 'Explain that, can you?'

Mr Campion coughed. He seemed a little embarrassed.

'I say, you know,' he ventured, 'there are just two things that occur to me.'

'Then out with them, son.' The Inspector lit a cigarette and wiped his face. 'Out with them. I'm not proud.'

Mr Campion coughed again. 'Well, the – er – heat, for one thing, don't you know,' he said with profound uneasiness. 'The heat, and one of your concrete walls.'

The Inspector swore a little and apologized.

'If anyone could forget this heat he's welcome,' he said. 'What's the matter with the wall, too?'

Mr Campion bent over the diagram on the boards of the throne. He was very apologetic.

'Here is the angle of the warehouse,' he said, 'and here is

the sandbin. Here to the left is the lamp post where Johnny Gilchick was found. Farther on to the left is the P.C. from Never Street examining a courtyard and temporarily off the scene, while to the right, on the other side of the entrance to Coal Court, is another constable, P.C. someone-or-other, of Phyllis Court. One is apt to – er – think of the problem as though it were contained in four solid walls, two concrete walls, two policemen.'

He hesitated and glanced timidly at the Inspector.

'When is a policeman not a concrete wall, Oates? In – er well, in just such heat . . . do you think, or don't you?'

Oates was staring at him, his eyes narrowed.

'Damn it!' he said explosively. 'Damn it, Campion, I believe you're right. I knew it was something so simple that it was staring me in the face.'

They stood together looking down at the diagram. Oates stooped to put a chalk cross at the entrance to the cul-de-sac.

'It was *that* lamp post,' he said. 'Give me that telephone. Wait till I get hold of that fellow.'

While he was carrying on an excited conversation we demanded an explanation from Mr Campion and he gave it to us at last, mild and apologetic as usual.

'Well, you see,' he said, 'there's the sandbin. The sandbin marks the boundary of two police divisions. Policeman A, very hot and tired, sees a man collapse from the heat under a lamp post on his territory. The man is a little fellow and it occurs to Policeman A that it would be a simple matter to move him to the next lamp post on the other side of the sandbin, where he would automatically become the responsibility of Policeman B, who is even now approaching. Policeman A achieves the change and is bending over the prostrate figure when his colleague comes up. Since he knows nothing of the bullet wound, the entrance to the cul-de-sac, with its clear view to the café, second-floor room, has no significance in his mind. Today, when its full importance must have dawned upon him, he evidently thinks it best to hold his tongue.'

Oates came back from the phone triumphant.

'The first bobby went on leave this morning,' he said. 'He was an old hand. He must have spotted the chap was dead, took it for granted it was the heat, and didn't want to be held up here by the inquest. Funny I didn't see that in the beginning.'

We were all silent for some moments.

'Then – the girl?' I began at last.

The Inspector frowned and made a little grimace of regret.

'A pity about the girl,' he said. 'Of course it was probably an accident. Our man who saw it happen said he couldn't be sure.'

I stared at him and he explained, albeit a little hurriedly.

'Didn't I tell you? When my sergeant phoned about the alibi he told me. As Josephine crossed the road after visiting the mortuary this morning she stepped under a bus . . . Oh yes, instantly.'

He shook his head. He seemed uncomfortable.

'She thought she was making a gesture when she came down to the station, don't you see? The mob must have told her to swear that no one had been in the upstairs room; that must have been their first story until they saw how the luck lay. So when she came beetling down to us she must have thought she was risking her life to give her Johnny's murderer away, while instead of that she was simply giving the fellow an alibi . . . Funny the way things happen, isn't it?'

He glanced at Campion affectionately.

'It's because you don't get your mind cluttered up with the human element that you see these things so quickly,' he said. 'You see everything in terms of A and B. It makes all the difference.'

Mr Campion, the most gentle of men, made no comment at all.

# The Santa Claus Club

## JULIAN SYMONS

*A brisk walk of half a mile takes us down Lower Regent Street, then left along Pall Mall and into that great landmark of London, Trafalgar Square. Here, in the Soames Building with its view across the invariably busy square, is the small office of Francis Quarles who has been described by* Suspense *magazine as 'the most gentlemanly private eye of them all'. Francis is a big man, bulky rather than fat, which in his cramped office tends to enhance his size even more. He is over six foot tall, and takes a pride in his appearance: favouring well-cut suits, silk shirts and colourful, patterned ties. He is never seen without a buttonhole (preferably a carnation) in his lapel. To some of the men of business and politics who consult him this makes Quarles seem a bit of a dandy, while the beautiful women from society and show business who seek his help find him sexually fascinating. He is, as his cases make clear, a highly deceptive character, much tougher than he initially looks and with a formidable brain that law-breakers tangle with at their cost. The first of Quarles' action-packed adventures, 'The Case of XX-2' appeared in* Ellery Queen's Mystery Magazine *in August 1952 and the first collection,* Francis Quarles Investigates, *was published in 1965.*

*Julian Symons (1912–1994) was widely known as 'the crime writers' crime writer' and won most of the major awards in the genre including the Cartier Diamond Dagger Award from the*

*Crime Writers' Association for a 'lifetime's achievement' in the field and several others from equally prestigious organizations like the Mystery Writers of America. Born in London, Julian worked as a secretary in an engineering company and as an advertising copywriter, before his friend George Orwell helped him to become a freelance book columnist and thereafter a biographer, poet and criminologist. As well as his various acclaimed non-fiction works such as* A Reasonable Doubt *(1960),* A Pictorial History of Crime *(1966) and* Bloody Murder *(1972), he has written a number of books featuring Inspector Bland in which he started his attempt to blend the literary values of the conventional novel with the excitement of the thriller – an achievement that has reached fruition in some of his latest books like* Death's Darkest Face *(1990). Although Julian later stopped living in the city where he grew up, he was a very clubable man – he was, in fact, a founder member of the Crime Writers' Association as well as a past chairman – a fact which gives an added piquancy to this adventure of his gentlemanly private eye which first appeared in 1960.*

IT IS NOT often, in real life, that letters are written recording implacable hatred nursed over the years, or that private detectives are invited by peers to select dining clubs, or that murders occur at such dining clubs, or that they are solved on the spot by a process of deduction. The case of the Santa Claus Club provided an example of all these rarities.

The case began one day, a week before Christmas, when Francis Quarles went to see Lord Acrise. He was a rich man, Lord Acrise, and an important one, the chairman of this big building concern and director of that and the other insurance company, and consultant to the Government on half a dozen matters. He had been a harsh, intolerant man in his prime, and was still hard enough in his early seventies, Quarles guessed, as he looked at the beaky nose, jutting chin and stony blue eyes.

They sat in the study of Acrise's house just off the Brompton Road.

'Just tell me what you think of these,' Lord Acrise said.

*These* were three letters, badly typed on a machine with a worn ribbon. They were all signed with the name James Gliddon. The first two contained vague references to some wrong done to Gliddon by Acrise in the past. They were written in language that was wild but unmistakably threatening. *You have been a whited sepulchre for too long, but now your time has come . . . You don't know what I'm going to do, now I've come back, but you won't be able to help wondering and worrying . . . The mills of God grind slowly, but they're going to grind you into little bits for what you've done to me.*

The third letter was more specific. *So the thief is going to play Santa Claus. That will be your last evening alive. I shall be there, Joe Acrise, and I shall watch with pleasure as you squirm in agony.*

Quarles looked at the envelopes. They were plain and cheap. The address was typed, and the word *Personal* was on top of each envelope.

'Who is James Gliddon?' he asked.

The stony eyes glared at him. 'I'm told you're to be trusted. Gliddon was a school friend of mine. We grew up together in the slums of Nottingham. We started a building company together. It did well for a time, then went bust. There was a lot of money missing. Gliddon kept the books. He got five years for fraud.'

'Have you heard from him since then? I see all these letters are recent.'

'He's written half a dozen letters, I suppose, over the years. The last one came – oh, seven years ago, I should think. From the Argentine.' Acrise stopped, then added abruptly, 'Snewin tried to find him for me, but he'd disappeared.'

'Snewin?'

'My secretary. Been with me twelve years.'

He pressed a bell. An obsequious, fattish man, whose appearance somehow put Quarles in mind of an enormous mouse, scurried in.

'Snewin – did we keep any of those old letters from Gliddon?'

'No, sir. You told me to destroy them.'

'The last ones came from the Argentine, right?'

'From Buenos Aires, to be exact, sir.'

Acrise nodded, and Snewin scurried out.

Quarles said, 'Who else knows this story about Gliddon?'

'Just my wife.'

'And what does this mean about you playing Santa Claus?'

'I'm this year's chairman of the Santa Claus Club. We hold our raffle and dinner next Monday.'

Then Quarles remembered. The Santa Claus Club had been formed by ten rich men. Each year they met, every one of them dressed up as Santa Claus, and held a raffle. The members took it in turn to provide the prize that was raffled – it might be a case of Napoleon brandy, a modest cottage with some exclusive salmon fishing rights attached to it, or a Constable painting. Each Santa Claus bought one ticket for the raffle, at a cost of one thousand guineas. The total of ten thousand guineas was given to a Christmas charity. After the raffle the assembled Santa Clauses, each accompanied by one guest, ate a traditional English Christmas dinner.

The whole thing was a combination of various English characteristics: enjoyment of dressing up, a wish to help charities and the desire also that the help given should not go unrecorded.

'I want you to find Gliddon,' Lord Acrise said. 'Don't mistake me, Mr Quarles. I don't want to take action against him, I want to help him. I wasn't to blame, don't think I admit that, but it was hard that Jimmy Gliddon should go to jail. I'm a hard man, have been all my life, but I don't think my worst enemies would call me mean. Those who've helped me know that when I die they'll find they're not forgotten. Jimmy Gliddon must be an old man now. I'd like to set him up for the rest of his life.'

'To find him by next Monday is a tall order,' Quarles said. ' But I'll try.'

He was at the door when Acrise said, 'By the way, I'd like you to be my guest at the Club dinner on Monday night . . .'

There were two ways of trying to find Gliddon; by investigation of his career after leaving prison, and through the typewritten letters. Quarles took the job of tracing the past, leaving the letters to his secretary, Molly Player.

From Scotland Yard he found out that Gliddon had spent nearly four years in prison, from 1913 to late 1916. He had joined a Nottinghamshire regiment when he came out, and the records of this regiment showed that he had been demobilized in August, 1919, with the rank of Sergeant. In 1923 he had been given a sentence of three years for an attempt to smuggle diamonds. Thereafter all trace of him in Britain vanished.

Quarles made some expensive telephone calls to Buenos Aires, where the letters had come from seven years earlier. He learned that Gliddon had lived in that city from a time just after the second world war until 1955. He ran an import-export business, and was thought to have been living in other South American Republics during the war. His business was said to have been a cloak for smuggling, both of drugs and of suspected Nazis, whom he got out of Europe into the Argentine. In 1955 a newspaper had accused Gliddon of arranging the entry into the Argentine of a Nazi war criminal named Hermann Breit. Gliddon disappeared. A couple of weeks later a battered body was washed up just outside the city.

'It was identified as Señor Gliddon,' the liquid voice said over the telephone. 'But you know, Señor Quarles, in such matters the police are sometimes unhappy to close their files.'

'There was still some doubt?'

'Yes. Not very much, perhaps. But in these cases there is often a measure of doubt.'

Molly Player found out nothing useful about the paper and envelopes. They were of the sort that could be bought in a thousand stores and shops in London and elsewhere. She had no more luck with the typewriter.

Lord Acrise made no comment on Quarles' recital of failure. 'See you on Monday evening, seven-thirty, black tie,' he said, and barked with laughter. 'Your host will be Santa Claus.'

'I'd like to be there earlier.'

'Good idea. Any time you like. You know where it is? Robert the Devil Restaurant . . .'

The Robert the Devil Restaurant is situated inconspicuously in Mayfair. It is not a restaurant in the ordinary sense of the word, for there is no public dining-room, but simply several private rooms accommodating any number of guests from two to thirty. Perhaps the food is not quite the best in London, but it is certainly the most expensive.

It was here that Quarles arrived at half-past six, a big, suave man, rather too conspicuously elegant perhaps in a midnight-blue dinner jacket. He talked to Albert, the *maître d'hotel,* whom he had known for some years, took an unobtrusive look at the waiters, went into and admired the sparkling kitchens.

Albert observed his activities with tolerant amusement. 'You are here on some sort of business, Mr Quarles?'

'I am a guest, Albert. I am also a kind of bodyguard. Tell me, how many of your waiters have joined you in the past twelve months?'

'Perhaps half a dozen. They come, they go.'

'Is there anybody at all on your staff – waiters, kitchen staff, anybody – who has joined you in the past year, and who is over sixty years old?'

'No. There is not such a one.'

The first of the guests came just after a quarter-past seven. This was the brain surgeon Sir James Erdington, with a guest whom Quarles recognised as the Arctic explorer, Norman Endell. After that they came at intervals of a minute or two: a junior minister in the Government; one of the three most important men in the motor industry; a general elevated to the peerage to celebrate his retirement; a theatrical producer named Roddy Davis, who had successfully combined commerce and culture.

As they arrived, the hosts went into a special robing room to put on their Santa Claus clothes, while the guests drank sherry.

At seven-twenty-five Snewin scurried in, gasped, 'Excuse me, place names, got to put them out,' and went into the dining-room. Through the open door Quarles glimpsed a large oval table, gleaming with silver, bright with roses.

After Snewin came Lord Acrise, jutting-nosed and fearsome-eyed. ' Sorry to have kept you waiting,' he barked, and asked conspiratorially, 'Well?'

'No sign.'

'False alarm. Lot of nonsense. Got to dress up now.'

He went into the robing room with his box – each of the hosts had a similar box, labelled 'Santa Claus' – and came out again bewigged, bearded and robed. 'Better get the business over, and then we can enjoy ourselves. You can tell 'em to come in,' he said to Albert.

This referred to the photographers, who had been clustered outside, and now came into the room specially provided for holding the raffle. In the centre of the room was a table, and on the table stood this year's prize, two exquisite T'ang horses. On the other side of the table were ten chairs arranged in a semi-circle, and on these sat the Santa Clauses. Their guests stood inconspicuously at the side.

The raffle was conducted with the utmost seriousness. Each Santa Claus had a numbered slip. These slips were put into a tombola, and Acrise put in his hand and drew out one of them. Flash bulbs exploded.

'The number drawn is eight,' Acrise announced, and Roddy Davis waved the counterfoil in his hand.

'Isn't that *wonderful?* It's my ticket.' He went over to the horses, picked up one. ' I'm bound to say that they couldn't have gone to *anybody* who'd have appreciated them more.'

Quarles, standing near the general, whose face was as red as his robe, heard him mutter something uncomplimentary. Charity, he reflected, was not universal, even in a gathering of Santa Clauses. Then there were more flashes, the photographers disappeared, and Quarles' views about the nature of charity were reinforced when, as they were about to go into the dining-room, Sir James Erdington said, ' Forgotten something, haven't you, Acrise?'

With what seemed dangerous quietness Acrise answered, 'Have I? I don't think so.'

'It's customary for the Club and guests to sing "Noel" before we go in to dinner.'

'You didn't come to last year's dinner. It was agreed then that we should give it up. Carols after dinner, much better.'

'I must say I thought that was just for last year, because we were late,' Roddy Davis fluted.

'Suggest we put it to the vote,' Erdington said sharply.

Half a dozen of the Santas now stood looking at each other with subdued hostility. Then suddenly the Arctic explorer, Endell, began to sing 'Noel, Noel' in a rich bass. There was the faintest flicker of hesitation, and then the guests and their hosts joined in. The situation was saved.

At dinner Quarles found himself with Acrise on one side of him and Roddy Davis on the other. Endell sat at Acrise's other side, and beyond him was Erdington. Turtle soup was followed by grilled sole, and then three great turkeys were brought in. The helpings of turkey were enormous. With the soup they drank a light, dry sherry, with the sole Chassagne Montrachet, with the turkey an Aloxe Corton.

'And who are *you*?' Roddy Davis peered at Quarles' card and said, 'Of course, I know your name.'

'I am a criminologist.' This sounded better, Quarles thought, than 'private detective'.

'I remember your monograph on criminal calligraphy. Quite fascinating.'

So Davis *did* know who he was. It would be easy, Quarles thought, to underrate the intelligence of this man.

'These beards really do get in the way rather,' Davis said. 'But there, one must suffer for tradition. Have you known Acrise long?'

'Not very. I'm greatly privileged to be here.'

Quarles had been watching, as closely as he could, the pouring of the wine, the serving of the food. He had seen nothing suspicious. Now, to get away from Davis' questions, he turned to his host.

'Damned awkward business before dinner,' Acrise said. 'Might have been, at least. Can't let well alone, Erdington.' He picked up his turkey leg, attacked it with Elizabethan gusto, wiped his mouth and fingers with his napkin. 'Like this wine?'

'It's excellent.'

'Chose it myself. They've got some good Burgundies here.' Acrise's speech was slightly slurred, and it seemed to Quarles that he was rapidly getting drunk.

'Do you have any speeches?'

'No speeches. Just sing carols. But I've got a little surprise for 'em.'

'What sort of surprise?'

'Very much in the spirit of Christmas, and a good joke too. But if I told you, it wouldn't be a surprise, would it?'

There was a general cry of pleasure as Albert himself brought in the great plum pudding, topped with holly and blazing with brandy.

'That's the most wonderful pudding I've ever seen in my life,' Endell said. ' Are we really going to eat it ?'

'Of course,' Acrise said irritably. He stood up, swaying a little, and picked up the knife beside the pudding.

'I don't like to be critical, but our Chairman is really not cutting the pudding very well,' Roddy Davis whispered to Quarles. And indeed, it was more of a stab than a cut that Acrise made at the pudding. Albert took over, and cut it quickly and efficiently. Bowls of brandy butter were circulated.

Quarles leaned towards Acrise. 'Are you all right?'

'Of course I'm all right.'

The slurring was very noticeable now. Acrise ate no pudding, but he drank some more wine, and dabbed at his lips. When the pudding was finished, he got slowly to his feet again and toasted the Queen. Cigars were lighted. Acrise was not smoking. He whispered something to the waiter, who nodded and left the room. Acrise got up again, leaning heavily on the table.

'A little surprise,' he said. ' In the spirit of Christmas.'

Quarles had thought that he was beyond being surprised by the activities of the Santa Claus Club, but he was astonished at the sight of the three figures who entered the room.

They were led by Snewin, somehow more mouselike than ever, wearing a long, white smock and a red nightcap with a tassel. He was followed by an older man dressed in a kind of grey sackcloth, with a face so white that it might have been covered in plaster of Paris. This man carried chains, which he shook. At the rear came a young-middle-aged lady who seemed to be completely hung with tinsel.

'I am Scrooge,' said Snewin.

'I am Marley,' wailed grey sackcloth, clanking his chains vigorously.

'And I,' said the young-middle-aged lady, with abominable sprightliness, 'am the ghost of Christmas past.'

There was a ripple of laughter.

'We have come,' said Snewin in a thin, mouse voice, 'to perform for you our own interpretation of *A Christmas Carol* . . . Oh, sir, what's the matter?'

Lord Acrise stood up in his robes, tore off his wig, pulled at his beard, tried to say something. Then he clutched at the side of his chair and fell sideways, so that he leaned heavily against Endell and slipped slowly to the floor.

There ensued a minute of confused, important activity. Endell made some sort of exclamation and rose from his chair, slightly obstructing Quarles. Erdington was first beside the body, holding the wrist in his hand, listening for the heart. Then they were all crowding round. Snewin, at Quarles' left shoulder, was babbling something, and at his right were Roddy Davis and Endell.

'Stand back,' Erdington snapped. He stayed on his knees for another few moments, looking curiously at Acrise's puffed, distorted face, bluish around the mouth. Then he stood up.

'He's dead.'

There was a murmur of surprise and horror, and now they all drew back, as men do instinctively from the presence of death.

'Heart attack?' somebody said.

Quarles moved to his side. 'I'm a private detective, Sir James. Lord Acrise feared an attempt on his life, and asked me to come along here.'

'You seem to have done well so far,' Erdington said drily.

'May I look at the body?'

'If you wish.'

As Quarles bent down, he caught the smell of bitter almonds. 'There's a smell like prussic acid, but the way he died precludes cyanide, I think. He seemed to become very drunk during dinner, and his speech was blurred. Does that suggest anything to you?'

'I'm a brain surgeon, not a physician.' Erdington stared at the floor. 'Nitro benzene?'

'That's what I thought. We shall have to notify the police.'

Quarles went to the door and spoke to a disturbed Albert. Then he returned to the room and clapped his hands.

'Gentlemen. My name is Francis Quarles, and I am a private detective. Lord Acrise asked me to come here tonight because he had received a threat that this would be his last evening alive. The threat said, 'I shall be there, and I shall watch with pleasure as you squirm in agony.' Lord Acrise has been poisoned. It seems certain that the man who made the threat is in this room.'

'Gliddon,' a voice said. Snewin had divested himself of the white smock and red nightcap, and now appeared as his customary respectable self.

'Yes. This letter, and others he had received, were signed with the name of James Gliddon, a man who bore a grudge against Lord Acrise which went back nearly half a century. Gliddon became a professional smuggler and crook. He would now be in his late sixties.'

'But dammit man, this Gliddon's not here.' That was the

General, who took off his wig and beard. 'Lot of tomfoolery.'

In a shamefaced way the other members of the Santa Claus Club removed their facial trappings. Marley took off his chains and the lady discarded her cloak of tinsel.

Quarles said, 'Isn't he here? But Lord Acrise is dead.'

Snewin coughed. ' Excuse me, sir, but would it be possible for my colleagues from our local dramatic society to retire?'

'Everybody must stay in this room until the police arrive,' Quarles said grimly. 'The problem, as you will all realize, is how the poison was administered. All of us ate the same food, drank the same wine. I sat next to Lord Acrise, and I watched as closely as possible to make sure of this. After dinner some of you smoked cigars or cigarettes, but not Lord Acrise.'

'Just a moment.' It was Roddy Davis who spoke. 'This sounds fantastic, but wasn't it Sherlock Holmes who said that when you'd eliminated all other possibilities, even a fantastic one must be right? Supposing poison in powder form was put on to Acrise's food? Through the pepper pots, say . . .'

Erdington was shaking his head, but Quarles unscrewed both salt and pepper pots and tasted their contents. 'Salt and pepper,' he said briefly. 'Hello, what's this?'

'It's Acrise's napkin,' Endell said. 'What's remarkable about that?'

'It's a napkin, but not the one Acrise used. He wiped his mouth half a dozen times on his napkin, and wiped his greasy fingers on it too, when he'd gnawed a turkey bone. He must certainly have left grease marks on it. But look at this napkin.'

He held it up, and they saw that it was spotless. Quarles said softly, 'The murderer's mistake.'

Quarles turned to Erdington. 'Sir James and I agree that the poison used was probably nitro benzene. This is deadly as a liquid, but it is also poisonous as a vapour – isn't that so?'

Erdington nodded. 'You'll remember the case of the unfortunate young man who used shoe polish containing nitro benzene on damp shoes, put them on and wore them, and was killed by the fumes.'

'Yes. Somebody made sure that Lord Acrise had a napkin that had been soaked in nitro benzene but was dry enough to use. The same person substituted the proper napkin, the one belonging to the restaurant, after Acrise was dead.'

'That means the napkin must still be here,' Davis said.

'It does.'

'Then I vote that we submit to a search!'

'That won't be necessary,' Quarles said. ' Only one person here fulfils all the qualifications of the murderer.'

'James Gliddon?'

'No. Gliddon is almost certainly dead, as I found out when I made enquiries about him. But the murderer is some-body who knew about Acrise's relationship with Gliddon, and tried to be clever by writing those letters to lead us along a wrong track.' He paused. 'Then the murderer is somebody who had the opportunity of coming in here before dinner, and who knew exactly where Acrise would be sitting.'

There was a dead silence in the room.

Quarles said, 'He removed any possible suspicion from himself, as he thought, by being absent from the dinner table, but he arranged to come in afterwards to exchange the napkins. He probably put the poisoned napkin into the clothes he discarded. As for motive, long-standing hatred might be enough, but he is also somebody who knew that he would benefit handsomely when Acrise died . . . stop him, will you?'

But the General, with a tackle reminiscent of the days when he had been the best wing three-quarter in the country, had already brought to the floor Lord Acrise's secretary, Snewin.

# The Incautious Burglar

## JOHN DICKSON CARR

*Moving on from Trafalgar Square brings us to Charing Cross Station and, just behind it, the stylish group of buildings which make up Adelphi Terrace. Here, at number 1, the gargantuan private detective, Dr Gideon Fell, has his office; and if he is not busy on a case, he will alternately be found discoursing on his love of good beer and tobacco or else telling jokes which he is constantly surprised make other people laugh. Fell, with his three chins, drooping moustache, and rumbling voice, bears a striking resemblance to the great English writer G. K. Chesterton, and like him, wears a huge cape and glasses perched on the end of his nose. His obvious eccentricity is underlined by the fact that he much prefers tackling cases where there is some hint of the supernatural involved, and he will happily travel hundreds of miles to prove that there is a rational explanation for the events after all. As Dorothy L. Sayers has observed, 'Dr Fell always arrives in time to dispel the ghosts with a fat chuckle and a blast of common sense.' Once met, he is never forgotten either, and there are a number of grateful clients who have been heard to say that they think of him as a mixture of Father Christmas and Old King Cole! The doctor's appreciation of good beer is another incentive for him to travel, making him something of a forerunner in the campaign for real ales . . .*

*John Dickson Carr (1906–1977), who has been called the master of the 'impossible crime' story, was another American whose inspiration to write detective fiction came, initially, when he was still a youngster and read G. K. Chesterton's stories of Father Brown and then, more specifically, when he settled in London with his English wife. When Carr made the decision to devise a detective of his own he made no secret of the fact that his man was modelled on Chesterton, 'in the hope I was creating a character everybody would like.' In 23 novels, beginning with* Hag's Nook *(1933), and dozens of short stories, John not only made Fell likeable but wholly memorable, too. (Sadly, John Dickson Carr was actually invited to join the London Detection Club in 1936 when G. K. Chesterton was its president, but just before they were due to meet – and doubtless discuss their doppelgänger, Dr Fell – the older man was struck down with his fatal illness.) In the story of 'The Incautious Burglar', the superweight sleuth is found once again running down a good pint of beer at the same time as he is hunting down a criminal.*

TWO GUESTS, WHO were not staying the night at Cranleigh Court, left at shortly past eleven o'clock. Marcus Hunt saw them to the front door. Then he returned to the dining-room, where the poker-chips were now stacked into neat piles of white, red, and blue.

'Another game?' suggested Rolfe.

'No good,' said Derek Henderson. His tone, as usual, was weary. 'Not with just the three of us.'

Their host stood by the sideboard and watched them. The long, low house, overlooking the Weald of Kent, was so quiet that their voices rose with startling loudness. The dining-room, large and panelled, was softly lighted by electric wall-candles which brought out the sombre colours of the paintings. It is not often that anybody sees, in one room of an otherwise commonplace country house, two Rembrandts and a Van Dyck. There was a kind of defiance about those paintings.

To Arthur Rolfe – the art dealer – they represented enough money to make him shiver. To Derek Henderson – the art critic – they represented a problem. What they represented to Marcus Hunt was not apparent.

Hunt stood by the sideboard, his fists on his hips, smiling. He was a middle-sized, stocky man, with a full face and a high complexion. Equip him with a tuft of chin-whisker, and he would have looked like a Dutch burgher for a Dutch brush. His shirt-front bulged out untidily. He watched with ironical amusement while Henderson picked up a pack of cards in long fingers, cut them into piles, and shuffled with a sharp flick of each thumb which made the cards melt together like a conjuring trick.

Henderson yawned.

'My boy,' said Hunt, 'you surprise me.'

'That's what I try to do,' answered Henderson, still wearily. He looked up. 'But why do you say so, particularly?'

Henderson was young, he was long, he was lean, he was immaculate; and he wore a beard. It was a reddish beard, which moved some people to hilarity. But he wore it with an air of complete naturalness.

'I'm surprised,' said Hunt, 'that you enjoy anything so bourgeois – so plebeian – as poker.'

'I enjoy reading people's characters,' said Henderson. 'Poker's the best way to do it, you know.'

Hunt's eyes narrowed. 'Oh? Can you read my character, for instance?'

'With pleasure,' said Henderson. Absently he dealt himself a poker-hand, face up. It contained a pair of fives, and the last card was the ace of spades. Henderson remained staring at it for a few seconds before he glanced up again.

'And I can tell you,' he went on, 'that you surprise me. Do you mind if I'm frank? I had always thought of you as the Colossus of Business; the smasher; the plunger; the fellow who took the long chances. Now, you're not like that at all.'

Marcus Hunt laughed. But Henderson was undisturbed.

'You're tricky, but you're cautious. I doubt if you ever took a long chance in your life. Another surprise' – he dealt himself a new hand – 'is Mr Rolfe here. He's the man who, given the proper circumstances, would take the long chances.'

Arthur Rolfe considered this. He looked startled, but rather flattered. Though in height and build not unlike Hunt, there was nothing untidy about him. He had a square, dark face, with thin shells of eyeglasses, and a worried forehead.

'I doubt that,' he declared, very serious about this. Then he smiled. 'A person who took long chances in my business would find himself in the soup.' He glanced round the room. 'Anyhow, I'd be too cautious to have three pictures, with an aggregate value of thirty thousand pounds, hanging in an unprotected downstairs room with french windows giving on a terrace.' An almost frenzied note came into his voice. 'Great Scot! Suppose a burglar—'

'Damn!' said Henderson unexpectedly.

Even Hunt jumped.

Ever since the poker-party, an uneasy atmosphere had been growing. Hunt had picked up an apple from a silver fruit-bowl on the sideboard. He was beginning to pare it with a fruit-knife, a sharp wafer-thin blade which glittered in the light of the wall-lamps.

'You nearly made me slice my thumb off,' he said, putting down the knife. 'What's the matter with you?'

'It's the ace of spades,' said Henderson, still languidly. 'That's the second time it's turned up in five minutes.'

Arthur Rolfe chose to be dense. 'Well? What about it?'

' I think our young friend is being psychic,' said Hunt, good-humoured again. 'Are you reading characters, or only telling fortunes?'

Henderson hesitated. His eyes moved to Hunt, and then to the wall over the sideboard where Rembrandt's 'Old Woman with Cap' stared back with the immobility and skin-colouring of a red Indian. Then Henderson looked towards the french windows opening on the terrace.

'None of my affair,' shrugged Henderson. 'It's your house and your collection and your responsibility. But this fellow Butler: what do you know about him?'

Marcus Hunt looked boisterously amused.

'Butler? He's a friend of my niece's. Harriet picked him up in London, and asked me to invite him down here. Nonsense! Butler's all right. What are you thinking, exactly?'

'Listen!" said Rolfe, holding up his hand.

The noise they heard, from the direction of the terrace, was not repeated. It was not repeated because the person who had made it, a very bewildered and uneasy young lady, had run lightly and swiftly to the far end, where she leaned against the balustrade.

Lewis Butler hesitated before going after her. The moonlight was so clear that one could see the mortar between the tiles which paved the terrace, and trace the design of the stone urns along the balustrade. Harriet Davis wore a white gown with long and filmy skirts, which she lifted clear of the ground as she ran.

Then she beckoned to him.

She was half-sitting, half-leaning against the rail. Her white arms were spread out, fingers gripping the stone. Dark hair and dark eyes became even more vivid by moonlight. He could see the rapid rise and fall of her breast; he could even trace the shadow of her eyelashes.

'That was a lie, anyhow,' she said.

'What was?"

'What my Uncle Marcus said. You heard him.' Harriet Davis's fingers tightened still more on the balustrade. But she nodded her head vehemently, with fierce accusation. 'About my knowing you. And inviting you here. I never saw you before this weekend. Either Uncle Marcus is going out of his mind, or . . . will you answer me just one question?'

'If I can.'

'Very well. Are you by any chance a crook?'

She spoke with as much simplicity and directness as though she had asked him whether he might be a doctor or a lawyer. Lewis Butler was not unwise enough to laugh. She was in that mood where, to any woman, laughter is salt to a raw wound; she would probably have slapped his face.

'To be quite frank about it,' he said, ' I'm not. Will you tell me why you asked?'

'This house,' said Harriet, looking at the moon, 'used to be guarded with burglar alarms. If you as much as touched a window, the whole place started clanging like a fire-station. He had all the burglar alarms removed last week. Last week.' She took her hands off the balustrade, and pressed them together hard. 'The pictures used to be upstairs, in a locked room next to his bedroom. He had them moved downstairs – last week. It's almost as though my uncle *wanted* the house to be burgled.'

Butler knew that he must use great care here.

'Perhaps he does.' (Here she looked at Butler quickly, but did not comment.) 'For instance,' he went on idly, 'suppose one of his famous Rembrandts turned out to be a fake? It might be a relief not to have to show it to his expert friends.'

The girl shook her head.

'No,' she said. 'They're all genuine. You see, I thought of that too.'

Now was the time to hit, and hit hard. To Lewis Butler, in his innocence, there seemed to be no particular problem. He took out his cigarette-case, and turned it over without opening it.

'Look here, Miss Davis, you're not going to like this. But I can tell you of cases in which people were rather anxious to have their property "stolen". If a picture is insured for more than its value, and then it is mysteriously "stolen" one night—'

'That might be all very well too,' answered Harriet, still calmly. 'Except that not one of those pictures has been insured.'

The cigarette-case, which was of polished metal, slipped through Butler's fingers and fell with a clatter on the tiles. It spilled cigarettes, just as it spilled and confused his theories. As he bent over to pick it up, he could hear a church clock across the Weald strike the half-hour after eleven.

'You're sure of that?'

'I'm perfectly sure. He hasn't insured any of his pictures for as much as a penny. He says it's a waste of money.'

'But—'

'Oh, I know! And I don't know why I'm talking to you like this. You're a stranger, aren't you?' She folded her arms, drawing her shoulders up as though she were cold. Uncertainty, fear, and plain nerves flicked at her eyelids. 'But then Uncle Marcus is a stranger too. Do you know what I think? *I* think he's going mad.'

'Hardly as bad as that, is it?'

'Yes, go on,' the girl suddenly stormed at him. 'Say it: go on and say it. That's easy enough. But you don't see him when his eyes seem to get smaller, and all that genial-country-squire look goes out of his face. He's not a fake: he hates fakes, and goes out of his way to expose them. But, if he hasn't gone clear out of his mind, what's he up to? What can he be up to?'

In something over three hours they found out.

The burglar did not attack until half-past two in the morning. First he smoked several cigarettes in the shrubbery below the rear terrace. When he heard the church clock strike, he waited a few minutes more, and then slipped up the steps to the french windows of the dining-room.

A chilly wind stirred at the turn of the night, in the hour of suicides and bad dreams. It smoothed grass and trees with a faint rustling. When the man glanced over his shoulder, the last of the moonlight distorted his face: it showed less a face than the blob of a black cloth mask under a greasy cap pulled down over his ears.

He went to work on the middle window, with the contents of a folding tool-kit not so large as a motorist's. He fastened two short strips of adhesive tape to the glass just beside the catch. Then his glass cutter sliced out a small semicircle inside the tape.

It was done not without noise: it crunched like a dentist's drill in a tooth, and the man stopped to listen.

There was no answering noise. No dog barked.

With the adhesive tape holding the glass so that it did not fall and smash, he slid his gloved hand through the opening and twisted the catch. The weight of his body deadened the creaking window when he pushed inside.

He knew exactly what he wanted. He put the tool-kit into his pocket, and drew out an electric torch. Its beam moved across to the sideboard; it touched gleaming silver, a bowl of fruit, and a wicked little knife thrust into an apple as though into someone's body; finally, it moved up the hag-face of the 'Old Woman with Cap'.

This was not a large picture, and the burglar lifted it down easily. He prised out glass and frame. Though he tried to roll up the canvas with great care, the brittle paint cracked across in small stars which wounded the hag's face. The burglar was so intent on this that he never noticed the presence of another person in the room.

He was an incautious burglar: he had no sixth sense which smelt murder.

Up on the second floor of the house, Lewis Butler was awakened by a muffled crash like that of metal objects falling.

He had not fallen into more than a half-doze all night. He knew with certainty what must be happening, though he had no idea of why, or how, or to whom.

Butler was out of bed, and into his slippers, as soon as he heard the first faint clatter from downstairs. His dressing-gown would, as usual, twist itself up like a rolled umbrella and defy all attempts to find the arm-holes whenever he wanted to hurry. But the little flashlight was ready in the pocket.

That noise seemed to have roused nobody else. With certain possibilities in his mind, he had never in his life moved so fast once he managed to get out of his bedroom. Not using his light, he was down two flights of deep-carpeted stairs without noise. In the lower hall he could feel a draught, which meant that a window or door had been opened somewhere. He made straight for the dining-room.

But he was too late.

Once the pencil-beam of Butler's flashlight had swept round, he switched on a whole blaze of lights. The burglar was still here, right enough. But the burglar was lying very still in front of the sideboard; and, to judge by the amount of blood on his sweater and trousers, he would never move again.

'That's done it,' Butler said aloud.

A silver service, including a tea-urn, had been toppled off the sideboard. Where the fruit-bowl had fallen, the dead man lay on his back among a litter of oranges, apples, and a squashed bunch of grapes. The mask still covered the burglar's face; his greasy cap was flattened still further on his ears; his gloved hands were thrown wide.

Fragments of smashed picture-glass lay round him, together with the empty frame, and the 'Old Woman with Cap' had been half crumpled up under his body. From the position of the most conspicuous bloodstains, one judged that he had been stabbed through the chest with the stained fruit-knife beside him.

'*What is it?*' said a voice almost at Butler's ear.

He could not have been more startled if the fruit-knife had pricked his ribs. He had seen nobody turning on lights in the hall, nor had he heard Harriet Davis approach. She was standing just behind him, wrapped in a Japanese kimono, with her dark hair round her shoulders. But, when he explained what had happened, she would not look into the dining-room; she backed away, shaking her head violently, like an urchin ready for flight.

'You had better wake up your uncle,' Butler said briskly, with a confidence he did not feel. 'And the servants. I must use your telephone.' Then he looked her in the eyes. 'Yes, you're quite right. I think you've guessed it already. I'm a police-officer.'

She nodded.

'Yes. I guessed. Who are you? And is your name really Butler?'

'I'm a sergeant of the Criminal Investigation Department.

And my name really is Butler. Your uncle brought me here.'

'Why?'

'I don't know. He hasn't got round to telling me.'

This girl's intelligence, even when overshadowed by fear, was direct and disconcerting. 'But, if he wouldn't say why he wanted a police-officer, how did they come to send you? He'd have to tell them, wouldn't he?'

Butler ignored it. 'I must see your uncle. Will you go upstairs and wake him, please?'

'I can't,' said Harriet. 'Uncle Marcus isn't in his room.'

'Isn't —?'

'No. I knocked at the door on my way down. He's gone.'

Butler took the stairs two treads at a time. Harriet had turned on all the lights on her way down, but nothing stirred in the bleak, over-decorated passages.

Marcus Hunt's bedroom was empty. His dinner-jacket had been hung up neatly on the back of a chair, shirt laid across the seat with collar and tie on top of it. Hunt's watch ticked loudly on the dressing-table. His money and keys were there too. But he had not gone to bed, for the bedspread was undisturbed.

The suspicion which came to Lewis Butler, listening to the thin insistent ticking of that watch in the drugged hour before dawn, was so fantastic that he could not credit it.

He started downstairs again, and on the way he met Arthur Rolfe blundering out of another bedroom down the hall. The art dealer's stocky body was wrapped in a flannel dressing-gown. He was not wearing his eyeglasses, which gave his face a bleary and rather caved-in expression. He planted himself in front of Butler, and refused to budge.

'Yes,' said Butler. 'You don't have to ask. It's a burglar!'

'I knew it,' said Rolfe calmly. 'Did he get anything?'

'No. He was murdered.'

For a moment Rolfe said nothing, but his hand crept into the breast of his dressing-gown as though he felt pain there.

'Murdered? You don't mean the *burglar* was murdered?'

'Yes.'

'But why? By an accomplice, you mean? Who is the burglar?'

'That,' snarled Lewis Butler, 'is what I intend to find out.'

In the lower hall he found Harriet Davis, who was now standing in the doorway of the dining-room and looking steadily at the body by the sideboard. Though her face hardly moved a muscle, her eyes brimmed over.

'You're going to take off the mask, aren't you?' she asked, without turning round.

Stepping with care to avoid squashed fruit and broken glass, Butler leaned over the dead man. He pushed back the peak of the greasy cap; he lifted the black cloth mask, which was clumsily held by an elastic band; and he found what he expected to find.

The burglar was Marcus Hunt – stabbed through the heart while attempting to rob his own house.


'You see, sir,' Butler explained to Dr Gideon Fell on the following afternoon, 'that's the trouble. However you look at it, the case makes no sense.'

Again he went over the facts.

'Why should the man burgle his own house and steal his own property? Every one of those paintings is valuable, and not a single one is insured! Consequently, why? Was the man a simple lunatic? What did he think he was doing?'

The village of Sutton Valence, straggling like a grey-white Italian town along the very peak of the Weald, was full of hot sunshine. In the apple orchard behind the white inn of the *Tabard*, Dr Gideon Fell sat at a garden table among wasps, with a pint tankard at his elbow. Dr Fell's vast bulk was clad in a white linen suit. His pink face smoked in the heat, and his wary lookout for wasps gave him a regrettably wall-eyed appearance as he pondered.

He said:

'Superintendent Hadley suggested that I might – harrumph – look in here. The local police are in charge, aren't they?'

'Yes. I'm merely standing by.'

'Hadley's exact words to me were, "It's so crazy that nobody but you will understand it." The man's flattery becomes more nauseating every day.' Dr Fell scowled. 'I say. Does anything else strike you as queer about this business?'

'Well, why should a man burgle his own house?'

'No, no, no!' growled Dr Fell. 'Don't be obsessed with that point. Don't become hypnotized by it. For instance' – a wasp hovered near his tankard, and he distended his cheeks and blew it away with one vast puff like Father Neptune – 'for instance, the young lady seems to have raised an interesting question. If Marcus Hunt wouldn't say why he wanted a detective in the house, why did the C.I.D. consent to send you?'

Butler shrugged his shoulders.

'Because,' he said, 'Chief Inspector Ames thought Hunt was up to funny business, and meant to stop it.'

'What sort of funny business?'

'A faked burglary to steal his own pictures for the insurance. It looked like the old, old game of appealing to the police to divert suspicion. In other words, sir, exactly what this appeared to be: until I learned (and today proved) that not one of those damned pictures has ever been insured for a penny.'

Butler hesitated.

'It can't have been a practical joke,' he went on. 'Look at the elaborateness of it! Hunt put on old clothes from which all tailors' tabs and laundry marks were removed. He put on gloves and a mask. He got hold of a torch and an up-to-date kit of burglar's tools. He went out of the house by the back door; we found it open later. He smoked a few cigarettes in the shrubbery below the terrace; we found his footprints in the soft earth. He cut a pane of glass . . . but I've told you all that.'

'And then,' mused Dr Fell, 'somebody killed him.'

'Yes. The last and worst "why". Why should anybody have killed him?'

'H'm. Clues?'

'Negative.' Butler took out his notebook. 'According to the police surgeon, he died of a direct heart-wound from a blade (presumably that fruit-knife) so thin that the wound was difficult to find. There were a number of his fingerprints, but nobody else's. We did find one odd thing, though. A number of pieces in the silver service off the sideboard were scratched in a queer way. It looked almost as though, instead of being swept off the sideboard in a struggle, they had been piled up on top of each other like a tower; and then pushed—'

Butler paused, for Dr Fell was shaking his big head back and forth with an expression of gargantuan distress.

'Well, well, well,' he was saying; 'well, well, well. And you call that negative evidence?'

'Isn't it? It doesn't explain why a man burgles his own house.'

'Look here,' said the doctor mildly. 'I should like to ask you just one question. What is the most important point in this affair? One moment! I did not say the most interesting; I said the most important. Surely it is the fact that a man has been murdered?'

'Yes, sir. Naturally.'

'I mention the fact – the doctor was apologetic – 'because it seems in danger of being overlooked. It hardly interests you. You are concerned only with Hunt's senseless masquerade. You don't mind a throat being cut; but you can't stand a leg being pulled. Why not try working at it from the other side, and asking who killed Hunt?'

Butler was silent for a long time.

'The servants are out of it,' he said at length. 'They sleep in another wing on the top floor; and for some reason,' he hesitated, 'somebody locked them in last night.' His doubts, even his dreads, were beginning to take form. 'There was a fine blow-up over that when the house was roused. Of course, the murderer could have been an outsider.'

'You know it wasn't,' said Dr Fell. 'Would you mind taking me to Cranleigh Court?'

They came out on the terrace in the hottest part of the afternoon.

Dr Fell sat down on a wicker settee, with a dispirited Harriet beside him. Derek Henderson, in flannels, perched his long figure on the balustrade. Arthur Rolfe alone wore a dark suit and seemed out of place. For the pale green and brown of the Kentish lands, which rarely acquired harsh colour, now blazed. No air stirred, no leaf moved, in that brilliant thickness of heat; and down in the garden, towards their left, the water of the swimming-pool sparkled with hot, hard light. Butler felt it like a weight on his eyelids.

Derek Henderson's beard was at once languid and yet aggressive.

'It's no good,' he said. 'Don't keep on asking me why Hunt should have burgled his own house. But I'll give you a tip.'

'Which is?' inquired Dr Fell.

'Whatever the reason was,' returned Henderson, sticking out his neck, 'it was a good reason. Hunt was much too canny and cautious ever to do anything without a good reason. I told him so last night.'

Dr Fell spoke sharply. 'Cautious? Why do you say that?'

'Well, for instance. I take three cards on the draw. Hunt takes one. I bet; he sees me and raises. I cover that, and raise again. Hunt drops out. In other words, it's fairly certain he's filled his hand, but not so certain I'm holding much more than a pair. Yet Hunt drops out. So with my three sevens I bluff him out of his straight. He played a dozen hands last night just like that.'

Henderson began to chuckle. Seeing the expression on Harriet's face, he checked himself and became preternaturally solemn.

'But then, of course,' Henderson added, 'he had a lot on his mind last night.'

Nobody could fail to notice the change of tone.

'So? And what did he have on his mind?'

'Exposing somebody he had always trusted,' replied

Henderson coolly. 'That's why I didn't like it when the ace of spades turned up so often.'

'You'd better explain that,' said Harriet, after a pause. 'I don't know what you're hinting at, but you'd better explain that. He told you he intended to expose somebody he had always trusted?'

'No. Like myself, he hinted at it.'

It was the stolid Rolfe who stormed into the conversation then. Rolfe had the air of a man determined to hold hard to reason, but finding it difficult.

'Listen to me,' snapped Rolfe. 'I have heard a great deal, at one time or another, about Mr Hunt's liking for exposing people. Very well!' He slid one hand into the breast of his coat, in a characteristic gesture. 'But where in the name of sanity does that leave us? He wants to expose someone. And, to do that, he puts on outlandish clothes and masquerades as a burglar. Is that sensible? I tell you, the man was mad! There's no other explanation.'

'There are five other explanations,' said Dr Fell.

Derek Henderson slowly got up from his seat on the balustrade, but he sat down again at a savage gesture from Rolfe.

Nobody spoke.

'I will not, however,' pursued Dr Fell, 'waste your time with four of them. We are concerned with only one explanation: the real one.'

'And you know the real one?' asked Henderson sharply.

'I rather think so.'

'Since when?'

'Since I had the opportunity of looking at all of you,' answered Dr Fell.

He settled back massively in the wicker settee, so that its frame creaked and cracked like a ship's bulkhead in a heavy sea. His vast chin was out-thrust, and he nodded absently as though to emphasize some point that was quite clear in his own mind.

'I've already had a word with the local inspector,' he went

on suddenly. 'He will be here in a few minutes. And, at my suggestion, he will have a request for all of you. I sincerely hope nobody will refuse.'

'Request?' said Henderson. 'What request?'

'It's a very hot day,' said Dr Fell, blinking towards the swimming-pool. 'He's going to suggest that you all go in for a swim.'

Harriet uttered a kind of despairing mutter, and turned as though appealing to Lewis Butler.

'That,' continued Dr Fell, 'will be the politest way of drawing attention to the murderer. In the meantime, let me call your attention to one point in the evidence which seems to have been generally overlooked. Mr Henderson, do you know anything about direct heart-wounds made by a steel blade as thin as a wafer?'

'Like Hunt's wound? No. What about them?'

'There's practically no exterior bleeding,' answered Dr Fell.

'But—!' Harriet was beginning, when Butler stopped her.

'The police surgeon, in fact, called attention to that wound which was so 'difficult to find'. The victim dies almost at once; and the edges of the wound compress. But in that case,' argued Dr Fell, 'how did the late Mr Hunt come to have so much blood on his sweater, and even splashed on his trousers?'

'Well?'

'He didn't,' answered Dr Fell simply. 'Mr Hunt's blood never got on his clothes at all.'

'I can't stand this,' said Harriet, jumping to her feet. 'I – I'm sorry, but have you gone mad yourself? Are you telling us we didn't see him lying by that sideboard, with blood on him?'

'Oh, yes. You saw that.'

'Let him go on,' said Henderson, who was rather white round the nostrils. 'Let him rave.'

'It is, I admit, a fine point,' said Dr Fell. 'But it answers your question, repeated to the point of nausea, as to why the eminently sensible Mr Hunt chose to dress up in burglar's clothes and play burglar. The answer is short and simple. He didn't.'

'It must be plain to everybody,' Dr Fell went on, opening his eyes wide, 'that Mr Hunt was deliberately setting a trap for someone – the real burglar.

'He believed that a certain person might try to steal one or several of his pictures. He probably knew that this person had tried similar games before, in other country houses: that is, an inside job which was carefully planned to look like an outside job. So he made things easy for his thief, in order to trap him, with a police-officer in the house.

'The burglar, a sad fool, fell for it. This thief, a guest in the house, waited until well past two o'clock in the morning. He then put on his old clothes, mask, gloves, and the rest of it. He let himself out by the back door. He went through all the motions we have erroneously been attributing to Marcus Hunt. Then the trap snapped. Just as he was rolling up the Rembrandt, he heard a noise. He swung his light round. And he saw Marcus Hunt, in pyjamas and dressing-gown, looking at him.

'Yes, there was a fight. Hunt flew at him. The thief snatched up a fruit-knife and fought back. In that struggle, Marcus Hunt forced his opponent's hand back. The fruit-knife gashed the thief's chest, inflicting a superficial but badly bleeding gash. It sent the thief over the edge of insanity. He wrenched Marcus Hunt's wrist half off, caught up the knife, and stabbed Hunt to the heart.

'Then, in a quiet house, with a little beam of light streaming out from the torch on the sideboard, the murderer sees something that will hang him. He sees the blood from his own superficial wound seeping down his clothes.

'How is he to get rid of those clothes? He cannot destroy them, or get them away from the house. Inevitably the house will be searched, and they will be found. Without the blood-stains, they would seem ordinary clothes in his wardrobe. But with the blood-stains—'

'There is only one thing he can do.'

Harriet Davis was standing behind the wicker settee, shading her eyes against the glare of the sun. Her hand did not tremble when she said:

'He changed clothes with my uncle.'

'That's it,' growled Dr Fell. 'That's the whole sad story. The murderer dressed the body in his own clothes, making a puncture with the knife in sweater, shirt, and undervest. He then slipped on Mr Hunt's pyjamas and dressing-gown, which at a pinch he could always claim as his own. Hunt's wound had bled hardly at all. His dressing-gown, I think, had come open in the fight so that all the thief had to trouble him was a tiny puncture in the jacket of the pyjamas.

'But, once he had done this, he had to hypnotize you all into the belief that there would have been no time for a change of clothes. He had to make it seem that the fight occurred just *then*. He had to rouse the house. So he brought down echoing thunders by pushing over a pile of silver, and slipped upstairs.'

Dr Fell paused.

'The burglar could never have been Marcus Hunt, you know,' he added. 'We learn that Hunt's fingerprints were all over the place. Yet the murdered man was wearing gloves.'

There was a swishing of feet in the grass below the terrace, and a tread of heavy boots coming up the terrace steps. The local Inspector of police, buttoned up and steaming in his uniform, was followed by two constables.

Dr Fell turned round a face of satisfaction.

'Ah!' he said, breathing deeply. 'They've come to see about that swimming-party, I imagine. It is easy to patch up a flesh-wound with lint and cotton, or even a handkerchief. But such a wound will become infernally conspicuous in anyone who is forced to climb into bathing-trunks.'

'But it couldn't have been—' cried Harriet. Her eyes moved round. Her fingers tightened on Lewis Butler's arm, an instinctive gesture which he was to remember long afterwards, when he knew her even better.

'Exactly,' agreed the doctor, wheezing with pleasure. 'It could not have been a long, thin, gangling fellow like Mr Henderson. It assuredly could not have been a small and slender girl like yourself.

'There is only one person who, as we know, is just about Marcus Hunt's height and build; who could have put his own clothes on Hunt without any suspicion. That is the same person who, though he managed to staunch the wound in his chest, has been constantly running his hand inside the breast of his coat to make certain the bandage is secure. Just as Mr Rolfe is doing now.'

Arthur Rolfe sat very quiet, with his right hand still in the breast of his jacket. His face had grown smeary in the hot sunlight, but the eyes behind those thin shells of glasses remained inscrutable. He spoke only once, through dry lips, after they had cautioned him.

'I should have taken the young pup's warning,' he said. 'After all, he told me I would take long chances.'

# The Bones of the Case

## R. AUSTIN FREEMAN

*Just as we began this tour in one of London's most lawless black spots, so it seems appropriate that it should end in the area which has come to epitomize law and order, The Temple. The last part of our walk, then, takes us along the Embankment to number 5A Kings Bench Walk in the Inner Temple Gardens. In this little island of tranquillity beside the Embankment can be found the chambers of Dr John Thorndyke who has been described by Chris Steinbrunner and Otto Penzler as 'the greatest medico-legal detective of all time'. Thorndyke is also the most handsome of all the London detectives: tall, slim, athletic and with a symmetrical face in the classic mould. He has superb eyesight, too, and extremely dexterous hands. The good doctor combines the professions of lawyer and forensic scientist and brings a painstaking attention to scientific and technical detail whenever he is tackling a case. He considers himself 'an investigator of crime' rather than a detective, and never travels anywhere without his inevitable green case full of miniature instruments and chemicals. Thorndyke is always more concerned with examining the minutiae of crime – the physical clues left at the scene – rather than the people involved, and never allows personal emotions to cloud his judgement. His exceptional reasoning powers are augmented by a deep knowledge of such subjects as archaeology, anatomy, botany, ophthalmology and Egyptology. Dr Thorndyke receives invaluable aid on his cases from Nathaniel Polton, his laboratory assistant and butler, and Christopher Jervis, his faithful chronicler. Introduced to the public in 1907 in* The Red Thumb Mark *– the first of 21 novels and 40 short stories – the fame of Thorndyke is such that he has since been the subject of several parodies and pastiches as well as being featured on television three times: first in 1964 played by the gentlemanly Peter Copley; in 1971 by the Shakespearean actor, John Neville; and the following years by Barrie Ingham, probably better known as the arms salesman, Hine.*

*Richard Austin Freeman (1862–1943), who was born in Soho, was actually a practising surgeon and eye-and-throat specialist who was forced to give up medicine because of ill health and instead turned his knowledge and imagination to writing crime fiction. Apart from the unique Dr Thorndyke, he is also credited with inventing the 'inverted' detective story in* The Singing Bone *(1912) in which the reader's interest is focused not on whether the criminal will be caught, but* how. *Freeman said he had the idea for Thorndyke when he was a student in the 1880's, but did not get down to committing the idea to paper until prompted by the success of his fellow physician Dr Arthur Conan Doyle with Sherlock Holmes. He was reluctant to agree that he had a model for his hero, but there is little doubt that he bears striking resemblances to Professor Alfred Taylor, the author of the definitive work,* Principles and Practices of Medical Jurisprudence *(1865), which was Freeman's 'bible' as a student. All of the Dr Thorndyke short stories which helped ensure his wider public fame in* Pearson's Magazine *have stood the test of time well, but there is perhaps no better case to finish with than 'The Bones of the Case' in which the investigator from the Temple finds himself involved in a murder case as grisly as any committed by Jack the Ripper – and thereby brings our tour of London After Midnight round full circle to a most suitable finale. The case will also be all the more welcome to admirers of Dr Thorndyke for it is one of only three short stories about him which were not collected in the mammoth volume,* The Best Dr Thorndyke Detective Stories, *published in 1973 . . .*

## PART I

MR PERCIVAL BLAND was a somewhat uncommon type of criminal. In the first place he really had an appreciable amount of common-sense. If he had only had a little more, he would not have been a criminal at all. As it was, he had just sufficient judgment to perceive that the consequences of unlawful acts accumulate as the acts are repeated; to realize that the criminal's position must, at length, become untenable; and to take what he considered fair precautions against the inevitable catastrophe.

But in spite of these estimable traits of character and the precautions aforesaid, Mr Bland found himself in rather a tight place and with a prospect of increasing tightness. The causes of this uncomfortable tension do not concern us, and may be dismissed with the remark, that, if one perseveringly distributes flash Bank of England notes among the money-changers of the Continent, there will come a day of reckoning when those notes are tendered to the exceedingly knowing old lady who lives in Threadneedle Street.

Mr Bland considered uneasily the approaching storm-cloud as he raked over the 'miscellaneous property' in the Sale-rooms of Messrs Plimpton. He was a confirmed frequenter of auctions, as was not unnatural; for the criminal is essentially a gambler. And criminal and auction-frequenter have one quality in common; each hopes to get something of value without paying the market price for it.

So Percival turned over the dusty oddments and his own difficulties at one and the same time. The vital questions were: When would the storm burst? And would it pass by the harbour of refuge that he had been at such pains to construct? Let us inspect that harbour of refuge.

A quiet flat in the pleasant neighbourhood of Battersea bore a name-plate inscribed, Mr Robert Lindsay; and the tenant was known to the porter and the charwoman who attended to the flat, as a fair-haired gentleman who was engaged in the book trade as a travelling agent, and was consequently a good deal away from home. Now Mr Robert

Lindsay bore a distinct resemblance to Percival Bland; which was not surprising seeing that they were first cousins (or, at any rate, they said they were; and we may presume that they knew). But they were not very much alike. Mr Lindsay had flaxen, or rather sandy, hair; Mr Bland's hair was black. Mr Bland had a mole under his left eye; Mr Lindsay had no mole under his eye – but carried one in a small box in his waistcoat pocket.

At somewhat rare intervals the cousins called on one another; but they had the very worst of luck, for neither of them ever seemed to find the other at home. And what was even more odd was that whenever Mr Bland spent an evening at home in his lodgings over the oil shop in Bloomsbury, Mr Lindsay's flat was empty; and as sure as Mr Lindsay was at home in his flat so surely were Mr Bland's lodgings vacant for the time being. It was a queer coincidence, if anyone had noticed it; but nobody ever did.

However, if Percival saw little of his cousin, it was not a case of 'out of sight, out of mind'. On the contrary; so great was his solicitude for the latter's welfare that he not only had made a will constituting him his executor and sole legatee, but he had actually insured his life for no less a sum than three thousand pounds; and this will, together with the insurance policy, investment securities and other necessary documents, he had placed in the custody of a highly respectable solicitor. All of which did him great credit. It isn't every man who is willing to take so much trouble for a mere cousin.

Mr Bland continued his perambulations, pawing over the miscellaneous raffle from sheer force of habit, reflecting on the coming crisis in his own affairs, and on the provisions that he had made for his cousin Robert. As for the latter, they were excellent as far as they went, but they lacked definiteness and perfect completeness. There was the contingency of a 'stretch', for instance; say fourteen years penal servitude. The insurance policy did not cover that. And, meanwhile, what was to become of the estimable Robert?

He had bruised his thumb somewhat severely in a screw-cutting lathe, and had abstractedly turned the handle of a bird-organ until politely requested by an attendant to desist, when he came upon a series of boxes containing, according to the catalogue, 'a collection of surgical instruments the property of a lately deceased practitioner'. To judge by the appearance of the instruments, the practitioner must have commenced practice in his early youth and died at a very advanced age. They were an uncouth set of tools, of no value whatever excepting as testimonials to the amazing tenacity of life of our ancestors; but Percival fingered them over according to his wont, working the handle of a complicated brass syringe and ejecting a drop of greenish fluid on to the shirt-front of a dressy Hebrew (who requested him to 'point the dam thing at thomeone elth nectht time'), opening musty leather cases, clicking off spring scarifiers and feeling the edges of strange, crooked-bladed knives. Then he came upon a largish black box, which, when he raised the lid, breathed out an ancient and fish-like aroma and exhibited a collection of bones, yellow, greasy-looking and spotted in places with mildew. The catalogue described them as 'a complete set of human osteology'; but they were not an ordinary 'student's set', for the bones of the hands and feet, instead of being strung together on cat-gut, were united by their original ligaments and were of an unsavoury brown colour.

'I thay, misther,' expostulated the Hebrew, 'shut that bocth. Thmellth like a blooming inquetht.'

But the contents of the black box seemed to have a fascination for Percival. He looked in at those greasy remnants of mortality, at the brown and mouldy hands and feet and the skull that peeped forth eerily from the folds of a flannel wrapping; and they breathed out something more than that stale and musty odour. A suggestion – vague and general at first, but rapidly crystallizing into distinct shape – seemed to steal out of the black box into his consciousness; a suggestion that somehow seemed to connect itself with his estimable cousin Robert.

For upwards of a minute he stood motionless, as one immersed in reverie, the lid poised in his hand and a dreamy eye fixed on the half-uncovered skull. A stir in the room roused him. The sale was about to begin. The members of the knock-out and other habitués seated themselves on benches around a long, baize-covered table; the attendants took possession of the first lots and opened their catalogues as if about to sing an introductory chorus; and a gentleman with a waxed moustache and a striking resemblance to his late Majesty, the third Napoleon, having ascended to the rostrum bespoke the attention of the assembly by a premonitory tap with his hammer.

How odd are some of the effects of a guilty conscience! With what absurd self-consciousness do we read into the minds of others our own undeclared intentions, when those intentions are unlawful! Had Percival Bland wanted a set of human bones for any legitimate purpose – such as anatomical study – he would have bought it openly and unembarrassed. Now, he found himself earnestly debating whether he should not bid for some of the surgical instruments, just for the sake of appearances; and there being little time in which to make up his mind – for the deceased practitioner's effects came first in the catalogue – he was already the richer by a set of cupping-glasses, a tooth-key, and an instrument of unknown use and diabolical aspect, before the fateful lot was called.

At length the black box was laid on the table, an object of obscene mirth to the knockers-out, and the auctioneer read the entry:

'Lot seventeen; a complete set of human osteology. A very useful and valuable set of specimens, gentlemen.'

He looked round at the assembly majestically, oblivious of sundry inquiries as to the identity of the deceased and the verdict of the coroner's jury, and finally suggested five shillings.

'Six,' said Percival.

An attendant held the box open, and, chanting the mystic

word 'Loddlemen!' (which, being interpreted, meant 'Lot, gentlemen'), thrust it under the rather bulbous nose of the smart Hebrew; who remarked that 'they 'ummed a bit too much to thoot him' and pushed it away.

'Going at six shillings,' said the auctioneer, reproachfully; and as nobody contradicted him, he smote the rostrum with his hammer and the box was delivered into the hands of Percival on the payment of that modest sum.

Having crammed the cupping-glasses, the tooth-key and the unknown instrument into the box, Percival obtained from one of the attendants a length of cord, with which he secured the lid. Then he carried his treasure out into the street, and, chartering a four-wheeler, directed the driver to proceed to Charing Cross Station. At the station he booked the box in the cloak-room (in the name of Simpson) and left it for a couple of hours; at the expiration of which he returned, and, employing a different porter, had it conveyed to a hansom, in which it was borne to his lodgings over the oil-shop in Bloomsbury. There he, himself, carried it, unobserved, up the stairs, and, depositing it in a large cupboard, locked the door and pocketed the key.

And thus was the curtain rung down on the first act.

The second act opened only a couple of days later, the office of call-boy – to pursue the metaphor to the bitter end – being discharged by a Belgian police official who emerged from the main entrance to the Bank of England. What should have led Percival Bland into so unsafe a neighbourhood it is difficult to imagine, unless it was that strange fascination that seems so frequently to lure the criminal to places associated with his crime. But there he was within a dozen paces of the entrance when the officer came forth, and mutual recognition was instantaneous. Almost equally instantaneous was the self-possessed Percival's decision to cross the road.

It is not a nice road to cross. The old-fashioned horse-driver would condescend to shout a warning to the indiscreet wayfarer. Not so the modern chauffeur, who looks stonily before him and leaves you to get out of the way of Juggernaut. He knows his 'exonerating' coroner's jury. At the moment, however, the procession of Juggernauts was at rest; but Percival had seen the presiding policeman turn to move away and he darted across the fronts of the vehicles even as they started. The foreign officer followed. But in that moment the whole procession had got in motion. A motor omnibus thundered past in front of him; another was bearing down on him relentlessly. He hesitated, and sprang back; and then a taxicab, darting out from behind, butted him heavily, sending him sprawling in the road, whence he scrambled as best he could back on to the pavement.

Percival, meanwhile, had swung himself lightly on to the footboard of the first omnibus just as it was gathering speed. A few seconds saw him safely across at the Mansion House, and in a few more, he was whirling down Queen Victoria Street. The danger was practically over, though he took the precaution to alight at St Paul's, and, crossing to Newgate Street, board another west-bound omnibus.

That night he sat in his lodgings turning over his late experience. It had been a narrow shave. That sort of thing mustn't happen again. In fact, seeing that the law was undoubtedly about to be set in motion, it was high time that certain little plans of his should be set in motion, too. Only, there was a difficulty; a serious difficulty. And as Percival thought round and round that difficulty his brows wrinkled and he hummed a soft refrain.

> 'Then is the time for disappearing.
> Take a header – down you go—'

A tap at the door cut his song short. It was his landlady, Mrs Brattle; a civil woman, and particularly civil just now. For she had a little request to make.

'It was about Christmas Night, Mr Bland,' said Mrs Brattle. 'My husband and me thought of spending the evening with his brother at Hornsey, and we were going to let the maid go home to her mother's for the night, if it wouldn't put you out.'

'Wouldn't put me out in the least, Mrs Brattle,' said Percival.

'You needn't sit up for us, you see,' pursued Mrs Brattle, 'if you'd just leave the side door unbolted. We shan't be home before two or three, but we'll come in quiet not to disturb you.'

'You won't disturb me,' Percival replied with a genial laugh. 'I'm a sober man in general; but "Christmas comes but once a year." When once I'm tucked up in bed, I shall take a bit of waking on Christmas Night.'

Mrs Brattle smiled indulgently. 'And you won't feel lonely, all alone in the house?'

'Lonely!' exclaimed Percival. 'Lonely! With a roaring fire, a jolly book, a box of good cigars and a bottle of sound port – ah, and a second bottle if need be. Not I.'

Mrs Brattle shook her head. 'Ah,' said she, 'you bachelors! Well, well. It's a good thing to be independent,' and with this profound reflection she smiled herself out of the room and descended the stairs.

As her footsteps died away Percival sprang from his chair and began excitedly to pace the room. His eyes sparkled and his face was wreathed with smiles. Presently he halted before the fireplace, and, gazing into the embers, laughed aloud.

'Damn funny!' said he. 'Deuced rich! Neat! Very neat! Ha! Ha!' And here he resumed his interrupted song:

'When the sky above is clearing
When the sky above is clearing
Bob up serenely, bob up serenely,
Bob up serenely from below!'

Which may be regarded as closing the first scene of the second act.

During the few days that intervened before Christmas, Percival went abroad but little; and yet he was a busy man.

He did a little surreptitious shopping, venturing out as far as Charing Cross Road; and his purchases were decidedly miscellaneous. A porridge saucepan, a second-hand copy of *Gray's Anatomy,* a rabbit skin, a large supply of glue and upwards of ten pounds of shin of beef seems a rather odd assortment; and it was a mercy that the weather was frosty, for otherwise Percival's bedroom, in which these delicacies were deposited under lock and key, would have yielded odorous traces of its wealth.

But it was in the long evenings that his industry was most conspicuous; and then it was that the big cupboard with the excellent lever lock, which he himself had fixed on, began to fill up with the fruits of his labours. In those evenings the porridge saucepan would simmer on the hob with a rich lading of good Scotch glue, the black box of the deceased practitioner would be hauled forth from its hiding-place, and the well-thumbed *Gray* laid open on the table.

It was an arduous business though; a stiffer task than he had bargained for. The right and left bones were so confoundedly alike, and the bones that joined were so difficult to fit together. However, the plates in *Gray* were large and very clear, so it was only a question of taking enough trouble.

His method of work was simple and practical. Having fished a bone out of the box, he would compare it with the illustrations in the book until he had identified it beyond all doubt, when he would tie on it a paper label with its name and side – right or left. Then he would search for the adjoining bone, and, having fitted the two together, would secure them with a good daub of glue and lay them in the fender to dry. It was a crude and horrible method of articulation that would have made a museum curator shudder. But it seemed to answer Percival's purpose – whatever that may have been – for gradually the loose 'items' came together into recognizable members such as arms and legs, the vertebrae – which were, fortunately, strung in their order on a thick cord – were joined up into a solid backbone, and even the ribs, which were the toughest job of all, fixed on in some semblance of a thorax. It was a wretched performance. The bones were plastered with gouts of glue and yet would have broken apart at a touch. But, as we have said, Percival seemed satisfied, and as he was the only person concerned, there was nothing more to be said.

In due course, Christmas Day arrived. Percival dined with the Brattles at two, dozed after dinner, woke up for tea, and then, as Mrs Brattle, in purple and fine raiment, came in to remove the tea-tray, he spread out on the table the materials for the night's carouse. A quarter of an hour later, the side-door slammed, and, peering out of the window, he saw the shopkeeper and his wife hurrying away up the gas-lit street towards the nearest omnibus route.

Then Mr Percival Bland began his evening's entertainment; and a most remarkable entertainment it was, even for a solitary bachelor, left alone in a house on Christmas Night. First, he took off his clothing and dressed himself in a fresh suit. Then, from the cupboard, he brought forth the reconstituted 'set of osteology', and, laying the various members on the table, returned to the bedroom, whence he presently reappeared with a large, unsavoury parcel which he had disinterred from a trunk. The parcel, being opened, revealed his accumulated purchases in the matter of shin of beef.

With a large knife, providently sharpened beforehand, he cut the beef into large, thin slices which he proceeded to wrap around the various bones that formed the 'complete set'; whereby their nakedness was certainly mitigated though their attractiveness was by no means increased. Having thus 'clothed the dry bones', he gathered up the scraps of offal that were left, to be placed presently inside the trunk. It was an extraordinary proceeding, but the next was more extraordinary still.

Taking up the newly clothed members one by one, he began very carefully to insinuate them into the garments that he had recently shed. It was a ticklish business, for the glued joints were as brittle as glass. Very cautiously the legs were separately inducted, first into underclothing and then into trousers, the skeleton feet were fitted with the cast-off socks and delicately persuaded into the boots. The arms, in like manner, were gingerly pressed into their various sleeves and through the arm-holes of the waistcoat; and then came the most difficult task of all – to fit the garments on the trunk. For the skull and ribs, secured to the back-bone with mere spots of glue, were ready to drop off at a shake; and yet the garments had to be drawn over them with the arms enclosed in the sleeves. But Percival managed it at last by resting his 'restoration' in the big, padded arm-chair and easing the garments on inch by inch.

It now remained only to give the finishing touch; which was done by cutting the rabbit-skin to the requisite shape and affixing it to the skull with a thin coat of stiff glue; and when the skull had thus been finished with a sort of crude, makeshift wig, its appearance was so appalling as even to disturb the nerves of the matter-of-fact Percival. However, this was no occasion for cherishing sentiment. A skull in an extemporized wig or false scalp might be, and in fact was, a highly unpleasant object; but so was a Belgian police officer.

Having finished the 'restoration', Percival fetched the water-jug from his bedroom, and, descending to the shop, the door of which had been left unlocked, tried the taps of the various drums and barrels until he came to the one which contained methylated spirit; and from this he filled his jug and returned to the bedroom. Pouring the spirit out into the basin, he tucked a towel round his neck and filling his sponge with spirit, proceeded very vigorously to wash his hair and eyebrows and as, by degrees, the spirit in the basin grew dark and turbid, so did his hair and eyebrows grow lighter in colour until, after a final energetic rub with a towel, they had acquired a golden or sandy hue indistinguishable from that of the hair of his cousin Robert. Even the mole under his eye was susceptible to the changing conditions, for when he had wetted it thoroughly with spirit, he was able with the blade of a penknife, to peel it off as neatly as if it had been stuck on with spirit-gum. Having done which, he deposited it in a tiny box which he carried in his waistcoat pocket.

The proceedings which followed were unmistakable as to their object. First he carried the basin of spirit through into the sitting-room and deliberately poured its contents on to the floor by the arm-chair. Then, having returned the basin to the bedroom, he again went down to the shop, where he selected a couple of galvanised buckets from the stock, filled them with paraffin oil from one of the great drums and carried them upstairs. The oil from one bucket he poured over the arm-chair and its repulsive occupant; the other bucket he simply emptied on the carpet, and then went down to the shop for a fresh supply.

When this proceeding had been repeated once or twice the entire floor and all the furniture were saturated, and such a reek of paraffin filled the air of the room that Percival thought it wise to turn out the gas. Returning to the shop, he poured a bucketful of oil over the stack of bundles of firewood, another over the counter and floor and a third over the loose articles on the walls and hanging from the ceiling. Looking up at the latter he now perceived a number of greasy patches where the oil had soaked through from the floor above, and some of these were beginning to drip on to the shop floor.

He now made his final preparations. Taking a bundle of 'Wheel' firelighters, he made a small pile against the stack of firewood. In the midst of the firelighters he placed a ball of string saturated in paraffin; and in the central hole of the ball he stuck a half-dozen diminutive Christmas candles. This mine was now ready. Providing himself with a stock of firelighters, a few balls of paraffined string and a dozen or so of the little candles, he went upstairs to the sitting-room, which was immediately above the shop. Here, by the glow of the fire, he built up one or two piles of firelighters around and, partly under the arm-chair, placed the balls of string on the piles and stuck two or three bundles in each ball. Everything was now ready. Stepping into the bedroom, he took from the cupboard a spare overcoat, a new hat and a new umbrella – for he must leave his old hats, coat and umbrella in the hall. He put on the coat and hat, and, with the umbrella in his hand, returned to the sitting-room.

Opposite the arm-chair he stood awhile, irresolute, and a pang of horror shot through him. It was a terrible thing that he was going to do; a thing the consequences of which no one could foresee. He glanced furtively at the awful shape that sat huddled in the chair, its horrible head all awry and its rigid limbs sprawling in hideous grotesque deformity. It was but a dummy, a mere scarecrow; but yet, in the dim firelight, the grisly face under that horrid wig seemed to leer intelligently, to watch him with secret malice out of its shadowy eye-sockets, until he looked away with clammy skin and a shiver of half-superstitious terror.

But this would never do. The evening had run out, consumed by these engrossing labours; it was nearly eleven o'clock, and high time for him to be gone. For if the Brattles should return prematurely he was lost. Pulling himself together with an effort, he struck a match and lit the little candles one after the other. In a quarter of an hour or so, they would have burned down to the balls of string, and then—

He walked quickly out of the room; but, at the door, he paused for a moment to look back at the ghastly figure, seated rigidly in the chair with the lighted candles at its feet, like some foul fiend appeased by votive fires. The unsteady flames threw flickering shadows on its face that made it seem to mow and gibber and grin in mockery of all his care and caution. So he turned and tremblingly ran down the stairs — opening the staircase window as he went. Running into the shop, he lit the candles there and ran out again, shutting the door after him.

Secretly and guiltily he crept down the hall, and opening the door a few inches peered out. A blast of icy wind poured in with a light powdering of dry snow. He opened his umbrella, flung open the door, looked up and down the empty street, stepped out, closed the door softly and strode away over the whitening pavement.

## PART II

IT WAS ONE of the axioms of medico-legal practice laid down by my colleague, John Thorndyke, that the investigator should be constantly on his guard against the effect of suggestion. Not only must all prejudices and preconceptions be avoided, but when information is received from outside, the actual, undeniable facts must be carefully sifted from the inferences which usually accompany them. Of the necessity for this precaution our insurance practice furnished an excellent instance in the case of the fire at Mr Brattle's oil-shop.

The case was brought to our notice by Mr Stalker of the 'Griffin' Fire and Life Insurance Society a few days after Christmas. He dropped in, ostensibly to wish us a Happy New Year, but a discreet pause in the conversation on Thorndyke's part elicited a further purpose.

'Did you see the account of that fire in Bloomsbury?' Mr Stalker asked.

'The oil-shop? Yes. But I didn't note any details, excepting that a man was apparently burnt to death and that the affair happened on the twenty-fifth of December.'

'Yes, I know,' said Mr Stalker. 'It seems uncharitable, but one can't help looking a little askance at these quarter-day fires. And the date isn't the only doubtful feature in this one; the Divisional Officer of the Fire Brigade, who has looked over the ruins, tells me that there are some appearances suggesting that the fire broke out in two different places – the shop and the first-floor room over it. Mind you, he doesn't say that it actually did. The place is so thoroughly gutted that very little is to be learned from it; but that is his impression; and it occurred to me that if you were to take a look at the ruins, your radiographic eye might detect something that he had overlooked.'

'It isn't very likely,' said Thorndyke. 'Every man to his trade. The Divisional Officer looks at a burnt house with an expert eye, which I do not. My evidence would not carry much weight if you were contesting the claim.'

'Perhaps not,' replied Mr Stalker, 'and we are not anxious to contest the claim unless there is manifest fraud. Arson is a serious matter.'

'It is wilful murder in this case,' remarked Thorndyke.

'I know,' said Stalker. 'And that reminds me that the man who was burnt happens to have been insured in our office, too. So we stand a double loss.'

'How much?' asked Thorndyke.

'The dead man, Percival Bland, had insured his life for three thousand pounds.'

Thorndyke became thoughtful. The last statement had apparently made more impression on him than the former ones.

'If you want me to look into the case for you,' said he, 'you had better let me have all the papers connected with it, including the proposal forms.'

Mr Stalker smiled. 'I thought you would say that – know you of old, you see – so I slipped the papers in my pocket before coming here.'

He laid the documents on the table and asked: 'Is there anything that you want to know about the case?'

'Yes,' replied Thorndyke. 'I want to know all that you can tell me.'

'Which is mighty little,' said Stalker; 'but such as it is, you shall have it.

'The oil-shop man's name is Brattle and the dead man, Bland, was his lodger. Bland appears to have been a perfectly steady, sober man in general; but it seems that he had announced his intention of spending a jovial Christmas Night and giving himself a little extra indulgence. He was last seen by Mrs Brattle at about half-past six, sitting by a blazing fire, with a couple of unopened bottles of port on the table and a box of cigars. He had a book in his hand and two or three newspapers lay on the floor by his chair. Shortly after this, Mr and Mrs Brattle went out on a visit to Hornsey, leaving him alone in the house.'

'Was there no servant?' asked Thorndyke.

'The servant had the day and night off duty to go to her mother's. That, by the way, looks a trifle fishy. However, to return to the Brattles; they spent the evening at Hornsey and did not get home until past three in the morning, by which time their house was a heap of smoking ruins. Mrs Brattle's idea is that Bland must have drunk himself sleepy, and dropped one of the newspapers into the fender, where a chance cinder may have started the blaze. Which may or may not be the true explanation. Of course, a habitually sober man can get pretty mimsey on two bottles of port.'

'What time did the fire break out?' asked Thorndyke.

It was noticed about half-past eleven that flames were issuing from one of the chimneys, and the alarm was given at once. The first engine arrived ten minutes later, but, by that time, the place was roaring like a furnace. Then the water-plugs were found to be frozen hard, which caused some delay; in fact, before the engines were able to get to work the roof had fallen in, and the place was a mere shell. You know what an oil-shop is, when once it gets a fair start.'

'And Mr Bland's body was found in the ruins, I suppose?'

'Body!' exclaimed Mr Stalker; 'there wasn't much body! Just a few charred bones, which they dug out of the ashes next day.'

'And the question of identity?'

'We shall leave that to the coroner. But there really isn't any question. To begin with, there was no one else in the house; and then the remains were found mixed up with the springs and castors of the chair that Bland was sitting in when he was last seen. Moreover, there were found, with the bones, a pocket-knife, a bunch of keys and a set of steel waistcoat buttons, all identified by Mrs Brattle as belonging to Bland. She noticed the cut steel buttons on his waistcoat when she wished him good-night.'

'By the way,' said Thorndyke,' was Bland reading by the light of an oil lamp?'

'No,' replied Stalker. 'There was a two-branch gasalier

with a porcelain shade to one burner, and he had that burner alight when Mrs Brattle left.'

Thorndyke reflectively picked up the proposal form, and, having glanced through it, remarked: 'I see that Bland is described as unmarried. Do you know why he insured his life for this large amount?'

'No; we assumed that it was probably in connection with some loan that he had raised. I learn from the solicitor who notified us of the death, that the whole of Bland's property is left to a cousin – a Mr Lindsay, I think. So the probability is that this cousin had lent him money. But it is not the life claim that is interesting us. We must pay that in any case. It is the fire claim that we want you to look into.'

'Very well,' said Thorndyke; 'I will go round presently and look over the ruins, and see if I can detect any substantial evidence of fraud.'

'If you would,' said Mr Stalker, rising to take his departure, 'we should be very much obliged. Not that we shall probably contest the claim in any case.'

When he had gone, my colleague and I glanced through the papers, and I ventured to remark: 'It seems to me that Stalker doesn't quite appreciate the possibilities of this case.'

'No,' Thorndyke agreed. 'But, of course, it is an insurance company's business to pay, and not to boggle at anything short of glaring fraud. And we specialists, too,' he added with a smile, 'must beware of seeing too much. I suppose that, to a rhinologist, there is hardly such a thing as a healthy nose – unless it is his own – and the uric acid specialist is very apt to find the firmament studded with dumb-bell crystals. We mustn't forget that normal cases do exist, after all.'

'That is true,' said I; 'but, on the other hand, the rhinologist's business is with the unhealthy nose, and our concern is with abnormal cases.'

Thorndyke laughed. '"A Daniel come to judgment,"' said he. 'But my learned friend is quite right. Our function is to pick holes. So let us pocket the documents and wend Bloomsbury way. We can talk the case over as we go.'

We walked at an easy pace, for there was no hurry, and a little preliminary thought was useful. After a while, as Thorndyke made no remark, I reopened the subject.

'How does the case present itself to you?' I asked.

'Much as it does to you, I expect,' he replied. 'The circumstances invite inquiry, and I do not find myself connecting them with the shopkeeper. It is true that the fire occurred on quarter-day; but there is nothing to show that the insurance will do more than cover the loss of stock, chattels and the profits of trade. The other circumstances are much more suggestive. Here is a house burned down and a man killed. That man was insured for three thousand pounds, and, consequently, some person stands to gain by his death to that amount. The whole set of circumstances is highly favourable to the idea of homicide. The man was alone in the house when he died; and the total destruction of both the body and its surroundings seems to render investigation impossible. The cause of death can only be inferred; it cannot be proved; and the most glaring evidence of a crime will have vanished utterly. I think that there is a quite strong *prima facie* suggestion of murder. Under the known conditions, the perpetration of a murder would have been easy, it would have been safe from detection, and there is an adequate motive.

'On the other hand, suicide is not impossible. The man might have set fire to the house and then killed himself by poison or otherwise. But it is intrinsically less probable that a man should kill himself for another person's benefit than that he should kill another man for his own benefit.

'Finally, there is the possibility that the fire and the man's death were the result of accident; against which is the official opinion that the fire started in two places. If this opinion is correct, it establishes, in my opinion, a strong presumption of murder against some person who may have obtained access to the house.'

This point in the discussion brought us to the ruined house, which stood at the corner of two small streets. One of the firemen in charge admitted us, when we had shown our credentials, through a temporary door and down a ladder into the basement, where we found a number of men treading gingerly, ankle deep in white ash, among a litter of charred wood-work, fused glass, warped and broken china, and more or less recognisable metal objects.

'The coroner and the jury,' the fireman explained; 'come to view the scene of the disaster.' He introduced us to the former, who bowed stiffly and continued his investigations.

'These,' said the other fireman, 'are the springs of the chair that the deceased was sitting in. We found the body – or rather the bones – lying among them under a heap of hot ashes; and we found the buttons of his clothes and the things from his pockets among the ashes, too. You'll see them in the mortuary with the remains.'

'It must have been a terrific blaze,' one of the jurymen remarked. 'Just look at this, sir,' and he handed to Thorndyke what looked like part of a gas-fitting, of which the greater part was melted into shapeless lumps and the remainder encrusted into fused porcelain.

'That,' said the fireman, 'was the gasalier of the first-floor room, where Mr Bland was sitting. Ah! you won't turn that tap, sir; nobody'll ever turn that tap again.'

Thorndyke held the twisted mass of brass towards me in silence, and, glancing up the blackened walls, remarked: 'I think we shall have to come here again with the Divisional Officer, but meanwhile, we had better see the remains of the body. It is just possible that we may learn something from them.'

He applied to the coroner for the necessary authority to make the inspection, and, having obtained a rather ungracious and grudging permission to examine the remains when the jury had 'viewed' them, began to ascend the ladder.

'Our friend would have liked to refuse permission,' he remarked when we had emerged into the street, 'but he knew that I could and should have insisted.'

'So I gathered from his manner,' said I. 'But what is he doing here? This isn't his district.'

'No; he is acting for Bettsford, who is laid up just now; and a very poor substitute he is. A non-medical coroner is an absurdity in any case, and a coroner who is hostile to the medical profession is a public scandal. By the way, that gas-tap offers a curious problem. You noticed that it was turned off?'

'Yes.'

'And consequently that the deceased was sitting in the dark when the fire broke out. I don't see the bearing of the fact, but it is certainly rather odd. Here is the mortuary. We had better wait and let the jury go in first.'

We had not long to wait. In a couple of minutes or so the 'twelve good men and true' made their appearance with a small attendant crowd of ragamuffins. We let them enter first, and then we followed. The mortuary was a good-sized room, well lighted by a glass roof, and having at its centre a long table on which lay the shell containing the remains. There was also a sheet of paper on which had been laid out a set of blackened steel waistcoat buttons, a bunch of keys, a steel-handled pocket-knife, a steel-cased watch on a partly-fused rolled-gold chain and a pocket corkscrew. The coroner drew the attention of the jury to these objects, and then took possession of them, that they might be identified by witnesses. And meanwhile the jurymen gathered round the shell and stared shudderingly at its gruesome contents.

'I am sorry, gentlemen,' said the coroner, 'to have to subject you to this painful ordeal. But duty is duty. We must hope, as I think we may, that this poor creature met a painless, if in some respects a rather terrible death.'

At this point, Thorndyke, who had drawn near to the table, cast a long and steady glance down into the shell; and, immediately his ordinarily rather impassive face seemed to congeal; all expression faded from it, leaving it as immovable and uncommunicative as the granite face of an Egyptian statue. I knew the symptom of old and began to speculate on its present significance.

'Are you taking any medical evidence?' he asked.

'Medical evidence!' the coroner repeated, scornfully.
'Certainly not, sir! I do not waste the public money by
employing so-called experts to tell the jury what each of
them can see quite plainly for himself. I imagine,' he added,
turning to the foreman, 'that you will not require a learned
doctor to explain to you how that poor fellow mortal met his
death?' And the foreman, glancing askance at the skull,
replied, with a pallid and sickly smile, that 'he thought not'.

'Do you, sir,' the coroner continued, with a dramatic wave
of the hand towards the plain coffin, 'suppose that we shall
find any difficulty in determining how that man came by his
death?'

'I imagine,' replied Thorndyke, without moving a muscle,
or, indeed, appearing to have any muscles to move, 'I imagine
you will find no difficulty whatever.'

'So do I,' said the coroner.

'Then,' retorted Thorndyke, with a faint, inscrutable
smile, 'we are, for once, in complete agreement.'

As the coroner and jury retired, leaving my colleague and
me alone in the mortuary, Thorndyke remarked:

'I suppose this kind of farce will be repeated periodically so
long as these highly technical medical inquiries continue to
be conducted by lay persons.'

I made no reply, for I had taken a long look into the shell,
and was lost in astonishment.

'But my dear Thorndyke!' I exclaimed; 'what on earth
does it mean? Are we to suppose that a woman can have
palmed herself off as a man on the examining medical officer
of a London Life Assurance Society?'

Thorndyke shook his head. 'I think not,' said he. 'Our
friend, Mr Bland, may conceivably have been a woman in
disguise, but he certainly was not a negress.'

'A negress!' I gasped. 'By Jove! So it is. I hadn't looked at
the skull. But that only makes the mystery more mysterious.
Because, you remember, the body was certainly dressed in
Bland's clothes.'

'Yes, there seems to be no doubt about that. And you may

have noticed, as I did,' Thorndyke continued dryly, 'the remarkably fire-proof character of the waistcoat buttons, watch-case, knife-handle, and other identifiable objects.'

'But what a horrible affair!' I exclaimed. 'The brute must have gone out and enticed some poor devil of a negress into the house, have murdered her in cold blood, and then deliberately dressed the corpse in his own clothes! It is perfectly frightful!'

Again Thorndyke shook his head. 'It wasn't as bad as that, Jervis,' said he, 'though I must confess that I feel strongly tempted to let your hypothesis stand. It would be quite amusing to put Mr Bland on trial for the murder of an unknown negress, and let him explain the facts himself. But our reputation is at stake. Look at the bones again and a little more critically. You very probably looked for the sex first; then you looked for racial characters. Now carry your investigations a step further.'

'There is the stature,' said I. 'But that is of no importance, as these are not Bland's bones. The only other point that I notice is that the fire seems to have acted very unequally on the different parts of the body.'

'Yes,' agreed Thorndyke, 'and that is *the* point. Some parts are more burnt than others; and the parts which are burnt most are the wrong parts. Look at the back-bone, for instance. The vertebrae are as white as chalk. They are mere masses of bone ash. But, of all parts of the skeleton, there is none so completely protected from fire as the back-bone, with the great dorsal muscles behind, and the whole mass of the viscera in front. Then look at the skull. Its appearance is quite inconsistent with the suggested facts. The bones of the face are bare and calcined and the orbits contain not a trace of the eyes or other structures; and yet there is a charred mass of what may or may not be scalp adhering to the crown. But the scalp, as the most exposed and the thinnest covering, would be the first to be destroyed, while the last to be consumed would be the structures about the jaws and the base, of which, you see, not a vestige is left.'

Here he lifted the skull carefully from the shell, and, peering in through the great foramen at the base, handed it to me.

'Look in,' he said, 'through the Foramen Magnum – you will see better if you hold the orbits towards the skylight – and notice an even more extreme inconsistency with the supposed conditions. The brain and membranes have vanished without leaving a trace. The inside of the skull is as clean as if it had been macerated. But this is impossible. The brain is not only protected from the fire; it is also protected from contact with the air. But without access of oxygen, although it might become carbonized, it could not be consumed. No, Jervis; it won't do.'

I replaced the skull in the coffin and looked at him in surprise.

'What is it that you are suggesting?' I asked.

'I suggest that this was not a body at all, but merely a dry skeleton.'

'But,' I objected, 'what about those masses of what looks like charred muscle adhering to the bones?'

'Yes,' he replied, ' I have been noticing them. They do, as you say, look like masses of charred muscle. But they are quite shapeless and structureless; I cannot identify a single muscle or muscular group; and there is not a vestige of any of the tendons. Moreover, the distribution is false. For instance, will you tell me what muscle you think that is?'

He pointed to a thick, charred mass on the inner surface of the left tibia or shin-bone. 'Now this portion of the bone – as many a hockey-player has had reason to realize – has no muscular covering at all. It lies immediately under the skin.'

'I think you are right, Thorndyke,' said I. 'That lump of muscle in the wrong place gives the whole fraud away. But it was really a rather smart dodge. This fellow Bland must be an ingenious rascal.'

'Yes,' agreed Thorndyke; 'but an unscrupulous villain too. He might have burned down half the street and killed a score of people. He'll have to pay the piper for this little frolic.'

'What shall you do now? Are you going to notify the coroner?'

'No; that is not my business. I think we will verify our conclusions and then inform our clients and the police. We must measure the skull as well as we can without callipers, but it is, fortunately, quite typical. The short, broad, flat nasal bones, with the 'Simian groove', and those large, strong teeth, worn flat by hard and gritty food, are highly characteristic.' He, once more, lifted out the skull, and, with a spring tape, made a few measurements, while I noted the lengths of the principal long bones and the width across the hips.

'I make the cranial-nasal index 55.1,' said he, as he replaced the skull, 'and the cranial index about 72, which are quite representative numbers; and, as I see that your notes show the usual disproportionate length of arm and the characteristic curve of the tibia, we may be satisfied. But it is fortunate that the specimen is so typical. To the experienced eye, racial types have a physiognomy which is unmistakable on mere inspection. But you cannot transfer the experienced eye. You can only express personal conviction and back it up with measurements.

'And now we will go and look in on Stalker, and inform him that his office has saved three thousand pounds by employing us. After which it will be Westward Ho! for Scotland Yard, to prepare an unpleasant little surprise for Mr Percival Bland.'

There was joy among the journalists on the following day. Each of the morning papers devoted an entire column to an unusually detailed account of the inquest on the late Percival Bland – who, it appeared, met his death by misadventure – and a verbatim report of the coroner's eloquent remarks on the danger of solitary, fireside tippling, and the stupefying effects of port wine. An adjacent column contained an equally detailed account of the appearance of the deceased at Bow Street Police Court to answer complicated charges of arson, fraud and forgery; while a third collated the two accounts with gleeful commentaries.

Mr Percival Bland, *alias* Robert Lindsay, now resides on the breezy uplands of Dartmoor, where, in his abundant leisure, he, no doubt, regrets his misdirected ingenuity. But he has not laboured in vain. To the Lord Chancellor he has furnished an admirable illustration of the danger of appointing lay coroners; and to me an unforgettable warning against the effects of suggestion.